VITELLIUS' FEAST

The Four Emperors Series

Book I: Palatine

Book II: Galba's Men

Book III: Otho's Regret

Book IV: Vitellius' Feast

VITELLIUS' FEAST
Book IV of the Four Emperors Series

L. J. Trafford

Two quotations from *The Twelve Caesars* by Gaius Suetonius, translated by Robert Graves (Penguin Classics, 1979). Copyright © The Trustees of the Robert Graves Trust and printed with permission from Carcanet Press Limited.

First published in 2019 by Sphinx, an imprint of
Aeon Books Ltd
12 New College Parade
Finchley Road
London NW3 5EP

Copyright © 2019 by L. J. Trafford

The right of L. J. Trafford to be identified as the author of this work has been asserted in accordance with §§ 77 and 78 of the Copyright Design and Patents Act 1988.

All rights reserved. No part of this publication may be reproduced, stored in a retrieval system, or transmitted, in any form or by any means, electronic, mechanical, photocopying, recording, or otherwise, without the prior written permission of the publisher.

British Library Cataloguing in Publication Data

A C.I.P. for this book is available from the British Library

ISBN-13: 978-1-91257-307-3

Typeset by Medlar Publishing Solutions Pvt Ltd, India

www.aeonbooks.co.uk

www.sphinxbooks.co.uk

For

My Mum

Philo's number one fan

CHARACTER LIST

The Vitellians
Aulus Vitellius*—Emperor
Galeria*—his Wife
Lucius Vitellius*—his brother
Triaria*—his sister-in-law
Fabius Valens and Caecina Alienus*—his commanders
Asiaticus*—his Freedman

The Flavians
Titus Flavius Vespasian*—hoping to be emperor
Titus Flavius Sabinus*—his brother
Titus Flavius Domitian*—his younger son
Antonia Caenis*—his long-term mistress
Antonius Primus*—his over-enthusiastic general

The wavering staff
Tiberius Claudius Epaphroditus*—a former secretary, now demoted
Tiberius Claudius Philo—Epaphroditus' former assistant, now a Domitian sitter
Artemina—a former towel holder, now bodyguard
Sporus*—a former empress, now dancer
Talos—Philo's former assistant, now assisting elsewhere

Servius Sulpicius Lysander—head of announcers
Midas—head of catering
Felix—chief overseer and head of slave placements

Elsewhere
Teretia—Philo's wife
Marcia—Philo's slave
Verenia—Lysander's betrothed and Teretia's cousin
Doris—Verenia's slave
Magnus—a soldier looking for love
Lucullus—a soldier looking for a new job
Lysandria—Lysander's mother, a former hairdresser with a deadly sideline
Nymphidia Sabina*—a woman in possession of exceptional talents

*Historical personages

PART I

THE REIGN

"Vitellius' ruling vices were extravagance and cruelty"
—Suetonius, *The Twelve Caesars, Life of Vitellius*

ONE

There were times when Domitian forgot he was a prisoner. Such as when he woke that morning. The slave had informed him that it was the fourth hour, with the same distasteful tone he'd used the previous morning when he'd announced it was the first hour. Domitian had yet to ascertain what hour the slave considered the appropriate one for rising. He rather fancied he'd be addressed in the same tone whatever time he woke.

His body slave was more than a little impatient with him and the shaver seemed almost put out by Domitian's overnight chin growth. Washed and dressed, Domitian plodded to the breakfast room, convinced that every single one of his uncle's slaves disliked him. He wished he possessed his uncle Flavius' affable way of talking to the staff. He tried so very hard to be friendly towards them but his conversation dried up after a line or two. None of the slaves seemed willing to keep the discourse running? Was it any wonder that he preferred his own company!

He entered the breakfast room with his mind fully occupied by his own wretchedness. Already seated were his uncle, his stepmother Caenis, and a visitor whose presence dissipated Domitian's everyday worries and brought back the full horror of his incarceration.

Evidently this showed in his features for Caenis chided him. "Come, come, that's no way to greet our guest."

Guest? Domitian would have given a bitter laugh, if he'd dared. This was no guest. Philo, for that Domitian had learnt was his name, had been sent by the palace to spy on them. The scribe appeared at his uncle's house periodically during the day, enjoying long chats with Caenis and Flavius. Though not with Domitian. Philo's manner towards Domitian had been polite, cordial, and even, Domitian admitted, friendly. He wished sometimes that he could respond in kind but his tongue was made silent by the knowledge that Philo was reporting back to the emperor's secretary, Epaphroditus. He was thus ever awkward in the scribe's presence, unable to relax and consumed with anxiety over how each of his utterances might be interpreted by Philo's boss.

"Do stop fidgeting on your feet and have some breakfast."

Domitian reluctantly sat beside Caenis, keeping his eyes averted from their visitor.

"So, what news do you bring this fine morning, Philo?" asked Flavius, leaning back in his chair and linking his fingers across his stomach.

Domitian's eyes shot upwards. News? Was this it? Had his father been formally declared emperor in the East? Or was it the current emperor, Vitellius? Had he reached Rome and decided upon Domitian's fate? Would the guards on the doors, who Philo had repeatedly assured him were no threat, turn on him?

The bread roll Domitian had been holding in his hand was reduced to crumbs that scattered between his fingers onto the floor, much to the delight of some swooping sparrows.

"Is there a baby yet?" Caenis asked Philo.

"Not yet," replied Philo between mouthfuls of melon. "Teretia's mother seems to think it could be a month or two still. We're not sure."

"Ho, ho!" laughed Flavius. "Ah to be young and in love, and up to the business so often you have no idea when a child was conceived. I remember those days!"

"Is she feeling this heat?" asked Caenis.

"She's finding it very hard to sleep. Thankfully, we are only on the first floor."

"Alas, we have several more months of summer to come," said Caenis. "Of course, usually we would escape the city heat for the coast." She popped a peach slice into her mouth. "Is there any reason Domitian couldn't enjoy the cooling air of Baiae?"

She posed the question in a way that implied there could be no reason.

"All his friends will be down that way," she continued, handing Philo a platter of fruit across the table. "I fear he'll be quite miserable stuck here with us old folk all summer."

Domitian felt he should say something, offer a convincing argument of his own as to why he should be let free from this house. Surely it would be easier to contain him in his father's isolated seaside villa? Or perhaps he should claim an illness that the heat made worse? Instead, all that came out of his mouth was a garbled, "I like the sea."

Flavius gave his nephew's shoulder a squeeze.

"I think it would be better for the lad. My house is rather cramped. He needs a bit of space, a change of scene to lighten his spirits. Caenis and I, we're seasoned at politics, but Domitian, he's young."

Philo shifted slightly on his chair under their scrutiny.

"I understand you'll not want to leave Teretia in her condition, but you'll have an assistant no doubt who can accompany my nephew."

"Or why don't both you and Teretia join him?" suggested Caenis. "She can escape the city heat too."

Philo gave a small cough to clear his throat. A sign, Domitian had learned over the previous months, that he was about to deliver bad news. The scribe had made the same gesture after Caenis' first effectively delivered commentary on why Domitian need not share her house arrest. This plea had been dismissed with an almost apologetic response: that although he may be a seventeen-year-old boy with no experience of war and politics, he was his father's son. There were those in Rome who would consider that enough to make him their figurehead.

"I'm sorry, Caenis, but that won't be possible. My instructions are that Domitian, yourself, and Flavius are to remain in Rome."

"A month away? The boy needs a break from all this," persisted Caenis. "We can have him back in Rome before Vitellius arrives. He need never know. Epaphroditus need never know."

She leaned forward offering Philo a conspiratorial smile.

Caenis had always been a benign and loving presence in Domitian's life, but these past months had opened his eyes to both her cunning and her intelligence.

Philo gave another cough, sinking Domitian's hopes for an escape. "Sorry, that won't be possible. The emperor is expected in Rome shortly."

A lump formed in Domitian's throat. Flavius' eyebrows knitted together above his nose. Caenis revealed nothing of her feelings as she enquired, "Vitellius is in Italy then?"

"Epaphroditus has gone to meet him," said Philo. "We heard he was nearing Bononia."

Domitian's brain whirled. Bononia? How far was that? How many days would it take Vitellius' army to reach Rome? And most important, what would it mean for him?

TWO

"Gods above! What a procession it was," laughed the barman. "There were these eunuchs, a big gang of them all kitted out in loincloths, and they danced through the streets. Behind them were women. But not good women. If you know what I mean." He aimed an exaggerated wink at Epaphroditus. "No, these were of the painted toga sort. Prostitutes. Our small town has never seen the like."

The barman, a portly man in his fifties, leaned back in his chair and grinned. "It was fantastic for business. All those soldiers. All those girls. Even those little eunuchs can knock back a drink. I've got enough coin to upgrade my premises now."

Just as well, thought Epaphroditus, taking in the grimy walls and filthy floor of the bar.

"The emperor?" he pressed, getting down to business.

This business was the sole reason he was sat in such dubious surroundings, in some forgotten town, in a part of Italy far removed from the villas and palaces he was more familiar with. "The emperor was with the soldiers?"

"I've never seen an emperor before."

"Did you see this one?" Epaphroditus asked.

The barman grinned from ear to ear. "Too right I did. I had him here in my bar! Imagine! An emperor! Huge big fat fella." He pulled his hands far apart to demonstrate the bulk. "He ate up my entire supply of whelks! All by himself! Can you imagine? A barrel of whelks?"

"Thank you," said Epaphroditus, getting to his feet. "Have this for your trouble." He pressed a gold coin into a sweaty palm.

Outside he wiped his own hand on his cloak and sucked in a mouthful of clean air. Around him, the townspeople were clearing up the debris left by Vitellius' passing army. They did so with smiles on their faces, even the slaves. Vitellius had left his mark on the town. But where was he?

They'd received notice some fifteen days past that the new emperor was hovering around the north of Italy. Epaphroditus had set off to intersect Vitellius' army before they reached Rome. So far, all he'd encountered were a series of depleted towns and happy businessmen like the barmen. There was quite a lot of coinage to be made from 30,000 soldiers, and word had spread. Epaphroditus had passed many enterprising sorts carrying their produce in wagons, or on their backs, as keen as he was to ingratiate themselves with the new emperor.

That they were keen to meet the approaching army boded well. The secretary had not expected such jollity when the army had marched from Germania under the command of Vitellius' two generals. Towns had been razed, women raped en masse, civilians slaughtered. Perhaps it was the presence of their emperor that had quelled Fabius Valens' and Caecina's blood-lust. Which suggested Vitellius had a better grasp on events than Epaphroditus had given him credit for when he'd been supporting Otho's claim to the purple.

Alas, Otho was no more and there was one man left standing: Aulus Vitellius. Who'd have thought it? Certainly not Epaphroditus. In all his dealings with Vitellius over the years in the courts of Claudius and Nero, not once had he imagined Vitellius had the ambition or the energy for such an audacious plan. That was why he'd initially assumed Valens and Caecina to be the instigators. But their behaviour since Otho's suicide suggested otherwise. Epaphroditus had expected both men to appear with their legions at the gates of Rome keen to install themselves in power. But they hadn't. They'd both dutifully and patiently waited for Vitellius to make his way from Germania to Italy. Which was contrary to everything Epaphroditus had thought he'd known about the bloodthirsty and avaricious Valens, and the handsome but empty-headed Caecina.

Part of the secretary's desire to rendezvous with the emperor stemmed from a wish to get close to these two men and a firmer grip on their motivations.

"Bumped into a kid putting up some notices," said Epaphroditus' slave. "The emperor is putting on some games, it appears."

"Where?"

"Bononia."

Bononia was half a day's ride away.

"Make sure my toga's ready," he instructed. "I have an appointment with an emperor."

* * *

Reaching Bononia Epaphroditus knew his slave was correct. There was an excitement in the air, a shifting frisson of thrill that only came when an emperor was present. Even with two Praetorians by his side, it took Epaphroditus a good hour to make his way through the crowds gathered outside the amphitheatre.

"Tiberius Claudius Epaphroditus to see His Imperial Majesty."

The steward, taking in the jeers and insults yelled at Epaphroditus for pushing to the front of the queue, said, "We'd better get you inside quickly before this turns into a riot. The gods know what methods those soldiers will employ to quell it."

A dollop of gob hit the back of the secretary's neck. His slave wiped it off as the Praetorians unsheathed their swords and looked murderously into the crowd.

"Leave it," ordered Epaphroditus as the steward beckoned them in.

* * *

The games had barely begun. They were still on the execution of the criminals, which was good. Epaphroditus, knowing Vitellius of old, knew how involved he got in the bloodshed. Once the gladiators were on, he'd have no chance of getting his attention.

The cheers and gasps of the crowd accompanied him as he was shown into the imperial box. A man of proportions more akin to a rhinoceros sat on a high-backed chair, his thighs spilling over the sides. This was Vitellius, emperor of Rome. Beside him sat a woman of a fleshy, matronly shape whom Epaphroditus knew to be the new empress, Galeria. Beside her was Vitellius' brother Lucius and his attractive wife, Triaria. Absent was Galeria and Vitellius' young son, but otherwise they were all here. The imperial family of only three months.

Vitellius' eyes were fixed on the action in the arena below. They flicked upwards when Epaphroditus was announced.

"Imperial Majesty," he said, bowing his head.

"I wondered when you'd show up," Vitellius laughed, his chins wobbling. "I knew you would. I bet Valens 3,000 sesterces you'd be the first of the palace staff to supplicate your way here."

He indicated behind his chair to where a man stood. This man was of far more interest to Epaphroditus than any member of Vitellius' family: Fabius Valens. So this was him. He was as Epaphroditus had expected. A lean, thin man with a grey pallor and hungry eyes. Those eyes were turned his way and the secretary could not miss the disdain in them. He might have been a woodlouse crawled out from a crack in the floor for all the respect Epaphroditus saw in those eyes.

It didn't faze him. He was used to such resentments. He'd been a slave once. Now he was one of those dubious freedmen; emancipated and taking jobs from real Romans. Ability, or lack thereof, never entered the equation for those such as Valens. Lack of ability never entered their thought processes.

So if this was Valens, the man standing to his left must be Caecina. Caecina, the bumbling commander whose men Otho's inferior forces had repeatedly bested in battle. If Valens hadn't arrived with reinforcements, maybe Otho would still be emperor. Caecina was quite as handsome as the reports suggested. A Greek athlete in the flesh. Such proportions of perfection and a countenance so pleasing that even Epaphroditus, who was a firm connoisseur of the female form, found it difficult to tear his eyes away. This gave him an opportunity to study the younger man. Caecina should be on top of the world. He was as close as you could get to an emperor. Yet, to Epaphroditus' surprise, the eyes in that handsome face seemed troubled. His stance, ever-so-slightly drooped.

"My generals," said Vitellius, sweeping his arm backwards. "My victorious generals, I should say." He gave a laugh. "Valens will tell you they weren't much of an enemy. So easily crushed."

Epaphroditus saw the pretty man pout, clearly upset by the reference to his own failure against Otho's forces. Valens' lips, however, were pulled back in a smug grimace.

"Gladiators and Praetorians!" he sneered. "My troops wiped the earth with them and their bathroom-buggering leader! That such a man could think himself emperor!" he spat.

Vitellius flicked his fingernails on the arm of his chair. "Now, now Valens. You should know that Epaphroditus was quite the pal of Otho's."

Valens' suspicious eyes fell on the secretary.

"But then he's quite the pal of anyone he thinks will do him favours. He'd snuggle up to that she-wolf Agrippina if he thought it would do him some good."

"I did indeed work for some years with Empress Agrippina," Epaphroditus replied, with enough hint of dark mystery to cause momentary worry in Valens' eyes.

"So you see, my men, he shall be quite the pal to us too," declared Vitellius. Then with some impatience, "You're blocking my view. I particularly wanted to see this."

Epaphroditus slid behind the imperial family, beside Caecina. He gazed down at the arena in front of him. They were still executing criminals. Not much of a spectacle. Not when the true crowd draws, the beast hunt and the gladiators, were yet to come. Vitellius' piggy eyes glistened with interest as a youngish woman was dragged into the centre of the arena. She wore a short pink gown that only just covered her rear. On top of her dark hair was pinned a flower garland.

Ahh, the historical allusion death section. Who was she? Niobe shot by Artemis' arrows? Iphegenia sacrificed to the gods? Eurydice bitten by a snake?

The answer was provided when the doors on the far side were pulled open and out came two men. In between them huffed an enormous black bull. This was the point at which Empress Galeria stood and departed. Her husband did not even look in her direction.

It was to be Paisphne, the queen who had lain with a bull and produced the Minotaur. There'd be no issue from this coupling though. Epaphroditus had seen it rehashed in the arena a dozen times. So far no woman had survived the beast's lust. Vitellius leaned forward in his seat, his mouth falling open in anticipation. Valens' grey lips were twisted into a smile as the girl was tied to four stakes hammered into the ground, her legs spread far apart.

The real Paisphne had hid in an artificially created heifer for her union. But where was the salacious fun in that? No, the crowd needed full unimpeded access to the action. The bull was brought forward. Glancing to his left, Epaphroditus was surprised to see Caecina look as sick as he felt. The handsome general averted his eyes as the show began. No such hesitation was evident in his fellow commander. Valens was relishing the death provided. His grey cheeks gaining a flash of pink. His eyes eager. And, Epaphroditus fancied, glancing at Valens' crotch, already aroused.

Interesting dynamics, he thought.

But then, no less interesting than the empress who chose to exit the vile seen before her while her sister-in-law Triaria sat forward in her seat, unabashed by the grotesque rape taking place.

THREE

Philo was generally a man who walked quickly. His days were so busy that speed was a necessity to complete every task assigned to him. The palace was an irritatingly large space to navigate and vital time could be lost in transit between offices. Thus Philo was light on his feet. It helped that he didn't have much in the way of weight to transport, being of small stature and frame. Today however, his gait was more of a trudge.

When Epaphroditus had assigned him the task of overseeing the Flavian family's house arrest, Philo had thought it a relatively mundane task. He'd also secretly felt it to be a waste of his time given how quickly correspondence built up on his desk. It fell much more easily under Epaphroditus' remit, he'd thought. His boss was far better at dealing with those patrician types than he was. Philo never knew what to say to them.

However, his boss was still fuming over what he saw as Caenis' betrayal. Caenis had been Epaphroditus' mentor, guiding and aiding his career. He'd considered her a friend. Yet while he'd been desperately trying to save Otho's throne, Caenis had been plotting to place her lover, Vespasian, on that same seat. In the wake of Otho's suicide, Epaphroditus was not in a forgiving mood. Which was why he'd assigned Philo to look after the Flavian family.

Truthfully, Philo was not enjoying this assignment. Though Caenis and Flavius had been extremely welcoming, Domitian's undisguised look of terror at his presence was denting that welcome. In fact, Philo found it all rather upsetting. Much like the assignment he was about to undertake now.

He paused outside the door. Held his hand up to the wood. Took a deep calming breath and rapped three times. His shoulders tensed as he waited for the anticipated response.

"COME THE FUCK IN!"

Though the door was firmly shut, Philo fancied he could feel a gust from that below ruffle his hair. He opened the door with his usual caution. Sitting behind an enormous desk sat Felix, head of slave placements and chief overseer. He was a large man, possessed of a girth that filled the whole length of his desk. A single one of Felix's arms was wider than all four of Philo's limbs laid together. He was a strong man. He was also a very loud, sweary man. One the sensitive Philo tended to avoid. However, today he was in need of Felix's expertise.

"Sit the fuck down then, Philo. Gany, move that that pile of tablets will you, son."

Ganymede, a boy of about ten years old, dashed forward and cleared the chair of impediments. Once this was done, he took his place beside the right elbow of his adoptive father. Both father and son glared at Philo.

"Well?" prompted Felix, rapping his knuckles on the desk.

"Well?" squeaked Ganymede.

Philo cleared his throat nervously. "I, err… I need, err…I need a slave girl."

Felix's glare relaxed into more of a hard stare. "So that's how it is. Your missus is expecting. She's not putting out for you like she used to. So you need a girl to work off your frustrations."

It took Philo a moment to decipher what Felix meant. When he did, his cheeks flamed hot and his mouth fell open. "No, no, that's not how it is!" he protested.

"It's awright, Philo. Nowt to be fucking embarrassed about. I got thousands of girls on my scrolls for you to choose from. Or would you rather I just choose one for you?"

"One with yellow hair," suggested Ganymede. "And a big bottom."

"Good thought, son. Ain't your missus' bottom on the fleshy side, Philo? Best fuckin' side to be on. Don't want no skinny thing, all fuckin' bones and none of the bits that make women all fuckin' womanly. So, a big bottom then? And breasts: melon-sized, hand-sized, or pointless puff-of-flesh size?"

"I want a slave girl to help Teretia and her mother with their chores. And with the baby when it's born," Philo said quickly before the conversation could descend any further. With Felix and Ganymede's attention on him, he said in a lower, calmer tone, "I wondered if you could advise me on what to look for. I've never purchased a slave before."

"'Ow much you got to spend?"

"Five hundred sesterces."

"Hmppf," Felix murmured and with a scrape of his chair, he was on his feet. "Right!" he declared. "There's a market on today. Let's see what we can get for your 500."

* * *

Philo hadn't anticipated Felix accompanying him on his shopping trip. He'd been hoping for a list of attributes and criteria he could mark his potential home helper against. Actually, though, he decided as he tried to keep up with Felix's long stride, it was a help. Philo, aware that he lacked both bargaining skills and menace, figured Felix would make sure he wasn't ripped off.

He'd hate to buy a girl and discover she couldn't manage the job. Teretia would be so disappointed. And he couldn't bear to upset his adored wife.

Teretia had been so very excited by the prospect of their becoming slave owners. Mostly, Philo suspected, because her cousin Verenia had her own slave girl, Doris, and was apt to show off about it. But aside from enabling Teretia to compete with Verenia, a girl about the apartment would be a great help for his heavily pregnant wife and elderly mother-in-law. It was something he needed to get right.

The slave market was being held in the Saepta Julia, close to the Pantheon temple. They'd discussed on their way there what Philo's requirements were.

"So you want a hardworking girl who can sweep floors, carry shopping, and cook a little. She must like babies and she must be a nice girl," recapped Ganymede.

"That's it," said Philo. "And I guess pretty, in being not ugly. I don't think Teretia would like an ugly slave. I mean Doris isn't beautiful but her dark hair does complement Verenia's blonde hair."

"You want to breed from her?" enquired Felix.

"I said I wasn't interested in that," said Philo. "I mean, obviously, I am interested in that, sometimes. But I have a wife and she, errmm, takes care of that. I don't need anyone else," he concluded piously.

Then, because he couldn't bear for anyone to think that Teretia was less than the perfect wife, he added, "I mean obviously it's more difficult because she's very pregnant now and her stomach gets in the way a lot and it's a bit uncomfortable for her. Well, actually, very uncomfortable. So we haven't been able to in a full way for a while. But that doesn't mean I'm not, err, satisfied. Because I am."

Felix made a hand gesture out of eye shot of Ganymede that suggested the favours Teretia might be bestowing upon Philo.

"I meant in the future," clarified Felix. "Did you want to build up your slave stock?"

"I just want one slave girl. That's all. There's only space for one bedroll in the kitchen. I can't fit any more in. Not until Lysander marries Verenia and moves out."

"That still fuckin' 'appenin'?" marvelled Felix, scratching at his beard. "I am a-fucking-mazed. You might wanna watch your purchase with Lysander. He's a full-on potent stallion. He populated the whole west wing of the slave complex single-handedly."

"Maybe Teretia would tolerate a plain girl," decided Philo. Seeing the mass of people gathered by the temple, "Oh, there's a bit of a crowd."

"Easily fuckin' sorted," said Felix using his bulk to clear a way through. Ganymede trotted through the newly created path. Philo followed behind.

At the front of the crowd was a small platform on which stood a shivering naked slave boy. To his left was a similarly unclothed group of men, women, and children. The auctioneer, catching sight of Felix, yelled out, "Bids suspended. We've got a palace buyer."

Cue plenty of disgruntled shouts and disparaging comments on palace types. Felix's response to this tirade of abuse was a series of keenly felt hand gestures, imitated by Ganymede. Philo kept his head down as the begrudging crowd were sent on their way.

"Fuckin' palace will buy up all the fuckin' good ones," a would-be owner decried as he departed. The few choice looks thrown at Felix suggested he was going to be the subject of a good curse tablet that evening.

"So, Felix. Gany," said the auctioneer nodding at the boy. "What can I do for you and your employer today?" He rubbed his hands together with glee.

"I need a slave girl for Philo here."

Noticing the freedman for the first time, he gave a double blink and his eyes took in a thorough examination of Philo's slight form.

"Oi, fuck off, mate. He might not be wearing his fuckin' liberty cap today but he's as free as fuckin' you and me. So don't you even fuckin' think it."

"Alright, Felix," smoothed the auctioneer. "But you know me, I can't help but appreciate a good bit of merchandise. Not had many Indians on my blocks."

Philo opened his mouth ready to correct him but Felix got in first, "Tarpobanian, you fuckin' idiot," shaking his head at such a rudimentary error.

The auctioneer gave the uncomfortable Philo another appraising look. "Pity. I got a flashy bugger on the Caelian who'd pay fifty thou for an Indian. Probably more for a Tarpobanian." He rubbed his palms together again. "Ah well. But come see what I've got today."

What he had were five slaves of the female variety. He lined them up with a flick of his whip at their calves.

"That one's a bit old," said Ganymede. "She won't have the energy to scrub your floors."

"Good call there, Gany," said Felix, ruffling the boy's hair.

Two further girls were dismissed as lacking muscles and being far too skinny, a state Felix had much commentary on. Which left two to choose from. Both were of similar height and build. One was dark of hair, the other blonde. Possibly, they were the same age. Philo couldn't tell. He looked to Felix for assistance.

"Nationality?" barked Felix to the auctioneer.

"They've both been in Rome since childhood. But birthwise, this one's a Briton; this one's from Germania. Both strong nations that build strong women."

"If that's what they fuckin' are," grumbled Felix.

To Philo's surprise, Felix addressed both in their alleged native tongues. Seeing his shocked face, Felix said, "What?

Handy to have a few languages under your belt. Then you know wot the fuckin' merchandise is plottin'. This one ain't a Briton," he stated.

He addressed her in a series of alternative languages, finally getting a hit. "Ha! I fucking knew it. She ain't been in Rome since childhood and she ain't no Briton." He gave the auctioneer a hard glare. "She's a Spaniard!" he told Philo. "You don't want one of them."

"I don't?"

"Nah. They all have to lay down for a nap three hours a day. Think of all that lost productivity! It's fuckin' freezing in Germania. They work 'ard to keep warm."

"So I want this one?"

"Hold yer 'orses, Philo. Let me take a closer look at 'er."

Felix checked the blonde girl over. Squeezing muscles, looking into her ears, opening her mouth and counting her teeth.

"Previous owner?"

"One," said the auctioneer. "Lost all his mint to Galba. He had to sell off everything he can."

"Plausible," said Felix. "He'll give you 200. With a guarantee he can return 'er within a month if she don't suit."

"Come on, Felix! I can't do that! If I do it for you, all my customers will want it. She's a virgin! You don't find many of those who've had previous owners."

Felix crossed his arms. "I'll go up to 300 but I still want that guarantee."

"350's my final offer."

"325."

"Done."

And they shook hands on it.

"Errr," interjected Philo. "What's her name?"

"Call 'er what you like, Philo. That's your privilege as a slave owner."

"Marcia is what her last owner called her."

FOUR

Philo and a fully clothed Marcia made their way to the Viminal Hill. Though he'd balked at keeping her in chains, he had taken Felix's advice and tied a rope to her wrists, keeping a firm grip on the other end of it.

"New master, she'll be scared like," Felix had told him. "Once you've got her home and your Teretia serves her a tasty meal, she'll be fine. But you need to get her home first."

Philo wasn't quite sure what to say to her. It seemed impolite to ask about her background. He feared it might upset her. New purchases in the palace had always been on the tearful side at first. Philo hoped Marcia would settle in nicely, like those new slaves at the palace had. Like he had, in fact, when he'd first arrived in Rome. Most of all, he hoped Teretia liked her.

He'd need not have feared. Teretia, seeing Marcia, clapped her hands with glee.

"She's wonderful," she declared.

"What a pretty girl," agreed Teretia's mother, Pompeia. "Come, come, sit down." And when Marcia didn't reply. "Does she understand us, Philo?"

"The trader said she's been in Rome since she was a child. So she should be fluent," worried Philo.

"Ahh, then she'll just be a little shy. A nice meal will cheer you right up."

An enormous bowl of salad accompanied by cheese and bread was placed on the table. Marcia sat down cautiously, her eyes drinking in her surroundings: a kitchen with its own stove, walls lined with hanging pots and pans, and an enormous table that dominated the room.

A beaker of water was placed before her. She took a gulp, then said quietly, "Thank you."

Her new owners smiled.

* * *

Later, when Marcia had been settled on to a bedroll in the kitchen with an instruction to call out if she needed anything, Philo sat on their bed watching Teretia plait her hair up for the night.

"I think I'll take Marcia out to the shops tomorrow, so she can get used to the neighbourhood," said Teretia.

"Maybe you should take her on the rope," said Philo. "You'll not be able to chase after her in your condition if she makes a run for it."

Teretia spun round on her stool. "She's not going to run away. Marcia is going to be terrifically happy here. Mother and I will make sure she is. I can't imagine why she'd even consider running away."

As a former slave, Philo could. He'd spent many hours lying on his bed dreaming up escape routes from his miserable life. Not that he'd ever come anywhere near to enacting his fantasies. The fear of being nailed to a cross was a strong deterrent.

Philo stood up. "Maybe I'll just go check she's alright. It is quite a hot night. She might be thirsty."

"I think that's very kind of you."

Philo took this compliment and the accompanying kiss. He then rushed off to check that the front door was firmly bolted and locked.

FIVE

On the wall was placed a melon. Beside that was a peach. And beside the peach, a singular grape. Domitian narrowed his eyes, fixing them firmly on the targets. He fired off three arrows with scarcely a pause between them. The wall was now fruitless. Searching in the shrubbery behind, he found the melon, peach, and grape. The arrow in the melon had stuck firmly, in the melon, jutting outward, and Domitian had a fancy he could create a melon hedgehog with some ease. The peach had been shot through, leaving a satisfactory hole in its centre. Meanwhile, the grape had been reduced to mush. He popped it in his mouth. Turning round, he was startled to find his stepmother sitting silently in a chair, watching him.

"Never interrupt a man holding a weapon is a mantra I've stuck to throughout my life," she said, smiling.

"It relaxes me," said Domitian defensively.

His fondness for archery had long made him the butt of his older brother's jibes. Understandably so, Domitian supposed. Titus was away fighting a real enemy in the desert of Judaea, whilst he was stuck here firing at fruit.

"I am glad," said Caenis folding her hands in her lap. "You need to unwind a little. These are very trying circumstances for you."

This was, in Domitian's opinion, a gross understatement of his daily terror.

"But, really, you must try and be polite to Philo. He is our best hope to extradite ourselves from this situation."

Domitian placed down his bow. "How so? He works for Epaphroditus who you betrayed. How could Philo possibly be our best hope? Our best hope is that father wakes up from his bout of insanity and declares Vitellius the rightful emperor. Like he should have done months ago!"

"That's not going to happen," she said with such certainty that Domitian felt his temper begin to bubble up.

"It's what Uncle Flavius wishes he would do! It's what I wish he would do! How could he do this to me? I'm his son. He's gone ahead and done this thing without one consideration for me and my safety!"

"Domitian," began Caenis softly, "He sent me back to Rome for exactly that reason: to keep you safe."

"Rubbish. He sent you back to organise two spies in Valens' and Caecina's camp, to build distrust between them and sow discontent in Vitellius' army. Why don't you just admit that? I didn't feature anywhere in his plans."

Caenis watched him angrily gather up his arrows before she replied. "That's not true. When your father is back in Rome he will tell you that."

"Back in Rome as emperor?"

"Yes, as emperor."

"You've gone mad. You've all gone mad." He picked up his bow and fired three shots, one after the other in a neat line down the watermelon.

"Philo is a scribe. He's been trained to follow orders. It's what he'll do without thinking. Except his boss is away, as he told us today. There are no orders. He's having to do his own thinking. He knew your father in Greece. He liked him. He likes us. I, we, can work with that."

Domitian eyed up the melon for a further barrage.

"Philo is high up in the palace bureaucracy. We need friends like him."

After comprehensively demolishing the watermelon with a further barrage of arrows, Domitian faced his stepmother. "What do you need me to do?" he asked.

"Just try not to look so horrified every time you see him. If you can manage that, it's a start."

Domitian stuck his finger into the watermelon carcass and sucked off the juice. "So, basically, I have no role whatsoever in whatever you and my father have planned."

He picked up his bow and walked past Caenis.

She waited for twenty-seven slow intakes of breath before releasing her screech of frustration.

SIX

Philo was gratified to find the next morning that his new purchase had not absconded. Walking into the kitchen he found his wife, mother-in-law, and Marcia all sat at the table tucking into bowls of porridge. Philo's eyes rested on Marcia.

"Philo!" beamed Teretia. "We've been teaching Marcia how to make porridge."

"She's a natural," said Pompeia, getting up to the stove and ladling out a bowl for Philo.

Philo's eyes went back to Marcia, who was spooning porridge into her mouth.

"What is it?" asked Teretia.

Philo's thoughts were made verbal by Lysander breezing in and commenting, "Jupiter's white bull! Are we letting the slaves sit now? That wouldn't be tolerated at the palace," he added, sitting down and reaching across the table for a piece of bread. "Philo, can you imagine the serving slaves sitting down with the emperor and empress and eating their breakfast?"

Philo couldn't. It was unimaginable.

"This isn't the palace, Lysander," said Pompeia, handing him a bowl of porridge. "It's the Viminal. We have our own way of doing things."

* * *

"She'll walk all over you if you're not careful," said Lysander as he and Philo made their way to work. "There's no point in having a slave if they sit down and you serve them. It's months until Saturnalia."

Privately, Philo agreed. At the palace there was a very strong demarcation of jobs and expectations were clear.

"I think Marcia needs a schedule," said Philo.

"I think Marcia needs a good whipping. Can you imagine what would have happened to us if we'd handed our dirty bowl to our master to wash up?"

A tut-tut escaped from between Philo's lips. The walls would have melted from the bollocking Felix would have meted out. Backs would have been stripped raw from the ensuing whipping.

"You need to take control of it. Before Teretia ends up massaging Marcia's feet!"

It was a subject that preoccupied Philo for the remainder of their journey. Thus, he missed much of Lysander's description of the sex he'd enjoyed with his betrothed, Verenia, the previous day. Reaching his office, he saw a man leaning against the wall outside using a fingernail to groom his teeth. Seeing Philo, he deigned to straighten up.

"Publius, you have something for me?"

Publius grinned. "I certainly do."

They settled into the small chamber that served as Philo's new office. A functional space that had thrilled Philo by being several square feet larger than his previous office: it gave him additional filing space.

Publius handed over a scroll to Philo. Examining its weight and width, Philo asked, "You found out all this on Vespasian?"

Publius gave a shrug. "It's nothing we didn't already know. He's an old geezer, so it's many years of stuff we ceased to care about decades ago."

"I guess that's to be expected." Philo's experience of Vespasian was of an unashamedly open man. He did not care to conceal. You took Vespasian as he was or you didn't. And whichever it was, it wouldn't have bothered the general in the slightest.

"There's some stuff on Titus that's a bit juicier. That Jewish princess for instance."

"My mother-in-law thinks it's romantic," said Philo. "It seems to be enhancing Titus' reputation rather than damaging it. Did you find anything Epaphroditus can use?" Philo asked with a hint of desperation.

Having been tasked with digging up dirt to besmirch Vespasian's reputation, Philo was keen not to disappoint his boss. It had been a long shot: the Vespasian Philo knew would own up to his mistakes and gruffly laugh them off. He was not a man likely to possess secrets. Witness his very open relationship with Caenis, an ex-slave. Many of Vespasian's class would have kept such a mistress behind closed doors, a private pleasure. Not Vespasian though. Even if he couldn't legally marry her, Caenis was his wife and treated as such.

"I did find something," said Publius with a sly smile. "But not on Vespasian or his Jewish princess-chasing son."

"Then?" asked Philo, confused.

"The younger son, Domitian. Have a read. I think you'll find I have earned my fee."

Two hours later, with a throbbing headache, sore eyes, and having gained a brain-twisting dilemma, Philo fully agreed. Publius had certainly earned his fee.

SEVEN

Epaphroditus sat at his desk, attempting to concentrate on the correspondence Philo had sent him. The situation in Rome, according to his assistant, appeared calm and orderly. Though there were some fears at the palace in regard to what a new emperor might mean for everyone's job.

Epaphroditus was not immune to that particular anxiety. Though he hadn't expected to keep his old role of private secretary, knowing that Vitellius would bring in his own team, he had hoped for a senior position of some sort. That he'd not been billeted with the emperor but rather here with the legions, ate into that hope.

A barrage of shouts from outside broke into his thoughts. Honestly, thought Epaphroditus, heading towards the door, shouldn't the legionaries be in their beds at this hour? They were meant to be marching onwards to Rome in the morning. Epaphroditus opened his door and cautiously stuck his head out.

The shouts grew louder, more combative. Looking to his left he could see in the glow of torchlights a small band of legionaries. He popped his head back in and watched through the crack as they ran past.

"Let's get them! Fucking Gauls!"

They had their swords raised. Dear gods, thought Epaphroditus, where are the centurions? Glancing to his right, he saw a form slumped against the wall, one hand clutching at a wineskin. His feathered helmet gave away his rank. So that's where all the centurions were. Epaphroditus felt a frisson of fear. This was not the hardened, disciplined troops of the Rhine he'd been expecting. This was a rabble of men supplied with too much alcohol and left to it. Where in Hades' name were Valens and Caecina? These were their troops to command, to control.

More yelling and pounding of feet on the ground. Through the crack, Epaphroditus saw a group of auxiliaries belt past pursued by legionaries with raised swords. One tripped and fell with a thump. Epaphroditus shut the door. This was not enough to blot out the auxiliary's screams. Or the victorious yells that followed them.

Epaphroditus turned to his wide-eyed, shaking slave.

"I think it might be a good idea to move the furniture in front of that door."

* * *

"It was an argument that got out of control," said Valens. "As I understand it, one of the legionaries was taking part in a wrestling bout with a Gallic auxiliary. The Gaul was considered too boastful in his victory."

"So they killed him," said Epaphroditus, arms crossed across his chest.

Valens gave him a glare. "They're Germans. They are a proud people."

"They are Roman soldiers under the command of Rome. They are required to act like it," replied Epaphroditus. "Two cohorts slaughtered! Two cohorts! Over the results of a wrestling match."

"It's been dealt with," snapped Valens. "The Gauls have been sent back."

"The Gauls aren't the problem. It's the rest of this army. I dare you to spend a night in that camp and sleep soundly."

"I journeyed from the Rhine with these men while you were softened in palace luxury!"

Epaphroditus hard glared him back. "They are out of control. You need to get them under control." *We are only a few days' march from Rome. The gods know what havoc they'll reap in the city unless someone takes them in hand.*

"I am not yours to command," responded a tense-lipped Valens. "And I would recommend you watch your manner, slave. I have the ear of the emperor. I can command your fate."

Epaphroditus waited until after Valens had stormed out before expelling a few choice expletives under his breath. Then he went off to see Valens' fellow commander with his complaints.

* * *

He found Caecina in a long-abandoned chamber, thick with cobwebs. He was sat on a battered wooden chair, polishing his sword with long strokes.

"Don't you have a slave to do that?" Epaphroditus asked.

"It calms me," said Caecina, not looking up.

"The soldiers—"

"We found your spy, by the way," interrupted Caecina.

"My spy?"

"Otho's then," said Caecina, his eyes fully fixed on his sword.

Epaphroditus wished there was another chair. It was awkward addressing the top of Caecina's head.

"Otho's spy?"

"Salonina was her name. Or rather, that was the name she told me."

Caecina's rag paused mid-polish, his fingers grasping at it. So that was what was troubling the handsome young man. Salonina.

During his time working for Otho's brief administration, Epaphroditus had received a multitude of reports on Caecina and the woman described as his wife. Both he and Philo had thought it was suspicious how Salonina appeared so suddenly by Caecina's side.

After discovering a female agent in the shape of Lysander's mother, Lysandria, working for Caenis in Valens' camp, Salonina seemed likely to be another such agent.

It was clearly a betrayal hitting Caecina hard. He was as wilted as a stick of damp celery. Epaphroditus felt a keen need to meet the woman who had so comprehensively manipulated the handsome young man.

"Where is she?"

* * *

Epaphroditus gave a gasp. "Nymphidia Sabina! I should have known."

Nymphidia, stretched out on a couch, took a sip from her enormous glass goblet.

"One usually doesn't drink this early, but, alas, entertainment is scarce." She took another sip. "Sit, sit. Tell me news of Rome."

Epaphroditus nodded to a slave, who carried over a stool and placed it beside Nymphidia's couch.

"I'd offer you a drink, darling, but I know you don't when you're working."

"Who says I'm working?"

Nymphidia gave an enchanting and beautiful smile, the sort that had no doubt ensnared Caecina. "You're here, aren't you? Have you snared yourself a good position under our new emperor yet?"

"Well, you'd know all about being under Vitellius."

Her laugh echoed around the room. "I fear such a pleasure would be impossible now. He was always chunky but now—" She puffed out her cheeks. "I wonder how Galeria produced that cute little boy. I can't see how it could be accomplished. I don't see she has the leg span to accommodate. I know!" she sparkled. "He'll take her from behind. But likely she'll have to do all the work. I can't see him even raising a sweat."

"Nymphidia."

She gave him a wicked look. "You can't tell me you've never pictured it."

"Not ever. Other people's sex lives do not interest me."

"I can believe that," she said, sipping from her goblet. "You do have such a busy sex life of your own, what with all those slave girls you just can't resist. It must be hard to find the time."

"Nymphidia."

"Quite, quite," she waved a hand. "Let's get to business. Tell me, what is new in Rome?"

"I have your employer under house arrest."

"My employer?" she asked casually, brow wrinkled to suggest confusion.

"Antonia Caenis. The woman who paid you to intercept Caecina Alienus and break his heart."

Nymphidia handed her goblet to the slave. She swung her legs over the edge of the couch so she was facing Epaphroditus.

"Is he really heartbroken?"

"He's miserable."

"Poor boy. I do worry for him. Perhaps you could bring him to me so we could have a talk."

"And you can twist his mind further against his colleague, Valens. Or perhaps now is the time to start bigging up Vespasian.

How slender he is in comparison to Vitellius. How better suited he is to the purple," suggested Epaphroditus dryly.

"I have no idea what you are talking about."

"Of course you don't," scoffed Epaphroditus.

Nymphidia stretched out a shapely leg. Resting her foot against Epaphroditus' groin, her toes began to curl.

"I don't think so," he said, lifting her leg up. "You're going to need all your energy to convince Vitellius not to execute you."

Her smile did not falter. "Darling, nobody is going to be executed. That cold beast Valens desires it, no doubt, but Vitellius retains a fondness for me."

"And you believe that fondness will overcome his disgust at your treachery?"

"It has so far," said Nymphidia sweeping her eyes over the luxurious chamber.

"And when they find out you weren't spying for Otho but for Vespasian?"

The smile dropped into a hard line as Nymphidia the politically savvy creature spoke, "Vitellius does not fear Vespasian. Why should he? Maybe Vespasian, or rather his agents, travelled to suss out the situation after the legitimate emperor Galba was killed by Otho. That was a sensible precaution to understand the situation. But now Vitellius is emperor. He has seven legions. Seven legions to hold the empire together. Vespasian can sit securely in the East with his own legions, happy in the knowledge that Rome is in safe hands."

Epaphroditus' green eyes met her sharp, intelligent gaze. "Except that's not what's going to happen, is it?"

Nymphidia broke his gaze and wriggled back on her couch, hitching up her gown to reveal two long, slender legs. The action was, Epaphroditus knew, planned to do exactly that.

"Why don't you come and join me?" she suggested, turning onto her side to face him. Her gown slipped off her shoulder, demonstrating the flimsiness of her attire, as well as providing a good portion of bare flesh.

So far, so Nymphidia.

She patted a space on the couch in front of her. "Come on, let us break into this dull day," she enticed.

Epaphroditus had intended to interrogate her, to wheedle out any further instructions Caenis had given her, to be uncompromisingly hard. Seeing Nymphidia's reclined figure, he was starting to suffer a hardness all right. Why shouldn't he? He deserved some enjoyment. And Nymphidia, from past experience, was a true professional in sexual matters. After all, it had been months since he'd last been with a woman. Not since Aphrodite had—

The thought of his dead wife killed his passion.

He stood, telling Nymphidia, "I shall be back later to question you."

"Give my love to Caecina," she called to his back. "Such a darling boy."

EIGHT

Lucullus looked down at the old woman. She reminded him of his Granny Sosillia. Though Granny Sosillia did not own such expensive-looking gowns or jewellery. She also didn't smell of apricots, as this lady did. No, Granny Sosillia's scent was of the cabbage she spent most of the day boiling, before slopping the watery green mush into your bowl. This lady was a lot politer than Granny Sosillia and her knuckle-rapping wooden spoon. It was thus with some regret that Lucullus was forced to tell the posh old lady, "No."

"No?" she repeated in a tone that suggested Lucullus had got it wrong.

"No."

"No, I'm not allowed to invite a friend to dine?"

"No."

"Am I allowed a friend for a breakfast chat?"

"No," squirmed Lucullus.

"Am I allowed to wave at my friend from the front door if she stands five paces away at all times?"

There was a gentle mocking in her voice. Lucullus smiled. "Sorry, but no. These are my orders. No one in or out, excepting tradespeople but they aren't to move beyond the kitchens. Oh, and Philo is allowed in."

Caenis gave a shrug. "That is a shame. I do so miss my friends."

Lucullus was sympathetic. Granny Sosillia had many friends. All of them bad-tempered old crones like her.

"Sorry, ma'am."

She looked sad, which made Lucullus sad.

"Perhaps you could pass this letter on to her for me." She handed him a tied scroll. "You are, of course, welcome to read it."

Lucullus handed the scroll back. "Sorry, ma'am. My orders—"

"And they couldn't be breached for a lady to send a greeting to a friend she is prohibited from seeing?"

"No, sorry."

She smiled sweetly in a way that Granny Sosillia never had in her entire, endless life and sighed, "Oh well."

When she was safely seated in the courtyard, Caenis' sweet expression was dropped, as were a few choice thoughts on Praetorians. That out of her system, she twirled the scroll round in her hands. How was she going to get her message to Lysandria?

Shuffling slightly on the bench she was assailed by a sharp prick to her thigh. Standing up, rubbing at the sore spot, she soon discovered the culprit. One of Domitian's discarded arrows. Damn boy! Why didn't he ever get a slave to clear up after him?

She picked up the arrow with irritation when an idea hit her. Was it possible? She surveyed the open courtyard. The walls were what? Ten feet high? If she stood on the bench? It was worth a try, wasn't it?

She unfurled her scroll, carefully wound it round the arrow, and used the ribbon to secure it. Now where was the bow? Ah, there it was. She'd never fired a bow before. How difficult could it be?

As it turned out, very. She couldn't even get the arrow to stay in place. It kept pinging out before she could fire the damn thing. So engrossed was she in this troublesome task that she didn't hear Domitian approach until he said, "What are you doing?"

Caenis dropped the bow with a start. She'd always been quick of mind, and it was entirely without hesitation that she told him, "Clearing up your mess."

Domitian gave her a long look. "No, you're not," he said.

She debated inwardly before saying, "I need to get a message outside. The guards are proving themselves surprisingly obedient by adhering to their orders. I thought I could possibly emulate your dexterity and skill with a bow and arrow to deliver this scroll. It appears I was wrong."

"A message to get help? To get us out of here?" The hope was all too naked on his face.

She quickly quashed it before it could take root. "No, my dear. Not that. We will get out of here, I promise. But the conditions are not right."

"What do you mean? Why aren't the conditions right?" he enquired with more than a hint of desperation.

"For our survival," she told him bluntly. "I need to make those conditions right. I need to get this scroll out there."

"To who?"

"You need not worry about that. It's all arranged."

"The agent who slept with Caecina? Or the one who poisoned Valens?" said Domitian evenly. "You may as well tell me. After all you and my father are the ones who got me locked up here surrounded by armed guards. I think I deserve the truth."

There was a teenage peevishness in his tone that Caenis was long familiar with. But his point was well made. "The poisoner," she told him.

Domitian took the arrow and bow from her hands. Bouncing the arrow on his palm to feel its weight, he asked, "Which side?"

Caenis pointed out the direction.

Domitian took three steps to the left, then looked upwards at the sky. He repeated the move, his eyes fixed on the roof. When they unfixed, he saw Caenis looking at him enquiringly.

"I'm trying to work out how high I need to shoot it to land on the street outside as opposed to our guttering. The scroll makes it heavier, so the arrow's journey may be more zigzaggy than I'm used to. The accuracy may not be so good."

Caenis left him to his pacing and pondering, and sat herself down on the bench. Eventually, he rubbed his hands on his thighs and emitted a, "Right!"

Caenis stood.

Domitian took a position in the middle of the courtyard. He loaded the arrow into the bow and fired. It shot upwards in a rather wobbly trajectory. Caenis held her breath, watching as the arrow arched down and dipped from view. Walking behind her stepson, she squeezed his shoulder.

"Well done."

* * *

The slave sat in the street. He'd been sat in that same spot every single day. So much so that passing residents had assumed him to be a beggar and he'd built up a nice amount of coinage for his freedom fund.

When the arrow appeared from over the wall and landed with a ping on the cobbles, he knew that this was what he'd been waiting for. He collected up the arrow and its message and rushed back to his mistress' house.

NINE

After another tense night of half sleep in camp, Epaphroditus was awoken by a banging at the door. "The emperor is intending to move on this morning," his body slave told him as he was dressed.

About time, thought Epaphroditus. True, Galba had delayed his arrival in Rome but he'd spent that time unifying the provinces under his rule. Vitellius was simply partying his way to the capital, lapping up the adoration en route. Or so Epaphroditus had heard, not having been in the emperor's presence since that day at the games.

Not that there was anything necessarily wrong with courting the mob. The people loved a show. It kept them passive. It could well bind them to this new emperor. But there comes a time when one has to pick up the pen and do some actual work. Even Nero had grudgingly complied with that.

* * *

The first person Epaphroditus came across was Empress Galeria.

"Imperial Mistress," he addressed her, lowering his head. "I understand we are departing this morning."

Galeria gave a tight smile. "My husband wishes to undertake a small excursion before we start back to Rome. It's not to my taste and I shall not attend. Neither will my son."

Epaphroditus had no chance to quiz her further for Vitellius' freedman, Asiaticus, swept in. "We're leaving," he said simply.

* * *

The cart bounced along the road, juddering whenever it hit a loose flagstone. Epaphroditus was encased with Asiaticus and Caecina. Neither was an enthralling travelling companion. They were quite a contrast: the flawlessly handsome Caecina and Asiaticus, possessed of a vicious scar that closed his eye and pulled up his lip into a sneer.

When he'd asked Asiaticus where they were going, the freedman was obtuse to the point of rudeness.

"You'll recognise it when we get there," he'd said.

Caecina, meanwhile, stared gloomily out of the window. Epaphroditus found himself doing the same. Had Vespasian declared himself, he wondered. Maybe he'd sent his troops on beforehand, to strike all the quicker. That's why they needed to get to Rome. Preparations needed to be undertaken. The legions who'd declared for Otho over Vitellius needed bringing on board, lest they veer towards the Judaean governor instead. Things needed to be done now. Epaphroditus felt a growing twitch of impatience as the wagon trundled slowly to its destination.

The cart came to a slow halt. The soldiers' shouts informed them they were here. Epaphroditus stepped down from the wagon. They were in the countryside, a gently sloping hill with a wooded copse and the straight lines of a vineyard in the distance. He gazed around, puzzled. Why were they here of all places? What could Vitellius possibly want to see here? And what was that incessant buzzing sound? His eyes fell on the field to the left of the road and the cloud of dark, fat flies that hummed above it.

"Ah, Epaphroditus," grinned the approaching emperor flanked by Lucius, Triaria and the thin-lipped Valens. "This is it! The sight of my magnificent victory!" He swiped a podgy arm in the direction of the fly-infested field.

This was where Otho's and Vitellius' forces had squared up to each other.

"Come, let us see," declared Vitellius, stepping forward and over a rotting corpse that lay in his way.

Valens walked alongside. "It was from this side I attacked, Caesar."

Epaphroditus walked behind, his whole body squirming from that buzzing and the stench that attacked his nostrils. He tried not to gag as they walked among the thousands of men who lay dead and decomposing in that field. He forced himself not to examine them, lest he recognise a friendly face from Otho's camp.

He was concentrating so hard on not tripping over that he missed most of Valens' commentary on the battle. He knew it all anyhow. He'd heard it from the scouts as they delivered the news of the defeat to Otho.

He remembered with a pang his friend's frozen expression and his terse reply, "I see."

"Gods, Lucius! Look at this one. He has no face," said Triaria bending over one body. "What type of weapon would do that, Valens?"

The general ceased in his commentary and examined the corpse. Its features were lost in one bloody mass of bone and gore. "None. More likely the wolves have been at him."

"What a feast for them," smiled Triaria, gazing around this field of death.

"For the birds too," continued Valens. "They go for the eyes. There's something in them that they can't resist. Sometimes they don't even wait till their victim is dead."

The bile hit the back of Epaphroditus' throat. He attempted to swallow it back down but there was too much. It escaped from between his lips as he bent over, retching. Standing back up, wiping the back of his hand across his mouth, he met the cold, grey eyes of Fabius Valens. Valens shook his head in disgust.

"They should make all slaves serve in the army. It would toughen them up."

"But would you trust them?" Triaria asked, aiming a kick at the slave girl who stood behind her.

Valens glared at Epaphroditus. "Not with my life. Not with anything that was mine"

This set Triaria laughing in a manner that had Epaphroditus wondering if she were drunk. She was certainly staggering somewhat but that could be down to the uneven surface and her heeled sandals. Her husband, in contrast to Triaria's glee, seemed almost bored by the excursion.

Vitellius cast his piggy eyes, onto his two generals. "Well? Where is it? What you promised me. Where is it?"

"It's this way Caesar, over there," said Caecina pointing.

"Too far," decided the emperor. "Asiaticus! Go get my ride."

Epaphroditus marvelled at the fortitude of the sedan chair bearers. How they managed to raise the gigantic bulk of Vitellius' body onto their shoulders was a feat worthy of Hercules. That they then managed to carry this weight right across the grass was truly inspiring. The gods knew how they'd been trained up to such strength. Men of that muscle would've made impressive bodyguards or gladiators. Epaphroditus couldn't keep his eyes off their endeavours. It saved him from viewing Valens' cold dislike and Triaria's mocking amusement.

He'd served worse, he told himself as he followed the emperor's chair. Triaria was no Agrippina. She'd need decades to practise her malice to come anywhere close.

Holding a hand above his eyes Vitellius declared, "Ha! I see it."

And so did Epaphroditus. It was Otho's tomb. So that had been the design the whole time. The bearers lowered Vitellius down in front of the small mound and tomb. The last time Epaphroditus had stood on this spot, it had been when Otho's ashes had been placed in this tomb. He remembered feeling numb, utterly disbelieving that the small urn contained the remains of his friend. It didn't seem possible that Marcus was gone. Epaphroditus had assumed he'd be extracting Otho from dubious situations of his own making when they were both old men.

He could've escaped this last scrape, this last adventure, but Otho had chosen not to. He'd ended his own life rather than risk any more of his troops. It was a nobility that Epaphroditus had never seen from his friend before. Otho had surprised him one final time.

Here he lay. That noble emperor. His victorious successor looked at the unadorned tomb with its simple epithet, "To the Memory of Marcus Otho."

"It's all he deserved," said Vitellius.

"I say!" said Triaria. "Why don't we have a picnic?"

"Good idea. I'm starving," grumbled Lucius.

Epaphroditus caught a gleam in the emperor's eyes. "Yes, let us dine. Right here. Right now. Let us celebrate my great victory."

Slaves were sent to the nearest settlement to demand supplies. They returned with half the village eager to impress, carrying food and furniture for the emperor. A great feast was laid out for the emperor, by the tomb of the man he'd defeated, beside a field of rotting legionaries of Rome.

* * *

Epaphroditus sat back on the wagon and, resting his head against the wood, closed his eyes.

"They were good fighters," came a voice.

Epaphroditus' eyes opened.

"They were good fighters, the Othonians," said Caecina. "They weren't as easily repelled as Valens claimed."

"I know," said Epaphroditus, keeping an eye on the allegedly sleeping Asiaticus. "But Caesar triumphed and that is all that matters now."

Caecina gave a faint smile, angling his handsome head towards Asiaticus, indicating that he understood.

TEN

"The boy was yawning when I left," said Felix, closing the bedroom door. "So I reckon he'll be out before I get to that bed."

In that bed sat Vallia in all her monstrous bulk, arms crossed over a bosom of such a size that whole ham legs could be lost in it for days.

"I hope that doesn't mean you've been exhausting him with work at that palace." She said "palace" in a tone that suggested she had as much respect for the home of the Caesars as she did for the local rubbish tip.

"'course I fuckin' ain't, woman," said Felix getting into bed beside her.

"And those three slices of pie he had for supper? I hope for your sake that wasn't because you forgot to give him lunch. Because that would be typical of your selfishness."

"Oh give it a fuckin' rest, woman," said Felix, placing his hand on her leg.

She brushed it away with a motion of such brusqueness it bruised his fingers.

"I'm getting mine tonight," he said, sucking on his knuckles.

"Are you now?" said Vallia, heading into screech territory. She shot and shooting a look of such fire it could have incinerated the sheets. "Ain't that typical of you. Take take take. Never mind what I might want."

"I know what you want," uttered Felix in a low growl moving towards her. "I know that glint in your eyes."

There had, over the years, been much speculation over the source of Felix's ever-present belligerence. A decade or so earlier, a general consensus had been reached: it had to be down to a stupendous sexual frustration. Because you couldn't. You just couldn't. No one could. Not even Felix. Not with Vallia. Surely? She was a gigantic ape of a woman. Possessing with a chin that was overdue a trip to the barbers and a complexion that had been unkindly compared to a blushing rhino.

The only reason the marriage had lasted, so the palace gossip ran, was because Felix was too scared to divorce her.

The gossip was entirely unfounded. From his very first sight of Vallia by the Aventine docks, Felix had been lustily smitten. For Felix liked big women. The bigger the better as far as he was concerned. The kind of woman who could smash a pig carcass into chops with a cleaver. The kind of woman who could carry three whole amphora of wine without breaking a sweat. The kind of woman who was his match for brute strength and fiery temper. The kind of woman who would meet his sweaty grapplings with a similar energy.

So, no. Felix foul temper had nothing to do with sexual frustration. He got plenty.

At the end of this particular wrestling bout, Felix rolled over with a contented sigh. "Ahh, woman."

Vallia slapped his hand off her humungous rear. "Animal! You'd think after all these years you'd get better at it. But no! Yet again, I am the only woman on the Aventine left unsatisfied by her husband!"

Felix was not fooled. He'd felt her body shudder all right. But he played along because that was how their marriage worked.

"I don't know why I fucking bother!"

"Neither do I."

A pause, then, "I suppose I'd better give it another go if the last one was such a fuckin' disappointment."

"Yes you had, you useless oaf."

At the conclusion of round two, they lay side by side in companionable silence as their limbs recovered from the activity. After a while Felix said, "I don't think I'll take the boy with me to the palace no more."

Vallia rolled onto her side to face him, the bed shuddering under her weight. "What? After all that going on about how you were going to give him a proper education? And how the teachers in the Aventine were thick as pig fat?"

"And I were fuckin' right. They are! You name one person who can read in this street."

Vallia thought for a moment: "Acer."

Felix rubbed his face with a palm. "Minerva's arse, woman. He's the fuckin' teacher. And a fuckin' crap one at that if he's the only literate fucker you can come up with."

"You said you'd give little Gany proper training for a proper job. That's what you said. I might have known it was all talk. Well, you can tell him his papa don't want to take him to work no more. I couldn't bear to see his little face."

"It ain't safe."

Vallia screwed up her eyes. "You've been taking him to work with you for months."

"The new emperor's going to be here soon and this new one, he ain't right," began Felix, and for once Vallia didn't interrupt. "Oh, he's been playing the fuckin' game for years. Perfect fuckin' lackey he is. Too lazy to be considered a threat but just competent enough to get up that ladder. Only I know him. I remember him." Felix tapped a hairy index finger against his temple. "When that demented Caligula were boss, there were no fuckin' restraints. Men could be what they truly fuckin' were. 'Course, in most cases, they was trembling cowards. Not him though. Not Vitellius. I'd already seen what he were capable of when that randy old goat Tiberius were in charge.

He nearly fuckin' killed one of my wine boys. Not cos he displeased him, or anything like that. No, it was his idea of fun. Under Caligula there weren't no depths he didn't sink to. And now he's the fuckin' emperor. He can do anything he wants. Anything."

Felix expected Vallia to argue. To get on at him for hours, as was per usual. (And for Felix, surrounded by meekly compliant slaves all day, this was one of Vallia's many attractions.) But she didn't.

She patted his hand and said, "Gany stays home."

ELEVEN

Epaphroditus stared out of the window of the wagon. The road was lined either side with tombs. The slowness of his transportation gave him plenty of time to study them. Temples in miniature with thick columns. Rounded mausoleums topped with statues. Sturdy rectangles covered in friezes. Soon he would pass the tomb of his son, Iugarthus, the marker that he was almost home.

It was, he mused, hardly a triumphant return.

* * *

A few days previously, he'd been lying on his bed trying to ignore the usual raucous rabble of noise outside. Since the night of the wrestling bout, the troops had scarcely been any better disciplined. True, nobody had been killed, but that was surely only a matter of time. He had placed his slave outside armed with a club. This did little to aid his sleep. He was just about to give up the idea of rest, when a summons had arrived from the emperor.

Vitellius had been enjoying a late supper, or long dinner, when Epaphroditus had entered. Serving the feast were a collection of small boys dressed as cherubs in white loincloths, with feathered wings strapped to their backs. On the couch next to Vitellius and Galeria, lay Lucius and Triaria.

The emperor expelled an, "Ahhh," that was part greeting, part belch.

Epaphroditus bowed his head. "Imperial Majesty."

"After our little trip yesterday, I have completed all that I need to in these shitty little towns."

A sentiment that shocked Triaria into a giggle. "Brother!" she exclaimed, smiling.

"It's the truth. I always speak the truth. I give credit for their efforts." He swept his arm across to indicate the banquet and the cherub servants. "But it is not up to palace standards. It is nowhere near palace standards."

Vitellius should know. There were few palace events he had excused himself from. Indeed, they kept a special couch for him at the palace with reinforced springs to hold his expanding bulk. It had gone into storage when Vitellius had departed to Germania. They'd need to get it out again now.

"I deserve... No, I am entitled to, so much more than these pathetic attempts at entertaining. Tomorrow we shall begin our preparations for our triumphal entrance into Rome."

Triaria clapped her hands together in glee.

"'Bout time," muttered Lucius.

Galeria was silent, picking at a piece of bread.

"I want you, Epaphroditus, to travel ahead of us and ensure that everything is properly arranged. I want the very best to serve me. I want proper entertainments," he said, thumping his fist on to the arm of the couch. "Get Felix working on it. I expect the best. And I will hold you accountable for it."

"Imperial Majesty, there is the more pressing concerns about the loyalty of the eastern legions—"

Vitellius cut him off. "Valens is dealing with all that. You concentrate on ensuring my expectations are met."

He'd been demoted from private secretary to entertainments coordinator. Fabulous.

* * *

The wagon came to a halt. The face of his slave popped up at the window.

"This is as far as we can go, master."

No wheeled vehicles were allowed into the city during daytime hours. It made for a noisy darkness as sellers struggled to get their goods to the relevant market.

"Would you prefer a chair or a litter, master?"

Epaphroditus stepped down from the wagon. In front of him stood the huge arches of the Porta Praenestina into the city. Already there was a bobbing queue of sedan chairs, their riders attempting a dignified sit, even as the local rabble abused them verbally.

"I think I'll walk. I want to head up to the palace first."

* * *

He walked through the familiar corridors, his mind very much elsewhere. So this was it. His new job. Entertaining Vitellius. Though it might have seemed a less daunting task than the tricky diplomacy he'd negotiated as Nero's chief advisor, Epaphroditus knew better.

Nero had possessed very particular interests, which he'd expected to be incorporated into his entertainment. Hadn't there been ordered mass whippings when the emperor had expressed his displeasure and disappointment in the festivities arranged for him? Hadn't there been executions for the underperforming? Yes, there had. Epaphroditus had signed off both orders without thought.

Epaphroditus knew that Vitellius would be no less exacting. He'd rather have been negotiating peace between Rome and her deadly rival Parthia.

Still, there were some positives. He'd been sat next to Vitellius at enough palace parties over the years to have some ideas as to what might be acceptable to the new emperor. Best to get some of it in place as soon as possible.

To this end, he sought out Felix.

* * *

"Eunuchs. What are our eunuch numbers like?" asked Epaphroditus, his eyes unwittingly drawn to the space beside Felix where Ganymede usually stood.

Felix scratched at his thick red beard. "Healthy number. They could do with an outing. What with that fuckin' old git of an emperor Galba not liking 'em and wanting them hidden away like some guilty secret. And then there were that emperor Otho fighting against fuckin' liking them. Well, they've been all holed up together for far too fuckin' long. They're like fuckin' chickens pecking the feathers off each other. Bit of dancing and that will be good for them."

"Excellent. Get them polished up. But Felix. No Sporus, alright? I don't need that sort of troublesome mischief."

Sporus was the most famous of the palace eunuchs. He'd been the lover of both Nero and Otho. He was likely eyeing up his next high-level conquest. But not on Epaphroditus' watch.

"Let the masseurs and beauticians loose on him to keep him out the way."

Felix gave a hmm. The closest he was ever likely to get to acknowledging an order had been given to him and he was going to follow it.

Epaphroditus had got to the door, intent on going home, when Felix said to his back, "Here, I don't want my eunuchs damaged. They're expensive to fuckin' write off. Classy goods. Not to be treated too roughly, if you know what I fuckin' mean."

"I don't know what you mean," replied Epaphroditus turning, his hand dropping from the handle.

"Our new emperor being who he fuckin' is," he expanded.

"I don't know what you mean. The new emperor likes dancing eunuchs. Who doesn't? They're generally a talented species of creature. I can't see him harming them."

"You've got a fuckin' selective memory, ain't ya?" Felix crossed his huge hairy arms.

"Just get the eunuchs brushed up, please," replied Epaphroditus tersely.

He was at the door when Felix said to his back, "He fuckin' better not try to strangle one of my boys again."

He couldn't help it, couldn't stop it. Epaphroditus' hand flew up to his throat, his fingers spanning across its width.

"Yeah, you remember alright," said Felix, as Epaphroditus shut the door behind him.

TWELVE

Walking back through the palace, Epaphroditus rubbed at his throat, attempting to push Felix's words away. He just needed to get home, have a hot bath, and wash off his journey.

Home was a sizeable mansion on the Esquiline Hill, a few streets away from the gateway into Rome. Standing outside the door he hesitated, pausing his hand midway to the knock that would alert his doorman. He hadn't been back to this house since the funeral. Afterwards, when the children had departed for the coast, he'd gone back to the palace. He hadn't returned.

Epaphroditus was a man forever moving forward. He'd made it a deliberate policy never to look back. But coming here to the home he'd built for Aphrodite was to move backwards. To immerse himself in memories of a time when he'd had a wife, a partner to share his life with. A woman he had never ceased to love, even after she was gone.

His chamberlain was very apologetic. "Master, you should have sent word. None of the rooms are ready."

"It doesn't matter. It's just me."

His eyes fell on the table that stood in the middle of the courtyard. This was where he and Aphrodite had shared their breakfast during the summer months, usually with a fidgeting child on at least one of their laps. The rest of their brood surrounding them, devouring the succulent fruit and arguing with each other. It was so vivid, so potent an image, that he could almost touch it. His hand drifted towards the chair. The chair that was always hers.

"Master."

Epaphroditus snapped back to the present. And to the heavy silence that hung over the deserted courtyard.

"I asked if you'd like some refreshments, master. I can get the cook to prepare something."

"I suppose so," responded Epaphroditus, sitting down at the table.

He placed his hand on the surface. It was warm, heated by the summer sun. His eyes fell on the chairs: empty. All of them empty.

He turned away, moving his head round so he didn't have to see them. Instead, he stared at a fat round flowerpot that stood some feet away. Faustina, his second eldest daughter, had once hid in that pot. She'd been two, maybe three, and enthused with a mischief they'd (wrongly) assumed she'd grow out of.

How they'd searched for her! Epaphroditus had cross-examined the doorman, who insisted, no matter what he was threatened with, that she hadn't passed him. It was as he and Aphrodite had collapsed onto these chairs, discussing how many slaves they should send out to search, that they had heard it. A giggle. An echoing giggle.

The relief was all encompassing as Epaphroditus had gently lifted the giggling Faustina out of her hiding place. Aphrodite had hugged the little girl tight as Epaphroditus kissed Faustina's dark curls, the two of them laughing with relief.

There was no laughter now. There was nothing but silence.

"Sir."

"Yes, yes, place the food on the table," he snapped, not looking up. Fighting to hold back the tears that were starting to form.

"Sir, it's me. Philo."

"Philo?"

Epaphroditus swung round to see the ever cringing, ever apologetic features of his assistant.

"I wondered, sir, if you might want to come and dine with Teretia and me. At our apartment."

* * *

Seated in Philo and Teretia's cosy kitchen, Epaphroditus asked, "How did you know I was back?"

Philo gave a small shrug. "I didn't. I've been stopping off each day to check. Today you happened to be there, sir."

It was the sort of thoroughness he'd come to expect from Philo.

"Could you pass Epaphroditus some bread please," Teretia directed the young girl lurking by the end of the table.

The girl did so.

"Our slave, Marcia," Philo responded to Epaphroditus' enquiring gaze.

"She's been a tremendous help already," said Teretia brightly.

"I like to help," said Marcia.

Epaphroditus felt his eyebrow raise at Marcia's presumption to speak and her lack of a "master" or "mistress". From Philo's squirming features, he knew this lack of courtesy was not lost on Marcia's owner.

Teretia pushed her hands on to the table. "We'll leave you men to talk work."

Philo gently placed his hands either side of his wife and helped her to her feet. Now upright, with her pregnant belly very prominent, a birth was imminent Epaphroditus calculated. He hoped Philo was prepared. Then he inwardly corrected himself: of course Philo would be prepared. No doubt there were a stack of linens ready to be used, a pile of swaddling blankets, and a wet nurse already sourced.

"I'm sure we'd find it quite dull, wouldn't we, Marcia?"

Marcia smiled. "I'd prefer to finish off those little booties for the baby."

"Me too!" gushed Teretia. "It is so much quicker with Marcia's help," she told Epaphroditus. "She knits twice as fast as me!"

The two girls departed, arms linked together. On hearing the door close, Philo gave a groan.

"Teretia seems to see Marcia as more like a sister than a slave," he said. "That's not to say Marcia hasn't been a terrific help. She has. But she's, err …"

"Not up to palace standards?"

"Yes, that's it."

Epaphroditus broke off another piece of bread. "You spend your entire childhood despising and loathing the palace overseers. Then you become a slave owner yourself and suddenly you have a full appreciation of their skills!"

"Yes, I think that's it," said Philo unhappily. "I'm not sure I'm up to disciplining her. I don't think I could. Teretia would never forgive me."

"You could always send her over to my house for training. My housekeeper Callista is a dreadful tyrant to the younger slaves. But she gets results."

"Really, sir?" brightened Philo. "Because that might work. Though she's keen, Marcia hasn't ever looked after a baby before."

"A subject Callista has ample experience of. It'll cheer up the old crone to have a protégée. She's apparently been rather glum since the children left."

"The children, are they…?"

"They're still in Baiae. I'll probably send for them after the summer. The emperor will be settled in Rome by then, and all will be calmer."

"The emperor is on his way back then?"

"He should be here in approximately five days."

"Five days?" Philo's eyes moved back and forth until they settled on an object at the end of the table, his note tablet.

Epaphroditus held up a hand. "There's no need to write this down."

Philo's writing hand twitched a few times, itching to work. He held it still with his other hand, placing both on the table.

"I may as well tell you now," began Epaphroditus. "Vitellius is bringing in his own man as private secretary. I have been redeployed. It's not, I'll admit, what I hoped for."

"That doesn't matter, sir. I am sure we'll do a great job wherever we are."

Epaphroditus pressed his fingertips together. "You're not coming with me, Philo."

The scribe's face fell with such naked hurt that Epaphroditus hurriedly added, "I need someone on the inside. Vitellius isn't taking this Vespasian situation seriously enough. None of them are."

"Sir?"

"If you can pass the important bits on to me, there's maybe a chance I can get myself redeployed again. They don't trust me. I was too close to Otho. I need to prove my worth."

Philo didn't appear any happier. "There's not much coming in from the East."

"Which is worrying in itself. Tell me, has Vespasian tried to contact Caenis?"

Philo shook his head.

"His brother? His son?"

Philo shook his head to both.

Chewing on a piece of bread, Epaphroditus said, "So he knows. He knows we know what he's planning to do."

"His legions are a good way away," supplied Philo. "That's quite a lot of time to get the resistance organised."

Epaphroditus looked down at his bread. "The thing is, he doesn't need to move at all. He has Egypt. That gives him control of the grain ships."

Philo's alarm was carried in his voice, as he concluded, "He can starve the emperor to surrender."

"Given how much Vitellius eats, that isn't going to take long."

Philo swallowed down a mouthful of lettuce. "But his family? He surely won't leave them to starve."

"No, he wouldn't. He'll have an escape route planned for them. Caenis will have it planned. She'll have left nothing to chance. No factor unseen. No eventuality unplanned for," he said, with a trace of bitterness in his voice. "Which is why I need you to stay put in your current role."

"Of course, I will serve in whatever capacity you choose, sir."

Epaphroditus gave a tight smile. "I knew I could count on you. Just be careful of Caenis. She is one extremely cunning woman."

THIRTEEN

When emperor Galba had arrived in Rome he done so with little fanfare or announcement. Keen to just get on with the job of sorting out Nero's mess, he'd not even sent forward word to the palace. Philo, who'd been tasked with the job of organising the new emperor's welcome, had thus endured a few hours of maximum stress.

Vitellius was different. This emperor camped a few miles outside the city in order to give his staff time to properly organise his greeting. And what a greeting it was to be! A banquet of such size, such lavishness that had never been seen. Not even in Nero's time!

It was causing Midas, head of catering, some stress, which he communicated to Epaphroditus. None of this fazed the new entertainments coordinator. Epaphroditus had climbed the palace ladder the hard way. Frankly, arranging a banquet for several thousand was a damn sight easier on the nerves than one of young Nero's night-time forays into plebeian drinking holes. Nobody in the first instance was in any danger of getting their knees bashed with a club by irate locals.

He took the panicking Midas in hand and set about organising a truly spectacular welcome for the new emperor. It was to be pure palace: larks' tongues, roasted flamingos, and more eunuchs than had ever been seen in one place at any one time before.

* * *

Marcia pulled the needle under the knot tied onto her thumb, creating another stitch. This was well on its way to being a snuggly blanket.

"Aren't you going to see the new emperor arrive, mistress? Everyone at the market says it is going to be a terrific sight."

Teretia, who was working on another blanket (because you can never have too many) shook her head firmly and gave a slight shudder as she said, "Philo is worried about me going too far from home this close to the arrival of my boy." Her expression brightened as she smiled down at her now globular stomach.

"Right girls!" bustled in Pompeia. She bashed her basket down on to the table. "I've filled my basket to the top with wool. Blue, red, yellow, green, and white. I reckon we can produce some lovely stuff today if we put our fingers to work." She began to unpack her purchases.

"Morning all," said Lysander, entering the kitchen accompanied by Philo. "Wow, that's a lot of wool. I wonder how many sheep it took."

He bounced a ball of white wool on his palm. Pompeia snatched it back off him.

"We don't intend on going out today," she told the men emphatically. "We are dedicated to the knit."

"Probably best," said Lysander. "The streets are going to be heaving today for the emperor's entrance. Not to mention all the soldiers."

"Lysander, if you're dropping in on Verenia on your way to the palace, could you ask her to come help with our knit."

"Mother, we don't need Verenia."

"Nonsense," scorned Pompeia. "She's a good knitter. I taught her myself. We need as many fingers working as possible."

"Good idea," agreed Lysander. "I'm not keen on my betrothed being out in the crowds. You know what young lads are like on these occasions. They can't resist trying to—"

"Ahem." Philo cleared his throat noisily before Lysander could launch into a full descriptive account of the molestations that were a standard feature of festival days.

"Do you have a role in the festivities, master?"

Philo inwardly warmed at hearing Marcia address him correctly. Clearly her morning with Epaphroditus' slave Callista had produced a positive effect on her. For which he was grateful. He really hadn't fancied having to discipline her. Just the thought of a whipping brought back terrible memories of the palace overseer, Straton. Straton had a very sturdy whip hand that had scarred Philo's back and buttocks permanently.

"I might look in later on events," said Philo to his slave, "but I rather thought I'd call in on Flavius first."

"You won't want to miss the banquet!" Lysander chimed in. "It is going to be epic. The eunuchs have been practising their bottom wiggles for days. It's brilliantly synchronised. And Mina's doing her whipping act. It's impressive. I saw her in the trial run yesterday."

Philo gave an involuntary shudder. Artemina, more generally known as Mina, was a former towel holder to Nero's empress Statilia. Philo had an uncomfortable relationship with her, forged the day she'd launched her naked form against him and grabbed hold of his penis with an upsetting amount of intent. Things had not improved when she'd become Straton's protégée in whip skills.

"I think I'd better give it a miss, Lysander. Flavius and Caenis are bound to be anxious with the new emperor arriving. Domitian too. I should be there to reassure them."

"I think that's a lovely, kind thing to do," Teretia beamed at her husband.

Philo gave her a gentle kiss on the lips, saying, "You will take care," with an anxious glance at her belly.

"I don't think it'll be today, Philo. I feel quite well and we haven't got our knitting done."

"Yeah, I hear that's how it works," said Lysander. "Childbirth only commences once a sufficient pile of baby clothes has been produced."

FOURTEEN

As Philo had predicted, Flavius' household was indeed edgy. Caenis admitted, "I've sent Domitian off to practise his archery. It's the one activity that soothes his anxiety. At least until we find him a girl!"

Flavius gave a chortle that ended sooner than it should have. "I would have got to work on finding him a wife; there's lots of lovely young girls of our class. But times being what they are…" He threw his hands up. "What has he got to promise them? Why would any girl's family wish to align with ours right now? He should be starting his public career."

There was an undeniable hint of despair in Flavius' voice. He looked older, more drawn than Philo remembered from the time when they'd both served Otho.

"This is just a temporary measure," Philo said. "Otho's nephew Salvius is contemplating running for aedile, I've heard."

Flavius gave a tight smile. "So my brother has to die for my nephew's life to continue as normal."

"That's not what I meant," flapped Philo.

The older man got to his feet, squeezing Philo's shoulder. He said, "I know it wasn't. He's a good lad, Salvius. I wish him well. I think I'll go lie down for a bit. I feel weary." He trudged away.

"I worry about him," said Caenis. "I worry about both of them." And then in an unexpected moment of candour, she said, "It's really not fair that Domitian and Flavius are suffering like this. They had nothing to do with any of it. It was Vespasian, Titus, and Muscianus."

"Muscianus, the Syrian governor?"

"That one, yes. And Tiberius Alexander, the Egyptian governor. Go tell your boss that. Possibly he'll benefit from Vitellius' generosity for that information."

A pained Philo shuffled his feet. "I still cannot release Flavius and Domitian."

Caenis gave an exasperated sigh. "Get Epaphroditus here. Let him and I talk alone. Perhaps I have additional information that may be of use to him."

Philo, knowing Epaphroditus' deep hurt at Caenis' betrayal, doubted he would come. Still, he promised her he would pass the message on.

* * *

The crowds had gathered by the Milvian Bridge ready to welcome the arrival of the new emperor. It was here the previous year that Emperor Galba had released his cavalry into the mass of civilians. Hundreds had been killed, including Teretia's father, another reason why she was happy to stay indoors knitting.

The waiting civilians this time feared nothing. News had been brought of quite a different entourage approaching the city.

"There's acrobats! And musicians. Not army trumpeters but proper musicians. They have a water organist playing on a wagon pulled by donkeys. I met a woman who's been following the march since the spring and she says it's the most fun she's ever had!"

Expectations raised, the crowd waited in high anticipation. They were not disappointed. The entourage of entertainers took a clear half hour to pass by before there was sight of the new emperor and empress.

The empress Galeria was seated in an open carriage, her son on her lap waving wildly at everyone. This had the crowd smiling and crying out best wishes for their "Little Caesar".

The emperor himself was sat on the largest, finest horse any of the crowd had ever seen, not even at the races. He wore the uniform of a general, made more impressive for the size of the armour that glittered in the summer sun. Vitellius had mastered the optimum look. He was neither glumly unimpressed nor gleefully overcome. Rather, he appeared as a man enjoying himself, but not too much. Epaphroditus would have been impressed.

Behind another carriage, containing Lucius and Triaria, rode the two men without whom this day would never had happened: Valens and Caecina.

Valens' eyes scanned the crowds. As a flurry of rose petals were thrown his way, he raised an arm of acknowledgement to the thrower. Then, seeing it was a girl, he slowed his horse down to take a better look. She possessed the type of thin, undeveloped frame Valens admired. He debated sending a soldier into the crowd to claim the girl for him, then dismissed that thought. There was no rush, no hurry. Valens had all the time in the world to enjoy whomever he wanted. There'd be no complaints now, no irate father or disapproving superior. Valens was the emperor's closest associate. He could do whatever he liked. No one could stop him.

What a homecoming this was! He'd left the city a penniless nobody and returned with unlimited wealth and power. Valens was impatient to exercise both. Glancing to his right, he noted his colleague's glum expression, quite at odds with the jollity all around.

"For Mars' sake cheer up, will you," hissed Valens. "You can't still be mooning over that bitch. So she tricked you and dented your pride. What's it matter now? Forget her. Move onto the next tight cunt. It's all for the taking."

"Is that what you did with that woman who fooled you into thinking she was curing you? When the whole time she was really poisoning you?"

Valens' jaw tightened as Caecina trotted his horse away.

* * *

Caecina pulled up alongside Asiaticus. The freedman nodded by way of greeting. He was not one for words, which for Caecina was a pleasant change from Valens. After a few moments of companionable silence, Caecina dared to ask, "Has the emperor decided what he will do with her?"

He didn't speak her name, mainly because he didn't know what to call her. To him she had been Salonina. This Nymphidia woman was a stranger to him, even though she wore Salonina's face.

"My master has always been fond of Nymphidia. No harm will come to her. He plans to let her return to her home. She'll be less trouble there than at the palace."

"I see," said Caecina.

So this was farewell. It should have cheered him that the source of his humiliation was being removed. But it didn't. Rather, there was a heavy stone in his chest that might once have been his heart.

FIFTEEN

Naturally, Verenia was an excellent knitter. Because she would be, Teretia sulked. Her mother's comments on Verenia's fine stitching had given her cousin the opportunity to show off again about her travels. How she'd learnt to knit during a particularly terrifying sea storm. Leaving Marcia open-mouthed and impressed.

It could have been a disaster of a knitting circle. Luckily, Verenia's slave Doris had been so rubbish at the work, she was demoted to the wool-holding task. Teretia gave a small satisfied smirk as she watched Marcia's blanket grow on to her lap from her slave's deft motions. As she did so, she felt a tightness below her stomach. Her hand fell onto the affected area, rubbing at it.

"Teretia love, are you all right?" asked her mother.

"I'm fine, mother. I might have been sitting down too long. He doesn't like being all squashed up."

"Why are you so convinced it's a boy?" asked Verenia, as Marcia aided Teretia to her feet. "It could just as well be a girl."

"He's a boy! I know he is," responded Teretia rubbing at her bump as another strange tightness occurred.

"From the way she's carrying all out front, mistress, I'd say it was a girl," was Doris' unwanted contribution.

"He's a boy," insisted Teretia, unable to stop herself stomping her foot, much as she'd done as a small girl when Verenia had similarly infuriated her.

Verenia offered her younger cousin a particularly condescending smile. "I am sure you're right but best not get your hopes up too high. Just in case."

"He's a boy!" repeated Teretia on the verge of tears. "A beautiful son for Philo."

Doris placed down the white wool she'd successfully wound into a near-enough ball shape.

"Will it come out Indian?" she asked.

"Philo's not Indian. He's from Tarpobane."

"An island off the coast of India," Verenia translated for Doris and Marcia. "I believe the peoples are very similar due to much interbreeding. *Very* common for near nations involved in trade. When I was in Alexandria—"

"Philo's not Indian!" protested Teretia.

"Now, now Teretia," soothed Pompeia. "Doris is just being curious about who the baby will look like. I'm quite curious myself. I think he might have your blue eyes but Philo's dark hair. Now come sit back down with us."

Teretia turned to the window to wipe away the budding tears from her eyes unseen. The Viminal streets below were strangely deserted. The few people that were out stood to the side of the road. Teretia was about to comment on this when she felt a tremble beneath her feet. A pounding vibration.

"What's that noise?" enquired Pompeia.

The women all got to their feet and gathered by the window, hanging their heads out to see if they could see the source.

"Marching," said Verenia. "Marching boots."

"It must be Vitellius' soldiers," said Teretia. "But why are they coming up this way? Shouldn't they be with the new emperor?"

The noise was now a thumping beat that vibrated the walls, the saucepans dancing on their nails. In the building opposite, the Viminal residents were also hanging out of their windows to see what was going on.

"Why are they coming this way?" pondered Verenia. "Teretia, did Philo say anything about— Teretia? Aunt Pompeia!"

Pompeia turned her attention away from the window to her daughter, standing very still, her face drained of its usual pinkish hue.

"Teretia love, are you well?"

Teretia's bottom lip trembled. "Oh mother!" she cried and burst into tears.

"Oh darling, whatever is the matter?" Pompeia put her arms around her daughter, stroking her hair as she sobbed.

"Eugh, why is there water all over the floor?" commented Doris.

"Oh," said Pompeia noting now the damp lower half of Teretia's gown. "Oh my. I think we'd better get the midwife."

"Err, Aunt Pompeia, how are we going to get the midwife with all of them?" asked Verenia, thumbing at the window.

In the street below were marching past thousands upon thousands of soldiers, taking up every inch of pavement.

"Oh," said Pompeia.

Teretia let out a wail.

"Don't panic, love. It's all going to be fine. It's a first baby so he's likely to make his way slowly. We've got plenty of time," consoled Pompeia, one arm around her daughter as she took in the great number of soldiers. "But it doesn't cost to be prepared. Marcia, Doris, let's push this table to the side of the room. Teretia's going to need space to pace. And Verenia …"

"Yes, Aunt Pompeia?"

"Towels and sheets, as many as you can find. And water! A jug of water please. Birthing is thirsty business."

As her bump tightened, Teretia cried out, "I want Philo!"

SIXTEEN

Philo had spoken to both Flavius and Caenis. He'd checked with the Guard to see if there'd been any breaches in security; there hadn't. He'd sat down in a quiet room and written up his report for the day. Then he'd spent a bit of time examining the room's frescoed walls, shifting a trunk to see more of the detail.

He should be setting off back to the palace. That was generally what he did at this time of the day. But he didn't really fancy walking into all the festivities planned for the emperor's arrival. Philo did not enjoy parties. They were noisy and were attended by too many people for Philo's comfort. When he'd lived at the palace, he'd often wandered off during Nero's extravagant revelries for a little light filing.

More recently he endured events, all the time thinking he'd much rather be at home. He doubted even Epaphroditus' well-executed welcome could compete with a night snuggled up to Teretia. Maybe he'd just check in on Domitian in case the young man had tunnelled out.

Asking assistance from the household slaves, he tracked Domitian down to a dining chamber. The young man lay on a couch, a note tablet balanced on his chest, chewing a stylus between his teeth. He looked thoughtful, relaxed even, until Philo cleared his throat. The previously calm expression morphed into the usual terrified one. He sat up so quickly that the note tablet slid off and hit the floor with a crash.

Philo retrieved it for him. Handing it over, he asked, "Schoolwork?"

Domitian gripped the side of the tablet, his eyes on the floor. "No, something else."

"Oh," said Philo, unsure of how to keep the conversation going and thus forestall his return to the palace. Then he remembered Publius' report, the one that contained lots of facts. Facts were something Philo was far more comfortable with than small talk.

"In my office," began Philo, sitting himself down on the low table in front of Domitian's couch, "it is standard procedure to compile thorough reports on all notable persons. I commissioned one about you."

Philo was rummaging about in his satchel so he missed the look of absolute horror that crossed Domitian's face.

"Ah, here it is," he said, producing a scroll. "I had an individual copy made of your particular report for easy referencing." He handed it over to Domitian.

Philo had, over the years, presented many individuals with such reports. Epaphroditus favoured them as a tool for snapping errant could-be traitor senators back in line. In Philo's experience there were two expected reactions. One, blinding rage complete with swearing refutations of the evidence collected. Two, the other was a sort of icy calm whereby the recipient nodded and then enquired what they could do for the emperor. On no occasion had he met with Domitian's reaction.

The young man, on completion of reading, bent over holding his head in his hands. Elbows pressing on his thighs, he began to cry. Actually, cry didn't cover it. Domitian sobbed. With loud inhalations of breath and a shaking form. Philo, unsure what to do, hugged his satchel to his chest and waited. Eventually the boy looked up, his eyes red and puffy.

"I suppose my father is going to find out about this."

Philo inwardly supposed Vespasian would. Once he handed over his report to Epaphroditus, his boss would no doubt make its content public as a foil to the lascivious charges being spread about Vitellius. In the battle of words between Otho and Vitellius, absolutely nothing had been off limits. Still, it didn't seem that this would cheer Domitian up much. Philo reached for a suitable response.

"It is a long way to the East," he tried. "Maybe it'll get lost in transit. That happens a lot. Which is why I always send duplicates a day apart, on separate ships or horses."

"He won't drop his claim because of me," said Domitian, wiping his nose on his arm. "You do know that, don't you? He's left me here to die, so I hardly think he'll step down to save the family a scandal."

The thought had never occurred to Philo.

"Oh gods!" despaired Domitian. "He's going to hate me even more than he does already. You see, he doesn't care for me at all. Uncle Flavius has been more of a father to me than him. I am utterly insignificant to him. Which is why it's so ridiculous that I'm being held here. Titus! Oh gods! Titus will find out. Oh, he'll bloody love it! Oh!" And here Domitian bent over once more. "I'm such a failure. Such an utter miserable failure."

This caused something of a stir within Philo, for it was how he felt about himself, though less frequently since he'd met Teretia. From what he had observed, Domitian could have done with a Teretia to boost his confidence. He was not the type of boastful young aristocrat Philo was accustomed to dealing with.

"I'm sure your father cares for you really," said Philo sympathetically. "It's just unfortunate that he's had to go abroad quite so much."

Domitian sat back up again. he didn't look any happier. He looked wretched. "You're going to make this public, aren't you? Everyone is going to know about my humiliation."

Humiliation? That was not a word Philo expected to hear. It was not a word Publius had used: dalliance, furtive, affair, yes, but not humiliation. Was the evidence Publius had collected a signifier of something quite different?

"I didn't know," sniffed Domitian. "I didn't know that's what he wanted. I'm such a fool. I was just so lonely. Uncle Flavius tries so hard, I know he does. But all my friends had gone to the coast for the summer and I didn't have anyone to talk to outside this house, and he was so friendly. I thought he liked me as a protégé. I thought he was going to help me with my public career. When I realised that wasn't what was happening, it was too late to back out. So I just went through with it."

Philo shifted. "Several times?" he asked in a soft voice.

Domitian nodded miserably. "I didn't want to upset him because he's an important man. I thought it might affect my career later. Because I need to have a public career like Titus, to prove to my father that I'm just as good as him. Except I'm not, am I? I allowed myself to be used in that way."

If Domitian were mincing his words, Philo knew full well what he was referring to, as Publius had given quite a thorough account. But in Publius' words, Philo had inferred quite a different scenario. One where Domitian had courted an older, distinguished man at the public baths. He'd met this man over a summer-long affair the previous year. The liaison seeming to have reached a natural conclusion when the temperature dipped. It didn't seem much. Nothing that dozens of young, sexually charged men hadn't involved themselves in before. But in Epaphroditus' hands, this could be twisted into a morally degenerate tale of the would-be emperor's pervert son.

Except now Philo had access to a third tale, and one that he was inclined to believe given Domitian's distress.

"He forced you?"

Domitian shook his head. "I wasn't expecting it. It came as a total shock when he first kissed me. I didn't know what to do. So I just went along with it. It seemed like the easiest thing to do."

Philo fiddled with the buckle of his satchel. He knew all about that, going along with things. It was what he'd done with Straton all those years, wasn't it? Going along with his every demand, no matter how distasteful he'd found it. Sometimes late at night when he couldn't sleep, he'd stare into the darkness. His lungs tight with tension at the realisation that it was this very meekness, this very compliant nature that Straton had mistaken for passion on Philo's part.

If he could have had his time again, Philo would have gone straight to Felix the first time Straton molested him. No doubt Domitian wished he'd handled his situation differently too. Philo could well imagine that the expression on his face when the Straton situation was messily revealed to Teretia was very much like the one Domitian was currently sporting.

"I don't suppose any of this matters anyhow," Domitian was saying. "Vitellius will likely have me killed in a few days."

"I won't pass it on."

Philo hadn't known that these were going to be his words until he spoke them. They came out with a firm decisiveness that was most unlike him.

Domitian's brow rose. "You won't?"

"No, I won't," said Philo in an even firmer tone. "The legionaries are going to resolve this conflict. Not words. They are of no consequence." Philo took the scroll back from Domitian. "I'll destroy this."

Domitian's troubled expression lightened as he said, "Thank you. Thank you so much. This means everything to me."

* * *

"How's she doing?" the midwife enquired, as she ascended the stairs with Pompeia and Marcia.

"She had a funny feeling during the night but put it down to wind," Pompeia explained. "She's suffered quite a bit with tummy troubles all through the pregnancy."

The midwife nodded. Digestive issues were no mystery to her. Very few bodily functions were.

"It got stronger during the day, this funniness. Then her waters went and she's in full play now."

Pompeia pushed open the door to reveal a fluster of womanhood. Teretia stood grasping the back of a chair, producing a grunting moo followed by a despairing cry of pain.

"It really hurts now. Mother, it really hurts."

"Now, now, Teretia, the midwife's here. It's all going to be fine."

The midwife dropped the heavy bag she'd been carrying. It made an alarmingly loud thump. Rolling up her sleeves she approached the suffering Teretia.

"It hurts, it really hurts. I didn't think it would hurt this much," said a wide-eyed Teretia, her lips wobbling.

"What you've got to think, my dear, is that these pains are what are bringing your lovely baby to you. Can you remember that?"

Teretia nodded, replying shakily, "I'll try. I do so want to meet my son. Oh, oh, another one's coming. There's another one coming!"

The midwife offered her a hand to grasp, saying to the others. "Right! I need someone to count and I need somebody to get me a nice cool bowl of water from that fountain in the street. It's a very hot day to be labouring in!"

The two slaves rushed out to get the water. Verenia began to count. Pompeia took hold of Teretia's other hand.

SEVENTEEN

The eunuchs had formed themselves into a pyramid five stacks high, the palace's high-vaulted ceilings being of a height to allow this, thankfully. The pyramid's peak, a youngish eunuch by name of Cyril, somersaulted off and landed lengthwise in the arms of two of his fellow no-balls. The gathered slaves clapped and cheered. All of them that is, bar one.

"Tsk," said Sporus, watching the eunuchs accept congratulatory back slaps and kisses to cheeks. "It's a cheap act," he declared, loudly enough to be given several death stares from his fellow imperial slaves. Sporus blew the offenders kisses from red painted lips.

"A very predictable act, don't you think, Mina? A very predictable, hackneyed, cheap act. Mina? Mina?"

His companion ignored this shrill order to agree, distracted by being stood on her head, her legs stretched up the wall. She kicked a foot against the plasterwork, propelling herself forward. Her feet hit the ground and she then pushed into a further flip, landing on her feet with a "Ha!" accompanied by a crack of her whip.

Though the thong of the whip landed a good ten inches from Sporus' golden sandaled feet, he nonetheless jumped in the air yelping. Mina rolled her eyes and set to practising her jump into the splits.

"It is monstrous," decided Sporus. "Absolutely monstrous. And a disaster. A positive disaster. And dreadful. Very dreadful for the emperor."

Mina threw back her arm, practising her whip move, ignoring the eunuch's shrill protests.

"How can it even be considered an entertainment if I'm not included? It can't. And to think those useless excuses for eunuchisation are performing!" he said, throwing another glare at the eunuch acrobats. "What does that say about our kind?"

"I thought you were unique," said Mina, practising a forward roll on the floor and springing to her feet with another, "Ha!"

"I am unique. I am a Sporus. Vitellius has never seen a Sporus. That's why he needs to see me tonight. I can be the first act. Then they can wheel on those sloppy no-balls and their stupid dancing and tumbling."

"Firstly," said Mina, straightening her Greek style helmet on her head. "He has seen you before. He's seen you at every banquet Nero held. And secondly. Secondly. Actually, I don't have a secondly. That's my point."

"But you agree I should be included in the entertainments." It pointedly wasn't a question. Sporus' self-obsession was such that he assumed naturally that everyone shared his views.

"Perhaps entertaining is beneath you," suggested Mina. What with you being an emperor's widow."

"Twice over," corrected Sporus.

"Once," corrected Mina. "You were never married to Otho."

He'd never been married to Nero either. Not legally, but there'd been a ceremony of sorts and a fabulous dress and everyone had got madly drunk afterwards. So that was near enough a legitimate wedding.

"Hmmm," pondered the eunuch. "You could be right."

Mina wriggled her shoulders round in order to loosen them up for her forthcoming performance.

"Or you could be wrong," decided Sporus. "Tonight is to showcase the palace stocks and their talents, so that the new emperor may properly select from the available slaves. It would be a travesty if he was left thinking that all the palace eunuchs can do is cheap, predictable tumbling with bells tied to their stupid, fat ankles. He needs to know that there is an alternative, a more cultured and refined product available. I mean, what if he heard those awful rumours that the Sporus died with Nero? What if he did? He might not know the Sporus still breathes! He has to see me."

Seeing a dangerous glint in her friend's eye Mina said, "Don't." In the sort of firm voice one uses to train a dog. It had yet to be proven to work on Sporus. Very little did.

"Don't what?" he asked lightly, innocently.

"Don't do whatever it is that you're thinking of doing. It would be a shame for Cyril, he's been practising like mad."

Sporus brushed off her arm. "It will be fine. I'll just sneak in after those poor excuses for eunuchisation have finished their deeply pedestrian routine—"

Sporus' intentions were interrupted by a deeply felt sigh of such dejection that both Mina and the eunuch turned round. There stood Philo, his satchel strap across his narrow chest, his eyes taking in the jumble of slaves getting in a final bit of practice.

"Oh," he said. "Is it still all going on?"

"Hullo, Philo," waved Mina cheerfully. "The entertainments haven't started yet."

"They haven't started," repeated Philo in the tone of a man just informed that his wife had been eaten by a Nile crocodile. A touch of shock, hysteria, and deep despair.

"The new emperor is still eating," supplied Sporus.

"Oh, that's awful. I thought it would all be over by now."

"You could hide in your office," supplied Mina.

Philo's horrified face untwisted slightly. "I could, couldn't I? There's no reason why I couldn't do that?"

"Ahh, there you are, Philo."

It was Epaphroditus, strolling past the eunuch pyramid accompanied by Felix.

"And you found Sporus, excellent."

Philo looked to his left to the golden gowned, tiara'd, strappy sandaled-up eunuch, noticing him for the first time. Sporus beamed at the confused Philo and then at Epaphroditus. He gave a stagey bow.

"And how can I help you?"

"Lock him in a cage," Epaphroditus ordered Felix.

"Right on ya. Awright there, Sporus, we can do this the easy way, where you just do what I fuckin' say. Or the 'ard way, where you don't and it all gets fuckin' messy. So what's it going to be?"

Felix rolled up his sleeves, one after the other.

Sporus gulped. Then bolted for it.

Felix shook his head. "Always the fuckin' hard way with that one." And shot off after him.

Epaphroditus, Philo, and Mina watched as Sporus ran into the eunuch pyramid, knocking it over and causing a shower of squealing beardless men. They hit the floor and formed a heap of outrage.

Felix grabbed into the pile of eunuchs and pulled out Sporus by his ankle. Holding him upside down to reveal that beneath his sparkly gown, the eunuch wore a matching glittery loincloth. Felix effortlessly swung Sporus onto his shoulder. They could see two golden sandals kicking impotently at the overseer's back as Felix strolled calmly away.

"Probably for the best," said Mina.

EIGHTEEN

While Sporus was unsuccessfully attempting to flirt his way past the four Praetorians Epaphroditus had placed on his door, Philo was being unhappily led into the main banqueting hall of the old palace. He found himself standing beside Lysander behind the couches of the illustrious diners.

"How come you haven't got a seat?" asked Lysander.

"Epaphroditus says imperial freedmen are to be sidelined. We're not to be too obvious as the emperor is bringing in his own team as the chief secretaries."

"That's what Galba did and look how that turned out for him," said Lysander. The announcer gave a shudder as he recalled the day he saw Emperor Galba being dispatched in the Forum. He shook off those bloody memories. "The entertainments have been good so far," he admitted. Then, lowering his voice, "Though watching our new boss feed is quite entertaining in itself."

Philo's eyes drifted over to the emperor's party and the rolling mass that was Vitellius. The emperor was cramming food into his mouth using the flat palm of his hand to shove as much as possible in. Crumbs scattered through his fingers and a pinky liquid descended down the back of his hand. Philo produced a shudder of his own.

Sat closest to the emperor was an elderly woman that Philo assumed to be Vitellius' mother. She did not look terribly impressed by her surroundings. Her mouth was twisted into a distasteful pout. Her eyes showing disgust and contempt. The empress on the other hand was blank-faced. The servers moved around her unseen. Staring off into the distance, her face gave nothing away as to her feelings.

Galba and Otho had been unmarried. There hadn't been an empress at the palace since Nero's spiky widow Statilia Messalina had departed for a luxurious villa by the coast. It must seem very strange for Galeria, mused Philo. One day you are an ordinary Roman wife and mother, the next day an empress. That was quite a switch. Philo recalled how long it had taken Statilia Messalina to settle into the complicated palace hierarchies and rituals. Statilia had at least been given time to get used to her new status. Galeria had truly been thrown into the life.

Philo found himself feeling rather sorry for her and all that she would now face. The army of slaves she'd suddenly acquired that would take over many of the functions she'd previously done for herself was the least of her troubles. Though there'd been considerable excitement in the slave complex that there was a young Caesar. Vitellius' son Germanicus was set to be the pet of half the slave girls in the palace.

Beside Galeria's couch was placed a man Philo had last seen across a battlefield ordering his troops to storm the town that Philo was trapped in: Caecina. Even in his reclined pose his great height was noticeable, as were his staggering good looks. Caecina was six feet plus of chiselled handsomeness. An Apollo made flesh. He could see the servers pausing in their duties to gawp at him. If Caecina were to reside in the palace, he'd need to be careful: every slave girl was going to want to conquer him. It didn't occur to Philo that Caecina might happily enjoy such conquering or even elicit it. For Philo, slave girls suddenly flinging off their clothes and launching themselves at you was something deeply upsetting and unnecessary, rather than an enjoyable way to spend an afternoon.

The man beside Caecina could only be Valens, his fellow commander. It was odd to see the two face to face, having read about their exploits in his correspondence for months. Valens was not blessed by the gods with Caecina's beauty. He was a thin man, unnaturally so, which might have been the result of Lysandria's attempt at poisoning him the previous spring. Valens was not shovelling in food like his master. He picked at it sparingly, grey eyes forever moving, scanning the faces that passed him by.

The rest of the party Philo knew: Lucius Vitellius and his wife Triaria. Triaria certainly seemed to be enjoying herself. Her brown eyes flashing with glee as they fell greedily on the food that was brought to her.

In the square space facing the emperor, Ampelius, a protégé announcer of Lysander's, stepped forward.

"This better impress me," muttered Lysander under his breath.

"Imperial Majesty," bellowed Ampelius. "And Imperial Mistress," bowing his body towards Galeria. "Next for your enjoyment, we present the Goddess Minerva and her special skills!"

Philo raised an eyebrow at Lysander. "Do I want to stay for this?"

"Don't freak out, it's nothing kinky. It's Mina and her whip."

To a dramatic drumbeat, Mina entered with long strides. She was dressed in a shortened white pleated gown, her features obscured by the large Greek-style helmet on her head. In one hand she held a silver shield and in the other a whip.

Taking note of Mina's long, bare, tanned legs the emperor's male companions looked on with interest. Triaria's mouth pursed. "Her dress will stay on, won't it?"

"Let's hope not," commented her husband, eagerly.

Triaria rolled her eyes.

On the final drumbeat Mina let out a, "Huh!" She cracked her whip on the ground. The marble gave it an impressive echoey thwack.

What followed was rather a revelation for Philo. He would never have imagined Mina could be so flexible and lithe. The routine was a series of tumbles and positions from which Mina snapped her whip on the floor. Philo found himself tipping his head to view as Mina balanced on one palm, her legs straightened in the air and slowly pivoted round.

"I never imagined a towel holder could do that," he commented.

"Pretty impressive that she's not caught herself on the whip," said Lysander. "Particularly when she did that cartwheel. It's a good job she's wearing a loincloth under that dress. That's all I can say. The emperor seems to like it."

Philo looked over and noted that Vitellius was indeed taking a keen interest in the performance. As were Valens and Caecina. He saw Valens lean over and say something to his colleague. During his teenage years Philo did not speak, and though officially noted as a mute there was an assumption by some that he couldn't hear either. As a result, people possessed a tendency to exaggerate their mouth movements when talking to him. During his silent years, he'd developed this into an ability to read lip movements from a distance. Sometimes it came in handy. Sometimes it did not.

Really, Philo could have lived without knowing what Valens wanted to do with Mina's body. What was perhaps more interesting than Valens' perversions was the look of disgust that crossed Caecina's face. Valens didn't see it, being too taken with Mina standing on her hands with her legs flayed outwards. But Philo saw it, and he noted it.

Mina finished her act with a bounced somersault in the air. She landed on two feet facing the emperor with a triumphant,

"Ha!" She knelt down in front of Vitellius, lowering her helmet's gaze to the floor.

The emperor grinned and clapped his hands together. The imperial party joined in. Finally, the rest of the guests and staff. Mina stood and took a bow to cheers.

"I wonder how the eunuchs will top that!" speculated Lysander.

"You just wait!" said Epaphroditus, squeezing in next to Philo. "It's going to be spectacular," he promised.

NINETEEN

Lysander and Philo had made it to the Subura on their way home before either of them spoke.

"That was quite a show."

Philo agreed that it was indeed quite a show.

"It was sort of like being back in Nero's day but madder. Do you think it'll be like that every day?"

Philo rather hoped not. His head was aching painfully from all the noise. Those jangly eunuchs were going to be quite a distraction if Vitellius insisted upon their permanent presence.

"I'd never thought of Epaphroditus as much of a party planner. But by Hercules, he pulled it off! Did you see the emperor's grin throughout?"

Philo had. It reminded him of a giant bullfrog that had caused a bit of merriment during a lesson one day at the imperial training school Lysander and he had both attended. Unlike his classmates, Philo had not liked that frog. Its green slimy features, its bulbous bloated body, and its grotesque expression had repelled him. He just wanted it gone so the lesson could continue.

The subject moved on to Verenia, or rather Lysander moved it on. Philo was still dwelling on the frog analogy. At the bottom of the Viminal Hill, they bumped into Pompeia Major, one of Teretia's many aunts.

"Hello, Pomp—"

She grabbed hold of Philo's arm. "Have you heard? Did they get word to you?"

Philo's puzzled face was answer in itself.

"Ooh, Philo, you need to get yourself home. Teretia's having the baby!"

"She's having the baby?"

"Yes, she—"

Philo had sped off before Pompeia could finish that sentence, his satchel banging against his hip. Outside their apartment building was Pompeia Minor. She was counting out some coins into another woman's palm.

"Pompeia?"

The stranger gave Philo a big grin. "I reckon you'll be the father."

"Father?" gulped Philo, his mouth dry.

"Yes, you are," smiled Pompeia. "Teretia's having a rest. She did brilliantly."

"That she did," confirmed the woman, closing her hand over the coins. "Until the next time."

Pompeia waved the woman off. Then turned to Philo.

"What are you waiting for? Get up those stairs and say hello to your son."

Philo blinked twice. "Son? I have a son?"

"Lysander," prompted Pompeia.

The announcer nodded. Putting his arm around his friend, he guided him to the door and up the stairs.

* * *

"Master!" grinned Marcia on seeing them.

The slave was mopping the kitchen floor clean of a number of alarming reddish patches.

Philo's mouth fell open. Lysander gently manoeuvred him through to the bedroom.

Teretia lay propped upright by several pillows behind her back. A thin white sheet covered her lower half. In her arms was what looked to be a bundle of towels. Verenia, who was sat beside Teretia, stood up and offered the spot to Philo.

"I've sent Doris out for some food to help Teretia get her strength back. We're going to have a big stew, even though it is far too hot in this weather." She went and stood beside Lysander, who put his arm around her, giving her a kiss on the cheek.

"Teretia? How are you?" asked Philo cautiously. "You are alright, aren't you?"

Her face was pink. Her hair damp with sweat. To Philo's eyes, she appeared quite exhausted.

"It seemed to go on forever and it hurt so much. But mother and the midwife were so good, they knew just what to do. And Verenia counted the pains so I should know that they would feel better by 16. But then they got faster, and there wasn't any gaps anymore. And I felt I was going to die with the pain."

Philo squeezed her hand.

"But then! Then he came out of me!" said Teretia more brightly. "And the midwife put him in my arms. And then I couldn't mind the pain at all."

She angled the bundle in her arms towards Philo. A small face became visible.

"I knew he would be a boy. Didn't I always say he'd be a boy?"

"Yes, you did," smiled Verenia. "And you were right."

Philo drank in that small face. The closed eyes, the tiny nose and lips. The skin that was neither as dark as his nor as pale as Teretia's. It was a light brown like the amphora in the palace cellars and complemented perfectly his black hair.

"Do you have a name? Teretia wouldn't tell us until you were home."

Teretia handed the bundle to Philo. It was the most precious thing he'd ever held. More so than any golden palace treasure.

Or even a brand-new, sharpened stylus set. Cradling his son carefully, unable to look away from that face, Philo told them, "Horace. Tiberius Claudius Horace."

"After the poet?" asked Verenia.

"After the plant?" asked Lysander at exactly the same time as his betrothed.

"A plant?" repeated Verenia, a touch of mockery in her voice.

"One we had as boys in our room at the palace," explained Lysander. "Philo won him in a competition."

"I liked that plant," said Philo rather defensively.

"He was a fine plant," reminisced Lysander. "Do you remember when we planted him in the courtyard? That was a good day. He was extra springy that day was Horace. I wonder if this Horace will be as springy." He smiled down at the baby.

Baby Horace opened his eyes. They were a warm brown colour with a green rim around the irises. Seeing the four people that were to be fundamental influences in his life, Horace began to cry.

Lysander looked to Verenia. "Shall we leave the new parents to it?"

* * *

"Great Vesta, the noises that came out of Teretia! I swear she was mooing like a cow at a sacrifice at one point," said Verenia, stepping over a discarded vegetable. "Not to mention all the gore."

Doris, walking a pace behind Lysander and Verenia, gave a shudder.

"But I suppose we can consider it worthwhile. Baby Horace is rather sweet," concluded Verenia, before adding in her usual bite. "Even if he is named after a plant."

"I wonder if Philo will take Horace the baby to meet Horace the plant," Lysander was pondering when he stopped so suddenly that Doris walked into the back of him.

Turning to face his betrothed, he took her hands in his. "It's not put you off, has it? Having children, I mean."

She gave a tinkly laugh. "Children? We don't need children, do we? We have Doris."

"I sort of thought we would," admitted Lysander. "I'm surprised you're not pregnant already. I am very potent. At the palace, my average was four fucks to impregnate. Sometimes it only took one…" Lysander trailed off as he spied a certain tightening around Verenia's mouth.

"That was too much information, wasn't it?"

Removing her hand from his, she told him, "You're not a slave anymore. How can I introduce you to my father if you're going to spout all this slave stuff? You know he has misgivings about us getting married."

Verenia's father, Verenius, was a travelling merchant and was currently somewhere near Alexandria. Nevertheless, a letter had found its way to him informing him that his daughter wished to marry. His response had been short and lacking, Lysander felt, in any congratulatory sentiment. It merely stated that he would meet this man before he would consider consenting to the marriage.

Since then, Lysander had been the recipient of a number of light scoldings on behaviour that Verenia was sure her father wouldn't approve of.

Lysander mumbled an apology, then dared to ask, "Children though. We will have children, won't we?"

Verenia expelled a sigh that was lost in a growing thudding noise.

"Soldiers."

Lysander offered a hand to Verenia and escorted her to the side of the street outside a shuttered-up shop. Doris followed. The three of them waited until from around the corner there appeared Praetorians.

Although they'd never been much good at marching, they usually moved at a suitable speed and near enough in formation to distinguish them from a rabble. However, the Praetorians making their way down the Viminal Hill were not moving in any kind of formation. They weren't even attempting a march. It was more of a shuffle. A dejected, despondent shuffle.

"They look sad, mistress," commented Doris.

They did indeed. There was little on display of their usual arrogance. Even the purple feathers on their helmets appeared withered. Verenia gave Lysander a nudge.

"Ask them what's going on."

Lysander was not keen to involve himself. In the last year, he and his fellow slaves had been held captive in the palace by Praetorians, watched them drag the corpse of their murdered prefect through the forum for a good kicking, and been the subject of not one but two stormings of the palace by the same guards.

However, Verenia's sharp elbow and his own anticipated loss of certain favours he was looking forward to if he didn't comply, spurred him into yelling, "Oi! What's going on?"

Guardsman Lucullus stopped. "We've been sacked. We've all been sacked!" he told them with an emotional crack in his voice. "Vitellius doesn't trust us. He's putting his own men in. Fuckin' German barbarians!" He spat with disgust.

Lysander inwardly did not blame Vitellius, given the Praetorians had deposed two emperors in the last year. He tried not to show this outwardly, effecting what he hoped was a sympathetic face.

"Where will you go?" asked Verenia.

"Me, I'm going to get drunk," replied Lucullus with a shrug. "Then, who knows what."

Lysander linked his arm onto Verenia. "We'd better get you home."

Who knew what chaos would unfold with thousands of commiserating ex-Praetorians let loose on the Viminal Hill.

* * *

Philo, lying beside Teretia, watched with awe as Horace's little lips sucked at his wife's breast. There had been a bit of fiddling about to get him to latch on. Pompeia had come in and aided the attachment with calm movements.

Teretia had been very clear that she did not want a wet nurse, even after Philo offered to pay for one. Secretly, her determination to feed Horace had pleased Philo. He'd never been fond of wet nurses. The ones at the palace had a tendency to get above themselves, particularly the ones charged with feeding imperial babies, such as Nero's late daughter Claudia. They were always rather snappish.

A few months later, Philo would fully understand their demeanour was not due to their station, but rather sleep deprivation. At this moment he was blissfully unaware of the particulars of having a baby in the house. He watched with interest as Horace would pause from his sucking, appearing quite asleep and then set off again suddenly.

"Tell me about your day," said Teretia.

"I rather think it won't compare with yours," replied Philo, gazing at his wondrous son.

"I'd like to hear."

"Alright," said Philo and proceeded to recount his conversation with Domitian earlier in the day.

"Oh that poor boy!" exclaimed Teretia at his conclusion, though Domitian was actually two years her senior.

"Do you think I did the right thing?" worried Philo.

"Of course you did. As you said to him, it's not going to make any difference to the outcome."

"But Epaphroditus did task me to uncover information on the family."

"And you did that. You're just using your judgement on how best to use that information. Epaphroditus trusts you to use your judgement, doesn't he?"

"I suppose so," said Philo, chewing on his lower lip.

TWENTY

"He's asleep," said Asiaticus.

"This is worth waking him up for," promised Epaphroditus, geared to deliver Caenis' revelations about the Syrian and Egyptian governors. It was information he felt sure would allow him to dump his shitty new job.

Not that the previous day hadn't been a stunning triumph for him. It had. But frankly, coordinating eunuch outfits was beneath his considerable skill set.

"I doubt it," was Asiaticus' straight reply.

Epaphroditus met Asiaticus' twisted scarred face without flinching. "I have important information regarding Vespasian."

"We don't say that name."

"Vespasian?"

"We don't even speak it. His Imperial Majesty commands that nobody speak that name. We do not discuss that situation."

A huge "but" hung in the air.

But how was the palace properly organising their response?

How were the army to be commanded?

How was anything going to be achieved if nobody could talk about the nature of the threat facing them?

Epaphroditus' inner administrator began twitching.

"That's unprecedented," he said in as neutral a voice as he could manage.

"These are unprecedented times."

"Indeed," agreed Epaphroditus. Using his smoothest, most trustworthy tone, he dripped in, "The other side are discussing the matter quite openly…" He left it hanging.

"I know. We had the news earlier."

For a brief moment, Epaphroditus thought that Philo had already handed over Caenis' information and was afflicted by a pang of annoyance. Asiaticus picked a scroll off the desk and handed it to him.

"It came last night. That man in that place has declared for our emperor."

"What?!?"

"Read it."

There came a groaning from the next chamber followed by a yell of, "Asiaticus!".

The freedman disappeared through the connecting door.

Epaphroditus read. Then read again. And then again. Because what he read made absolutely no sense to him. Vespasian's legions had declared loyalty to emperor Vitellius. As had the legions in Egypt and Syria.

He was still boggling over this when Asiaticus reappeared.

"Eunuchs," he said. "The emperor wants to see his eunuchs."

He took the scroll from Epaphroditus' hands. "That's your job. Go do it."

* * *

In the gloom of a single oil lamp, Epaphroditus could just about see the mass. It had many limbs and was possessed of many heads. It writhed and moaned and made obnoxious smells. The stench was dreadful. Epaphroditus stepped out of the eunuch quarters, shutting the door behind him.

"What happened?" he asked Felix.

"Apparently, the little fellows were all excited after their dance for the emperor. They ordered a plate of fuckin' oysters to fuckin' celebrate it like. Them weren't good oysters."

This was exactly why the slaves were served plain portions of soup or gruel, thought Epaphroditus. Nobody ever got sick on gruel. Sick of it, certainly. But not sick on it.

"Tell me there's seven or eight little eunuchs that don't like oysters and are all psyched up for a repeat performance for the emperor."

Felix scratched at his beard. "I got one eunuch that ain't fuckin' puking his guts up."

* * *

Sporus stood to attention in a dazzling red gown sewn with jewels and matching tiara.

Epaphroditus turned to Felix. "No."

"He's the only eunuch in the palace who hasn't got oyster projectiling out his bum."

Epaphroditus gave Sporus a long look. The eunuch pushed back his shoulders and thrust out his chest.

"Still no."

Sporus' shoulders sank slightly.

"I had trouble enough with him under Nero. I'll not have him complicating my life again."

"I can dance!" butted in Sporus.

"He can," confirmed Felix. "He was one of my top dancing boys until he got that empress job."

Epaphroditus glared at Sporus. It was the damnedest piece of mischief wrapped up in a gown and wig. But what choice did he have? Vitellius wanted eunuchs. This creature was the only one left standing.

"I'd better not regret this," he warned the eunuch.

Sporus smiled dazzlingly. "You won't, sir. Trust me."

Epaphroditus would have sooner trusted the Praetorians to babysit his children.

* * *

It was the end of an important meeting. Present were Valens and Caecina, Lucius, Triaria, and Vitellius himself, flanked by Asiaticus.

The top topic of discussion had been the disbanding of the Praetorian cohorts.

"A master stroke!" declared Triaria.

"The Guard have been proven craven and untrustworthy," supplied Valens. "They were all in Otho's camp to a man. They only swore to be loyal to Your Imperial Majesty under duress."

"How could we ever have felt safe with them swarming about the palace," said Triaria, shivering despite the summer heat. "We would be constantly on edge wondering what they were plotting."

"It's also an excellent way to reward the men for their hard work," said Caecina. "Why should such lazy and dishonest brutes soak up all the benefits and perks of being in the Guard? Our men are proper soldiers, they are far more qualified to look after the emperor."

"Well said," responded Valens, looking at his colleague.

Caecina nodded at the compliment. It was the first sign of a thaw in relations between the two men.

"How was it taken? This disbanding? The troops, how did they take it?" yawned Vitellius.

"With bitterness, Imperial Majesty, but peacefully," said Valens. "They dare not make too much fuss with their replacements present."

Vitellius gave a lazy smile. "I bet they didn't."

"I shall sleep well in my bed tonight," declared Triaria, then looking about the chamber, commented, "I thought we were having those tumbling eunuchs back to entertain us?"

She got to her feet. "Where are they?" she asked and then, spotting Epaphroditus stood behind a line of Vitellius' body slaves, she pointed a finger. "You. You there. Where are the eunuchs? My brother distinctly asked for eunuchs."

"I did," confirmed Vitellius, giving another yawn and scratching at his groin.

"You. You explain why this has not happened."

Epaphroditus had served Nero for many years. It had left him a repertoire of slick excuses for any occasion. However, he had no need to deploy one, for this was the moment when the tambourinist entered with his instrument. He stood to the side of the room giving it one of those one hand in the air wiggles that his kind were always fond of. Then he gave three bangs: the chamber doors were flung open and in danced a small figure.

Even Epaphroditus, who was more familiar with Sporus than he'd ever wished to be, gave a double take. The eunuch favoured feminine gowns and flashy jewellery, a hangover from his time posing as Nero's dead wife Poppaea. These trinkets had been abandoned along, with his usual red, ringletted wig.

Instead, he wore saffron-coloured trousers of the Parthian style, tapered at the ankles with ribbons, that billowed at his knees. On his top he wore nothing, displaying his slender, tanned, hairless chest. His dark curly hair was pulled back tightly into a ponytail.

Epaphroditus wasn't sure what he'd expected. The kind of duties Sporus had performed for Nero had been of the sexual variety and involved a heavy dose of play-acting. He supposed he'd expected something similar. That was what Sporus did. He pleased men with his body.

But Sporus' body was put to quite a different use. To the slow beat of a tambourine he began to gently twirl, his arms arching high into the air, twisted like the branches of a tree. His bod ambulating, he emitted first a quiet, "Elalalllallah."

But as he twirled and as the beat of the tambourine got faster the sound grew louder in volume and the twirls became faster and faster until he was but a blur of yellow. Yet still his arms and hands, beautifully poised, were somehow still visible.

Epaphroditus felt a growing appreciation. That damned eunuch was good. Sporus' simple dance and song showed up those other eunuchs as the unflatteringly flashy, over the top, obvious crew they really were. Sure they could synchronise a tumble and a dance, but none of them could have performed such an achingly haunting and beautiful dance.

The tambourine beat was quickening now. Until one final bang and Sporus stopped. He was stood on one leg, the other making a triangular shape with his foot pressed against the inside of the opposite thigh. He was so perfectly balanced, so still, it was as if the rotations, the blur of energy, had never happened. As if he had never moved at all.

Triaria gave a gasp and was then on her feet applauding. Valens and Caecina did likewise, the younger man shouting out, "That was marvellous! Astounding!"

Epaphroditus slapped his palms together. That damned eunuch had done it. He'd bloody done it.

Sporus placed his leg on the floor with a noted grace. Then he lay himself face down, arms outstretched before the emperor. Lifting his head just a little, he kissed Vitellius' toe.

The emperor gave a greedy grin. "And you would be Sporus. The Sporus Nero was so fond of."

Placing kisses gently on the remaining four toes down to the littlest, Sporus replied, "At your service, Imperial Majesty."

Placing his other foot near Sporus' mouth for further treatment, Vitellius replied, "Yes, you will be."

TWENTY-ONE

"There you go, Marcia. Some big fat sausages."

"Thank you, Tadius," said Marcia, taking the packet from the butcher and placing it in her basket.

"Do give my best wishes to your mistress and little Horace for me."

"I certainly shall," she promised, stepping out into the street.

The warmth hit her cheeks and she closed her eyes against the glare of the sun, enjoying the moment. In her old house, she was hardly ever let out of the kitchens, let alone trusted to leave the premises. The only time she ever escaped those pans and the scrubbing brush was when her old master called her to his private bedroom. There he would lie on the bed with the shutters closed and she would rub his wrinkly thing up and down until it spurted its juice all over her fingers.

That was the only time she ever saw her old master.

When she'd first seen the new master, she'd naturally assumed he'd want the same. And worse, what with him being foreign looking. Everyone knew that them from the East were strange and not normal. She'd been dead worried when the master had purchased her. Her fellow goods had offered her sympathetic but ultimately smug smiles that it wasn't them being taken off to who knew where by a perverted Easterner.

She'd been truly terrified about what might await her as she was pulled by a rope through the city.

As it turned out, what awaited her was the mistress. The most smiley, kind girl Marcia had ever met. Marcia had instantly warmed to her and her caring mother. She wasn't as sure about that blond lodger who was having it away with the mistress' mean-mouthed cousin. Then there was the master. He stared at her in a disapproving way and wasn't nearly as friendly as the mistress. In fact, he rarely acknowledged her presence at all. But the mistress loved him and from what she'd observed so far, the master doted on his wife. So she was prepared to throw over her doubts regarding his foreignness and him having been a slave just like her.

She was fully aware of how lucky she was. Marcia had a lovely mistress, who talked to her all day like a proper person, who trusted her to cradle little Horace in her arms, and to go out shopping all by herself. She really hadn't needed to have her fortune spelled out to her by that hard-faced old hag, Callista. But even that hectoring lecture couldn't dent Marcia's enthusiasm for her new life. Since putting into practice Callista's lessons (such as standing up when her owners entered the room and keeping her eyes downwards when addressed), the master had thawed a little, seemingly more pleased with her. A satisfying outcome. For Marcia would have been devastated to discover her adored mistress was bound to a cold, cruel foreigner!

Next stop was the grocer. She needed some vegetables to go with the sausages. And plenty of them to build up her mistress' strength. Marcia was worried for her mistress. She seemed much paler since baby Horace was born.

Crossing the street, she noticed three soldiers. They walked in a clump, staring up at the height of the apartment buildings and tripping on the kerbs. They must be very hot dressed in those animal skins, thought Marcia.

The Viminal residents were stepping out of their way, viewing them uneasily. Not Marcia. They looked a bit lost as they marvelled at their surroundings. Stopping by the fountain, they pointed to the water-spouting nymph. She knew from the master that the soldiers were German, like her. Not that she remembered much about Germania at all. But she'd somehow retained enough of the language to understand the soldiers were not discussing the clever sculptor who'd created the nymph, but rather the more attractive assets of her.

Marcia's cheeks went pink as she stood in the street clutching her shopping basket.

"You understand, don't you?"

She turned to see another soldier. He towered above her, with the broadest shoulders she'd ever seen. He was smiling at her, "You're German, right?" he asked in her own tongue.

"Originally," she replied in Latin. She explained to him, "My spoken is not so good. I probably have a terrible accent and pronounce words all wrong."

The soldier took her basket from her hands. "Let me carry this for you, pretty German girl."

Her cheeks flushed pink again.

"My name is Magnus. And yours?"

"Marcia."

* * *

The slaves dashed back and forth clutching armfuls of gowns. Mina, sitting cross-legged on the floor, felt quite dizzy watching them skittering about.

"And I'm to be the emperor's personal dancing boy," said Sporus, as he pulled yet more dresses from his wardrobes and threw them onto the bed for slave collection. "He wants me near his quarters so he can call for me whenever he wants a dance."

"Dance?" queried Mina. "Is that a euphemism?"

"Eu-what?"

"Euph— oh, never mind. You'll be employed for more than dancing is what I meant."

Leaning over, smoothing down the skirt of a gown, Sporus said, "His Imperial Majesty said that he had heard much about my work for Nero."

"That'll be a yes, then," said Mina. She shuffled on her bum out the way of the bustling slaves who'd been tasked with moving Sporus' plentiful possessions.

Sporus, giving a kick to a slave he felt wasn't performing well enough, said, "I shall do whatever pleases His Imperial Majesty."

Mina screwed up her nose. "Gross."

"You've done worse," shrugged Sporus. "It'll be like old times. The Sporus will once again be loved by an emperor! It's what Sporuses need. They simply cannot function without it. You should get a job with the new empress. It'll be totally like old times then. Me, the emperor's most beloved. And you, the empress's slave."

Mina rolled her eyes at this very Sporus put down.

"She's nice, the new empress. Quiet but nice."

So Mina had heard too. Galeria's attendants reported her as polite, sweet, kind, and minimally demanding. Quite a change from her predecessor: the barbed, sharp-tempered, very demanding Statilia Messalina. But even this was not enough to tempt her.

"I'm done with towel holding and message running. Maybe I'll train to be an overseer or go in the arena or be an inflictor of punishments." She flicked an imaginary whip across the room.

"Bit seedy," said Sporus, disapprovingly. "Especially when you could be glamming it up in the inner court. With Caecina even …" he dripped in.

Mina was visited by an instant vision of the oh-so handsome Caecina. His chiselled jaw, strong hands, blue eyes, and probably awesome body.

"I could put in a word for you …"

Mina imagined herself atop the gorgeous stallion, riding him to the brink and then—

"No," she said, shaking off the image. "I don't think so. The reality is bound to disappoint. Nobody that handsome will ever be worth screwing. He'll have never had to put the effort in, what with every woman in the world prepared to hitch up her skirt and pop out her boobs for him. I bet he just lies there on the bed like the beautiful statue he is."

"You'd get to gaze at him appreciatively from that position," said Sporus. "Not something, alas, I am able to do."

"Probably a blessing with Vitellius," shuddered Mina. "Does he have to lift his stomach up so you can find his thing?"

"He loves me," stated Sporus.

Mina doubted that, but who was she to puncture her friend's delusion. Pulling herself to her feet she told him, "Enjoy," and ran her tongue around her lips suggestively.

Sporus slapped her on the arm, and then said in a quieter voice, "You will come visit me though, won't you?"

Hearing an unusual tinge of anxiety in his tone, she gave him a hug. "Of course. How else am I going to get all the gossip."

Sporus waggled his eyebrows. "I'll tell you everything," he promised.

Mina kissed him on both of his soft cheeks. "Maybe edit out the gratuitous emperor nudity or at least make sure you fill me in after I've had my breakfast!"

TWENTY-TWO

It was a dream he hadn't had for years. A hand gripping at his throat, squeezing tighter and tighter. The burning rasp as he gulped for air. The panic that burgeoned when no air came. That mocking laughter that got louder and louder and—

Epaphroditus awoke with a start, gasping and gulping for air. When it had filled his lungs, the cold sweat of terror began to subside. He turned onto his side to face… nothing. There was nothing there. Just a space in the bed. Here it came again. That pang. That aching hole that had lodged itself in his core. He rolled onto his back and let the tears escape down the side of his face, dampening the pillow.

Would he ever adjust? ever get used to that hole? And if he did, if he woke and didn't automatically reach for her, would that mean she was truly gone? He didn't want that. He didn't want to accept that this thing had happened. That his wife was dead.

The bleakness smothered him. He was approaching his fiftieth year, he could feasibly have another ten years of this, of this utter emptiness, this insufferable hole. And in that moment, he didn't want to get up. Didn't want to place his feet on the ground. Didn't want to get dressed. Didn't want to go to work. He didn't want to do anything.

He closed his eyes, pressing fingertips over the lids, hoping to go back to sleep. To be unconscious and unknowing. To just not be for a time seemed preferable to everything. What was the point of anything anymore?

"Master."

Epaphroditus' eyes pinged open. Callista was standing at the end of the bed.

"Philo is here to see you, sir." With a pursed mouth, she added, "With that lazy slave of his." Then far more happily, "And baby Horace."

Epaphroditus sat up and commanded, "Send my dresser in."

Philo was sat in the courtyard, Horace cradled against his shoulder, the freedman gently stroking his back. Marcia was stood a few steps away, ready to be of assistance if required. On seeing Epaphroditus, Philo made to stand.

"No, you stay there. You don't want to wake the little one."

Horace shuffled his little bottom against the palm of Philo's hand.

"Sorry, sir, to disturb you. I thought, I rather thought it might be easier to meet here. The palace is rather noisy these days."

It certainly was. It was one singular party that seemingly had no end. If Epaphroditus had thought his arrangements for the emperor's arrival were to be the most taxing element of his new job, he'd been quickly disabused of that. He was frankly surprised that there were any hogs left in the Italian peninsula, the rate Vitellius' court was consuming them.

"Also, I thought Teretia could do with a bit of a break," admitted Philo. "It's nice for Horace to get a bit of air." He stroked Horace's dark hair gently.

"Callista, bring some refreshments for us."

"Certainly, master," replied Callista. "Perhaps you can assist me." She was looking at Marcia.

Marcia looked at Philo for permission. Philo gave her the nod and she followed Callista out.

"How is your purchase doing?" asked Epaphroditus. "More satisfactory?"

"Much more after her chat with Callista, sir. And she loves Horace. She sings him lullabies in German."

Epaphroditus raised his eyebrows. "I can't say I'd have thought the Germans capable of producing baby-soothing songs. From what I remember of them, most of their ditties concerned lopping off the heads of their enemies and using their blood to make sausages with. Are you sure it's a lullaby she's singing to him?"

"Oh yes. I, err, have a bit of German," Philo shyly admitted.

Epaphroditus, familiar with Philo's natural self-deprecation and superior language skills, took this to mean he was fluent. "Is Marcia aware you can understand her home language?"

"I haven't mentioned it yet," said Philo. "It's not come up. I have been rather busy with Horace and the house-sitting."

"Now that's what I wanted to talk to you about," said Epaphroditus, sitting forward. "What do we make of this announcement from the East that Vespasian has relinquished his claim?"

Philo thought for a moment. He replied just as Callista and Marcia appeared carrying trays of drinks and food, "I thought it odd, sir."

The slaves laid out the food. Epaphroditus picked up a piece of bread and bit into it, gesturing for Philo to continue with his thoughts.

"The timing seems off, sir. Why wait all these months for Vitellius to reach Rome and then declare for him? Why not declare the moment Valens' and Caecina's forces were victorious if it was his intention the whole time? He's made himself suspect for no gain."

"Quite. The likelihood is that he'll lose his governorship too. Vitellius surely can't trust Vespasian with an army still."

"I don't think the emperor thinks much on Vespasian at all," said Philo carefully.

"I can believe that. The entertainments I've had to put on for the court leave precious little discussion time."

"The message was definitely genuine, sir?"

"From what I saw, I don't doubt it. It would be nice to believe that those creatures Valens and Caecina were faking information to win Vitellius' praise, but it is not the case. Vespasian has declared for Vitellius. I don't believe for a single moment he's backing down. I know the man of old. He's pig-headed and stubborn. But he's shrewd. So what's he doing?"

After a moment Philo said, "Buying himself a bit of time, sir?"

Epaphroditus picked a fingernail between his front teeth. "Got to be, hasn't it? He declares for Vitellius and Vitellius doesn't see the need to move against him immediately. Even if he were to be replaced as governor immediately, the news wouldn't reach Judaea for at least a month. And who's to say the Judaean legions would accept a new governor anyhow? They've got a battle-winning, Jew-killing one providing them with bounty aplenty."

"It would give him some breathing space to secure further backing, sir."

"That it would," pondered Epaphroditus. "In the East though or further afield?"

"That's an important question, sir."

"One that it might be useful to have answered for the emperor. If he's not bothered by the threat from the East, he might be shook up by one closer to Rome."

That might be exactly the sort of news that the deliverer would be praised greatly for. Epaphroditus intended to be that man, if only to escape further roasting piglets.

"See what you can find out from Caenis," he instructed Philo. "They must have had a plan of which provinces they would tackle in which order. We need to know how many have gone over as soon as possible."

TWENTY-THREE

The guards had changed. That was the first thing Domitian noticed about the new regime. The previous lot hadn't been exactly friendly, but in comparison to their replacements, Domitian now ranked them as civil. His new jailors hadn't even the proper Praetorian uniform with its purple-plumed helmets and scorpion-embossed breastplates. They arrived in standard legionary armour, sharp gladius sword included. This they enjoyed pressing to the throats of each and every person who appeared at the front door. How long the local tradesmen would deliver supplies under such ill-treatment was debatable. Domitian fully expected to starve to death.

The slaves weren't happy either. Not that they ever were in Domitian's experience. They'd been complaining to his uncle about their treatment at the guards' hands. Apparently everyone was under suspicion, even uncle Flavius' chief steward Stephanus who was past 70 and lame in one leg. If the atmosphere in his home prison had been uneasy before, it was now positively teetering on an edge.

Such ill ease had brought the three of them together for Domitian was reluctant to be on his own in any of the chambers. Not with these guards about the house. He'd stuck close to his uncle, sitting beside him in his study, assisting him with his correspondence.

"Your father will be pleased that you're taking an interest," said Flavius, handing him a small scroll to be sealed.

Domitian, handing the scroll to a slave, said, "I doubt he'd care. He has other matters on his mind."

"Your father cares deeply for you, Domitian. I know that for a fact."

Domitian took back the wax-blobbed scroll and stamped his uncle's seal ring into it with such force that Flavius' desk wobbled.

"You don't have to pretend, uncle. I know how it is. Titus is the favoured son. I may as well not exist."

Flavius smiled. "You don't half talk a lot of nonsense."

He fiddled about in the drawer of his desk, producing a narrow scroll which he handed to his nephew. "Read it. It's one of many similar correspondences."

It was a letter from his father to his uncle. The bulk of it was concerned with Vespasian's recent campaign in Judaea. The paragraph describing Titus' heroics had Domitian twitching, until he reached the final part.

"In regards to Domitian, ensure his schooling is not substandard. Most of those so-called pedagogues are nothing but charlatans. He's got a sharp brain but it needs activity. Employ one of your slaves if you think fit. I'll leave it in your hands, brother."

Domitian rolled the small scroll back up.

"He writes to me regularly with instructions," said Flavius. "I try to comply with his wishes as best I can. So you see, you are very much in his thoughts."

A dazed Domitian thought for a moment, then said, "It doesn't feel like it."

Flavius squeezed his shoulder supportively. "It's not untrue that your brother was given more honours, but that's nothing to do with you or your father. It just so happened that Titus was your age when your father's fortunes were moving upwards, and he was able to take full advantage of those court connections. He was also old enough to follow your father to his foreign postings. You were not, so he left you with me, so that I might educate and support you in the same way he would if he were here."

Domitian rolled the scroll around. Staring down at it, he said quietly, "I miss him."

"I know you do."

"I wish… I wish he hadn't done this thing."

He looked up and met his uncle's eyes.

"So do I," he said.

* * *

It took Philo three times as long as normal to walk to the house on the Esquiline Hill. There were soldiers everywhere, clogging up the streets, hanging around in gangs. They were impossible to avoid. After filling up the Praetorian barracks, some had decided to camp in the surrounding streets. They made quite an obstacle to Philo's journey as he stepped carefully over the still-dozing legionaries. The Viminal residents were wisely staying indoors. Philo nodded a greeting to Tadius the butcher, who was shaking his head at the four soldiers sitting on the pavement outside his shop.

A cohort-sized number were moving en masse, kicking everything and everyone out of their way. Being too nervous to walk around them, Philo trudged behind them and the path they left in their wake, down the slopes of the Viminal Hill.

Any assumptions that they were ambling, for it was definitely not a march, to the palace were swept away when they took a right into the notoriously seedy Subura district. With all the looting they'd committed en route to Italy, they'd have plenty of coinage to pay the Subura whores and barmen. And it was only the second hour of the day!

They'd have to sort it out, thought Philo as he turned the corner into the relevant street. The soldiers would have to head back to their original postings. Otherwise, who knew what mischief the German tribes would get up to. Unless, he pondered, Vitellius was keeping them in Italy to face down Vespasian's eastern legions.

It would make sense. Part of Otho's demise had been due to his vastly undersized army. Valens and Caecina had reached Italy before Otho's reinforcements could. Vitellius was perhaps keen not to repeat the same mistake. Which was fine for the emperor, but it was going to mean an uncomfortable few months for the civilians of Rome, having to coexist with so many legionaries.

Outside Flavius' house were more soldiers, accompanied by Fabius Valens. Philo had tried to have as little to do with Valens as possible. He had already acquired a reputation for cruelty and perversion at the palace. Felix was steaming about the place, intermittently exploding about the damage done to his goods. He was threatening to cut off Valens' access to the imperial slave girls until he "fuckin' sorts out his fuckin' twisted head."

Valens' grey eyes fell on Philo.

"You boy. Go bring me Flavius Sabinus."

"Flavius?"

"That's what I said. Go get him. The emperor has summoned him."

TWENTY-FOUR

They were in the courtyard garden, all three of them. Caenis sat in the shade, her legs stretched out on the bench with a scroll laid open on her lap. Domitian was tucking into a plate of bread and honey. Flavius was sitting on a wicker chair in the full blaze of the sun, enjoying its warmth, a glass of cordial in his hand.

"Morning, Philo," Flavius greeted him. "You're a bit later today. I hope that new baby of yours hasn't been keeping you up at night."

"A little," said Philo with a wan smile. "Flavius, the emperor wishes to see you. I'm here to take you to the palace. Fabius Valens is waiting outside."

The scroll fell from Caenis' lap onto the floor as she sat up. "What does he want?"

Philo, trying to ignore Domitian's wide-eyed horror, addressed Flavius directly. "You're not alone in this. Apparently, Celsus and Dollabella have been called in too. Anyone who sided with Otho is being asked to swear an oath of allegiance."

Flavius got to his feet. "Very well."

"Uncle," bleated Domitian.

Flavius forced a smile. "I'll be back. Don't worry."

As they stepped outside the front door, Valens' lip curled upwards.

"The emperor has much to say to you," he told Flavius.

* * *

Valens personally led them through the palace. He placed three of his soldiers on each side of Flavius and Philo, impeding them from the view of all loitering about the palace corridors. They were led to one of the larger chambers in the new palace. The huge double doors were swung open and they were led into a very crowded room.

Flavius looked enquiringly at Philo. The scribe shrugged in response. Around the sides of the room were positioned Praetorians. Stood in front of that sneering line were men in purple-edged togas: the Senate. At the end of the chamber was lying Vitellius, flanked by Triaria, Lucius, and Caecina. Of the empress there was no sign, nor the young Caesar.

It was not this end of the room that was attracting Flavius' attention though. His eyes were drawn to the figure stood alone in the centre of that square of people. He too wore a purple-lined toga denoting his status.

"Dolabella," mouthed Flavius.

Valens gave the back of Flavius' knees a push with his own.

"That way. To the emperor."

Flavius headed towards the emperor. On seeing him, Vitellius gave a lazy smile.

"Ahh, city prefect. Good of you to come. And so helpful. You can help us clear up this matter. Come stand beside my couch so that I may see you."

Flavius did so, positioning himself between the emperor and Triaria. Philo took a spot to the side of the room that made him unobtrusive, but also gave him a good view of Dolabella.

Though Dolabella's and Philo's paths had crossed only a few times, Philo still naturally had a stack of facts about the senator stored in his head. He wondered whether the most pertinent of these would prove to be Dolabella's marriage to Vitellius' first wife.

"City prefect," drawled the emperor. "We find ourselves in quite a quandary. Some most serious—"

"Heinous," interrupted Triaria with a snarl.

"Very well, heinous charges have been levelled against Dolabella here."

"Traitor!" spat Triaria, her furious eyes directed at Dolabella.

The senator's form shrank a little.

"We can't agree whether he is guilty or not."

"Guilty!" cried Triaria.

She walked over to the cowed Dolabella and lifted his chin with her fingers, forcing him to look at her. "Guilty as a dog," she declared, pushing Dolabella's chin. He staggered a few steps backwards. The Praetorians lining the walls sniggered and cheered.

Vitellius did not reprimand his soldiers, to Philo's surprise. The scribe looked around nervously at the standing guards. Philo had a long-standing fear of Praetorians born of a life spent at the palace in their company. He tried to avoid them as much as possible, or at least ensure there was a moderating force present to contain them.

He tried to imagine what their former prefect Nymphidius Sabinus would have made of such a show. He would have been steaming mad at them. He'd have had them all roundly beaten at a minimum. Even Tigellinus, the fun-loving crony of Nero, wouldn't have stood for it.

But these weren't your ordinary everyday brutes of guards. These were soldiers of the toughest legions in the entire empire. Now under the command of a man who seemingly possessed no energy to inflict authority over them. Philo felt a shudder run down the length of his back. He was beginning to realise why the gathered senators looked so worried.

"My sister, as you see, Flavius, is very clear in her verdict. Caecina here less so."

The handsome man shrugged. "I don't see that there's the evidence to charge him."

"Idiot," said Triaria. "Varus made a convincing case."

Vitellius flapped one of his fleshy hands. "Varus, let's hear it again so Flavius here can get up to speed."

Varus stood forward and presented his claim. Very simply, Dolabella was a traitor intent on overthrowing the emperor. The evidence for such a startling accusation was that Dolabella had sided with Otho during "recent troubles", as Varus termed it. He'd been sent on to Aquinum to organise troops for Otho. Now he had returned to Rome. This return was deemed suspicious since the emperor had not summoned him.

Further doubts were cast on Dolabella's character by the fact that he hadn't immediately come to swear his allegiance to Vitellius, but had instead spent several days in Ostia. What was he doing there? Varus maintained he was trying to win round further troops to add to the legions in Aquinum.

That was it. No witnesses were mentioned. No signed confessions. If Dolabella had been inciting an invasion and overthrow of the emperor, he would have had to talk to thousands of people. Yet Varus mentioned none. It was, in Philo's view, flimsy at best.

"So there you have it, Flavius. The case against. What do you say, city prefect? Is he guilty of treason?"

All eyes fell on the elderly frame of Flavius.

"Of course he is guilty," declared Triaria, stood with her hands on her hips opposite Dolabella. "Look at him!" she screeched, turning back to face the emperor and Flavius. "He is a guilty dog. Look how he hangs his head in shame at his actions. Convict him, Flavius Sabinus."

"Well, I... I..." Flavius began to splutter.

"You hesitate?" flamed Triaria. "Why do you hesitate? Every moment is vital. His troops could be on the move right now, ready to attack the emperor!"

Vitellius, to Philo's eyes, did not look much like a man in fear of a plot against his life. He looked amused, his fat lips twisted upwards as Triaria raved at Flavius. What a strange woman she was. Even Statilia Messalina in one of her high rages had never appeared thus. She truly looked as if she might strike Flavius the way she had pushed at Dolabella. These were men of the Senate! Distinguished public servants humiliated in front of their peers.

The atmosphere was ugly, tense. Philo's senses, born of a palace upbringing were telling him now was the time to get out, to run. But seeing Flavius— kind, honest and hardworking Flavius— Philo found his feet stuck to the ground.

"It's simple, Flavius. Is he guilty?" pressed the emperor.

"Guilty, guilty," said Triaria, stamping her foot on the floor hard. "Guilty, guilty."

The Praetorians joined in banging their staffs on the marble floor. "Guilty! Guilty! Guilty!" they yelled at increasing volume, making Philo's ears thump with the noise.

Vitellius watched with a smug smile, then held up his arm. The guards fell silent.

The emperor regarded Flavius with greedy black eyes. "I'm beginning to wonder if my sister is correct. You are hesitating. It makes me wonder why. Of course, yourself and the traitor worked closely together under the rule of the usurper, that false emperor ..."

"DEATH TO OTHO!" cried the guards en masse and partook in another round of staff thumping.

Philo, watching closely, saw the emperor speaking to Flavius but he couldn't hear the words above the din. The emperor's head was tilted, so he couldn't read his lip movements either. Whatever was said, it upset Flavius greatly. Philo could see his hand trembling against his side. When the guards fell silent again Vitellius said, "He has decided. He has the verdict on the traitor. Let him speak."

Flavius was pushed forward into the square centre of the chamber. He stood gazing round at the hostile faces and then at the cowering Dolabella. He raised his head, his eyes looking imploringly at Flavius.

"The verdict! Give out the verdict!" screeched Triaria from the side.

* * *

The purple and gold litter made its way through the streets of Rome, its curtains firmly closed. Its inhabitants, Philo and Flavius, were silent. Not a word had been spoken since Valens had escorted them both out of the palace to their waiting transportation and the necessary Guard escort. Flavius' knees had given way on sight of them. A quick-minded Philo had grabbed hold of his elbow and assisted him into the litter.

"Thank you for your help," Valens had sneered before shouting at the bearers, "Get to it!"

"We should be back at the house soon," Philo said, breaking the silence.

Flavius chewed on his lower lip then bent over, taking his head in his hands. "Oh gods," he groaned and began to cry.

Philo banged on the roof of the litter. It was lowered to the ground. He leaned forward and placed his hands over Flavius' quivering ones.

"We'll wait here until you're ready to go back to the house."

"Thank you, Philo. I'm sorry about all this," said Flavius choked out, before he gave way once more to weeping.

Philo kept hold of his hands as the old man cried.

"You have nothing to be sorry about," insisted Philo. "There was nothing you could have done. They were intent on convicting him. Nothing you said would have made any difference to the outcome."

"I was a coward…" said Flavius. "I let that man, I let that innocent man be killed without a word of protest."

"As did your fellow senators," pointed out Philo.

Flavius removed his hands from Philo's. "I'm an old man. My time is nearly over. I hope it will be a good death. Today makes me think maybe not."

"Flavius—"

"Don't. Don't tell me that we're all perfectly safe. Don't remind me again how Otho kept safe Galeria and her son. Otho was a gentleman. He had honour. He died because he could not bear to see men suffer. This emperor is not of that mould. This emperor induces suffering so that he may enjoy it. What else was it that happened there? Dolabella had done nothing. He wanted to have him crawl in front of him. He wanted to break him as he did me. And he did break me. That is my shame to bear."

"Flavius, we do what we can to survive," said Philo with some feeling.

As a slave, Philo had said things he didn't believe in, done things he didn't want to, and offered not a word of protest as colleagues were dragged off for execution in front of him. That was a slave's life. He hadn't thought he'd see a day when men like Dolabella and Flavius would be treated just as badly. That whole scene had unnerved Philo immensely. It was like nothing he'd ever witnessed before. Not under Nero nor his under predecessors.

"I'm not afraid for me. My time is at an end," Flavius was saying. "It's Domitian I fear for. He's just a boy. An innocent against that monstrosity. He hasn't got a chance."

The despair was all too evident in Flavius' voice. Something shifted inside Philo.

"Nothing will happen to Domitian. I will keep him safe. I promise you that."

Flavius looked at him curiously.

He banged on the roof of the litter and they were raised up.

"You have my word," said Philo.

TWENTY-FIVE

Gazing up at the arched ceiling with its indented jewels, Mina had to admit that Sporus had done very well for himself.

Following her upward gaze, Sporus said, "They're not real you know. They're painted on."

"Never! I can see the sides of that sapphire."

"Painted," said Sporus, sitting on the bed cross-legged. "Only the best painters can manage such an effect. But the emperor says I won't have to settle for so little very long."

Mina's eyes swept across the huge space Sporus had been allocated. A space so big it housed no less than five wardrobes and a long marble table that Mina suspected was larger in length than her own chamber.

"I can see you're struggling," she said with a heavy dose of sarcasm, for Sporus was too shallow to pick up on light mockery. You had to trowel it on. Much like whoever had been responsible for the eunuch's make-up that morning.

Sporus favoured a heavy use of kohl to accentuate the exotic slanting of his eyes. But today, the surrounding flesh had been painted in various shades of blue: from an almost turquoise colour through to dark blue beneath. It wasn't until he blinked that Mina noticed the eyes painted on the lids.

"The emperor says the new palace is too ordinary for him. He considers it an ugly space not suited to the ruler of the world," Sporus was saying.

"It will be a difficult space to tart up any further. What with all the gold, those walls that squirt perfume on you, and the banqueting room with the actual waterfall in."

"Oh he's not going to tart it up. He's going to demolish it and start again."

"He's going to rebuild the new palace?" boggled Mina.

"But better. More fitting."

It would be pointless to ask Sporus where Vitellius was going to get the money from. Sporus would neither know nor care. As long as he was equipped with pretty dresses and jewels very little crossed his mind. Sometimes Mina wished her needs were as simple as her friend's.

The ten-foot-tall entrance to Sporus' rooms creaked open and Ampelius the announcer stepped in.

"Aulus Vitellius Asiaticus," he said with a pompousness learned from Lysander.

Sporus uncrossed his legs and smoothed his blue gown to his ankles. He gave a quick fidget to his dark wig. The man who then entered was quite unlike any other that Mina had ever seen. Though he was of average height and build, with neatly cut dark hair, it was his face that made him stand out. Or rather the scar that dissected it from forehead to chin, slicing the nose in two on its path. Mina tried not to but the shudder ran through her before she could suppress it. Working on the front line of the palace, one was surrounded by the most beautiful of slaves. A physical disability such as Asiaticus' was unknown in circles where even the gladiators were swoonworthy.

"You're on," he told Sporus.

The eunuch leapt off the bed gracefully. One of the five wardrobes was opened and a slave stepped out holding a cloak made entirely out of peacock feathers. The feather cloak was draped across Sporus' shoulders then pulled across.

"That explains the eyes, I think," said Mina. "You're a peacock?"

"Tssk, as if," said Sporus, bending down his head so that the slave could place a silver crown upon it. "I am Goddess Juno, Queen of the Heavens," he declared pushing back his shoulders and holding a pose that Mina acknowledged was suitably regal.

"So the emperor likes you to dress up?"

"I'm a different goddess every day," grinned Sporus. "It's brilliant."

"You know what you've got to do?" enquired Asiaticus from the doorway.

"Of course," sang Sporus, skipping over. "I'm a professional! See you later, Mina." He disappeared in a puff of perfume and a swish of feathers.

Mina pulled herself off the couch she'd been reclining on. Walking past the grotesque Asiaticus, she enquired, "What does he have to do?"

Mina couldn't tell from Asiaticus' expression whether he was annoyed by the question or not. He did answer it however. "Today he plays Juno who has caught her husband Jupiter in the act of making love to another. Juno will vanquish her rival by showing off her far superior beauty and attributes. It will be a contest between the two as to who is the most pleasing to the king of the gods."

"Who's playing Jupiter?"

"The emperor of course."

"And the love rival?"

"Some slave," dismissed Asiaticus. "Pretty but inferior. Juno will triumph."

Well that was something, thought Mina as she walked back to her room. Sporus would triumph. He would win back his god/emperor lover. It wasn't a lover Mina would ever contemplate imagining herself in the act with, yuck. But if it made Sporus happy to be back in the centre of the court again, then she was happy for him.

Entering the corridor that led to her chamber, Mina was surprised to see Philo lurking outside her door. Actually, lurking wasn't the right word. Lurking suggested a degree of calmness. Philo was not calm. Even from a distance he looked fidgety, agitated. He was looking the opposite way to her, so she helpfully yelled down the corridor, "What are you up to?"

Philo shot a foot off the ground, and fell against the wall holding one hand over his heart. Mina sidled up to the shaking freedman.

"Tiberius Claudius Philo! What are you doing hanging outside the bedroom of a slave girl?"

Mina didn't believe for a moment that Philo was after an assignation, but she couldn't resist teasing him. "I'm flattered that you should seek me out to satisfy your sexual needs and naturally I am happy to fulfil them. Do you want me on top?" She stroked his arm. He pulled it back with a jerk. "No? You on top? You behind me? A bit of genital sucking and licking?"

She pouted her mouth and made a sucking motion complete with sound effects. This gave Philo the chance to interrupt, in a rather high pitched tone, "I have a mission for you." And then in a lower, half whisper he added, "An undercover mission."

* * *

"An undercover mission?" Mina repeated once they were inside her room.

Philo flapped his hands about. "Not so loud," he whispered.

Mina looked about her chamber. At the bed, the wardrobe, the table.

"There's no one here."

Philo pointed to the door. With a sigh Mina stood up, walked over, opened the door and peered out into the deserted corridor.

"There's no one there either."

"What about that door?"

"It leads to the old empress's chambers. It's empty. The new empress prefers the old palace rooms. But if it makes you happy, I'll check."

She disappeared through the connecting doors, returning moments later. "Empty," she announced, settling herself onto her bed. "So what's this undercover mission?"

"It's of the utmost secrecy. You must tell nobody. Absolutely nobody. Nobody at all. Not anybody. Anything. At all. Not a single detail. Not that we've even had this conversation. Discretion. Absolute discretion."

"Alright, I get it. Lips sealed. I can keep a secret you know."

Philo looked unconvinced.

"I can!" she insisted. "I know what you're thinking of. You're thinking of that time I flung myself at you and you ran away, and I told everyone in the palace that you were impotent."

That was, uncannily, exactly what Philo was thinking of.

"But nobody swore me to secrecy over that."

Philo would have done had he not been so keen to escape the firm grip Mina had on his penis at the time.

"So you see that is no evidence. Besides which, did I tell everyone the reason you ran away was because you were a nervous virgin untouched by female hand? I did not." Then seeing Philo's jaw drop open in horror, she admitted, "Sporus told me. Teretia told him. I'm assuming you told her." She gave a shrug. "It's rather sweet. Extraordinary. But sweet. I didn't tell anyone, did I?"

She crossed her arms. "And I saved your life by dragging you out of a prison cell that time. Fully managing not to blab my big mouth as to where you were hiding to those that wanted you dead. I deserve points for that one."

Philo inwardly conceded. "It's very important," he stressed. "Lives depend on it. Your life depends on it. You must not speak of it. Ever."

"Oh for Minerva's sake!" Mina rolled her eyes. "I get it. I swear on Vesta's girdle that I shall tell no one the words you are about to speak. Though they better be bloody worth it after all that build-up."

Philo laced his fingers together, his brow creasing with worry. "I need you to protect someone."

"Protect? Like a bodyguard?"

Philo supposed so. Though his misgivings were renewed by the bright eagerness she enthused her question with.

* * *

He got her past the Praetorians posted on Flavius' door easily. His explanation that she was a dresser for Caenis was accepted without questioning. Mina's uncharacteristically demure presentation in a plain, unflattering brown gown with her hair sensibly tied in a bun and her eyes dutifully averted to the floor, aided their deception.

"You'll stay here with the family," Philo told her as they made their way through Flavius' ample townhouse.

"You haven't said yet who I will be protecting and from what," complained Mina. "Is it gangsters? I'd be fabulous fighting gangsters. Or gladiators? That would be a challenge but I am soooo up for it. Straton taught me some ace skills that I've not had a chance to use yet. He used to be a gladiator, did you know that? Felix told me. He was the best gladiator in Rome at one point. He was, like, mega famous."

Philo hadn't known that. But knowing that did not alter his feelings about his deceased tormentor.

"In here," he said, pushing open the door for her.

Mina found herself in a cluttered study. There were papers and tablets lying about in heaped piles. Sitting cross-legged on the floor surrounded by this chaos was a boy. On sight of Mina and Philo, a bleat escaped from between his lips, his eyes widening.

"What is it?" he asked getting to his feet. "What's happened? Is it my father?"

His accent, to Mina's ears, was pure posh boy. He looked about her age, maybe younger, with a rather square chest and a head of black curls.

"Is it him, then? Is this who I'm protecting?" she asked Philo.

"This is Titus Flavius Domitian," Philo introduced. "His father is Titus Flavius Vespasian."

"You say both of those names like they should mean something to me. They don't."

Philo might have inwardly scoffed at her ignorance, but then he remembered Vitellius' ban on even mentioning Vespasian's name. The news was being suppressed, so it was entirely likely that few at the palace knew what was going on in the East.

"Vespasian is the governor of Judaea. He's been declared emperor by the eastern legions. Which has put Domitian here in a rather awkward and dangerous position," explained Philo. "He's been held here under house arrest since the spring."

"Who is this?" interrupted Domitian, recovering himself.

"This is Artemina. She will keep you safe from harm."

Domitian crossed his arms across his chest. "How can she protect me when Vitellius decides to have me killed? She's just a girl!"

Mina surveyed Domitian. His status as "pure posh boy" was confirmed but she added "grumpy" to her mental categorisation

Then the significance of this job hit her. "Philoooo? Oh, Minerva's shiny helmet, Philo! This is treason, isn't it? It's a totally treasonous thing to do if I protect grumpy posh boy here against the emperor's command."

Philo pulled at the neck of his tunic, looking extremely unhappy. "It has its risks," he admitted.

Mina plumped her bum onto a nearby chair, flattening several scrolls. "I'm surprised at you, Philo. In fact, I'm shocked. Extremely shocked. You're the emperor's private secretary's secretary. Isn't it in your job description to do anything and everything the emperor wishes? Isn't there a dedicated passage to not being treasonous? This is going to look pretty bad for you at your next appraisal."

"Artemina, if you feel this is contrary to your—"

"Oh, I'll do it," said Mina brightly. "Fighting Praetorians. Kicking soldiers' arses. Spiriting grumpy posh boy here to safety against the odds. It all sounds fabulous. How soon till you depose Vitellius then, Philo?"

"There's nothing of that sort going on," stressed Philo. "I just need you to keep him safe."

"How's she going to do that?" interrupted Domitian. "She's just a girl. And not a very strong one."

The disdain in his voice niggled Mina. "Philo, hand me my whip."

Philo opened the satchel that was slung over one shoulder. He rummaged inside and produced a whip, handing it over to Mina.

"'Course it's a small space and crowded," said Mina, surveying the messy study. "You should really get a slave in to tidy it up. Slack standards. It wouldn't be tolerated at the palace, would it, Philo?"

She took position in the corner of the room and narrowed her eyes.

"Grumpy posh boy, you might want to stand by that wall. Otherwise I'll be messing up my protection remit."

Domitian did as he was told, albeit with a grudging trudging of feet.

Mina stood in the corner by the door, turning her feet inward to find the correct balance. Her eyes scanned the crowded study for a suitable target. Having found one, she gave a shrug and then, with a blurring speed, pulled back her arm and cracked her whip forward. The tongue shot backwards. Mina stood holding a tied scroll in her hand. Domitian's eyes went back to the pyramid stack of scrolls on his uncle's desk. It now lacked a peak. The remaining pile slowly slipped onto the floor with a soft thwack.

"I'm going to have to tidy those up now," he grumbled.

Mina turned to Philo. "Are we sure he's worth protecting?"

TWENTY-SIX

A noisy breakfast was taking place over on the Aventine Hill. Felix and Vallia were embroiled in a heated exchange of words that had begun when Felix had opened his eyes that morning.

"You kept me awake all night with your snoring! All night! Not a wink of sleep did I get!"

She had, over enormous bowls of porridge dribbled with honey and scattered with fruit, lamented ever marrying him. She should have known he'd be a snorer from the way he'd blown his nose on their first meeting. But had she listened to her instincts or indeed that dreadful honking sound? No, she had not. And look where it had got her!

"In an apartment four times the fuckin' size of any of your flea-bitten family," Felix reminded her in between mouthfuls of her delicious porridge. "And we could have lived somewhere far nicer if you hadn't insisted on living in this fuckin' dump of a district!"

"To be near my ailing papa!"

"Well, he ain't ailing no more, is he? He ailed off across the fuckin' River Styx ten years ago! We got no reason to stay 'ere in this cesspit. We could move somewhere much nicer for the lad."

Two sets of belligerent eyes fell on the form of a small boy sat on a pile of cushions, tucking into his own bowl of porridge.

"That's it, Gany. You eat it all up," encouraged Vallia, affectionately.

"I'm gonna be big and strong like my papa!"

"'Course you are, son," smiled Felix.

Ganymede scraped the last of his porridge off the sides of the bowl. "Can I come to work with you today, papa?"

Felix cleared his throat, earning a glare from Vallia. "Err, not today, son. Another time, mebbe."

Ganymede's little face fell. "But papa, you've been saying that for months now. Wasn't I any good when I was your assistant?"

Seeing his son's pleading face tugged deep inside Felix's chest. "You were the best assistant I ever had."

This was true enough. None of the others had lasted even the morning working with Felix.

"I could help with the filing, papa."

"I'm sorry, Gany, but, err, you need to get better at your letters a bit. Besides, your mama needs you here today."

"I do, love," said Vallia. "I've got lots of things you can help me with today. Things I really couldn't manage on my own."

"See, son."

"Yes papa, yes mama," was the dejected Ganymede's response.

* * *

Gany's sad face stayed with Felix during his walk to work. He hated having to leave him at home. He'd grown used to Gany's small presence beside him, his pair of little helping hands. He missed him during the time he was at work, and that ate at Felix's insides. But at least Gany was being looked after by Vallia. His wife would make sure nothing happened to the boy. Something Felix, working at the palace, could no longer guarantee.

The palace corridors were obstructed by the usual slumped forms of comatose Praetorians. Some had at least managed to prop themselves up against a wall before passing out. Others lay sprawled out in the middle of corridors. The slaves walked round them carefully.

Not so Felix. He made sure his boots connected with every single one of them, hard. Generally in their crotch area if he could get a good kick in. Those that opened their eyes took one look at Felix's death stare and decided they'd not make a fuss in regard to their throbbingly painful genitals. Such was the effect of the chief overseer, even on the hardened German legionaries.

Having hopefully sterilised thirty or so guards, Felix arrived at his office. There was on the corner of his desk a pile of tablets. He flicked through a few of them. Most were demands from the various departments for more stock, demands none of them would have dared to present to Felix in person. From the number of replacements sought, you'd think a plague had swept through the slave complex. It hadn't. Vitellius had.

He'd been right to keep his boy away, hadn't he? No matter how sad his little face had been.

It was better than exposing Gany to all this. Felix threw a tablet down in disgust.

"Felix?"

He looked up to see that smooth green-eyed Greekling, Epaphroditus, stood in the doorway.

"Don't you ever fuckin' knock?"

Epaphroditus gave the open door two raps with his knuckles, then entered.

"Today's schedule."

He handed Felix a scroll. The chief overseer's eyes scanned down the list of banquets, entertainments, more banquets, further entertainments, yet more banquets, a spot of entertainments, and a banquet to finish off the daylight hours.

"Does he ever do any fuckin' work?" he enquired. "One thing to be said for Nero, he'd always pause in his orgying to sign paperwork."

"That he did," said Epaphroditus with a hint of nostalgia.

"So does he do any fuckin' work? You know the stuff that runs a city and a fuckin' huge empire with barbarians every side of it being hairy and agitating?"

"I couldn't say," responded Epaphroditus. "I just do the entertainments now."

Felix gave a hmph. "This ain't normal. You know that, don't you? Of course you fuckin' do. You've seen nearly as many useless emperors as I have come and go. This ain't normal. And it ain't sustainable."

Epaphroditus did not flinch under Felix's hard stare, commenting neutrally, "I couldn't possibly say."

Felix gave another hmph. "One thing to be said for that bloke we're supposed to pretend we don't fuckin' know. You know, Vespasian, who's sitting out East with plenty of fuckin' soldiers. One thing I'll say for him, he always treated the stock well."

Epaphroditus placed one hand on Felix's desk. "Things will calm down."

"Your eyes might be green but I know you're not. And you know as well as I know that there is only one way this thing is fuckin' headed."

The two seasoned palace insiders met gazes. "Not necessarily," conceded Epaphroditus.

"We'll be washing the blood off the walls before too long," said Felix. "You know I'm right, don't you?"

Epaphroditus offered no denial.

* * *

Felix's words stuck with Epaphroditus.

"This ain't normal."

What was normal anyhow? he asked himself as he stood on the corner of the Palatine Hill gazing down into the new palace grounds. This was usually a pleasant spot, with the gently lapping waves of the lake and the rolling green of the gardens. A spot to calm oneself from whatever mayhem was occurring inside the palace.

Epaphroditus was one of the few who considered Nero's pleasure palace and gardens a vast improvement on what had stood there before. Who wanted to look down upon yet more rickety tenement blocks of apartments? Wasn't Rome full enough of such squalor already? Though one could feel sorry for those citizens who had lost their homes in the great fire that had swept through the district, the aftermath was much pleasanter on the eye. Or it usually was.

Today, Epaphroditus' view was ruined by the army tents dotting the landscape and the soldiers milling about beside them. The usual calm and birdsong was obliterated by shouts and yells. They'd had no choice but to let them camp in the palace grounds. The Praetorian barracks were full and every possible space had been taken on the Campus Martius.

Alright, Felix was partially correct. This bit wasn't normal. So many soldiers inside the city. Inside the palace. When were they going to return back to their provinces? And who in Jupiter's name was keeping the damned Germans on their side of the river if most of the Rhine legions were in Rome? Epaphroditus' fingers twitched. Somebody needed to get on top of this. Somebody needed to make sure the empire didn't crumble at the edges like a Saturnalia honeycake.

He made his way to his old office. Opening the door, he found the small antechamber deserted. The desk that took up much of the room was clear. Unnaturally so. When this desk had belonged to Philo, it had been piled high with scrolls and tablets, despite his former assistant's obsession with tidiness. Epaphroditus knew that Philo's new desk in his new office was exactly the same.

Pulling open the desk drawers revealed absolutely nothing in them. Odd.

"Sir!"

Epaphroditus looked up to see a slave clutching an armful of scrolls.

"Where are you going with those?"

The slave's arms being full, he could only angle his head towards the door to Epaphroditus' old office. Epaphroditus opened the door for him, then followed him in.

Gazing about in astonishment Epaphroditus expelled a "What the—?"

His former office was full to bursting with correspondence. There were scrolls on the desk piled so high that you couldn't see the pleasant frescoed wall behind. The couch beside the desk had taken the overflow, until that too was full. Then they'd been placed on any other bit of furniture and finally the floor. Which was where the slave placed the latest batch by the ornately carved legs of the marble desk.

There was a set way of organising the post. Standard reports were received firstly at the messengers' hall to be sorted for the relevant department to deal with. Epaphroditus would notify the head of messengers as to what needed to come to him first for reviewing. This could be based on the seal, the destination it had come from, or the sender. After that Philo would open these selected missives and determine which Epaphroditus and the emperor needed to deal with personally.

"Who told you to leave the post here?"

"The emperor's secretary," was the reply.

"And he is?"

"On holiday by the coast, sir."

"Of course he is. These are being dealt with by his assistant and the most crucial sent onto him?"

He asked the question knowing full well what the answer would be, given Philo had been recommissioned.

"No, sir," confirmed the slave. "We just leave them here. Oh, unless they are from the eastern provinces."

Epaphroditus raised an eyebrow. "What happens to the post from the eastern provinces?"

"We pass them on if it's positive news."

"And if it is not positive news?" he asked.

"We bring them here, sir."

Epaphroditus gazed around once more at the mess: an empire run by nobody.

TWENTY-SEVEN

Caecina did not look best pleased to see him.

"I'm in a rush. Make it quick," he said as a slave fastened his plaid cloak on.

Epaphroditus had spent the walk back to the new palace grounds carefully formulating his words. Then he'd scrapped his chosen words, realising that the direct approach was the best way of addressing the young consul. Too many words confused him.

"Nobody is dealing with the correspondence," he said. "There are piles and piles of unopened post containing possibly essential information for the emperor."

Caecina looked at him blankly. "The secretaries?"

"Are under no one's instruction, sir."

And enjoying the free time this afforded them, he'd discovered. A mass skive-off he'd taken straight to Felix to deal with. Caecina's expression was vacant, leaving Epaphroditus wondering if he should have approached Valens instead. Maybe Lucius. Or the talon-tongued Triaria.

"That's not how it should work," he said finally.

"No, it is not," agreed Epaphroditus. "It should be working quite differently. It is crucially important that we get the matter under control. There could be information regarding Vespasian's movements in the East. Movements that the emperor needs to know about. If you would like me to supervise and resolve this—"

Epaphroditus didn't get a chance to complete his escape from entertainments, for at that moment in strode Valens and he was treated to a hard, grey stare.

"What's he doing here?" he asked Caecina.

"Something about the post, I think." Then to Epaphroditus, "Was that it?"

Epaphroditus opened his mouth to reply, but was cut off by Valens.

"The post is of no concern to him. He deals with entertainments. Talking of which, Asiaticus wishes to talk to you in regards to the entertainments for the emperor's birthday."

"Wouldn't it be easier if I talked to the emperor directly?" suggested Epaphroditus, adding in a smooth, "So there's no misunderstanding concerning his requirements."

Valens looked him up and down. "No. I think not. The emperor has been very clear in his dislike of you."

This seemed grossly unfair given the efforts Epaphroditus had put in on his behalf. But then, he'd never served a grateful master, so it didn't greatly surprise him. Nor did it depress him. His career had involved much flitting back and forth in imperial favour. And he still possessed a keen sense that he could win round Vitellius. If he could ever get access to him.

He wasn't officially dismissed but took his leave when Valens and Caecina started a conversation of their own as if he were not present. So he slipped out into the corridor still entertainments coordinator.

TWENTY-EIGHT

Valens took Caecina to a bar off the Subura. It was full of soldiers, because everywhere in Rome was full of soldiers these days.

"To us and our fortunes!" declared Valens, clunking his cup against Caecina's.

As Valens took a gulp of his wine, Caecina took in their surroundings: dingy, dirty, common. Hardly fitting for the two consuls of Rome. Valens seemed happy enough though, his colourless eyes bright for once.

"What are we doing here? Really? We should be attending posh dinners not dives like this. We're consuls."

Valens grinned. "I get it. You're worried the girls here won't live up to your high standards. But I checked them out last night and they'll do you."

"I'm not interested," said Caecina.

"It's the best thing for you, stuffing your cock into some whore. It'll help you get over the last whore. There's some of the more mature ones if that's your fancy," sneered Valens.

A bristling Caecina retorted, "I'd rather a woman than a child."

Valens brushed off Caecina's accusations. "To each their own," he said. "Let us not fight. We are partners. Extremely successful partners. Who'd have thought all those months ago in Germania that we'd be here now, consuls of Rome."

Caecina had thought it. He'd be unable to contemplate any failure of any sort. He'd set off for Rome fully convinced of their triumph. And what a triumph it had been! Yet something still nagged at him. It was Salonina in part, he acknowledged, but it was also something else. Something that had nothing to do with her and his broken heart at all. Shallow as he was, Caecina struggled to identify this deeper emotion, unused to such complexity in his character. Caecina was a man who ate, had sexual relations, slept, undertook the rudiments of work, and then ate, had sexual relations, and slept all over again.

He forewent the water in his wine and took a large sip.

"I heard some of the legionaries got sick," said Caecina.

"A summer fever," said Valens. "It has hit those camped on the Campus Martius the hardest. It seems to be the air down that way that disagrees with them. That and the heat. Germans aren't used to the Italian sun."

"How many have died?"

Valens turned suspicious. "What do you care?"

Caecina placed down his cup on the table. "They may yet have to face the eastern legions. If they're puking up their dinners and expiring, they are not much use to us."

"Vespasian declared for Vitellius months ago."

"Yes, but what has he been up to since?" pressed Caecina.

Valens shrugged. "Fighting Jews like he was before. And good luck to him."

"That entertainments fellow told me that the correspondence isn't being dealt with at all."

Valens signalled to a waiter, pointing to their empty wine jug. "That's what he said, did he?"

Caecina nodded. "It's a concern, isn't it? Vespasian could be marching his way to Rome right now."

"Except he isn't," said Valens, as the empty jug was replaced. "He's in Judaea having declared for Vitellius."

"But—" Caecina begun.

"But nothing," interrupted Valens. "That entertainments man wants his old job back. He was Nero's private secretary, apparently. He's trying to panic you into promoting him."

"I'm not panicking," insisted Caecina, his ego bruised.

"Well, it sounds like that from this side of the table. Next you'll be telling me of all the dreadful omens you've heard about that foretell our doom." Valens leant his elbows on the table and glared at his younger colleague. "The facts are this. We won. Vitellius won. Every governor in the whole damn empire has acknowledged that. He has the full loyalty of the legions including the hardest, meanest, best soldiers of all! The ones that we marched all the way from Germania to here." He thumped his fist on the table. "To Rome, the greatest city that ever was." This he shouted so that the soldiers in the bar cheered the sentiment.

Valens took the congratulatory yells with a smug grin and a raised arm. Which was when Caecina had possibly the only revelation he'd ever experienced. This was why they were in such a diseased dive. So Valens could seek the congratulations of the soldiers. That's what he'd wanted this whole time. To triumph. To win, to be praised. And he knew he wouldn't be getting it from his own class. That's why they were here. To ignore anything that didn't fit Valens' victorious opinion of himself.

Caecina hadn't thought beyond victory either. But that was very much the man he was. Action now, think never. Valens was the brains, the planner of their huge endeavour. It was he who'd first suggested they overthrow emperor Galba. Who'd pointed out that their superior legion numbers would make victory certain. Who'd persuaded Caecina that Vitellius would make the perfect emperor. He'd planned everything. But he hadn't, realised Caecina with a jolt.

He watched his colleague shine under the light of attention. This was it. This was Valens' plan for after they'd triumphed. Revel in the glory. There was no further plan. There was absolutely no reason for making Vitellius emperor other than this for Valens. With a horrible sinking feeling in his stomach, Caecinia realised that his elders didn't know better at all.

TWENTY-NINE

Traitor. Treachery. Treason. Philo couldn't shake off those words of Mina's. They hung over his every moment. A permanent accusation. He'd been called a traitor once before. Galba's men, Laco and Icelus, had accused him of conspiring to make Otho emperor. He'd been entirely innocent of that charge.

Offering protection to Vespasian's son was not of any assistance in making him the sole, legitimate emperor, so Philo told himself. Vespasian had an army. Vitellius had an army. Only a clash between the two would settle who was the emperor. Nothing Philo did would influence that result. He was an insignificant palace employee. Yet he was still haunted by those words: traitor, treachery, treason.

A concerned Teretia attempted to coax Philo's worries out of him. They were lying side by side in bed, baby Horace's cradle within rocking distance. Teretia asked, "What if Vespasian contacts you?"

Philo, schooled in the palace protocols of not mentioning that man, gave a start at his name being spoken out loud.

"You can't say things like that, Teretia," he said, sitting up in bed and gazing frantically around in the dark.

"There's no one but us here," she pointed out.

"It is dangerous to talk like that. Someone could overhear."

"What, my mother? Or Lysander?"

"There's Marcia …"

"Marcia wouldn't tell tales on us!" exclaimed Teretia. "She's family."

Philo, though he possessed distinctly less trust in Marcia than Teretia, let that one go. "Nonetheless—"

"If he contacted you, would you help him?"

Philo lay back down beside Teretia, saying in a half whisper, "I have no means to do so, even if I wanted to."

"Do you want to though, help him?"

"I serve the emperor. Vitellius is the emperor."

That came out firmly, with an air of finality about it. Philo began to feel reassured, safer, less treacherous. Until Teretia's next question.

"When you knew him in Greece, did you like him?"

Philo was transported back to the days when he had been a member of Nero's travelling court during his tour of Greece. Vespasian and Caenis had also been a part of that court. Philo had got to know them both reasonably well over those two years.

"Epaphroditus didn't get on with him," said Philo, still unable to speak Vespasian's name out loud. "Because he refused to listen to 'palace speech'. That's what he called it when you use a lot of words to say very little. He wouldn't play along with the official greetings and pleasantries that make up palace speech. He'd talk right over Epaphroditus, or sigh loudly and grumble that he had other things to do, so could he get to the point before sunrise." Philo found himself smiling at the memory. "At first I thought this was incredibly rude. But when I got to know him better, I knew he wasn't being mean. He just didn't need or want any of that court flattery and panegyric that the other senators demanded as their right. He just wanted the facts, the meat he said, of the conversation. I suppose it comes from all those military campaigns he led. If the enemy is invading your territory, you don't want to waste words on titles and protocols. He's a lot like his brother, Flavius. Both of them are men that get on with the job and do it well. I wish I worked with more like them. It would make things much easier."

Teretia took hold of Philo's hand. Lacing her fingers between his, she asked, "You liked him then?"

"Yes," said Philo. "Yes, I did. He was kind to me at a point I needed kindness."

He paused. Teretia waited for him to continue the story. Which he did, eventually.

"I liked Greece. It was a break from things that were back home."

"That man?" asked Teretia, which was how she always referred to Straton.

"Yes," confirmed Philo, quietly. "I didn't want to go back home to that. I decided not to. It was Vespasian who found me, who stopped me from going through with that," said Philo somewhat obliquely, knowing how much tales of his past suicide attempts upset his wife. "He sat with me the whole night. He wouldn't leave me, even though I really wanted him to. He didn't need to do that. But he did."

A small sniffing noise signified Teretia was crying. "Then I owe him much, because without him we would never have met. And Horace would never have been born!"

The two doting parents considered the horror of a world without Horace.

Then Teretia asked, "Do you think he'd make a good emperor?"

There followed a long pause. So long that Teretia wondered whether he'd gone to sleep. But he did reply. Eventually.

"Yes."

"Better than Vitellius?"

This was the moment that Tiberius Claudius Philo, in the privacy of his own bedroom, on the lower slopes of the Viminal Hill, committed his first treasonous act.

"Yes," he said. "He would make a far better emperor."

* * *

They'd talked about it well into the night. Well Philo had talked. Teretia had listened. Sometimes while nursing baby Horace. Sometimes while settling him back into his cradle.

"I never felt like this about Nero, and he could be ever so cruel. But he was the proper legitimate emperor with a bloodline back to the great Augustus. I suppose that's why I never questioned his actions. But now we've had all these men wanting to be emperor and none of them share even a drop of blood with Augustus. I suppose I have been mentally ranking them this whole year and a half since Nero died."

"You know what makes a good emperor, Philo, because you've worked with so many."

He had, and he could no longer suppress his feelings. Vitellius was not a good emperor. Vespasian would make a better one.

It was thus a rather subdued Philo who sat eating breakfast the next morning. He stared down at his bowl, eager not to catch Lysander's eyes. His friend knew him too well and would notice he was troubled. Maybe even realise what was at the heart of it. He was a traitor.

"How did my little grandson sleep last night?"

"Quite well," Philo told Pompeia, not looking up. "He was awake about eight times I think. But he was quicker to settle."

"He'll sleep more once he starts getting some food in his belly. That won't be long now," reassured Pompeia.

"I'm sure that'll help. I thought it best to let Teretia rest."

"I'll keep the porridge bubbling for her, master."

"Thank you, Marcia."

"I can get all the food in today and cuddle baby Horace when the mistress needs to sleep."

"Well, that is your role," mumbled Lysander under his breath.

"Thank you, Marcia."

"Mind you be careful though," said Pompeia. "What with all those soldiers about. They've been causing a lot of trouble they have. I'll go see my sister this afternoon instead so I can come with you, Marcia."

"There's no need, Mistress Pompeia. I shall be quite fine."

"There's not a lot of point in sending a slave shopping if you end up going yourself," said Lysander. "You may as well save yourself the space and money."

The spoon Marcia had been using to stir the porridge pot dropped.

"That's a bit unfair, Lysander," said Pompeia. "Marcia was—"

There was a sharp tap on the door.

"I wonder who that is come to see us so early?" pondered Pompeia.

Lysander stared pointedly at Marcia, "Ahemm."

Marcia got the hint. "I shall go see, mistress."

"Because that is your role," grumbled Lysander. When she'd disappeared into the hall, he exclaimed, "Honestly Philo! She acts as if she's doing us all a favour by her continued presence."

Marcia returned with Doris, whose presence this early in the day caused alarm, exacerbated by the slave's solemn demeanour.

"Is Verenia alright?" asked a concerned Lysander.

"A message from my mistress," announced Doris, handing a note tablet to Lysander.

The announcer untied the leather ribbons.

"It's not bad news, is it, Doris my dear?" asked Pompeia. Fruitlessly as it turned out, for Doris held her tongue impassively.

All eyes fell on Lysander. Even Philo was distracted from his private treasonous thoughts. "Lysander?" he asked with real concern in his voice.

Lysander flipped shut the note tablet, meeting three interested sets of eyes.

"He's back," he said. "Verenia's father has returned home."

Then he excused himself, leaving three puzzled expressions.

"Surely it's a good thing that mistress Verenia's father has returned?" queried Marcia.

"It is," confirmed the implacable Doris, breaking her silence.

"So why is master Lysander so sad?"

"I'll go find out," said Philo.

* * *

Philo found his friend in his room, busy packing his various bottles of voice tonics into his workbag.

"It's a positive thing that Verenius had returned," said Philo. "You can get started on organising the wedding."

"I suppose so," said Lysander quietly.

"That is what you want, isn't it? To marry Verenia?"

Since his friend had taken up with his wife's cousin Philo had lived in mortal dread of Lysander abruptly dumping Verenia and causing all manner of familial complications. So he waited for Lysander to answer with some trepidation.

"More than anything."

Philo felt his shoulders untense. "Then…?"

Lysander turned to face Philo, his expression troubled. "What if he doesn't like me? What if he won't allow us to marry?" Before Philo could reply, further worries escaped from Lysander. "What if Verenia's pregnant? We used all the precautions we could, but what if she didn't stick her sponge far enough up? What if the olive oil was off? What if my cock leaked a bit before I got it out? What if we can't marry and Verenia's pregnant? What will happen to her?"

Philo's mouth fell ever so slightly open. In the near three decades he'd been friends with Lysander, he had never given the slightest indication that he thought of anybody but himself. When Philo had been thrown into a jail cell the previous year,

Lysander had not wasted any time worrying about his oldest and indeed only friend. No, he'd made an instant move on the not-at-all widowed Teretia.

"You really love her, don't you?"

"More than anything," admitted Lysander. "So what happens if Verenius doesn't like me?"

Philo squeezed his friend's arm. "He will. We'll make sure he does."

He'd said it with a rare determination, lacking his usual apologetic air. Lysander did not look convinced.

"And how are we going to do that?" he asked.

THIRTY

Of course he couldn't let it be. A roomful of unopened post was just too upsetting for Epaphroditus. It offended the core of his being. However, he realised, as he stood once more surveying the papyri carnage of his old office, it was a task he was unable to tackle completely on his own. Not least because he already had a very demanding job arranging entertainment for Vitellius.

It was a job that was annoyingly public and failures clear for all to see. Surprisingly, he was actually grateful to Sporus. Previously he'd considered the eunuch an impediment at best; now he found himself delighted with his performance. Epaphroditus knew of few others who could act such a variety of roles and with so much conviction. In another life had he not been eunuchised, Sporus could have carved out an excellent career on the stage. Even better, now Asiaticus had taken over the care of the eunuch, Epaphroditus was free from blame for any of Sporus' future mischief. Winner.

Still, Epaphroditus really couldn't spare several days away from his position to sort out the post. So he needed help: efficient, organised, trustworthy, and hardworking help.

The deeply pained expression on Philo's face was, Epaphroditus knew, akin to the one he himself had sported when he'd set eyes on this mess.

"None of it has even been classified by province prior to opening?" the freedman breathed in horror.

"Not a single one," confirmed Epaphroditus solemnly.

"But ... but ... but," floundered Philo.

"Exactly," said Epaphroditus. "Can you spare time away from the Flavian household to help me sort it out?"

A still dumbfounded Philo managed a nod.

"Great. I've got snacks and drinks in. I suggest we start with the—"

"East," Philo supplied.

They'd worked together for so many years that no instructions needed to be given. They just got on with the job, chatting amiably as they did.

"Lysander is surely good son-in-law material," said Epaphroditus in response to Philo's retelling of the morning's main event. "He's reasonably placed in the imperial court. He's in a key position to accept hefty bribes and push any contracts the emperor's way that Verenia's father might benefit from."

"I thought so too," said Philo, scanning a scroll and then placing it into the "not of key importance" pile. "I suggested he invite Verenius and Verenia to dine at his mother's home."

"Excellent idea. Lysandria's latest husband has a lot of connections in business that Verenius is bound to share. Plus I have to admit that Lysandria is an excellent hostess. As long as you keep her away from the food."

Epaphroditus threw an arched look Philo's way. Both of them knew Lysander's mother, Lysandria, to be a poisoner. They'd caught her only a few months before attempting to poison Fabius Valens under instructions from Caenis. However, she shared a long and sometimes intimate history with Epaphroditus, and had taken care of Philo after his mother's death. So neither of them had felt compelled to denounce her. Also, given she possessed the kind of skills that could well be useful in the future, it seemed sensible to keep her onside.

"I said Teretia and I would go along for moral support. Though Teretia is already fretting about leaving Horace at home," said Philo, his eyes scanning along an open scroll. "Err, sir. I think this one is for the 'important' pile."

Epaphroditus placed down his own scroll, a request to grant citizenship to three men of Alexandria who'd proved themselves worthy. "Oh yes?"

Philo paraphrased the account for him. "Muscianus, the governor of Syria, has been reported as making a speech at the theatre in Antioch. Among many complaints, he has made a claim that Vitellius intends to settle his German troops in Syria and move the legions currently based there somewhere less hospitable."

"And I suppose the Syrian troops were less than happy about this," murmured Epaphroditus, breaking open another seal. "Oh, and here it is reported that the governors of Syria, Judaea, and Egypt have been making nice with local client kings. We were right. Vespasian bought himself time to secure support and cash."

"And armaments," said Philo holding aloft another scroll. "It appears to have been extremely well organised. Local officials are overseeing production. I can't think of any other reason they would be producing quite so much weaponry in Syria other than a plan to attack, sir. Plus Muscianus' agitating with no evidence to back up his claims is pretty damning, sir."

"It is," agreed Epaphroditus. "It all dates to the beginning of the summer, and we're now falling into colder days."

"You think they're already on their way?"

"It's quite possible. The answer is quite possibly in this room."

They both looked at the heaps of scrolls that surrounded them. Philo looked down at his hands a moment, then asked Epaphroditus quietly, "You will be taking this to the emperor, sir?"

The former secretary was so caught up in their discovery, his brain already whirling round possible responses to the situation, that he misheard Philo's words as a statement rather than the question it had been.

"Yes, I'll have to get past bloody Fabius Valens first."

A silence, then Philo said, "Err, I might have a better chance of getting the information to the emperor, sir. Sorry. Because I'm still classed in the secretariat and you're, err, not. And, erm, the emperor doesn't seem to dislike me quite as much as you, sorry."

Epaphroditus had never been insulted quite so apologetically. It made him smile. "You are right, Philo. As ever. The important part is the emperor understands what is going on. If you can get it to him easier than I can," he shrugged, "go for it."

Philo got off the floor.

"Yes, sir," he said, firmly averting his eyes from his previous boss.

THIRTY-ONE

It had been magnificent. He had been magnificent. Truly, he had. Sporus couldn't remember a time when he'd danced so well. It had been a tour de force of floating veils, of lithe limbs gracefully formed, of pure raw emotion channelled into dance.

The audience had gasped. They had clapped. That bossy wife of the emperor's brother had declared it "just marvellous". It had been. Marvellous. Laid out on his plush bed, Sporus' narrow chest heaved up and down from the exertion. A dressing gown landed on his face. He moved it off to see Asiaticus standing by the end of the bed. Sporus had become used to the freedman's presence. The scar didn't bother him. After all, his previous dresser had been Calvia Crispinilla and she had a pinched, sour face not unlike the puckered bottom of a cat.

"You want something to eat?"

"No," said Sporus, propping himself up onto a fluffy pillow. "Maybe a slither of food. A snack of some sort. A slice of bread. Nothing too heavy. Some meats perhaps. And fruit. But just a small platter of bread and meats and fruit."

"With cake?"

"Definitely."

"As you wish."

"Was there any visitor for me?" enquired Sporus. "Mina, perhaps?"

"No, there wasn't."

Poor Mina, she was probably working, doing something incredibly menial that Sporus could never lower himself to. Perhaps she'd found a new lover. It had been at least two months since she'd had a boyfriend. Still, she could at least visit him to tell him all about her latest dreadful conquest. Sporus tucked a stray hair behind his ear and wondered if the emperor would call for him that night.

Asiaticus had just returned from instructing the kitchen staff in regard to Sporus' food request, when he was told the emperor wanted to see him. He found Vitellius laid out on a couch, a table overflowing with food in front of him. Though the table was well within reach of his podgy hand, a small boy dressed as cupid had been charged with bringing the emperor nourishment. He did so by placing the chicken leg or bread slice in his mouth and then pressing his mouth near Vitellius' own, the emperor taking the food from the boy's lips with his own, one hand caressing the boy's buttocks as he did.

Seeing Asiaticus the emperor said, "There you are. You like my winged boy?"

Asiaticus nodded, for no other response was acceptable.

Vitellius grinned. "Maybe I'll give him to you. You haven't fucked anything recently have you?"

"No, Imperial Majesty." No other response was acceptable. "You called for me Your Imperial Majesty."

"I did," confirmed Vitellius and then to the boy, "Wine!"

The boy took a sip of wine from a goblet and then pressed his mouth against the emperor's to transfer the liquid.

"It's a good vintage," smiled the emperor, his eyes fixed on the boy lasciviously.

"Imperial Majesty," prompted Asiaticus.

"Ah yes. I wanted to talk about that eunuch."

"Sporus?"

"Yes him. He bores me. I was intrigued for a while. But I'm done with all that dancing and flouncing. It tires me."

"You want me to send him back?" enquired Asiaticus.

"No, no, not at all." Vitellius waved his thickened hand. "I want him to be more diverting. More interesting. More fitting to my tastes. You know what my tastes are, Asiaticus, don't you?"

Asiaticus lowered his head, "Yes, Imperial Majesty."

Vitellius patted the couch and beckoned for the cupid. "You see, he was my boy once," he told the cupid. "A boy like you." Vitellius used a finger to lift up the cupid's chin. "But" even prettier. Yes, he was the prettiest boy I ever saw. I delighted in his beauty. "But then he had to go spoil it." A glare was directed at Asiaticus. "Didn't you?"

Head still lowered Asiaticus replied, "Yes, Imperial Majesty."

"He ran away, the silly boy. I found him of course. I wasn't going to let such beauty escape me. Not when he was mine. Mine by rights. I brought him home, my runaway boy. And then do you know what he did?"

The cupid shook his head on Vitellius' outstretched finger. "Tell him. Tell him what you did."

Asiaticus said quietly, "I cut myself."

"He did that to himself, can you credit it? He cut his own face. An idiotic thing really, wasn't it? I suppose he thought it would make me not want him. And of course it did. How could one look upon that face and grow hard? But it also meant that no other fucker wanted him either. He's unsellable goods. His very act of escape bound us together. We are stuck with each other."

"Yes, Imperial Majesty."

"Good. Now bring me that eunuch. I want to enjoy myself."

THIRTY-TWO

Mina was bored, very bored. Almost towel holding for the empress bored. Guarding the son of a potential emperor had sounded pretty awesome when Philo had explained it to her. Even more because of Philo's clear internal dispute as to whether he should offer her the job. She had interpreted this to mean that it was a deeply dangerous (and thus exciting) mission.

The mission had not lived up to her expectations. The emperor's son had proved to be less than dashing. Domitian existed in a permanent mood, keen to let her know just how much he resented her presence. In ordinary circumstances, she'd have used her whip to reciprocate her displeasure at the grumpy posh boy. But irritatingly, in her guise as Caenis' attendant, she had to behave as an attendant. Attendants didn't tend to attack their mistress' stepsons.

She also had a long list of chores to complete in order to convince the Praetorians guarding the house that she was what she said she was. All in all it was pretty tedious, and she didn't even have a pal like Sporus to complain to about how dull it was.

She was carrying some folded linens to Caenis' chamber through the colonnaded side of the courtyard, when she heard an odd noise: "ping, thwack."

It was coming from somewhere within the courtyard. Intrigued, she dumped her pile of fresh linens on a stone bench to get dirty, and pushed her way through the shrubbery. Crouching behind a very Horace-like bush she surveyed the scene.

Grumpy posh boy was standing with his back to her. She saw his arm pull back and then "ping, thwack". She shuffled out from behind the bush to get a better view. Ah, it was a bow. The ping being the release of the arrow, the thwack being the noise it made when it hit the target. The target being a wooden post.

He held four arrows in one hand. With a speed that verged on the blurred, he transferred them to his firing hand and shot one after the other. They hit the post one underneath the other in an absolutely perfect vertical line. Mina's mouth fell open in appreciation. As Domitian walked over to retrieve his arrows, Mina stepped out from the foliage and began clapping. A shocked Domitian spun round and promptly dropped his weaponry.

Ignoring his stunned expression, Mina said, "That was impressive. Seriously impressive. I'm really impressed."

"It's just a hobby," muttered Domitian, packing away his arrows.

"It's a cool hobby."

Domitian looked up at her, puzzled.

Mina sensed he was doubting her sincerity. "I mean it," she stressed. "I'd like to see more of what you can do. Show me. I mean, could you hit that"—she looked around for a target—"leaf on that plant there?" She pointed to the corner of the courtyard.

"Which leaf?"

The question had Mina near bouncing on her toes with excitement. She walked across the courtyard to the intended victim, selecting a leaf and waggling it. "This one."

Domitian picked an arrow out of his quiver. "Stand back," he ordered.

Mina stood back in the colonnaded section watching as Domitian placed himself directly in front of the tree. He placed the arrow in his bow and pulled back the string and then let it go with a ping. To Mina the arrow was just a blur. She couldn't tell where it hit, though she saw the branches of the tree sway.

"Did you get it?" she asked.

Domitian retrieved the leaf from its landing place. He handed it to Mina and she examined the clear cut of its stem. Then she took it back to the tree to confirm it was the exact same leaf she'd chosen. It was.

"Flaming chariot wheels!" she exclaimed, grinning at Domitian. "That was brilliant."

His shoulders relaxed. "My brother Titus tells me that archery is lame and unRoman."

"Titus sounds like an arse."

Domitian's bottom lip descended. "He's a war hero."

"Really?" said Mina, deeply uninterested. "Don't they have archers in the army?"

"Yes, yes they do."

"Then he's an arse if he doesn't realise their worth," concluded Mina, sitting down on a stone bench.

Domitian shook his head of curls in shock, utterly unused to anyone describing Titus as anything less than a shiny golden statue of perfection. He sat down beside her on the bench, his bow resting between his legs.

"I want to learn," said Mina.

"Eh?"

"Archery. I want to learn. I want to be able to do what you can. I want you to teach me."

"I suppose—" began Domitian.

"Excellent," interrupted Mina, bouncing to her feet. "Shall we have the first lesson now?"

She had her hand on his arrows before he could think of an objection.

"Though I am warning you up front, O grumpy posh boy. You teaching me to use a bow is no excuse for coming up behind me and touching up my girl parts!"

"Well, err, no. Of course not," said Domitian.

Mina grinned. "Good. Your boy parts are safe from my extremely strong and sharpened kneecaps."

Domitian winced.

* * *

He careered along the corridors. Not his usual mince but rather a staggered gait that paid no heed to the other slaves taking this route. Bashing into them, he didn't pause to apologise or even to acknowledge them as he pushed onwards. He sucked in deep lungfuls of air, trying to hold it together. Just to hold it together long enough to reach his destination.

He didn't knock, because he never had. He'd always entered this room by swinging open the door and arranging himself artfully in the frame. He did not pose today. Today he just barged open the door.

"Mina?"

The room was empty, dark. "Mina?" he tried again, his heart beating with a sliver of hope.

The silence thundered in Sporus' ears. A small hiccup of a cry erupted from his chest before he collapsed onto the floor, sobbing.

When he'd been summoned by the emperor, he'd been excited, happy, gleeful even. Sporuses were at their most gleaming under the imperial light. He'd been on full beam, attired in a gorgeous green gown with matching veil pinned to his wig. Vitellius had given a smile on sight of him and Sporus, knowing himself to be gorgeous, was ready to please. It's what Sporuses did. They pleased.

He'd expected to undertake a bit of dancing, maybe some acting, before getting down to the pleasing element. But that was not what happened. That was not what had happened at all.

It was all too awful. This wasn't how you treated a Sporus. Sporuses were for dressing up, for petting, for loving and cherishing. They weren't made for that. Not that. His hand shakily rose to his throat and to his cheek. The skin was sore, bruised, broken in places. Even in the dark of Mina's room, he could see the stains on his dress. His beautiful green dress. He'd been so thrilled when Asiaticus had presented it to him that morning. Now he wanted to burn it, to incinerate it. To incinerate it. To blackened ashes.

The eunuch sat on the floor, staring into the darkness. His hands shook uncontrollably in his lap as the tears dripped down his cheeks. Vitellius did not cherish him. Vitellius had hurt him. He had hurt him a lot. Sporus did not shine. Sporus did not gleam. Sporus did not feel like a Sporus at all.

THIRTY-THREE

Marcia rolled over on her bed roll. No, still not comfy. It was just too hot. Sweltering hot. Sweaty hot. She gave up on any further sleep and went to open the shutters.

It was really early. She knew that because the delivery wagons were still parked outside the shops. They'd all have to move before it got too light. Wagons were only allowed into the city during the dark hours. Marcia would often curse their noise as she lay on the kitchen floor trying to sleep. This house was very noisy compared to her last. There she'd been muffled in a villa of so many rooms that she was always far away from the street. She'd decided she preferred noise though. Here she was connected to the world. A part of the Viminal community she was growing to love.

She cooked up breakfast as normal. The master was first up, followed by Mistress Pompeia, the lodger, and then the mistress herself.

"Horace only woke up three times!" the mistress announced brightly.

Marcia was as thrilled for her as everyone else. Except for the lodger, who commented that he was well aware of that given he'd been woken up three times as well. Marcia threw evil looks at the lodger's back on her mistress' behalf.

She was glad the lodger would soon be going and not just for his room, which would then be hers. A room of her own! The lodger, as she always thought of him despite him having a name, was not worthy of her master and mistress. He might work at the palace but she'd discerned he wasn't nearly as high up as her master. Though you'd never know it from the way he talked to the master. Disrespectful it was!

There had been much talk about the lodger's engagement to her mistress' cousin. A party was going to be held at the home of the lodger's mother. In attendance would be the snooty cousin's father. This seemed to worry the lodger very much. Marcia would have wondered why, but all her concerns were taken up with her mistress. Her mistress did so want to go to the party but she didn't think she could bear to be so long away from baby Horace.

Of course the lodger didn't understand, pointing out that the master spent many hours at work away from baby Horace and was still partially functioning.

Marcia understood though. She missed baby Horace when she was out shopping. He was the sweetest, most adorable baby even when he was crying, which he did a lot. Marcia like to walk around with Horace snuggled into her shoulder and sing him songs. The mistress said she had a lovely singing voice and encouraged her to sing Horace songs from her homeland. Which she did. And which she felt sure calmed baby Horace quicker than any Roman song.

The mistress was quite forthright that she couldn't leave Horace, even after the master said how nice it would be for her to have a night out. That was what swayed it for Marcia. Because her mistress did deserve a nice night out in a pretty dress. She'd offered up her services and said she would look after baby Horace in the slave quarters of the lodger's mother's house. That way, if the mistress was missing Horace, he could be brought in instantly.

The mistress clapped her hands together with glee and declared that to be just the perfect solution. The master was similarly pleased. Even the lodger was happy because apparently his mother had been nagging and nagging about seeing Horace.

After that there was much discussion about dresses, the mistress fearing that she wouldn't be able to fit into her nice gowns. Mistress Pompeia had suggested a new one was required. This was when the mistress had suggested a pretty new party dress for Marcia too.

Marcia near burst inside with bubbled excitement. A new dress of her own! And she was allowed to choose the colour and everything! It was thus an extremely happy Marcia who skipped along the Viminal streets, her shopping basket hung over her arm.

"Marcia!"

She turned to see Magnus walking towards her. A sight that made her smile all the more.

"Let me carry your basket for you," he smiled.

Though Marcia very much appreciated Magnus' daily help with the shopping, she couldn't help wondering whether there ought to be some soldiering duties he should be undertaking instead. Indeed, shouldn't all the soldiers be doing more than hanging about the streets? Some of the traders she knew had relocated their stalls off the Viminal. Sick of the abuse, harassment, and petty pilfering of the troops. Another reason Marcia was glad of Magnus' company. Nobody gave her any bother when she walked by his side.

She beamed up at her protector. He was so handsome. Tall and broad with blond hair and the bluest of eyes. Even bluer than the mistress' eyes. Gazing into that blue, Marcia began to feel herself fall in love.

* * *

"Trust me," said Domitian to Mina.

She'd heard that one before, hadn't she? It was a phrase that fell easily from the lips of men.

"I won't hurt you."

Ha!

"I've been practising," said Domitian.

She bet he had.

"Let me have your hand."

He took Mina's left hand by the wrist and placed her palms against the post.

"Now splay your fingers as wide as you can."

Mina did so.

Domitian walked back to his spot and picked up his bow. Mina winced.

"Are you sure you can do this?" she asked. "Because there is no need to show off. Not to me. I know how good you are."

"Keep still," warned Domitian, as he placed the arrow in the bow.

Mina began to feel her fingers tremble. She concentrated all her mind on keeping them still. Then she screwed her eyes shut.

Ping, a gust of air, thwack. Repeated four times.

She dared to open her eyes. Her hand was still pressed against the post but in the gap between each digit was now embedded an arrow.

Mina gave a squeal and then bent her knuckles in order to free her hand. Running up to Domitian, she bounced into his arms. He automatically placed his hands on her side to aid her leap, then hastily removed them, remembering her very particular threat to his nether regions.

Mina took a step back.

"Sorry," muttered Domitian, staring at his feet.

Mina regarded the youth who stood in front of her.

He was passably attractive, she supposed, and young. Which would be new. Mina's chosen partners tended to be at least double her age, and high enough in stature to significantly aid her career. The likes of Epaphroditus, who had secured her the towel keeping job and Titus Vinius, Galba's aide, who had raised her further up the ladder.

Domitian didn't have much to offer her on that score. He could be the son of an emperor. Or alternatively he could be the son of a soon to be executed traitor. Either way he was stuck in this house with no means to offer her much. Except for what she was fairly sure was a well-muscled frame, an unbelievable talent in archery, and a head full of dark curls that she rather fancied twisting her fingers in.

However, wasn't it ethically unsound? Wasn't she supposed to be protecting him? Even considering running her hands through those curls crossed a boundary, didn't it? A boundary that should never, ever be fully stepped over.

Mina looked at Domitian.

"I could do it again if you liked. The hand shot," he said with such earnestness Mina felt her innards tremble.

"Later," she said.

She threw off any notions of boundaries, ethics, and propriety. Taking a step forward, she cupped his face in her hands and kissed him. He did not hesitate in his response and they dived into a smooch of such passion that neither of them could doubt what was coming next. Certainly not Mina, who could feel Domitian's anticipation digging into her.

"Your bedroom?" she suggested.

Domitian nodded, as eager as a stray dog at a sacrifice.

* * *

The curls were quite as delightful as she'd anticipated. Mina tangled her fingers in their softness as her lips pressed against Domitian's.

She broke the connection to kick off her sandals, and to tell him, "Just so you know I'm still on duty and if some Vitellian murderers come through that door, I shall fight them naked."

Kicking off his own sandals and fiddling with his belt, Domitian said, "I'd expect nothing less from you, Artemina."

"Mina. You may as well call me Mina, given we're going to be naked together." She pushed her dress down over her shoulders, to her waist and then to the floor.

"Mina," said Domitian, with the first genuine smile she'd seen from him, as he took in her nakedness.

"Oi, grumpy posh boy," Mina said, hands on his hips. "You too."

Domitian really didn't need any encouragement to disrobe. Mina was pleased that she'd been absolutely right in assessing that his rather solid frame was deceptive. Beneath that tunic were housed arms thick with muscles, and a wide chest with defined contours. He'd depilitated of course. Every man did these days. But that just made the curls on his head all the more enticing and she threw herself at him with such force he staggered backwards, his naked buttocks hitting the cool plaster of the wall.

"Bed?" Domitian managed to ask between kisses.

"Bed," confirmed Mina, grabbing his hands and pulling him forwards.

Mina, otherwise engaged so not looking where she was going, fell backwards onto it, Domitian tumbling on top of her.

"Perfect," grinned Mina locking her legs around his hips and pulling him inwards.

* * *

As they lay catching their breaths back, Domitian tried to find the suitable words.

He settled on, "Thank you."

"Ditto," said Mina, her chest heaving up and down from the exertion. "Let's be clear though. This isn't a love thing, alright? I've been there with the love thing and really it wasn't worth it. It's definitely not a love thing. It's a," she snapped her fingers trying to locate the correct term for what had just passed between them.

"Hobby?" suggested Domitian. "Practice?"

"Practice is necessary in all things," agreed Mina. "Let's think of it as exercise for me, because I can't perform my usual whip exercises due to the guards, and for you—"

"It's taken my mind off my situation. For a bit."

"And that's a good thing. Because tension is not a good thing. Let us think of it as exercise for me and tension release for you. That's the deal, take it or leave it."

Domitian took a sly glance at Mina's toned, lithe body lying beside him. "I'll take it."

THIRTY-FOUR

Sporus had made a decision. He was going to escape. It was a decision that had been brewing for days, swirling about inside him. He could not endure, he would not endure, Vitellius anymore.

Sporus was a catamite. One of those delicate boys that emperors like to collect. He'd been trained in the arts of lovemaking at a very young age, and was thus used to being used by all manner of men. But he's never been so ill used as by Vitellius. Not even by the slaver who'd put him on the block and been the first to sample the young boy's delights.

Sporus had written this and other unwanted experiences off as a necessary casualty of his career. You did not enter day one as the wife of the emperor. You had to work your way up through the dregs at the bottom to reach the bubbly foam at the top.

He was bathing at the top now in frothy foam and life had never felt so bleak. Or so lonely. Where was Mina? She hadn't been to see him at all. Nobody had. Sporus spent his days lying on his huge bed, eyes brimming with tears, his whole body hurting, waiting. Waiting until Asiaticus appeared with his next summons to the imperial bedchamber.

When Nero, or indeed Otho, had been emperor, such a summons would have sent flutters of delight in Sporus' breast.

A summons from Vitellius did not. It caused a dark, heavy dread that settled at the bottom of his stomach. In his breast fluttered not delight but fear. He did not hide that fear. He'd discovered that was what Vitellius enjoyed. He enjoyed seeing Sporus' fear. If he did not see it, he sought to cause it.

It was horrible. It was more horrible than anything Sporus had been subjected to in his short life. He would escape.

It would be easy enough to accomplish. After all, the previous year, Sporus had successfully escaped from captivity among the eunuch priests of the Great Mother. Compared to scaling the ten-foot walls of their Palatine Hill complex, escaping from a palace he knew down to the smallest chamber was a doddle.

No, the escaping part didn't worry him at all. It was what happened next. Where would he go? The palace was all he'd ever really known. There had been a before the palace, a before the block, a name he'd owned before he was Sporus. But like all of his pre-eunuchisation memories, he'd chosen to forget it.

The palace was his everything. He'd assumed he'd always be there. That he'd gain his freedom and become one of those mega-rich imperial freedmen who always caused so much trouble. That halted him in his planning. He wouldn't ever be an imperial freedman with all the prestige that held. He wouldn't be palace anymore.

What would he be?

He shoved those thoughts away. He'd be fabulous wherever he was. He was Sporus. He didn't need a palace to shine. Why, he'd been quite the celebrity when he'd stayed with Philo on the Viminal Hill after his escape from the Galli.

That was it! That's where he would go. To Philo and Teretia's apartment on the Viminal. Teretia would look after him. He'd be an excellent addition to their household. He could advise Teretia on fashion and sex. Philo would be most thankful to him for the latter. It was Sporus' firm opinion that the scribe's character would be much improved by a good fucking.

He'd go to the Viminal. Of course he had no idea how to get there but he was sure some kind passer-by would know. Sporus was happy to repay any such kindness with a mind-melting, cock-exploding "Sporus", the likes of which Teretia would be shortly loosening Philo up with.

Sporus began to feel hopeful and rather excited about his new life. He imagined how thrilled the Viminal residents would be to have him back in their midst. It would be glorious. But first things first, he had to get away from that abomination of an emperor.

He chose his least flashy dress and cloak. He didn't want to be robbed on his way to the Viminal by some common thief. Of course, Sporus' least flashy outfit was everyone else's best party dress, but the lack of accompanying jewellery left him distinctly less sparkly. He debated for a long time whether he should take anything with him. But he didn't own a bag to carry them in. Anything Sporus had previously needed moving, he'd used a slave for. It puzzled him how things were done without slaves. Teretia would know though, and Philo seemed to have adapted to the life.

He pushed open the doors to his room and minced his way down the corridor. Head held high, untiared, and ready for his new life. At the end of the corridor he pushed open the doors. Two guards stood there.

"Excuse me," he said, walking in between them.

"Oi!" said one guard. "Where do you think you're going?"

Sporus improvised. "For a walk. I need to get a bit of sun. My complexion is awful!" He turned his head and patted a cheek. "Dreadful!"

"No, you don't," said the guard. "Get back in your room."

"I will," said Sporus using his most delightful smile. "After my walk."

"Now," said the guard.

Sporus looked to the other guard for support. "I'll just be a short while. Just a casual saunter in the sunshine to air my face. I'll be back before—"

The guard punched him in the face, sending the eunuch scuttling backwards. From the floor Sporus looked up at them in shock, a hand across his bruised eye. The guards bent down, their faces a few inches from his.

"Get back to your room. Unless you want more."

"But you can't. You can't do that. I'm a Sporus. I'm the favourite of the emperor. You can't hurt me. It's not allowed."

The guards shared a look, nodded at each other, and then laid their fists into the eunuch's slight body. Sporus lay cradling his head, knees curled up to his chest, trying to protect himself from the blows.

After they were done, when he lay sobbing on the ground his ribs pulsating with pain, he was issued with a warning.

"Don't you ever fucking open those doors again or we will kill you. You understand?"

Sporus managed a slight nod. They picked him up and, pushing open the doors, threw him back into the corridor.

He lay there for what seemed like hours, in shock and in terrible pain. Until that terrible day he'd been forced to flee with his beloved Nero, Sporus had never known unhappiness or discomfort. He'd never imagined that this could be his life.

Eventually he slowly crawled along the corridor back to his room. There he lay on his bed a mass of hurt and despair as blackness fell all around him.

THIRTY-FIVE

"I need to speak to Antonia Caenis and Flavius Sabinus," said Philo with an unusual degree of firmness.

This firmness made no impression on the slave, given Philo turned up every day and did just that. Nonetheless he sensed an increased fidgetiness in their regular guest so he led Philo to Flavius' study.

"I'll go fetch them, sir."

"Thank you."

Left alone, Philo gazed round Flavius' study. It was tidier than when he'd last been here. Domitian had clearly been busy. He picked up a note tablet that was lying on the chair beside the desk.

"Psst, Philo."

He turned to see Mina hanging on to the door frame.

"Philooooo," she hissed in a half whisper.

"Hullo, Artemina. You have something to report to me?"

She looked over her shoulder and said, "I had sex with grumpy posh boy."

The note tablet fell from Philo's fingers, hitting the floor with a crash.

"And it was tremendous," continued Mina as Philo disappeared beneath the table to retrieve his tablet. "It's like that time at the Cerealia Games when that rhino refused to take part in the beast hunt and just rammed its head against the arena wall again and again. It's just like that. Magnificently poundy. I know that small penises are all the rage but you know what, I'm not sure that's warranted. It might make a statue all nicely proportioned and that, but I've come down against them in sex terms. I'm coming down firmly on the side of a good firm length. And girth! You can't discount girth."

That Mina managed to say all this while Philo was under the desk was testament to how little he wanted to be part of this conversation. When it seemed he couldn't reasonably keep pretending to retrieve the tablet, he reluctantly verticalised himself.

A question formed on his lips but he never got to ask it because Mina grabbed hold of his arm and entreated him. "You must tell Sporus. He needs to know. Because if grumpy posh boy's father gets to be emperor that means I've had an emperor's son! Tell Sporus. He'll be sick with jealousy. Maybe tell him grumpy posh boy is, like, Apollo gorgeous. But with a big penis. And don't forget to tell him that I've switched from small penises now because he'll like to know that. Have you got all that, Philo?"

Philo's head flopped down in the approximation of a nod.

"Excellent! Thanks," she bounced. "Right, I'd better go check on him. He nodded off after our latest pounding but you know, Vitellian assassins could strike at any moment!"

She dashed out. Leaving a stunned Philo and a host of images he really wished he didn't have branded into his mind as Caenis and Flavius entered.

"Did she tell you the big news?" asked Caenis. "About her bedding Domitian."

"Yes," said Philo. "She did and I cannot apologise enough. She shouldn't be doing that with him. Because I gave her a job to undertake, which definitely did not include that. I'll make sure she goes back to the palace and is replaced with someone more suitable. Someone who won't be doing that with him."

"No!" said Flavius and Caenis in unison.

They looked at each other and laughed. Flavius spoke for them both. "We are delighted at the situation."

Philo's eyebrows rose in surprise.

"My gods, the atmosphere has lightened since those two took at bed wrestling."

"I caught him whistling this morning," confided Caenis. "And it was a jolly tune too."

Flavius guffawed.

"It is the best possible thing that could have happened to him."

"A most practical girl," approved Caenis. "But we digress, sorry Philo. We were told you wanted to see us."

Philo looked around the small study cautiously.

"Don't worry," said Flavius. "We won't be overheard. Our new jailors are far too lazy. They prefer to harass citizens outside the front door."

Philo knew this to be true. He'd passed two of the new Praetorians laying their fists into a local on his way in. They'd taken a similar view on people happening to walk on the Palatine Hill also.

"Feel free to speak whatever is on your mind. My nephew's bed antics included."

Philo leaned forward in his chair. "I have news from the East."

Caenis and Flavius exchanged a look.

"Philo," said Caenis with concern. "I know the difficult position you are in. You don't need to do this."

Philo gave a tight smile. "I've thought about it a lot and I believe I do. I do need to do this." And then, in case they hadn't understood his meaning, he clarified it beyond any misunderstanding. "I want to help you. To help you all."

"You have a wife and son, please don't forget that," said Flavius kindly.

"I know I do and that is one of the reasons I want to help. Vitellius, he's, well he's… He's not what an emperor should be," explained Philo. "I'm not convinced he even wants to be emperor. I've not seen him exercise or even enjoy the powers granted to him. He's too busy eating and throwing parties and injuring the workforce to bother with any of the duties of an Imperial Majesty. The paperwork is in a dreadful state," he concluded with some feeling.

Caenis sat back in her chair, her elbows leant on the arms. She pressed her fingertips together in an action that reminded Philo instantly of Epaphroditus.

Flavius said, "He was a decent enough aedile. And quaestor actually. I'd say he's been a generally adequate official his whole career."

"He's played a role. He's always played a role," said Caenis. "When he doesn't need to, his mask slips. I remember him during Caligula's brief reign, if we can call those bloody years that. He was the emperor's friend, his closest friend. He felt safe. He didn't pretend back then. I saw him, as others did, for his true self."

"And now he's at the top," said Flavius grimly. "He has no need of any man's esteem, any man's influence. He can do as he pleases."

"And he does!" replied Caenis. "It surprises me, Philo, that Epaphroditus supports Vitellius quite as unquestioningly as he does. He knows as well as I do what Aulus Vitellius truly is."

"What is that, madam?" asked Philo.

Caenis sat forward in her chair and said, "A man who ought not to be emperor."

Those few words conveyed everything that Philo had thought, had felt these past few months. "What can I do?" he asked.

"I take it that the news you have is related to arrangements in the East?"

Philo nodded. "I told Epaphroditus I'd pass on what we'd discovered to the emperor. I didn't," Philo admitted. "I told him

Vitellius was unconcerned by our findings. Which is believable. He only ever wants to hear good news from the East. He ignores everything else. I doubt he would have stirred had I given him a full report," Philo justified to himself.

"The money raising has been successful?" asked Caenis.

"Several client kings have lent their support financially."

Caenis gave a satisfied nod of her own. "That is good. That is what we planned. And Egypt?"

"Aligned with Vespasian."

"Good. They'll be preparing for a spring campaign as planned. We need to do our part here."

Flavius gave a hmmph and said, "We need to get word to our friends in the city. Philo?"

"Who do I need to see?"

"No, it is too dangerous for him to be that involved," said Caenis. Then after a moment's thought, she asked Philo. "Tell me is Lysandria being watched?"

Philo shook his head. "The guards were replaced and Epaphroditus has no authority to order a watch. He thought it enough for me to watch you." He gave a tight smile. "I can visit Lysandria quite easily and without suspicion. She's family. Even more so when Lysander marries Verenia."

"I don't want to write anything down," said Flavius. "The guards may be slack here but if he were caught with anything on his person—"

"Don't be silly, Flavius. Philo is palace trained. He can commit to memory anything we tell him to."

"I can," confirmed the scribe.

His natural modesty prevented him from revealing that he'd memorised all of Homer and could recite any passage from memory unprompted. It was a talent he'd acquired as an adolescent to fill his lonely evenings. While his contemporaries were exploring the opposite sex, themselves, and the effects of undiluted wine, Philo has instead used his time to learn things. He could read ten languages, name every consul going back to the formation of the republic, and juggle six balls at once if called to do so. So far, Philo's impressive juggling skills remained undiscovered but his ability to memorize large bodies of text was about to be fully utilised.

THIRTY-SIX

Lucullus sank his feet into the stream. The cool water instantly soothed the pulsating redness of his blisters. Beside him on the bank, Decius removed his sandals, lowering his own feet into the water emitting an, "Arrr," as he did so. The other ex-Praetorians did the same. Or lay on their backs on the bank feeling the sun warm their faces.

* * *

After they'd been so casually dismissed, there had been much discussion and arguing as to what to do next. Some had proposed an appeal to the emperor. Others that they should perhaps prove their usefulness to Vitellius by suppressing a riot (of their own making). But both these suggestions were shouted down. There was simply no appetite for prostrating themselves before this new imperial fat-arsed master.

The talk had turned to Emperor Otho and what a proper emperor he'd been. They reminisced about that daring day the Guard had overthrown Galba and made Otho emperor. Then onwards to the fierce battles they'd engaged in on his behalf. Talk of Otho led to talk of Otho's end and a general lament for their fallen hero.

"We could have won," Decius had commented, wiping away a tear. "He didn't need to do that. He didn't!"

They'd all had a good weep before they'd decided that the only course was to disband. Embraces were had and farewells offered. Lucullus, watching as his former comrades began to shuffle off, had felt like weeping all over again. His world was ending. It was all dribbling away like the final drops of a satisfyingly lengthy piss. He thought back to the day he'd been enrolled into the Guard under Emperor Nero. How proud he'd been. How happy. He and Proculus standing side by side in their scorpion breastplates and purple-plumed helmets, puffing out their chests, knowing they'd well and truly won at life.

Proculus was dead. Gone. As was everything else now. Lucullus had nothing. No best friend. No job. No emperor to serve. He gave a sniff.

Seeing his despondency his fellow guardsman Decius had punched him on the shoulder.

"Cheer up mate, We had a good run at it, didn't we? New flip of the note tablet and that. What will you do now?"

Lucullus had shrugged. "Go back home I guess. My ma has a farm in the Po valley. She's always nagging me to send more money back so she can buy more slaves to work it."

"Nice farm is it?"

Lucullus had smiled. "Yeah, it is."

He told Decius all about it. From the gentle slope of the fields to the evil geese that chased off all unwanted visitors. At the end of this tale of pastoral bliss punctuated by lethally shaped beaks applied to the soft fleshy buttock, all within earshot were enthralled. Decius was struck by an idea. "Hey, your ma doesn't need more slaves to work that land."

"She doesn't?"

"We can do it!" Decius had declared. "All of us." He swept a hand across forty or so Praetorians. "Why not? We can be like Romans of old, toiling the land and sweating nobly. And at the end of a hard day's work, we can watch the sun set while sharing flagons of wine."

Lucullus was not sure his ma would be that pleased by a load of drunken ex-soldiers cluttering up the farm. But there was, he had admitted, something in Decius' vision. He could picture them all working together, hauling farm equipment about, clearing up the yard, being useful and, more important, being together.

"Let's do it!" Lucullus had said brightly. "Let's all go to my ma's farm and start again."

Such was the surprising zeal for farm work that their numbers swelled into 100 or so. A hundred men marching northwards were apt to be served first at taverns and be provided with food from the farms they passed. All of which had made for a jolly atmosphere, despite the blisters.

* * *

Now, as Lucullus lay back on the river bank, he tried to picture how happy his ma would be by the presentation of 100 strong men ready to help her. She'd have to lock those damn geese away though, he thought: twelve of those fuckers could easily decimate 100 Praetorians. As images of geese causing carnage floated around his mind, he became aware of a noise. It wasn't much. Just a rustling. But something about it had Lucullus sitting upright. There it came again.

"Decius, what's that—"

He didn't get to finish his question. Out of the surrounding wood appeared soldiers. A mass of soldiers. Shields held high. Eyes glaring. Lucullus and the others jumped to their feet and pivoted round. Soldiers to the side. To the Rear. To the front. They were surrounded. Lucullus' eyes fell on the spot where he'd dumped his gear and, more important, his sword. It was well out of reach.

"DO NOT MOVE!" yelled a centurion stepping in front of the line of legionaries. "YOU ARE SURROUNDED BY THE 13TH LEGION SWORN TO IMPERATOR VESPASIAN! STATE YOUR LEGION AND COMMANDER."

The ex-Praetorians looked at each other. Decius nodded at Lucullus, who took on the mantle of spokesman.

"We have no legion. No rank. No commander. That bastard Vitellius stripped us of everything!"

A yell of agreed grievance exploded from the ex-Praetorians.

The centurion smiled. He stepped forward accompanied by four legionaries and walked towards Lucullus and his band of would-be farmers.

"Men," he said, stretching out his arms. "How do you fancy joining us and taking back what is rightfully yours off that fat fucker Vitellius?"

The pastoral dream that had sustained them for so many miles drifted away and to a man they responded, "Fuck, yeah!"

* * *

Beside the campfire over a steaming bowl of army rations, the 13th Legion filled their colleagues in on events.

"We were for Otho," said a centurion, name of Acer. "We were on our way to save him. But he didn't wait for us."

"Good man, Otho," said Lucullus. "He was the best of men."

"The true emperor," cried out another guard.

"I would have died for him. We all would have died for him."

Cue yelled affirmations from the ex-guards.

"Quite," said Acer. "There was no way the 13th Legion were going to support that usurping fat fuck Vitellius."

The camp rang out with boos at the emperor's name.

"Then word reaches us from the East. Seems there's a new emperor in the making," continued Acer. "So we reckon we'll back him. Better him than align with the fucking German legions."

"Too right!" joined in the Praetorians, still sore from the fucking German legions having taken their jobs.

"Then we get word from this eastern emperor. He says he's coming to kick Vitellius' fat arse in the spring. And he wants us to hold off the Vitellians in this north bit of Italy. Which we were well up for."

"YEAHH!!!"

"But our commander, Beaky (that's wot we call 'im, Beaky—everyone calls Primus Beaky), gets to thinking. Spring is a long way off. A lot could happen before then. Like them fucking Germans building up their numbers. So he thought, why wait? Why don't we hit 'em fuckers now. Take them by surprise like."

"We missed one battle. We aren't going to miss another!"

Acer stirred his spoon round his bowl. "So my Praetorian pals. You up for avenging the proper emperor, Otho? You up for some fighting? Some bloody hard fighting against them fucking Germans?"

The Praetorians grinned and thumped their fists against their chests.

"Too bloody right we are!"

Acer and his pals got to their feet and thrust their swords into the air. "For Imperator Vespasian."

The Praetorians copied the motion. "For Imperator Vespasian."

It was only the second time any of them had heard that name.

THIRTY-SEVEN

Caecina had endured a rather restless night's sleep. This was most unusual for him. Generally his head hit the pillow and he was out, untroubled even by dreams. Caecina was not a man of dreams. Dreams involved forethought. Caecina was very much a man of the moment. He rarely contemplated anything beyond breakfast. He just did. So far that "just doing" had served him well.

Here he was, Caecina Alienus, not even 30 and a consul of Rome! He was the city's golden boy with the ear of the emperor.

Except, thought Caecina, as his slave dabbed perfume strategically about his naked body, he wasn't sure he wanted the ear of the emperor. He wasn't sure he wanted to be anywhere near the emperor.

In Germania, Vitellius' excesses seemed comic, especially when compared to the tough, hardened German soldiers that surrounded him. In Rome, Caecina was finding him less amusing. For a man of Caecina's energy, spending the whole day at a banquet was torture. No matter how good the food was, he sat in fidgety silence wanting to "do". Surely there was something to "do"?

When Caecina had worked with Galba in Spain, there had been much to do. It had been all doing: piles and piles of scrolls to go through, numbers to add, messages to dictate, petitions to hear. Really, part of the reason Caecina had let Galba seduce him was to enliven all that doing. Surely being emperor contained just as much, if not more, doing.

Who was doing the doing?

Not Vitellius for sure. He was busy lying on a couch, with endless food and boys brought to him to save him from moving even an inch of his flabby flesh.

"Master?" enquired the perfumer, standing back, bottle in hand.

Caecina gave a sniff. "Yes, fine. Send someone in with my clothes."

"Yes, master."

A blue and yellow plaid tunic and accompanying trousers were brought in. Caecina's gaze fell upon them. He'd been so pleased the day he'd first tried on these Celtic garments. They'd instantly felt right. He'd truly felt that he'd found himself the day he pulled up those trousers. Today their appearance caused a damp feeling of dismay that settled in his stomach.

"Take them away. Bring me a tunic instead. An ordinary Roman tunic."

He told himself that this was a sensible decision. The woollen trousers were far too hot for a Roman summer. But this wasn't the truth of it at all. They were a symbol of his epic adventure leading 30,000 men through hostile tribe territory to fight a battle and make Vitellius emperor. That had been the greatest, craziest, most exhilarating time of his young life.

"But what was it all for?" he said out loud.

"Master?" queried the sandal buckler.

"Nothing, nothing," he dismissed.

As he got to the door his chamberlain told him, "Fabius Valens sent word that he is going into town this evening if you wish to join him."

"I don't," he replied.

He walked down the corridors of the palace, his slaves showing him the safe route through the drunken soldiers that lay slumped in his path. Where were his big brave Germans? Those loyal brutes he'd marched all the way from Germania? He thought their culture, their beliefs, to be superior to those of his own people. Yet look how easily they'd been corrupted!

Caecina could have cried. Except at that moment he caught sight of a face he recognised.

"You! Indian boy!"

Philo halted. "Sir?"

"You work for Epaphroditus, don't you?"

"Yes, sir."

"The post. The post thing. That was sorted?"

"Yes, sir. Epaphroditus and I went through it all."

"And Vespasian in the East. What news was there? Is he challenging the emperor's right to rule?"

Philo blinked twice, then said, "No, sir. There was nothing. Vespasian is loyal."

Caecina gave a handsome smile. "Good. That's good, isn't it?" he asked.

"Yes, sir. Yes it is."

* * *

Epaphroditus stared down at his note tablet. At the top he'd inscribed in the wax: The Emperor's Birthday Party. The rest of it was blank, much like Epaphroditus' mind. From what Asiaticus had said, Vitellius was expecting something spectacular. The likes of which had never been seen in Rome before. Something the people would talk about for decades. Even centuries. No pressure then.

Epaphroditus used the sharp end of his stylus to scratch at his head. It didn't help. Over the course of his near 50 years in imperial service, Epaphroditus had attended hundreds of banquets, feasts, parties, and orgies. That should have provided plenty of material to nick ideas from for Vitellius' birthday. The only problem was that Vitellius had been there too. A bulky presence through Caligula's demented and debauched affairs. During Claudius' penchant for naked nubile girl dancers. Even for Nero's artistic endeavours. He'd seen it all. He'd participated in it all.

So how in Jupiter's name was Epaphroditus going to come up with something novel?

Midway through a groan, an idea hit him. He quickly pressed his stylus into the wax.

Dress-up pigs.

He reviewed it, expelled a, "Yay," then rubbed it out. Turning to his slave he instructed, "Go summon Midas. Two heads have got to be better than one. Certainly better than this one." He tapped the stylus against his temple.

* * *

Midas fidgeted on the chair.

"Go," instructed Epaphroditus pointing his index finger at him.

"Errr. Umm. Naked flute girls. Naked flute girls playing while standing on their heads. Naked flute girls with scenes painted on their naked flesh so that when they stand together they make a full picture. Naked flute girls doing things with their flutes! Naughty things!"

Well, that explained much about Midas' off-duty musings, thought Epaphroditus. "No flute girls, naked or otherwise. What else have you got?"

"Errr." Midas' eyes flickered back and forth.

Epaphroditus took pity. "Alright, the food then. That is your department."

"Trojan hog?" suggested Midas with a hopeful air. "You slice open a pig and its intestines slip out. Except it's not intestines, it's sausages!"

"Seen it," dismissed Epaphroditus. "Which means Vitellius also has. But it might be worth working on. Some sort of twist on it." He fingered his chin.

"You cut open a pig and what you think are horrible flies are actually currents. Blood that gushes out but isn't blood—"

"A river cascading out," said Epaphroditus, picking up Midas' train of thought. "A wave."

"That cascades downwards like a fountain," said Midas, his eyes bright.

"Red. Because it's striking and reminiscent of a sacrifice to the gods. What is red? Wine, sort of. Grapes, though more purple than red. Berries. Some sort of berry. The edible non-poisonous sort."

"Pomegranates?"

Epaphroditus clicked his fingers. "Pomegranates! Proserpina! That's our theme."

"Sir?"

"Proserpina was kidnapped by Pluto and taken to the underworld. Her mother Ceres, goddess of the harvest, mourned her loss so much that the land was barren, and the people starved. Jupiter demanded that Pluto hand Proserpina back to her mother, but the young goddess had eaten a pomegranate seed and this tied her to the underworld. She could not return to Ceres and the mortal world. So a deal was struck between the brothers, Pluto and Jupiter. Proserpina would spend half the year with her mother on the earth and half the year with her husband Pluto in the underworld. For that half of the year the earth is once again barren. But each spring when Proserpina returns to her mother, the earth lets forth her harvest."

"Gives us an opportunity to show off the abundance of the earth, sir."

"It does indeed. Vitellius can represent our time of plenty after the barrenness of a civil war. We can show off the extent and variety of food shipped in from all over the empire."

"Exotic fruit?"

"Make sure it tastes good though. And if not, make sure it's just for display and not actually tasted."

"Yes, sir."

"The emperor could be presented with a massive plate that has on it some food from every point in the empire and beyond. His own personal harvest from his vast domain."

Midas chewed on his lower lip. "We could start off with some five or six courses for the guests. Then our Proserpina is kidnapped and the food is cut off."

"Sad singing to denote Ceres' mourning?" suggested Epaphroditus.

"And then we have our pomegranate blood fountain cascading wave river thing to kick off Proserpina's return and the abundance of the empire!" Midas bounced his bum on the chair. "I wonder where we can find a three-headed dog to be Pluto's pet Cerberus?"

"Imaginative costuming?" supplied the entertainments coordinator. "Alright, this has legs as an idea. From you I want a full menu for our feast of plenty by tomorrow. Flesh out our pomegranate fountain idea. Also, we need to talk entertainments."

"Yes, sir. I already have several ideas."

"No naked flute girls."

Midas' lips closed.

"We need a Proserpina. Someone who can pull off her despair and then joy convincingly. I want the guests and the emperor to really feel it. To really feel her pain."

Midas' and Epaphroditus' eyes met and they said in unison, "Sporus."

THIRTY-EIGHT

Asiaticus' eyes scanned down the tablet. Epaphroditus had given up trying to read his expression: that scar made him appear forever sneering. Instead he waited for the verdict in silence, hands clasped behind his back.

"This menu is satisfactory," concluded the freedman.

"I shall get Midas on to it straight away. Right after I brief Sporus."

He moved towards the double doors that led to the eunuch's room. Asiaticus stepped in front of him.

"He's asleep."

"Ahh, that old excuse," smiled Epaphroditus. "Just drag him out of bed by his ankle. That's what Calvia used to do. A slap on the bum with a curling tong or just the threat of it does wonders for his cooperation."

Asiasticus did not move, nor respond.

"If I could just—"

"No."

"No?"

"I shall brief him when he wakes."

"But—"

"In consultation with the emperor, who I know will have his own ideas in regards to its performance."

Epaphroditus fixed his eyes on Asiaticus, refusing to flinch at his damaged eye. "Look, friend," he began, with a stress on the friend. "I have no desire to step on your toes. I have no desire to Sporus-sit. That's your job. Mine is organising entertainments. And I need to go through the schedule with those entertainments. It will ensure the emperor's requirements are met. We'd hate for him to be disappointed on his birthday, wouldn't we? Especially if it were due to Sporus not being fully prepared—"

He left the implied threat hanging.

"No," repeated Asiaticus. "I shall do the briefing."

Epaphroditus' jaw stiffened with suppressed fury for a moment, then he smiled widely, saying lightly, "As you wish."

* * *

"Proserpina and Pluto, you say?"

"Yes, imperial master," said Asiaticus.

"That sounds like fun," declared Triaria. "The age of abundance."

"I like it," said Vitellius. "Make sure there's goods from every province. Let us ram it down the throats of those client princes in the palace that we own them and their country. There will be no mistaking that Rome rules the world."

"Hear, hear," said Triaria.

"It was suggested that the eunuch might make a good Proserpina," added Asiaticus.

Vitellius' piggy eyes were suddenly focused. He neglected to even yawn, belch, or shove anything edible in his mouth as his brain ticked over the possibilities.

"I believe it will make an excellent Proserpina," he said. "We need a Pluto. One to contrast with the fair and beautiful Proserpina. Her tragedy must be emphasised. Else why would Ceres lay the earth barren in her mourning?"

"The eunuch did show a great deal of tragedy in his recent performance as Niobe. The way he wept as his children were shot by Apollo and Diana. I was very moved," said Triaria. "It is an excellent actor."

Vitellius held out his goblet for refilling. "Who said anything about acting. If my guests are to fully experience the drama, it needs to be real."

"Real?" queried Caecina.

"The Rape of Proserpina," said Vitellius taking a gulp from his goblet, a slave rushing forward to mop away the red liquid that escaped from the corner of his mouth. "We shall present a true tragedy: a maiden being cruelly ravished and incarcerated. It'll make the reconciliation at the end all the sweeter and joyous."

Valens gave a thin-lipped grin. "That sounds a most satisfying performance."

"It shall be. Dependent on the correct man playing Pluto. Asiaticus, get to it. Find the perfect Pluto to brutalize our dear Proserpina. The prisons must be full of ugly brutes. Why shouldn't one of them get to enjoy one final sweetness before execution?"

* * *

Epaphroditus made his way back to his office fuming at Asiaticus' obstruction. Jumped-up, chalk-footed, phallus-breathed cock muncher! Ugly, twisted, freak of a creature! Debauched chicken's arse of a man!

The walk to his office and imagined abuse heaped on Asiaticus helped dissipate his temper. Flames of anger extinguished, he began to wonder instead. Why wasn't he allowed to see Sporus?

Even as a deliberate attempt to show Epaphroditus his place in the administration (somewhere between a pan scrubber and a stylus sharpener), it made no sense. Surely Asiaticus wanted

Vitellius pleased? If the emperor was pleased, he could take all the credit. Epaphroditus wouldn't be able to stop him. Should the emperor be displeased then Asiaticus could dump all the blame on him. And again, Epaphroditus wouldn't be able to stop him. Though either course was a winner for Asiaticus, pleasing the emperor and gaining the praise for doing so was surely preferable. So why bar Epaphroditus from fully briefing Sporus? It made no sense.

But enough of eunuchs and stupid freedmen. He had too much to organise to get caught up in this mystery. He needed to coordinate with Midas. Right now. There was too much to do. Except, when was the last time he'd seen Sporus?

Asiaticus had taken over the minding of Sporus, which as far as Epaphroditus was concerned was absolutely fabulous. He had been extremely happy to relinquish the role. But now he thought about it, he hadn't seen Sporus since Asiaticus had taken him off his hands. Though barred from direct contact with the emperor, Epaphroditus had nevertheless slid unseen into his own organised entertainments to check there wasn't a fuck-up. Searching his memory, he couldn't place Sporus at any of them.

This felt odd. Part of being emperor was showing off your assets. The things you owned that nobody else did, or could afford to. You put such assets front of house. Sporus was all front of house. He was the flashy diamond tiara you showed off at dinner parties even though it gave you a headache. Yet he hadn't been on show.

Hand poised on his office door, Epaphroditus paused. Something wasn't right. His hand fell from the door and he set off towards the slave complex.

* * *

Felix was involved in one of his usual shouty arguments with an underling when Epaphroditus entered his office. Actually, argument is the wrong word. It was more of a monologue delivered at seven-times normal volume straight into the hapless Xeno's face. It blew him back a step and earned him more bellowed insults on how his fuckin' uselessness extended to being fuckin' unable to stand on a fuckin' spot for even a fuckin' moment.

Epaphroditus waited patiently by the door for the conclusion of Xeno's torment. Eventually there was a pause that allowed the redness to fade slightly from the non-bearded part of Felix's face. Xeno was told to get the fuck out and improve his fuckin' attitude and face. The now haggard-looking overseer trudged past Epaphroditus, his head hung low.

"Oh, it's fuckin' you, is it?" said Felix, moving a pile of tablets from one side of his desk to the other. "Well what the fuck is it?"

Epaphroditus deposited himself on a chair. "When did you last see Sporus?"

Felix's eyebrows burrowed down above his prominent nose. "I don't know off the top of my fuckin' head. I got fuckin' thousands of slaves. I don't keep tabs on all their movements."

"I haven't seen him for months."

Felix gave Epaphroditus a long look. "You're in charge of him," he said.

"Asiaticus took him off my hands. When did you last see him?"

Something in Epaphroditus' concerned tone penetrated Felix's thick skin. The head of slave placements sat down opposite the erstwhile secretary, and pondered. "He's quite the eunuch for making his presence felt."

"He is," agreed Epaphroditus, with a faint smile. He was recalling the time Sporus had gatecrashed one of Nero's imperial parties and ended up in a cat fight with the empress Statilia Messalina.

Felix broke into that memory. "I ain't seen him for months. And I don't like the fact that you ain't either. It's not fuckin' right."

"No, it's not," agreed Epaphroditus, noting Felix's worried expression and knowing he was right to raise the issue.

"I'll see what I can find out. I assigned him a beauty team, they must have seen him. I can't believe Sporus could cope with a chipped nail or unbrushed hair."

A thought struck Epaphroditus. "Artemina, the one who was the empress's towel holder."

"The one you fuckin' used to fuck?"

Epaphroditus made a small noise to indicate the truth in that invective. "She and Sporus are friends I seem to remember. Maybe she can reassure us of his situation."

"Doubt it," said Felix. "She's in fuckin' Baiae."

"Baiae?"

"At one of Nero's summer villas."

Epaphroditus frowned, "Why?"

"How the fuck should I know," growled Felix. "You should know the fuck why. Philo signed her out."

Epaphroditus was stunned. Not by Felix's sweary outburst, he'd been exposed to that for nearly half a century. It hadn't exactly desensitised him to Felix's temper, but rather he accepted it as a considered factor in getting anything done.

No, what had stunned him was that Philo had signed Artemina out. He would only have done so if ordered to. Epaphroditus was Philo's superior and he'd given no such order. Which could only mean that Philo had decided to send Artemina to Baiae himself. This was so radically out of character for Philo that Epaphroditus was lost for words.

"I'll let you know what I find out about Sporus," Felix was telling him.

Epaphroditus nodded absently as he stood. "Thank you," he said, though the Sporus situation had been overtaken by another concern.

THIRTY-NINE

Lysandria unfurled the cloth on the table revealing a series of metal needles, pins, and sharpened scissors of varying sizes. This was her hairdressing kit.

"Nothing too dramatic, please," pleaded Teretia.

She was sitting on an ample chair, in an ample chamber within the ample Caelian Hill home of Lysandria and her current husband, Gaius Baebius. Lysandria stood in front of her, screwing up her nose.

"I think you could pull off a high arch of curls, Teretia my dear. You've got the length." She picked up a strand of Teretia's golden hair and played with it between her fingers.

"I wouldn't want to look too different," persisted Teretia. "What if Horace didn't recognise me and he cried. That would be awful!"

Teretia and Lysandria looked over to the side of the chamber where Horace sat on Marcia's lap. Teretia gave him a little wave and he smiled. This caused a flurry of, "Awwws," and, "How adorable," from all the women present, including Lysandria's own staff.

"He looks the spit of his father, doesn't he?" smiled Lysandria, taking little Horace's tiny hands in hers. "You look like your daddy lots and lots."

Horace gave a gurgle.

"He has the curl on his neck like the master," offered up Marcia, touching the errant dark hair on the back of Horace's neck.

"Oh, that is adorable!" gushed Lysandria. "But back to business!" She turned to Teretia. "How about a series of plaits on the top of your head, with ringlets curling down onto your neck. It is the height of elegance and something my mistress wore."

"Oh yes please," said a relieved Teretia, who'd feared a towering edifice similar to the one Lysandria wore. "And for Marcia?"

"Well, I'm afraid, Marcia, that I cannot let you outdo your mistress but you do have a lovely head of hair to work with. I think it's a shame when owners keep their slaves' hair cut short. Such a shame," she repeated, looking at her own short-haired slaves. "Gaius Baebius insists though. He says it's hygienic but I think it's because he knows I'd spend all my time styling them. He thinks hairdressing is unbecoming for a wife of his." Lysandria rolled her eyes.

"Is Baebius coming tonight?" asked Teretia.

"He is," confirmed Lysandria. "He's been a bit peaky these last few days, not very well at all."

Teretia shifted on the chair and averted her eyes. She'd heard from Philo of Lysandria's past as a poisoner. It was a difficult image to marry with this sweet, fluffy, caring middle-aged woman. But one couldn't deny that her husbands appeared to have been uniquely unlucky with sudden, fatal illnesses.

"He has made a surprising recovery though," said Lysandria, gazing at her row of tools. "Especially for tonight."

"That's good timing."

"Isn't it," said Lysandria, approaching with the scissors. "Let us hope it lasts."

* * *

"You're going to have to talk to her," said Lysander as the slave shaved his chin.

Philo, sat beside him, formed a, "Mmm," noise.

"That's three people who've seen her with this soldier. Three. Tadius, Vologses, and Pompeia. You don't want your slave hanging around with soldiers."

Philo certainly did not.

"I'll ask Teretia to talk to Marcia. It will come better from her. If I say anything it'll seem like I'm ordering her to stay away from this man."

"Which you will be," pointed out Lysander. "You are allowed to tell your own slave what to do. What will she turn out like if you don't correct her disrespectful manner? You need to show her the right path. It's an insult to you and Teretia that she's carrying on without your permission."

"We don't know that they have been carrying on. They have been seen together, that's all," corrected Philo.

"Gods you're naïve. What do you think they're up to? A handsome German and a pretty young slave girl?" Lysander shook his head. "You should probably have sex with her. She's of that ripening age. It makes her easy prey to any horny soldier who treats her nice. If you stuffed her she wouldn't need to go elsewhere for her pleasure. Plus your cock could do with the exercise what with Teretia still mashed up down there from squeezing out Horace."

"She's not all mashed up," protested Philo.

"You said—"

"I said she was a bit sore. Which is understandable."

What Philo was finding less understandable now was the instinct that had led him to share such intimate details with Lysander.

"Sore, mashed up, whatever. The key point is that your slave is hanging about with a dubious dirty legionary because she isn't getting any sex at home. Now what are you going to do about that?"

Philo was hit with a brief image of the naked Marcia he'd seen at the slave market: small breasts, skinny thighs, and angular hip bones.

He shuddered. "I'll get Teretia to have a girly chat with her," he decided. "If she is really suffering from lack of, ermm, that, then perhaps we could find a more suitable partner than this German."

"Or you could just whip out your own cock and sort the problem out yourself without having to involve Teretia or anyone else," countered Lysander.

* * *

Freshly barbered up, Lysander and Philo were led to the dining room. Here they found Lysander's stepfather already reclined. Lysander nodded at him. Baebius nodded back. This was as warm as their relationship got.

Thankfully the women entered. They were led by Lysandria carrying Horace in her arms. Teretia came in next. She was dressed in a light blue gown the same colour as her eyes. Her golden hair was plaited over her head, and weaved into the plaits were tiny pearls. Similar sized pearls were threaded onto the ringlets that curled down on her neck. Round her neck was a blue stone and pearl necklace. Philo's breath caught in his throat. His wife was beautiful. The most beautiful woman he had ever set eyes on. Lysander elbowed Philo's ribs and he was snapped back to the present and the entrance of Marcia with a less spectacular version of her mistress' hairdo lacking the pearl additions.

Teretia linked onto Philo's arm. He kissed her cheek. "You look beautiful," he told her.

Her cheeks went pink with happiness. Handing Horace to Marcia, Lysandria greeted her son with a kiss on each cheek. Then she stepped back.

"You look much better without those horrible hairy sideburns," she said running a finger on the now smooth, clean skin on the side of Lysander's face. "I know they were very Nero but alas we are no longer in the age of Nero."

An announcer entered. "Gaius Verenius, a trader. And his daughter Verenia."

Lysander would usually have had plenty to say about the announcer's lacklustre delivery but nerves silenced him.

Lysandria gave him a hug. "Courage, my love."

Verenia entered clinging onto the arm of a tall, suntanned, physical-looking man. Verenius' gaze was on the luxurious furnishings of Baebius' home rather than his hosts. Lysandria stepped forward.

"Sir, you are welcome."

Verenius gave a taut nod but did not reply, which confused Lysandria who was accustomed to the elaborate greetings of the palace. She hid this fluster well, saying, "I am Julia Lysandria and this is my husband Gaius Baebius."

Baebius unreclined himself. Taking Verenius' hand he gave it a firm shake. "I understand we are in the same line of business; the export/import industry."

Verenius warmed up. "Indeed I am," he proclaimed in a booming voice. "Though I cannot claim my operation is quite to the scale of yours!" he added, gazing at the black and gold walls of the dining room.

"Had my fair share of luck," said Baebius.

"My son, Servius Sulpicius Lysander."

Lysander stepped forward, head bowed. "It is nice to meet you, sir."

Verenius turned back to Baebius, saying "I'd like to hear more about that luck," and leaving Lysander standing awkwardly out of line. On his arm, Verenia winced. Lysandria took charge.

"Introductions first, then dinner and then you can talk business, don't you agree my dear?"

She fixed her eyes on her husband.

"Yes, my dear. Quite right. Verenius, it is a pleasure to welcome into my home yourself and your lovely daughter, who my wife and I hope to know better."

Verenius gave a grunt.

"This here is Tiberius Claudius Philo, our current emperor's private secretary's secretary, and husband to your niece."

"Hello, Uncle Verenius," said Teretia. "It's nice to see you again after all these years."

"Sorry to hear about your father. He was a good and decent man, Teretius."

Teretia pressed her lips together. Philo gave her hand a supportive squeeze.

Baebius clapped his hands together. "Now that's done, let us get the food in. I am starving. I haven't eaten in days because of this nasty stomach bug I picked up."

There followed a dinner party of a restraint not seen at the palace for a good four administrations. The food lacked dramatic flair but the liberal use of meats and spices demonstrated Baebius' wealth. The musicians were similarly low key, but if you listened hard enough their supreme talent was detectable.

Philo, who had attended many of Lysandria's parties, assumed this sobriety was in honour of Verenius and Verenia. A usual gathering of Lysandria's contained all the excesses of the courts she'd grown up in. It was a rare do that didn't conclude with the hostess staggering about drunkenly clutching a pair of red-hot curling tongs, promising superior hairstyles to all and accidentally branding her guests.

The talk was respectable too, with a discussion on Verenius' recent travels and a general appreciation of baby Horace. Even the political chat was safe, with Philo cautiously revealing that the new regime was keeping both him and Lysander busy. Lysander himself was curiously silent. During a conversation on the merits of particular overseas ports Teretia said to her husband, "Verenia looks nervous."

She did. Her usual air of superiority and cool poise was lost. Her hands fiddled with the fabric of her gown, her eyes flittered about, coming to rest on Lysander. She gave him a tight smile.

"She doesn't look well. Maybe it's the heat. I'll suggest we go for a walk in the cool."

Seeing Verenia's pained expression, Philo concurred with the sense of this suggestion.

"Cousin," said Teretia, breaking into Verenius' and Baebius' discourse. "Shall we take a walk in the cool before the next course? It is rather sweaty."

"Good idea," said Verenia, fanning her face with a hand.

"The courtyard is nice and cool at this time," said Lysandria. "I'll come with you girls."

As the ladies made to depart, followed by Marcia and Doris, Lysandria shot her husband a look. Baebius nodded in response.

Once they'd swished out, Baebius said, "Alright, Verenius, let us talk about this marriage business."

Lysander gulped down a mouthful of wine.

FORTY

In the cool garden that was situated in the centre of the house, Teretia and Verenia watched as Lysandria carried Horace about, pointing to the plants and flowers that had been expertly cultivated. Teretia smiled at Horace's intent expression.

"Isn't Horace funny? I swear to Minerva he understands everything you say to him," said Teretia.

When Verenia did not respond Teretia turned towards her cousin. Verenia was pale, tense looking.

"Are you unwell?" she enquired, concerned.

"I suppose that the men are discussing the marriage arrangements."

"I think they probably are. I'm sure an arrangement can be met. Uncle Verenius has enough money for a dowry and he looked very impressed by Gaius Baebius."

"Yes, he did," said Verenia.

She leant her head back against the wall and closed her eyes.

"Well then," said Teretia brightly. "There is no need to worry about Uncle Verenius objecting."

"I'm not worried about father. I never have been. He's keen to have me off his hands. He'd let me marry anyone at all if it meant he didn't have to fork out supporting me."

"I don't understand."

Verenia turned her head to face Teretia. "It's Lysander. I think, no, I know," she corrected herself. "I know he'll break it off once he knows the truth."

"What truth?"

* * *

"I love your daughter and I wish to marry her, sir."

"Let me deal with the negotiations," said Baebius. "It's what I do. Verenius, it's as the boy says. He wants to marry your daughter. My wife is very taken by her and for my part she seems pleasant enough. Match wise you'll do well out of it. You will be linking your name to the Baebius name and that is something in this city. It opens doors. Plus you get my wife's and stepson's palace connections. Those are not to be sniffed at. We all know those superior freedmen who demand so much to get past them."

Verenius nodded. "It's near impossible to get to the people with clout these days."

"With this marriage you get a fast track round the lower ranks straight to those that make decisions. Philo here, my stepson's closest friend, is the emperor's private secretary's secretary. That's the kind of level we're talking about here: the very upper echelons of the administration. This is a very advantageous match for both your daughter and yourself. The dowry should reflect that."

Verenius took a sip of wine. It seemed to take an inordinately long time for him to swallow the liquid. Once he had, he said, "That is excellent reasoning, sir. Let me be honest with you, Baebius. When I heard my daughter had taken to embroiling herself with a freedman I was dubious."

Lysander fidgeted on his couch.

"But then I thought, why not," continued Verenius. "If he can provide for her, he can have her. Daughters are nothing but an expense, and mine is no exception. I'd already got her off my hands with an extremely satisfactory marriage to a very suitable young man. Then she's back again and he's refusing to pay the dowry back. I was pleased she'd sorted herself out. 'Course it's not the usual way to cut your father out of the betrothal."

"You were overseas," pointed out Lysander. "We, I mean, Verenia couldn't contact you."

Baebius gave Lysander a long look.

"Please ignore my stepson. He's unaware of the proper way to conduct a marriage. Matters such as these are dealt with differently in the palace."

"I imagine they are, Baebius. It's a different world."

"That it is. But you were saying?" prompted Baebius, throwing Lysander a warning look.

"I was saying that I was happy for my daughter to marry a freedman and I'd set myself to agreeing to the match. Only then I learnt we were talking about an imperial freedman and one that was related to your good self, Baebius. This has put me in a very awkward position."

"The dowry amount is fully negotiable," assured Baebius. "I am a reasonable man, and as I said, my wife is very fond of Verenia already. As is Lysander."

"It's not the money, good sir. It is the guilt I would feel contracting an arrangement with your honourable self knowing that my side of the deal was sullied."

"Sullied? We are all aware that Verenia has been married before. Nobody is expecting her to be intact." Baebius looked over to Lysander for confirmation.

"I know she's not a virgin. We've talked about it, about her first marriage. It doesn't matter to me. We just want to be married, please sir," pleaded Lysander.

Seeing his friend's distress Philo chipped in, "I am happy to vouch for Lysander. Epaphroditus who was private secretary to Nero will also vouch for his character."

Verenius shuffled his buttocks and then looking directly at Lysander he said, "She's barren. My daughter cannot bear children. Did she tell you that?"

It was evident to both Philo and Baebius from the drop of Lysander's features that this was entirely new information for him.

"Baebius, if he'd been any other freedman I wouldn't have spoken up. But I couldn't deceive you, sir. It wouldn't be proper."

Lysander rushed to his feet, colliding with Verenia in the doorway.

"Lysander?"

"Excuse me," he said, pushing past her.

"Father!"

"I'm sorry, Verenia. He had to be told. It was only fair."

His daughter said calmly. "I see."

Then she turned on her heels and departed, Doris trailing behind her.

Lysandria threw up her hands. "What is going on?"

FORTY-ONE

The party broke up pretty quickly after Verenia's exit. They left Lysandria being comforted by Baebius as she sobbed, "My poor, poor boy."

All the way back to the Viminal Hill, Verenius maintained that he had committed a noble act.

"I couldn't let him be tricked into marriage, could I?" And then to his niece's unsympathetic face, "I've lost out too! I could have been in business with Gaius Baebius!"

They dropped him off at his house. There was no sign of the litter that Verenia had taken. Walking up the stairs to their apartment, Teretia said, "Uncle Verenius dealt with that very badly."

Philo agreed.

"Poor Verenia! That was just awful."

"It would have been better if he'd pressed Verenia to tell Lysander herself," said Philo. "If he truly felt that strongly about it."

Teretia paused on the stairs. "You don't believe Uncle Verenius feels that strongly about it?"

"I'm not convinced," was all Philo would say.

"Doris says he's very mean to her mistress," contributed Marcia, who was walking behind them carrying a sleeping Horace. "Apparently he's still angry at the mistress Verenia for the end of her first marriage."

"And this is his revenge?" gasped Teretia. "That's awful. Isn't it, Philo?"

"It is awful," her husband agreed as they reached their door. He pushed it open and entering the kitchen noted Lysander's sandals by the feet of the table. "He came home," he said indicating the footwear.

"You'd better go talk to him," said Teretia. "He must be devastated."

* * *

Philo gave the door two gentle taps and waited for a response. When none came he looked down the corridor to where his wife and slave were standing.

"Just go in," hissed Teretia.

Philo pushed open the door, sticking a head round the door cautiously. "Lysander?"

His friend was sat on the bed, his back against the wall. As he looked up Philo noted the red eyes. He'd clearly been crying.

"Can I come in?"

Rubbing at an eye Lysander gave a shrug. Philo took this as agreement and sat himself down beside his friend.

"I'm sorry," he said. "I'm sorry about what happened back there."

Lysander swallowed down a sob. When he trusted himself to speak he asked, "Why didn't she tell me?"

"I suppose she was worried you'd break it off with her if she told you the truth."

Lysander tilted his head back against the wall, staring up at the ceiling. "She hinted to me that she didn't want children. I thought I'd be able to talk her round after we were married or else she'd just fall pregnant anyway. Because that's what I'm good at, making women pregnant. It's the only thing I've ever been good at!"

"That's not true."

Lysander blew a long sigh from between his lips. "I always thought I'd have children. You know, ones that were mine and not the palace's. Ones I could be a proper father to, like my father was to me. Briefly."

Lysander's father had been executed by Nero for being in possession of a superior singing voice to the emperor. He'd had many faults, Hypheston, including a tendency to muck around with Lysandria's emotions, but Philo couldn't deny he'd been a very affectionate father towards Lysander.

"I was so looking forward to that part of marriage. Like with you and Teretia and Horace. I wanted us, Verenia and I, to have our own Horace, and others. A whole team of children that were ours to enjoy, to see grow, to be proud of."

He broke down, holding his head in his hands as he sobbed. Philo put a consoling arm around him.

"Except none of that is going to happen now. Because the woman I love is barren."

"You do still love her then?" enquired Philo, tentatively.

Lysander rubbed at his eyes, "She's the only woman I've ever felt a connection with. Ever."

"What will you do?"

"I don't know," said Lysander. "I thought tonight was going to be the best night of my life." His voice began to crack again. "Instead it's one of the worst. I've lost everything!"

FORTY-TWO

It did not take Felix long to establish the facts. He summoned the hairdressers, the make-up artists, the wardrobe keepers, the jewellery holders, the sandal polishers, and the hair pluckers he'd assigned to Sporus. They stood in front of him, heads bowed. Felix smelt fear. Not unusual for anyone standing a few feet away from him. But his keen nose, honed from decades of dealing with slaves, also detected a whiff of guilt too.

Parking his bum on the edge of his desk, the wood giving an audible creak in response, Felix cracked two of his knuckles. "Go on, let's fuckin' 'ave it," he barked.

There followed a silence so brief you'd have struggled to crack an egg in it. Hairdresser Delia broke first. "He sent us away. The one with the scar."

With one having broken their agreed silence, the others present talked over each other to get their side of the story out and deflect the blame away from themselves. Their stories were identical: Asiaticus had prevented Sporus' beauty team from doing their jobs. None of them had seen the eunuch for months.

"And why the fuck didn't any of you fuckin' come and tell me this?" Felix bellowed at the quivering slaves.

Because, Felix managed to extract, they'd been ecstatic not to have to deal with the troublesome eunuch. Sporus was not the best of clients. He was demanding, he was shrill, and he was mischievous. Nobody wanted to work for him. So they'd kept the secret between them and enjoyed their sudden bonus of leisure.

Felix simmered through this sorry tale of deception waiting until its conclusion. Then he belted out a bollocking the likes of which hadn't been heard in the palace since Halotus, Emperor Claudius' food taster, had spectacularly failed at his job. The beauty staff were each given a stroke of the whip for every day they'd skived off.

Well, he had the fuckin' facts, didn't he? He should inform Epaphroditus. Except Felix didn't want to do that. Sporus was his merchandise and he'd failed him. He'd failed him big time. What a clueless fuckin' idiot he'd been! So busy sorting out dancers and flute players and patching up that fucker Valens' cast-offs that he'd not noticed the eunuch's plight.

Felix couldn't wait for Epaphroditus to fuck about with his smooth fuckin' tongue. Fat good it had done him with Vitellius, demoted from private secretary to entertainments coordinator. No, this needed sortin' out right fuckin' now! What the fuck was that fat fucker of an emperor doing with his merchandise?

Actually Felix had a fair idea and it was turning his stomach with disgust. During mad Caligula's time he'd seen firsthand how Vitellius liked to enjoy pretty young boys. Nero's favourite sex game of dressing up as a wild animal and suckingly attacking the genitalia of some trussed up slaves seemed a bit of harmless fun in comparison. A bit of fluff to fill up time with, where nobody got hurt and none of his merchandise got damaged.

Vitellius, in Felix's considered opinion, was one twisted fucker. He keenly recalled the time he'd had to fight Vitellius off from strangling one of his wine boys. The sick fucker had wanted to watch the life fade from the boy's eyes as he had his way with him. Felix hadn't put up with such perversions then, and he certainly wasn't going to put up with them now!

He stomped down the corridor that led to Sporus' suite. It was empty. Presumably the fuckin' guards were off drunk somewhere. There was no sign of that ugly fucker Asiaticus either. Good. Felix wrenched open the double doors. A figure on the bed sat up with a jolt. Felix blinked twice.

"What the fuck?"

The figure was barely recognisable as Sporus. He was dressed in a grubby loincloth, ribs jutting out above it, and higher up, a neck that was ringed with bruises. The skinny legs were similarly bruised and showed off red circles that looked to Felix's eyes like bite marks. Sporus gave a small sob.

"Felix?" he croaked.

Felix approached the bed. "It's alright, boy. It's al-fuckin'-right. I'm here to get you out. You able to walk?"

Sporus shook his head.

"No problem. You're no heavier than my Gany. I'll carry you."

Sporus lifted up a scrawny leg. There was a leather belt tethered round his ankle.

"Fucker!" Felix swore. "Fuckin' fucker."

He took the leather between his two hands and tugged at it to judge its strength. Following its length took him to a brass ring hammered into the wall. He grabbed hold of the ring and pulled. A crunch and a crack later, Felix stood holding the loose belt. Behind him the wall now owned a jagged circle of missing plaster.

He got rid of the dislodged plaster on the ring by smashing it against the wardrobe. Belt cocked over his wrist he rubbed the dusty plaster of his hands using the bedsheet.

"Right. Let's get you outta here."

He put Sporus on his back, the eunuch's arms holding on round his neck.

"Can you take me to Philo's?" said Sporus in a huskier tone than usual. "I'm going to be his and Teretia's in-house help. I'm going to teach them about sex and how it should be done, so they have lots more cute babies. I'm sure they won't mind purchasing me from the palace. They so need my services."

"Let's get outta here first," said Felix. "Then I'll have my Vallia feed you up a bit."

Felix stuck his head out. It was all clear. It remained so until they were halfway down. The doors at the end opened and in stepped Asiaticus. Sporus gave a whimper into Felix's shoulder.

"What are you doing?" he asked, taking a step towards them.

"What's it fuckin' look like?" retorted Felix, walking towards Asiaticus.

"It looks like you're stealing the emperor's property."

"Yeah and so what if I fuckin' am?"

They were now face to face. Sort of. Felix's height was such that Asiaticus was forced to tilt his head back to look at him.

"Put that eunuch down."

"No."

Asiaticus wasn't given a chance to repeat the order. One of Felix's booted feet was forced against his groin. The freedman collapsed on the floor groaning. Felix stepped over him, kicking Asiaticus in the head as he did so.

Sporus looking back over his shoulder at the heaped freedman. "Felix," he bleated.

The head of slave placements shrugged. "I done worse to better and I'm still 'ere."

Reaching the doors at the end of the corridor Felix stuck his head out. The guards he'd passed earlier were still there, filling up space.

"Alright," he grumbled. "Follow my lead."

He stepped through the doors.

"Sick slave comin' through," he yelled. "Some nasty fever thing. Probably catching."

On Felix's back Sporus gave a cough.

"Reckon it's wot you guards 'ave been all fuckin' dying of."

The Praetorians pushed their backs into the walls to avoid contamination. It left a clear path through for them. Sporus dared to open his eyes. Ahead was the door to a side chamber that led to a courtyard, and beyond that a passageway for the slaves that ended with an exit door onto the Palatine Hill. They were going to make it! Sporus hoped Teretia would have a good dinner bubbling on the stove, he was so very hungry.

"GUARDS! STOP THEM!"

Felix looked over his shoulder to see a green-looking Asiaticus, blood dripping down his face from the boot-induced cut to his forehead. He was pointing straight at them.

"Awright. Hold tight. I'm gonna have to run for it."

Felix bowled his way along, using his shoulder to shove Praetorians out the way, kicking out a leg to fell them at the crotch or the knee. Sporus squeaked and closed his eyes again. Ahead was a line of four Praetorians holding their swords out in front of them.

"STOP THERE!" one commanded.

Felix halted. The guard approached. "A wise move, my friend," he said as he resheathed his sword.

Felix waited until he was a few steps in front of them. Then he lowered his head downwards and ran straight at him. His head connected with the guard's leather breastplate, knocking him off his feet. The three remaining Praetorians looked at Felix.

"ARGHHHHHHHH!" he yelled and ran straight for them at such a speed that they didn't have time to react. He crashed straight through their wall, scattering them.

"Can I look yet?" asked a rather jiggled Sporus.

"Not yet. We got more of the fuckers!"

They certainly did. There came before them a marching square of 16. Felix looked over his shoulder to see a similar square approaching from the rear. He backed towards the side wall.

"Sporus, I'm gonna put you down. Stand behind me so those fuckers can't see you. When they're all distracted takin' me on, you run for it. Just get out. Understand?"

"What about you?"

"Don't worry about me. Just get out."

The Praetorians were almost on them. Felix bent his knees slightly. Sporus let go of his neck and slid down his back, standing behind the overseer shaking with fear. Felix looked at the mass of guards facing him. He snorted and bellowed at full Felix volume. "LET'S BE FUCKIN' 'AVIN' YOU THEN!!!!"

As they reached to grab him, he hit out wildly with thick knuckles. Breaking their formation he pushed forward, leaving a gap behind him. This was Sporus' moment and he took it, pelting down the corridor, his bare feet slapping on the marble floor. He decided to head for the slave complex. There'd be no guards there and also friends who would help him. Maybe. Sporus had always been somewhat of a dividing force among his fellow slaves.

He shot round the corner and ran down a long arched corridor. Then he heard it. Footsteps, running footsteps behind him. He dared to look over his shoulder—a few feet behind him ran Asiaticus.

No! No, he wouldn't be caught. He was going to escape. He was going to live on the Viminal with Philo and Teretia. And what a tale he had to tell them!

Something crashed into his back. Sporus was thrown to the ground with a thump. Then there was a weight on top of him and a horribly familiar voice.

"Got you!" huffed Asiaticus.

Sporus screamed.

FORTY-THREE

Two days after Felix was jumped upon by twenty Praetorians, Epaphroditus made his way to work ignorant of events. He'd uncharacteristically taken some time off. For the newly widowed, the first year is a series of punches to the heart. The one that had firmly thumped Epaphroditus was his wife's birthday. The one he should have been spending with her. The first without her.

There was no denying his reaction to this date. No mincing of words. No pretence. He'd cracked into pieces and spent two whole days in bed weeping. When he wasn't weeping, he was stuck at the bottom of a very dark hole of despair.

He inwardly cringed remembering the state to which he'd been reduced. It was only with the assistance of his slave Callista that he'd managed to crawl his way out of the darkness.

On the afternoon of day two of his grief wallow, Callista had sat down on the end of his bed.

"Master, may I speak?"

He raised an arm to signal his approval.

"Master, we are all concerned for you. You have not left this room. You have not eaten. We all, all of us, miss her."

There was a crack in her voice that penetrated Epaphroditus' weepy stupor. He sat up and saw that Callista was crying. She rubbed at her eyes, wiping the tears away. "Sorry, master."

Of course Callista missed Dite. She'd been by her side these last 15 years, her closest aide and probably confidante.

"This is such a sad house, master. Wouldn't it be better to bring the children back? To have the house full of noise. Rather than this, master."

He understood. While he'd at least had his job, shitty as it was, to fill the Aphrodite-shaped void in his life, Callista had been left in the house with no mistress and no children to care for. She'd had nothing to distract her from her grief.

"I would so like to see if little Rufus is talking now, master," she continued.

Epaphroditus looked round his dark, silent bedroom. It didn't feel right. This wasn't how it was supposed to be. He was supposed to be woken up by Claudia and Julia jumping on his stomach yelling, "Daddee, Daddee."

He was supposed to be snuggled up with Dite and baby Rufus, listening to his two eldest girls arguing, and debating with Dite which one of them would get out of bed to sort out the row.

Callista was right. It was a sad house. He missed the laughter. He missed the constant fights between his seven children. He missed his children. The touch of them when they hugged him. The smell of them.

"Master?"

Epaphroditus cleared his throat. It had been two days since he'd used his voice. It sounded strange to him as he said, "Why don't you go down to the Baiae house to be with them? It's what we'd usually be doing these summer months. Take any of the other staff that will be of help to you. I can manage here."

"But master, the children will want to see you too."

"I'd send for them, I would, but Rome … and the emperor. These are not happy times."

Callista nodded. "Thank you, master."

After she had gone he called for his body slave to dress him, reflecting on his words. Why didn't he send for the children?

Rome was secure, an emperor in place. Philo had reported no further news of Vespasian from the East. All was settled. And yet. He recalled Felix's words, "This ain't normal. You do know that?"

He had, even if he hadn't been prepared to admit it to himself. Now he could, inwardly, unspoken. Things were not normal. It wasn't normal to have soldiers spilling all over the city. To have Praetorians openly brawling in the palace corridors. To have so many of the imperial slaves cruelly brutalised. To have so little of the basic administration of the empire undertaken. To have rooms full of unopened post. It wasn't normal. And at the centre of this web of mayhem sat the fat, black spider Vitellius. The emperor who sat and watched but did nothing.

Epaphroditus, once washed, shaved, and dressed, made his way to a palace he no longer recognised, to arrange yet another party for that spider. That at least would be something completed successfully. Or so he had thought until he set eyes on Midas. The catering chief's usual springy blond curls were slicked to his head with sweat, his face ruddy, his eyes panicked.

"Thank Jupiter you're back!" said Midas, turning his eyes upward to the heavens. "Felix has been arrested and nobody knows what the fuckerty fuck is going on!"

* * *

Having sat the panicking Midas down with a cup of wine, Epaphroditus began the task of unpicking what he'd missed.

"Felix has been arrested?"

Midas gave a nod. "He's in one of the cells in the basement. If you listen hard you can hear him yelling. Or so everyone says. And his wife has been up here too."

Midas' wide-eyed look told Epaphroditus that Vallia's recent visit had been as memorable as her last trip up to the palace during Felix's ill-advised grapple with a laundry girl. After that appearance, Felix had kept his hands firmly off the goods.

"How did they get her to leave?" asked Epaphroditus. A cohort of Praetorians had been needed the last time to march Vallia away from inflicting further damage on her husband.

"They didn't," said Midas. "She's sat on the steps outside the Palatine Hill entrance. The notable guests to the emperor are being diverted to other doors."

Epaphroditus rubbed his palm across his hair. "Alright. What happened that ended up with Felix in the cells and Vallia on the steps?"

"He tried to steal Sporus."

Epaphroditus' eyebrows rose upwards.

"Everyone is saying that he's had this massive passion for Sporus the whole time."

Epaphroditus' eyebrows dropped to their usual position.

"Everyone is saying that since the emperor took charge of Sporus, Felix couldn't bear not seeing him. So he tried to steal him. And he very nearly got away with it too. Amplieus says Felix was at the doors when the Praetorians caught him. Who'd have thought Felix loved Sporus?"

Nobody, thought Epaphroditus. Because it wasn't true. Sporus would have to put on three times his body weight, and change sex properly for Felix to even notice him that way. Unless fat, female Sporus also possessed bulging biceps and the oxen-lifting strength of Hercules, Felix really wasn't going to exert himself. The only women who'd ever met Felix's standards had been the laundry girls and latterly the fearsome Vallia, whose temper and strength was thus that nobody dared evict her from the palace steps.

He reeled off a list of instructions for Midas, who seemed calmer for having been given some direction. Then he sat back in his chair and put his mind to the Felix situation. Felix had been caught trying to remove Sporus from the palace shortly after Epaphroditus had asked him to check on the eunuch.

That was no coincidence. The two were as linked as a steel slave chain.

Epaphroditus had known Felix his entire life. Felix was, underneath his growling insubordinate exterior, a loyal palace employee carrying out the orders given to him from up high. He might grumble about the emperor. He might grumble about the stupidity of the order. But he always followed them. There was one exception to Felix's loyalty that Epaphroditus knew of. He was very particular about the care of his slaves and more particularly about the merchandise being damaged.

If Felix had discovered an extremely valuable piece of merchandise like Sporus was being ill used, he would have no qualms about removing him. It was exactly what he'd done for Epaphroditus once, way back during a time the secretary chose not to remember. His hand went up to his throat nonetheless. He cursed it and turned his mind back to the issue at hand.

If Felix had been prepared to take on the entire Praetorian Guard, then clearly Sporus was in some grave danger.

There were three points to consider:

1) Did he care?

2) If he did care, did he care enough to do anything about it?

And, 3) How in Jupiter's name was he supposed to organise a delightful party for the emperor with the head of slave placements under lock and key?

FORTY-FOUR

The eunuch had ceased crying the previous day. Since then, it had lain on the bed staring at the ceiling and sometimes the wall. It had not spoken. Asiaticus thought back to his earliest dealings with it: demanding dresses, food, and entertainments in that shrill voice. It pleased Asiaticus to see this hollow creature. It showed that it had ceased to think of its own needs. Now it would only think of the needs of the emperor. That was how it should be.

The freedman sat on the bed, facing away from Sporus.

"You have given in. It is better this way. It makes it easier to endure."

The eunuch rolled onto its side. Looking over his shoulder at it, Asiaticus saw that its eyes were sad.

"It won't be forever. I promise you that. Soon he will tire of you in that way. Then there will be opportunities for you. As there were for me."

The eunuch spoke. "Did he do that to your face?"

"No," said Asiaticus to the wall. "I did it to myself. I was foolish. I resisted. I swore he would never reduce me. I ran. But he found me. I sliced into my face thinking he would not want to take me back. But he did. I was stupid. I could have had what I have now." He looked down at his hands, each finger sporting a jewelled ring. "I could have had it all so much sooner had I not resisted. Things are so much better now." He looked over his shoulder at the eunuch. "You will see. This performance today will be the beginning of your new existence."

Sporus sat up. "Performance?" he asked. "What performance?"

How he kept his face straight, totally devoid of the horror he felt, Sporus never knew. But he had. He'd looked blankly at Asiaticus as the freedman explained the "special performance" for Vitellius' birthday.

It would be just like his dressing-up days when the emperor had been entranced by his Juno, his Daphne, and his Niobe. Before he'd been earmarked for iller treatment. He'd be Proserpina in a gorgeous gown of the lightest green, with ears of wheat tied into his hair to highlight the goddess' connection with the harvest. He would be able to show off the best of his dancing. Even better, this was to be held in the arena so that so many more people would have the chance to witness his talent.

Then would come on evil Pluto to abduct him.

"The emperor likes his entertainments to be real," Asiaticus had said. "How else can we appreciate the devastation of Ceres if we have not witnessed the horror inflicted on her daughter? We owe it to the gods to better understand their suffering."

Asiaticus could wrap it up in whatever fancy divine analogy he pleased, but Sporus understood it well enough. He was to be raped in front of thousands of spectators for the enjoyment of the emperor.

Even as Asiaticus had detailed the performance for him, Sporus had had but one thought: No.

No, he wouldn't be out on public display in the arena like some freakish dwarf or pig-ugly gladiator.

No, he wouldn't dance for pleb grocers or pleb butchers or pleb's slaves.

No, he wouldn't be penetrated by whoever the fuck they'd got playing the God of the Underworld in front of all those people.

No.

For he was a Sporus! Sporuses were marvellous creatures of refined tastes and possessed of great beauty. Sporuses were for admiring, for cosseting, for loving in the proper way. This Sporus had been empress. He had been wife to the rightful emperor Nero!

They were fools, all of them, if they thought he would play his part in this tawdry performance. As if.

Asiaticus was wholly wrong in his belief that Sporus was broken. It would have taken decades to dissolve an ego as monstrous as Sporus'. Over the past day, as he'd lain staring at the ceiling, he'd been plotting. Plotting and planning his escape.

He'd ditched, with a heavy heart, his Viminal Hill plan. It was a shame because he really would have been an excellent addition to Philo's household. But where he was going was so much better than that cramped apartment. He even felt a little sorry for the palace. How much duller it was going to be for them without a Sporus! But that was life and they'd just have to get used to it. Tough.

He fingered the gauzy green material of the dress Asiaticus had handed to him. Green was so not his colour. He threw open the wardrobe and took in the array of fabulous outfits folded on its shelves. Red. Definitely red. Red had always been his colour. He removed the green dress, replacing it with the red. Next the wig selection. Red again, the colour of Nero's sadly deceased wife Poppaea's hair. Next up, the jewellery. Golden bangles studded with rubies matched with a similar necklace and of course a tiara. One final item, a red silky scarf that he tied round his neck and flicked over his shoulder.

Staring into the bronze hand mirror, Sporus blew himself a kiss. Gorgeous. As ever. As would always be. Forever young. Forever gorgeous. The Sporus had reached its prime. Gold sandals were slipped on to his feet. He stepped on to the chair. Turning round he wound the end of the scarf round, a metal ring that was hammered into the wall for holding lit torches. Scarf firmly knotted, he turned back round and took one final look at the world he'd so sparkled in. A lump formed in his throat. Then he remembered what faced him that day. The jeering faces. The calls. The humiliation. That world, that ugly world, had no place for a Sporus. They didn't deserve one.

Taking a deep breath, he stepped off the chair.

* * *

Epaphroditus was troubled. He was troubled by all manner of things. Chiefly that the head of slave placements was locked away, and somehow the lost slaves were coming to him instead with their issues. Barraged by complaints and pleas for direction, Epaphroditus decided to go somewhere he couldn't be found. It was the only way he was going to get any of his own work done.

He took refuge on an upper floor of the old palace, sitting on a windowsill, taking in the air and the blue summer sky. Dite had always loved summer best. It was the time of year when they'd escape down to the coast as a family, and for those few days would be beholden only to her. No emperor. No Felix. No palace at all. Just her. Her and the children. Maybe after the emperor's birthday do, he'd go down to Baiae and see them. Surely Midas could cope with Vitellius' endless entertainment demands for a short while?

He was pulled out of his thoughts by yelling. Looking downwards he could see the unmistakable figure of Vallia remonstrating with the guards on one of the palace doors. Beside her stood a smaller, slighter figure: Ganymede, the son. Where he'd come from, Epaphroditus had no idea. He presumed Felix had purchased the boy. There'd been another son, one born by Vallia. But that had been decades back. A boy with red flaming hair like his father's and a mischievous freckled face.

That boy had died and there'd been no other children. Not until Ganymede showed up fully formed as son of Felix.

Epaphroditus wondered what would happen to them if Felix were executed. Presumably the head of slave placements had left them well provided for. Otherwise the boy may well find himself back on the slavers' block.

Walking past Felix's family, Epaphroditus saw another familiar figure: Asiaticus. The freedman hurried past the yelling Vallia, down the steps that led to one of the many routes to the Forum. He disappeared from view. Which left an opportunity for Epaphroditus that he might not get again. With Sporus' key watcher out, he maybe had a chance to find out what was happening with the eunuch.

* * *

He took the chance, hurrying down to the new palace, swatting slaves with questions out of his way as he proceeded. What an absolute mess the palace was in without Felix's bellowing instructions. Someone would have to sort it out. Epaphroditus had a horrible feeling it was going to fall to him as one of the few senior members of the palace staff who'd somehow survived the events of the last year. But first things first: Sporus.

The guards on the double doors gave him a long look.

"We were told not to let anyone in," said one.

"But not me," said Epaphroditus. "I'm the entertainments coordinator."

He didn't elaborate or even explain, but spoke with such confidence that he could see the guards swaying in their duty.

"If you could let me in, I can then get on."

He looked them squarely in the eyes. "Now please. I have so very much to organise that I can't be hanging around here," he said with undisputed authority. "Now," he repeated in a firmer but still polite tone.

The guards looked at each other. Then they looked at the calm, confident figure of Epaphroditus.

"Sorry, sir," they grumbled and stood aside for him.

"Not a problem," Epaphroditus assured them as he disappeared through the doors.

The corridor on the other side was deserted as Epaphroditus moved swiftly down it. Who knew how long Asiaticus' errand would take. He could be back at any moment. Obviously, Epaphroditus had concocted an explanation as to his presence, but he preferred not to use it unless pressed. Best to avoid the freedman altogether rather than give any hint of insubordination.

"Sporus," he said, pushing open the door. "Sporus?"

The bed was empty, as was the couch positioned on the other side of the room. As his eyes scanned the chamber for signs of the eunuch, he picked up a flash of red. Turning his head he saw it, or rather him.

"Oh fuck—"

He ran forward and grabbed Sporus' rear, lifting him higher, trying to take the weight off the neck.

"It's alright, it's alright. I'll get you down. I'll get this."

With Sporus' lower half balanced on his chest, Epaphroditus stretched out a leg. Wrapping his foot around the chair leg he pulled it forward. It lay on its side. He'd have to let go of Sporus to stand it up. He could do that. It would just take a moment. To Sporus he said, "I'm going to let go of you just briefly. Just so I can get you down. Alright?"

He gently eased his grip on Sporus, lowering him. Letting him go, he righted the chair then grabbed back hold of Sporus and hoisted him upwards.

"It's alright, the chair is here, Sporus. I'm going to put your feet on there. You stand and I'll get this thing off your neck."

He manoeuvred Sporus to the chair.

"OK now. Put your feet down. Sporus. Sporus. You can step down now. Sporus."

There was no response from the eunuch.

"Sporus. Sporus. Step down now. Sporus."

The eunuch's weight was pressed against Epaphroditus' chest.

"Sporus." He slapped a hand on the eunuch's leg. "Sporus!" Another slap. "Sporus."

He gave him a blow this time, what should have been a stinging blow to his leg. It should have had him squealing and complaining. But it didn't. There was no response at all. "Sporus?" asked Epaphroditus softly. "Sporus?" Then one final time. "Sporus?"

He let go of Sporus' legs. The weight fell and banged against the wall. Epaphroditus stood back, his hand over his mouth.

"Oh gods, Sporus."

Then he slid to the ground with a thump, turning his face away from where the eunuch hung.

FORTY-FIVE

The kitchen on the Viminal Hill was inhabited by Pompeia's five sisters, all named Pompeia, when Lysander and Philo passed through on their way to work.

"Hello boys!" said the Pompeia that was Teretia's mother cheerfully, waving a wooden spoon at them. "Did you want breakfast?"

Seeing as every chair was taken by a Pompeia, they both declined. Teretia, who was sitting on a chair by the window, was given a goodbye kiss. As was Horace on his little head. The boy kicked his legs out with glee in such a delightful manner that Philo couldn't stop himself picking up his son and giving him a proper hug. A red-eyed Lysander watched from the doorway as Philo reluctantly gave Horace back to Teretia.

"Bye boys. Have a lovely day!" called the Pompeias in unison at the departing men.

When they had clattered down the stairs, the sisters all looked at each other.

"Poor man," they coo-ed.

"He really is properly heartbroken," said the Pompeia who was Teretia's mother. "He's barely eaten these last few days. And he usually has such an excellent appetite. Such a pity."

"You'd have thought that Verenia might have come over," said Teretia.

"Now, now, Teretia, let's be kind to Verenia. She is as much a victim of this as poor Lysander."

"That Verenius!" scoffed the eldest of the Pompeias. "This is all his fault! I have a good mind to march over to his house and give him a right mouthful."

As a Pompeia had done each and every morning since the dinner party revelation. It was surprising that Verenius hadn't yet jumped back on his boat and departed for foreign shores. The Pompeias were a fearsome force. The Furies were a bunch of tame kittens in comparison.

Berating Verenius again was agreed by all to be an excellent plan. Thus, they departed, scornful reprimands at the ready. In the quiet they left behind, Teretia nursed Horace while Marcia wiped down the kitchen table.

"Mistress."

"Yes, Marcia."

"I was wondering if you needed anything from the shops today."

"So you might meet with your handsome German soldier," Teretia smiled as she moved Horace onto her other breast.

"It would be nice to see him," admitted Marcia. "All this business with Master Lysander and Verenia makes me miss him all the more."

"I know exactly what you mean. I held on to my Philo all night long. I didn't want to let him go."

"I have your permission, mistress?"

"Of course," said Teretia, smiling down warmly at her son. "Who am I to stand in the way of true love?"

* * *

On their way to work, Philo attempted some small talk with the unusually solemn Lysander. "It's the emperor's birthday today. Are you involved much?"

"Not until the banquet," said Lysander. "There's sacrifices in the morning. Then Valens and Caecina have organised games right across the city. The heralds will be handling that. My team is not on announcing duties until much later."

"Nice to have some free time," suggested Philo after a long pause.

Philo wasn't much good at small talk, even with Lysander. His friend had always been the one to drive the conversation, and indeed dominate it. Philo was used to being the quiet one in their friendship. Strangely, he was beginning to miss Lysander's boastful, arrogant chit-chat. He was about to embark on a comment on the weather, namely isn't it a bit cooler today, when he was saved by a, "Pssst."

They both turned their heads to see an approaching Doris. The slave stopped in front of Lysander.

"If your mistress is lurking behind a wall waiting to talk to me, tell her I don't want to see her. Not yet."

"My mistress anticipated this. She begs you read this."

She handed Lysander a small cylinder scroll. Bowing her head, she left them.

Lysander dropped the scroll into his bag.

"Isn't it lucky you have all that free time this morning?" said Philo. "It'll give you time to read Verenia's scroll."

All he got in response was a, "Hmmm."

* * *

Like Lysander, Philo had little to do with the emperor's birthday celebrations, which suited him fine. He intended to avoid them as much as possible. In fact, he intended to spend the day at Flavius' and then sneak off back home. He just needed to pick up some paperwork from his office at the palace.

He pushed open the door to find Epaphroditus sat on his desk, a scroll in his hand.

"Sir?"

"There you are," said Epaphroditus in a tight voice, not looking up. "I've been waiting for you. You were some time so I thought I'd do a bit of reading while I waited. I picked up this report by Publius." He waved the scroll in the air. "It makes interesting reading. Certainly more interesting than what you reported back to me."

Philo felt his throat tighten. He clenched his fists shut to stop his hands shaking and in a voice he struggled to control, said, "If you mean the business with Domitian, sir, I didn't think it to be relevant to the emperor's cause."

"You're quite right. Publius' report is of little consequence. That curly-haired boy offering his bum up to Coccanius Nerva is hardly likely to forestall Vespasian's invasion."

Philo should have been relieved by this, but there was something in his boss' voice that kept him on edge. "Sir?" he asked hesitantly.

Epaphroditus placed Publius' report on the desk beside his thigh. "Are you on your way to see Flavius and Caenis?" he asked.

"Yes, sir. I usually do at this time."

Epaphroditus slid his buttocks off the desk. "Excellent," he said. "I'll come with you. I'm so very eager to hear from Caenis herself on how she turned my own assistant against me."

"Sir?" bleated an alarmed Philo.

"You were so very long," said Epaphroditus in a tight voice. "So I decided to catch up on the latest reports from the East."

Philo's stomach flipped over.

"They were much more interesting than Nerva finally getting his cock sucked. So packed full of details. Pertinent details. I can see from your face that you know to what I refer, Philo."

Philo stared at the floor.

"I can think of only one reason that you would deliberately keep such crucial information from me. You've been turned, haven't you? You're actively working for Vespasian against our emperor."

Philo did not reply.

"You always were a lousy liar, so I have to fully commend you for the subterfuge of the last few months. I am really very impressed." The fury was evident in Epaphroditus' voice. "Checking in with Caecina, I discover that he had no clue about Vespasian's machinations. He told me the 'Indian boy' had told him there was nothing to report. You never passed on our findings to Vitellius, did you?"

Philo hung his head down, staring at the floor.

"I suppose this is your revenge on me for accidentally involving you in Otho's plot against Galba. I never meant for you to get arrested. I never meant for you to get hurt. I was shocked and upset that you were and, believe me, I know full well my part in that."

Philo dared to look up. He supposed he'd known this moment was a distinct possibility when he'd agreed to work for Caenis. That didn't make it any easier. He looked up to face the man he admired most in the world. The man who'd plucked him from the bowels of the scribes hall and promoted him. The man who'd treated him with unfailing kindness. The man who'd contributed to his freedom fund. The man he'd betrayed.

"It had nothing to do with that," said Philo, meeting his boss's hurt eyes. "I have never blamed you for what happened to me. Never. I just… Things aren't…" he struggled to put his emotions of the last few months into words. Epaphroditus waited silently. "He isn't my emperor," said Philo, his eyes brimming with tears. "I never thought I would ever do anything like this."

"Neither did I," said Epaphroditus quietly.

"What will you do? Turn me over to Vitellius?" Philo gave a gulp. "Please leave Teretia alone. And Horace. Please."

Epaphroditus gave a nod. "I'm not a monster. They're safe. Consider that a promise."

Philo took several lungfuls of air, his whole body shaking. He'd been here before of course. The previous year, Epaphroditus' and Otho's actions had convinced Praetorian Prefect Laco that Philo was plotting with them. He wasn't and he'd been devastated by the accusations that had been thrown at him. He'd been beaten by the guards to elicit information he did not possess.

This time, he possessed information. But he wasn't going to give that up. Not for anything. He knew what was coming. He knew what to expect. He knew about broken jaws and battered ribs. He knew about pulsating blows and dizzying pain.

After a few moments he said quietly, but with determination, "I'm ready. I'm ready if you want to call the guards." He gave a shaky smile, his eyes beginning to well up again. "Can you tell Teretia that I'm sorry."

Epaphroditus' eyes swooped upwards. Then he covered his face with his hands, breathing heavily through them. Eventually he removed them. Standing beside Philo, his eyes cast downwards Epaphroditus said, "We're going to see Caenis, like I said."

FORTY-SIX

The journey to the Esquiline Hill was tense. They took a litter. Epaphroditus sat at one end not looking or speaking to Philo. Philo himself struggled to contain the swirling thoughts that were battering at his head. How would they do it? How would they execute him? Technically, as a freed citizen he should escape crucifixion. But Icelus, Galba's aide, had been freed and that hadn't saved him from the cross. These were different times. Times when the old rules no longer applied. Times when the ever-loyal and dedicated Tiberius Claudius Philo had turned traitor.

Arriving at their destination, they found no one but an old door slave.

"Where are the Praetorians?" Epaphroditus demanded of the doorkeeper.

It was Philo who answered. "They start on Flavius' wine cellar about this hour. We see little of them until the replacement cohort turn up at the seventh hour."

Epaphroditus gave a tut and walked past the decrepit door keeper.

* * *

The door banged on its hinges. Thump. Thump. Thump. The noise bothered neither Mina nor Domitian. The former had her palms pressed against the wood. The latter stood behind thrusting deeply into her. Mina insisted on always facing the door when they had sex.

"I'll see it first if there's any trouble!" she'd said.

Domitian had not objected. He liked that particular position. He also liked the way, after sex, while his heart was still thumping from the exertion, Mina would leap up and declare she was famished, or demand another archery lesson from him. No lying side by side in each other's arms. No sentiments expressed. It was wonderfully uncomplicated. So much so that Domitian couldn't find it in himself to mind that while he was fornicating with a slave, his older brother Titus was bonking a queen of the East. This was most unlike him.

He climaxed with a groan, gripping hold of Mina's hips, his head collapsing against her shoulder. She wriggled forward so that he slipped out of her.

"Let's go fire some shots!" she said, miming the action.

Domitian grinned and began to look for his hastily discarded clothes.

His affair with Mina was so utterly unlike the last liaison he'd inadvertently embroiled himself in. Domitian had genuinely had no clue about Nerva's feelings towards him. He'd thought the older man was being kind to him, in much the same way Caenis and Flavius were. He'd assumed it was for the same reason too: to compensate for his father's lack of interest in him.

As time went on, Domitian began to wonder whether Nerva had singled him out in recognition of his abilities. Used to being overlooked and forever compared to Titus, Domitian had lapped up the attention. Nerva was after all stupendously well connected. He could aid his forthcoming public career no end. He'd possessed no inkling that Nerva's interest in him had nothing to do with securing an aedileship. Not until that day.

He'd been sitting with Nerva in his leafy garden talking about the usual subjects: poetry, mutual acquaintances, and the inescapable politics of the day. The older man's expression had suddenly turned serious. He'd taken hold of Domitian's hands as he spelled out his suffering journey from the gradual realisation of his feelings towards him, to the joy of spending time with him and the pain this love caused him at all hours of the day. All of which made Domitian feel unaccountably guilty for being the cause of this pain.

Seeing Nerva's nervously earnest expression at the conclusion of this declaration, Domitian had felt an intense weight of pressure upon him. He was fond of Nerva, super fond. He liked spending time with him. But he'd never once thought of him in that way. That, however, was an awkward thing to admit to the man who'd just burst open the secrets of his heart to him. Which was how he'd ended up embroiled in a snog on a bench with a family friend.

It had been nice to be loved. Domitian, lonely and forever ignored, had certainly enjoyed the attention. He'd even enjoyed the physical side of it, for Nerva was a gentle and courteous lover. At every conclusion that love was reaffirmed with words of praise for his beauty, for his intelligence, for his complete desirability. Who wouldn't have lapped that up? In Nerva's house, Domitian was cast as the most important person. One who was welcomed with a warm smile, a kiss, and the physical demonstration of desire pressed against him.

Oh yes, it had been nice to be loved. At first. However, the cosy, safe cocoon of Nerva's embrace was lost the moment Domitian stepped outside the door. Then he became tormented by guilt and fear as to what all this could mean for his reputation. Lying on his bed back at his uncle's house, Domitian looked back with horror on acts he had willingly engaged in. If anyone found out! He cringed inwardly at Nerva's protestations of love. What if Nerva talked? What if he told his fellow well-connected friends about his affair with that son of Vespasian's?

Titus would kill himself laughing if his little brother's first elected position was tinged with such a scandal.

He'd steeled himself to end the liaison. Nerva would understand. Nerva knew how important reputation was in Rome. He'd climbed the cursus honorum of public positions. He'd know how eager candidates were to dig up dirt on their competition. Domitian couldn't hope for success with such a huge stain on his virtue. Nerva would understand. Except that every time Domitian saw that warm smile greeting him, his inner resolve crumbled and he'd somehow find himself curled against Nerva's naked body again, accepting heartfelt protestations of love.

In the end he'd taken the coward's way out. Unable to cope with both the fear of discovery and the fear of upsetting the one person in the world who'd ever loved him, Domitian had taken to avoiding Nerva. If he didn't see Nerva, he couldn't end up in bed with him, so his reasoning went. The tactic had been remarkably successful. And if he occasionally lay awake at night feeling guilt for blanking Nerva. He consoled himself that it was nowhere near as bad as the guilt he had felt the second after Nerva had ejaculated down his throat. Virtuous young men of character standing for an honourable role in government should not know how to pleasure honourable standing members of senatorial rank to such a climax.

In comparison to the daily round of joy and guilt that had tormented Domitian, the frantic fun couplings with Mina were as refreshing as a drink from a fountain on a scorching day. He walked behind her as they carried their bows.

Coming towards them down the corridor was Epaphroditus accompanied by Philo. Domitian froze on the spot, his knuckles going white from the grip he had on his bow. Epaphroditus' eyes were not on him though.

"Artemina, not in Baiae I see. More lies," he declared, turning back to throw a furious glance at the cowering Philo.

"What's going on?" asked Mina.

"Follow me. All of you," barked Epaphroditus.

FORTY-SEVEN

Flavius and Caenis were relaxing in the sunny courtyard garden when they were interrupted by the party of four.

"He knows," said Philo, before Epaphroditus could speak.

"There is a certain symmetry to it. Betrayed from above by my mentor. Betrayed from below by my assistant."

He was angrier than Philo had ever seen in all the years they had worked together. Domitian's usually ruddy cheeks paled. Even Mina had cottoned on that this was a very serious situation and bit at her lower lip. Caenis laced her fingers in her lap and met Epaphroditus' flaming glare.

"I have no influence on Philo. He is very much his own man," she said evenly, unfazed by his hostility. "Perhaps you have not noticed."

"It's true, sir," said a wretched-looking Philo. "Anything I did, any help I offered, was entirely my decision. Caenis played no part."

"That's what she'd have you believe. She is an exceptionally clever and manipulative woman," said Epaphroditus, his eyes not leaving Caenis. "She got me too, way back. I betrayed my own master because of her. I thought it was the right thing to do at the time. Now I'm not so sure it was. The descendants of

Aelius Sejanus could not have made more of a hash of running the empire."

"Sejanus!" spat Caenis, her face crinkling with disgust. "If you believe Sejanus would have made a good emperor then you truly are as deluded as I thought."

"Deluded? I have no delusions. I see everything as clear as a glass goblet. My assistant, egged on by yourselves, has committed treason against the emperor. No doubt after his interrogation, I shall have the names of the other conspirators. The emperor will be so very grateful to me."

Philo made a small bleating noise. Sitting down, he buried his face in his hands. His small frame shook as he wept. Mina stared in shock at the broken Philo, then at Epaphroditus, his upper lip pulled back in a snarl.

The previous year she'd imagined herself in love with Epaphroditus. She'd pictured a future with him. She'd anticipated a lifetime of really hot sex. He in turn had left her to her fate at the hands of the Praetorian Guard the day Nero had fallen. Had faked his own death and hadn't thought she was worth informing of his very much alive status, leaving her to grieve and suffer his loss. And then when they'd been reconciled, he'd knowingly infected her with a venereal disease. But even after all that, she had not been as horribly disillusioned as she was at this exact moment.

"Why don't we kill him?"

Epaphroditus spun on his heel to face her.

"Well? Why don't we?" She raised her bow upwards, placing an arrow in the taut string. Then she pointed it directly at her former lover.

"Artemina," he said, cautiously.

"He said so himself, the emperor doesn't know yet. I'm betting nobody does. I'm betting he came straight here. We all know the guards are sleeping it off. They probably didn't even see him arrive. Nobody knows he's here. If we kill him, we're all safe."

There followed a tense pause to this suggestion.

Eyes fixed on the arrow head aimed at his chest, Epaphroditus said, "The ramifications—"

"Would be worse how?" countered Mina. "You're talking about torturing Philo! What in Venus' active fucking vagina is going on? He's just had a baby. Well, Teretia has. I'm not going to let you take him away. I'm not going to let you take anyone away. Philo ordered me to keep Domitian safe. I'm extending that order. I'm keeping him safe too. And Antonia Caenis. And Flavius Sabinus. Because they are the bloody good guys! What kind of world is it if Philo is considered an enemy?"

She pulled back the bow string tighter, narrowing her eyes.

"Think you can hit me if I run?" sneered Epaphroditus. "I can get to the guards before you load a second arrow."

"I've got a back-up," retorted Mina, giving Domitian's shin a kick. "And he is deadly accurate, I assure you."

Another kick to his shin had Domitian picking up his bow and loading it. "I practise a lot," he said half-apologetically.

With two armed archers aiming squarely at him, Epaphroditus felt a sheen of sweat forming on his forehead. He threw his eyes skyward and gave a short barked laugh.

"Of all the ways I thought I'd leave this life, this is by far the least expected. Shot down by a slave I used to screw and Flavius Vespasian's lesser son. Who could even imagine it?" He returned his gaze to Mina, the sneer relaxed, the green eyes imploring. "Do it," he said. "You're right, it's the only way to save yourselves. If you let me go I will go, straight to the emperor and denounce you all. Do it. Shoot me."

Mina pulled the string back as far as it would go. Epaphroditus closed his eyes and said in a voice heavy with wear. "Do it. Just do it."

Mina looked to Domitian. He nodded back at her and pulled his own string taunt.

"No!"

The cry was of such volume that it startled both Mina and Domitian. Their hands dropped their bow strings and two arrows were projected outwards. The first, from Mina, hit a stone column, pinging a chip in it. The second, from Domitian's bow, thwacked on to the ground, bounced off and embedded itself in Caenis' wicker chair missing her by inches.

Epaphroditus opened his eyes.

"No!" said Philo again, stepping in front of Epaphroditus. "No, you're not to. No."

"Philo, he's going to have you executed," said Mina. "We have to stop him."

"No, that's enough," said Philo. "Stand down. I'm ordering you to stand down."

Mina lowered her bow. Epaphroditus exhaled the breath he'd been holding. Philo turned to face his former boss. Epaphroditus placed a hand on his shoulder, mouthing a, "Thank you."

Mina placed her hands on her hips. "Well, what happens now?" she demanded.

Flavius got to his feet. "Now we talk. Epaphroditus, will you sit and listen to an old man who has always respected you?"

Epaphroditus gave him a suspicious look, his hand still resting on Philo's shoulder.

"Come, let us all talk with honesty," said Caenis. Then looking at Epaphroditus, "We've always been honest with each other, haven't we?"

Epaphroditus gave a tight smile. "Sometimes brutally so. I seem to remember you warning me off Aphrodite because I'd ruin her."

Caenis smiled back. "I will admit to being wrong at least once in my life."

They sat on the wicker garden furniture around a low circular table on which slaves laid out refreshments. Their shaking hands as they placed down the beakers suggested they were in need of a hard drink too. It had been quite a morning.

Mina and Domitian sat some distance away on a stone bench by the fountain. Mina's hand on her belt ready to pull out her whip if needed.

Seeing the two young people seated side by side, Epaphroditus said, "They're screwing each other, yes?"

Flavius, with a twinkle in his eye, confirmed this was indeed the case. "They think we don't know but twice a day the furniture bangs itself against the wall."

Epaphroditus took a sip of wine to hide his smile. "Go on then. Talk to me. Tell me why you've embroiled Philo in treachery."

On the chair beside him, Philo gave a shudder at that word.

"I am most intrigued to know what you said to him. It must have been stupendous because I've never known him to be the slightest bit disloyal to any emperor. Even Galba who had him beaten to mush."

"Sir, they honestly didn't say anything to me. I just… Things aren't… Things aren't right." Philo struggled to explain. "Vitellius. He's… He's not right, sir. He's not right to rule Rome."

"He's no worse than Nero or Caligula," insisted Epaphroditus.

Caenis leaned forward in her chair. "You and I have known each other a long time. So many years. I've watched you grow from that scamp of a boy I first knew, to the man you are now. You only got there because you're a survivor. You never got greedy. You never lost your mind to power. You watched and you learned. And you survived when so many fell. I put that down to Claudia Aphrodite," smiled Caenis. "She gave you that one thing you needed to protect. That one thing to survive for. The Epaphroditus she loved and the one I love would never have begged to be shot with a bow. He would have talked his way out of the situation with that smooth tongue of his. Grief has clouded your reactions. It's clouded your judgement. Aulus Vitellius is going to fall and he's going to take you with him."

She sat back in her chair and Flavius picked up the thread.

"He's playing the part of the playboy emperor well. I give you that. He makes a nice Nero. But you and I both know, because we both worked for that administration, that Nero knew the responsibilities of government. Yes, maybe he took a bit of incentivising some days. But he knew that paperwork had to be done. That delegations had to be met. That petitions had to be heard. From what Philo has told us, Vitellius is doing none of this. He has abandoned the machinery of government for the love of luxury. He is not fit to be emperor. It's as simple as that."

Epaphroditus' first thought was, "Of course you'd say that when your brother is aiming for the throne."

But looking into Flavius' watery blue eyes, his inner cynicism dissolved. He'd worked with Flavius for decades through several administrations. Each time, Flavius had moved his loyalty to the next emperor and served him just the same. He had in the last year served Nero, Galba, and Otho. Epaphroditus had never heard him complain about any emperor. Until Vitellius.

And Philo? Philo was the epitome of duty. He did whatever was asked of him, no matter how distasteful. Under Nero there had been plenty of actions their department had been involved in that stank. But he'd never baulked at them. And, crucially, he'd never judged an emperor for dishing them out. Until now. Until Vitellius.

Epaphroditus shut his eyes for a moment and saw again Sporus. That scarf tied tight around his neck. Tongue hanging between black lips. Eyes bulging in their sockets. There had been nothing remaining of the eunuch's staggering beauty. It was ugly. It was all ugly.

Opening his eyes, he looked beyond the earnest expressions on the faces of Caenis, Flavius, and Philo, over to where Artemina sat beside Domitian.

He stood.

"Artemina. I'm sorry. Sporus is dead."

The crumpled expression on her face and the shock on those of Caenis, Philo, and Flavius as he detailed what had led to Sporus' suicide was all he needed in the end.

No reasoned arguments about Vespasian's superior forces or Vitellius' administration. Just the sad tale of a once-feted and beloved eunuch who found himself with an emperor who wished to debase and humiliate him. And who jumped off a chair in his best red gown and sparkly sandals to escape.

Mina fled crying, followed by Domitian. Philo sat stunned, tears flowing down his cheeks. Flavius shook his head, appalled. Epaphroditus looked to a horrified Caenis.

"I'm in," he said.

FORTY-EIGHT

"There were three of us," said Mina. "Alex, Sporus, and me. Except Sporus wasn't Sporus at first. He had another name. He was another boy. It wasn't until after his eunuchisation that he became Sporus. It's a joke you see: Sporus means seed. But he doesn't have any seed. A joke."

They were sitting in Domitian's room. Mina on a chair placed in front of the door, Domitian on a low stool. He held tight on to her hands as she talked. He'd expected her to cry more, to sob into his shoulder, but she wasn't that kind of girl. She wanted to tell him about her friends. It was very important she said. So he listened.

"Alex had red hair and freckles all over his face. He was the nicest, kindest boy. He'd do anything for you. Anything. Well, not exactly anything because he had quite a moral core. I don't think Sporus and I knew how much until last year. Alex was a messenger boy. He hated his job. He wanted to do something else. I worked in the nursery. Which I hated. Sporus was a dancer. Which he loved. And there were three of us," she repeated. "Three friends since we were children. Since before Sporus was Sporus. Since before Alex had freckles. And before I, before I became me."

She rubbed the tears from her eyes with the back of her hand. "We had so many adventures, shared so much gossip, had so much fun. And I have to tell you this, grumpy posh boy. You have to hear it all. All about how Sporus fell in love with Nero. How Alex failed in love. And how I got my job with Empress Statilia Messalina. All of it. Because there is no three of us anymore. There's just me." She looked up at Domitian, her face pained in grief. "I'm the only one left."

* * *

They talked long into the night, the slaves lighting the lamps around them as the light faded.

"This is a different army to the one that marched with Valens and Caecina from Germania," said Flavius. "They've lost discipline."

Picturing the drunken lumps littering the palace corridors at all times of the day, Epaphroditus had to agree. "Also, he's lost numbers to that fever sweeping the city."

"We could up that," suggested Caenis lightly. "A new strange bout of illness that disposes quickly."

Epaphroditus raised an eyebrow. "I take it you're suggesting we procure the services of Gaius Baebius' wife?"

"Purely as a supplier. I can't risk sending her up to the palace in case she bumps into Valens."

"As entertainments coordinator I have full access to the kitchens. A place Valens wouldn't be able to find if he had it tattooed on his arm," offered up Epaphroditus. "Soldiers don't have food tasters."

"It evens it out a little," smiled Caenis. "But stronger methods are needed."

"Caecina," said Philo quietly. "Caecina is the weak link. I think he, and whatever forces he commands, could be turned."

"How so?" asked Flavius.

"Caecina is as unnerved as we all are by Vitellius' habits. He rarely turns up to the orgies any more. I've heard that he's really trying quite hard at his consular work."

Epaphroditus had to ask. "Is he any good at it?"

"No, not really," admitted Philo. "He's, err, not very gifted. But his secretaries are rather taken by him, and not just because he's so handsome. They think him kind-hearted and are quite happy to fill in for his deficiencies."

"Valens? Actually you don't need to tell me. I know what Valens is up to." Epaphroditus gave a shudder.

"You think Caecina is for turning?" pressed Caenis.

Philo gave a shrug. "I think it's possible. But anything is possible at the moment."

"Too true," said Epaphroditus. "So let's concentrate on the probable. We have an emperor closing his ears to all negative reports who is about to get a very rude awakening—in how long?"

Caenis shuffled on her stool. "Sooner than was anticipated, I'm afraid."

FORTY-NINE

Caecina screwed up his eyes and read the document one final time. Nope. He still didn't understand it. He looked up at the hopeful face of his secretary, Talos. He didn't like to disappoint the lad after all the time he'd spent explaining the document to him.

"Excellent," said Caecina, forcing a smile out, causing half the slaves present to swoon and the other half a sudden race to their hearts. "It's all as you said it was. So where do I sign?"

This gave Talos the enviable task of leaning over the handsome man in order to indicate the relevant point. He did so while cursing that as a man he lacked a bosom to seductively expose as he leant over. The best he could do was to wear ever shorter tunics to show off his legs. The joke going round the slave complex was that Talos was going to turn up to work in only a vest and sandals by the winter.

"Pen? Where's my pen?"

Talos scanned the desk for the missing article.

"Is this it, sir?" asked the announcer Ampelius, approaching with it in his hand.

Talos cursed inwardly at such an obvious set-up that had Caecina beaming his smile at Ampelius rather than him. He shot the announcer a hard look. Ampelius smirked in response. It was gearing up to becoming a standard night of thwarted flirting and fierce rivalry for Caecina's smallest attentions. But then the messenger burst in.

To the puzzled expressions that greeted him, the messenger, red of face declared, "I can't find anyone! There's no one anywhere!"

"They'll all be at the emperor's birthday entertainments," said Talos. "Hand it over and I'll see it's properly distributed." Then to Caecina in a far softer tone, "I'm very sorry at this boorish intruder, sir."

"Is it an important message?" asked Caecina, looking over Talos' shoulder.

The messenger, looking suitably grave, responded, "As important as it gets."

* * *

The emperor returned from his birthday games in a fury. The replacement Proserpina had been unsatisfactory. The glorious act he'd been gleefully anticipating was nothing but a humping mating. She hadn't even put up a fight, as surely the goddess had done. Rather, the slave had just lain there naked and silently accepted the cock of the underworld god. It was distinctly non-entertaining. If he wanted to see slaves have dull sex, he could have done so without having to leave the palace or his comfy couch.

In the end, he was so annoyed and disappointed that he'd ordered Proserpina to be sent to the underworld permanently, courtesy of several sword thrusts to the stomach. That she would never now be reunited with her mother, Ceres, and that the world was now thrust into permanent winter troubled him not a jot. Fuck that girl! And fuck that eunuch that had ruined the whole spectacle. He was firmly blaming Asiaticus for that loss. It was his fucking job to watch the eunuch. To ensure that it was available for the emperor's sole pleasure. He had failed. He had failed totally.

Vitellius would have stomped down the palace corridors kicking slaves out of his way as he went. However, he'd gained far too much weight to walk any distance. He had to be content with yelling insults from his sedan chair as it was carried along. Triaria and husband walked behind similarly aggrieved.

"I do hope that entertainments coordinator has some suitable plans for the banquet," she said. "Else I fear my brother will fully show his displeasure tonight."

She sounded gleeful at the prospect. The chair was lowered in the emperor's private bedroom. Standing by the gargantuan bed was Caecina.

"I did try to stop him, Imperial Majesty," said the chamberlain of the room. "But he insisted."

"I need to get changed for the banquet," said Vitellius gruffly. "Now is not the time. Nor is it ever the time for you to be present in my bedchamber unannounced."

"Apologies, Imperial Majesty, but I wanted to catch you before the banquet began."

Before Vitellius got too drunk to comprehend the message that he had to impart.

"Caecina?" It was Valens marching in. "You sent for me?"

The two commanders stood a few feet apart, Vitellius in front of them forming a triangle.

"Well?"

Caecina cleared his throat, then said, "Vespasian's forces are in Italy. They are headed in our direction."

PART II

THE RESISTANCE

Autumn to winter AD69

"They felt they were in no way inferior to the troops of Spain who had appointed Galba; and the Guards who had appointed Otho; and the troops in Germany who had appointed Vitellius"
—Suetonius, *The Twelve Caesars, Life of Vespasian*

FIFTY

The air of the chamber was thick with a nasal-clogging incense. It was combined with the whiffs of roasted meats that were carried in on golden platters. This was day two of the banquet, and yet the emperor's piggy eyes continued to light up on sight of more dishes.

"Gods! I swear he must have eaten three whole cows by now," Lysander commented to Midas.

"It's incredible, isn't it? It's like Saturnalia every day. But with only one man allowed to have any fun."

Lysander, seeing the suffering faces of the dancing eunuch troop, was inclined to agree. It was a far cry from the emperor's welcome party when the staff had jostled for prime position. Now they jostled not to be picked. Nobody wanted to entertain for Vitelllius. It was exhausting. All feared being singled out for special attentions, like Sporus. Nobody wanted to end up like Sporus.

Even Lysander had instructed his announcers not to be too flashy in their announcements. The key thing was not to stand out, not to attract attention. What an administration this was that nobody wished to serve it! Vitellius was fortunate that his palace was staffed by slaves who had no option but to comply.

Viewing the imperial family, Lysander saw no joy in their faces at the jiggling of the eunuchs. The empress and the emperor's brother and wife sat stony-faced. Even the young son of the emperor was sullen and tired. Only the emperor showed any animation.

Lysander shook his head. All of this for one man. He'd seen enough. It was no wonder there were machinations afoot. Lysander had no role in what was going on, but he'd noticed the furtive glances, the secret messages being slipped into palms, the hushed conversations. There was definitely some top-level plotting going on. At some point he'd have to choose a side. Not yet though. He slipped outside and back to his office.

He had too much to do: a stack of posh types who the emperor might or might not see. Whatever was decided, their names, titles, and connections would need to be memorised and the diction and emphasis agreed. Lysander didn't trust his useless protégés to do this without close supervision.

Yet rather than exacting high standards, Lysander found himself drawn to Verenia's letter again. He'd lost count of the number of times he'd read it. Lots. Many. Too many perhaps. Each reading did not diminish its emotional impact on him. Nor did it lend any clarity to what he should do. He unrolled it again.

He could imagine Verenia writing it. Her pale face taut with misery as she admitted that she was barren. How she must have fought for her composure as she detailed how she had not always been hollow. How she'd once carried a child in her womb and loved it beyond anything she'd ever loved before. That child had been a light in her otherwise dark and oppressive life. It brightened her future and gave her hope. She'd been so looking forward to being a mother. To caring for an infant. To being his or her everything.

She'd never had the chance to hold her child. She'd never been a mother. Her brutal husband, Lucanus, in a fit of anger had punched her in her growing belly. Her beloved anticipation was killed in her womb. Never to be born. Never to cry. Never to need her.

She didn't go into much detail of this event. Lysander imagined it to be far too painful for her to divulge, but the announcer could imagine. He'd been present in the chamber when Nero had kicked his heavily pregnant wife, Poppaea, in the stomach. The empress had died in agony in a pool of blood as the staff stood round helplessly.

That punch to Verenia's stomach had rendered her infertile and subject to many more punches from her enraged husband. Until she'd had the courage to leave him, angering her father and blemishing herself in the eyes of the Viminal Hill society.

Lysander rubbed at his eyes. That bit always made him cry. He wanted nothing more than to hold Verenia in his arms and tell her how brave she was. But he couldn't shake off the image of those golden-haired children sat on his lap. The gods had bestowed on Lysander two gifts: a voice and potency. Both had served him well, and he'd thanked both Apollo and Priapus for the honour. It seemed wrong to disdain gifts from the gods. It was the sort of thing that got those heroes of old into terrible scrapes.

These were not the days to alienate the gods. Though Vitellius had banned all mention of him, everyone knew Vespasian's army was on the march. The whole of Rome needed the gods' protection. Lysander had even taken to praying to Philo's weird gods who resided next to the normal Roman gods in their apartment's shrine. They needed all the help they could get.

Then there were those other feelings that manifested themselves every time he looked upon Horace sleeping. Or feeding. Or smiling. Or sitting on his lap having a cuddle. A tightness in his head and a lump hardening in his throat. He wanted this. He wanted children.

This being Rome, you could just head down to the nearest rubbish tip and pick up an abandoned baby. However, Lysander came from a long line of palace-bred slaves and thus possessed an inbuilt snobbishness regarding foundlings. Felix always said they were foundlings for a reason, and they never progressed very far up the palace hierarchy.

What to do? He was in love with a woman who couldn't give him the one thing he'd always wanted. Either he lost her, or he lost his dream. Either choice was tinged with sadness. Which was probably why Lysander dithered over making that decision. Everything was just all too awful!

* * *

"Valens, we have to go now," insisted Caecina. "They're in Italy!"

Valens, knuckles white as he gripped the edge of the desk, said, "I am well aware of that. But there are things to organise. We can't just go marching off with no plan. It'll be Placentia all over again."

It was a dig. Caecina had failed to take the town of Placentia, despite his overwhelming numbers of experienced troops. The handsome young consul regarded his colleague: Valens' hard eyes, his greasy grey hair, his sallow pitted cheeks. He really was repulsive, inside and out. Rotten, like so much of Rome these days.

"I'm going north. We need to fight them before they gain too much territory. They need to be defeated. To be vanquished. Lest any other legions defect to that man."

"Defect? Why would they defect? We have the German legions. The greatest, hardest, meanest fighters in the empire."

"Had," corrected Caecina. "I don't know what we have now. Maybe a campaign will help recover their glory. But I am going. This can't wait for you to get better."

Valens' narrowed his eyes. "What do you mean?"

Caecina stared him out. "You're sick again. Everyone knows it. You spend all night vomiting up your guts."

"There is nothing wrong with me," insisted Valens through tightened lips.

Caecina gave a sceptical guffaw. "Bloody look at yourself man! You're practically a cadaver. And you're holding onto that desk for dear life because you're frightened you'll collapse if you let go. You're sick! You were laid up for months last time."

That was a dig at Valens who'd been lying sweating in his bed while Caecina had marched his own troops into battle.

"I was poisoned!" pointed out Valens. "I was poisoned by that bitch. This is nothing."

As he said the words he suddenly paled. He bent over and began retching.

Caecina didn't wait for his colleague to cease. "I can't wait for you. I march today."

"Then you'll cock it all up like you did previously, you foolish boy!"

"Whatever," was Caecina's less than masterful final word as he stormed out.

Valens slid to the floor. Three slaves rushed forward to assist him. He felt dreadful. Almost as dreadful as before. But it couldn't be poison this time. Not with the palace cohort of food tasters assigned to him.

* * *

In an alcove down a narrow corridor in a forgotten part of the palace, a bag was handed over. Midas opened it and peered in.

"Spoons," said Lysandria. "He'll not be asking for rich foods given how he feels. Porridge and soup most likely. He's snobbish enough not to share cutlery with any of the food tasters. Which is when you hand him one of these. When he scoops up his soup, it'll mix with the potion."

"Will it kill him?" asked Midas.

Lysandria gave a tinkly laugh. "We don't want to kill him. That's far too obvious. Not yet anyway. He needs to slowly linger downwards to that eventuality." Then to Midas' shocked expression, she said. "I'll be back in two days with more. Take care. He must suspect nothing. Make sure you change tasters the moment he voices any distrust in them."

"I shall," promised Midas.

Lysandria pulled the hood of her cloak over her head and slipped out the back door.

FIFTY-ONE

The guards were more than happy to let Epaphroditus pass.

"He's been quieter," said one. "Less of the bellowing."

"More yelling," said another. "So I reckon he's on his way down."

"Asiaticus asked for another update," said Epaphroditus casually. "It's a waste of time I know."

"No, no," disagreed the guards. "It'll be good to know when he's definitely gone. Someone will have to take the body and that."

"Be a bit pongy, a fellow that size."

"And we need the space. The emperor's locking 'em up en masse. But we daren't put anyone in with him. So we're having to dispatch them quicker than usual. Which gets messy when the emperor changes his mind."

Epaphroditus nodded sympathetically. He knew all about fickle-minded emperors.

"You are doing a splendid job keeping him contained."

"I daren't open the door," confided the other guard. "He's an animal."

"Probably why Asiaticus gave me this task. I get all the shitty jobs."

"Shame," they sympathised. "If you could let us know if he's dead."

"I'll be sure to tell."

"Only he's supposed to be dead already," said a guard.

"I daren't open the door," repeated the other guard.

"We thought he'd starve to death a lot quicker than this."

"He always has been strong-willed," said Epaphroditus. "He'll be hanging on out of spite."

"Too bloody right," agreed the guards.

Epaphroditus gave them a little wave as he walked down the long corridor to where Felix's cell lay. They waved back.

"Don't get too close to the door. He might go for you," they helpfully suggested.

"Idiots," said Epaphroditus under his breath. "You replace the idiot Praetorians with even greater idiots. Who'd have thought that possible?"

He made his way around another corner, passing three other cells to reach the one at the far end. When there, he put down the bag the guards hadn't thought to search and pulled out a slice of pie. Then he pressed his face against the bars of the small window in the door.

"Felix," he hissed into the darkness. "Felix."

From within the blackness a shape began to move.

"Felix."

"Wot you fuckin' got for me today?" asked the former head of slave placements and chief overseer.

"I believe its gourd pie," said Epaphroditus, holding up the slice and examining it. He gave it a sniff. "Appetising. And still warm."

Felix's red-bearded face appeared at the barred window. "Just shove it the fuck through will ya. I'm fucking starving."

Felix wasn't starving. He wasn't starving because Epaphroditus visited him several times a day with food hand-baked by Vallia. He squeezed the pie slice through the bars. Felix took hold of it and sat on the floor of his cell to tuck in.

After finishing the first huge bite and taking the time to wipe crumbs from his beard, he commented, "Ask me wife whether she can get hold of some slim, thin cooking pot things. That way I could have me some fuckin' stew. She makes lovely fuckin' stew, Vallia."

Epaphroditus was well aware of this fact, having dined with Felix's wife several times in the last two months. He told himself he was being a good citizen and palace employee checking in on how Vallia and little Ganymede were faring since Felix's incarceration. Actually, the incentive was Vallia's stupendous cooking. In Epaphroditus' mind, the mystery of why Felix stayed married to the wife he endlessly complained about was solved. Frankly, he'd contemplate marriage to Vallia for a single spoonful of her stew.

"I'll ask her," he told Felix, inwardly deciding he'd sample the goods before handing it over.

"Wot news out there?"

Epaphroditus shrugged. "It's absolute chaos."

"Not surprised with Aulus Vitellius in charge," said Felix in-between mouthfuls of pie. "He always was a lazy fucker."

"And without your expert input," added Epaphroditus. "I am trying to fill the chasm you left, giving reassurance to the staff. But it is not easy."

"It's a hard fuckin' job keeping the fuckin' staff in line. Ain't I always fuckin' said that?"

"Yes," smiled Epaphroditus through the fog of nearly fifty years of memories. "You always have."

Felix sat on the floor of his cell finishing off Vallia's pie. Then he said to the hole in the door, "Wot 'appens now? You keep feedin' me, even them idiot fuckin' guards are gonna think at some fuckin' point I should be fuckin' dead by now. Wot then? Can't see you takin' a fall for me."

Epaphroditus, back leant against the wall beside the door, stared at the brickwork opposite as he said, "You took a fall for me once. Maybe I owe you."

A grunt came from within the cell. "Are we acknowledging that what we both know happened, happened?"

For once it was a sentence devoid of profanities, and the Aventine street accent was dropped in favour of a voice born of the imperial training school they'd both attended.

To the wall, Epaphroditus said, "Maybe."

"Always knew you were wasted as a wine boy," said Felix. "I don't like it when quality merchandise gets extinguished on some fucker of an emperor's perversions. Didn't like it back then. Don't like it now. But you never answered my question: what now?"

Epaphroditus looked back through the door to where Felix was barely visible sat on the floor, a heap of powerful muscles and brawn.

"Vitellius is going down. I'm taking him down. He has no right, no purpose in being emperor. When it comes to it, when the moment comes, will you help me?"

It was a daring request. Felix never involved himself in politics. He'd watched emperors come and emperors go, but had never once partaken in their fall. He'd always been an impeccably loyal palace employee. It was with quite some trepidation that Epaphroditus awaited the reply. It came with a force and volume that was the essence of Felix.

"Too fuckin' right I will."

FIFTY-TWO

Caecina pulled his plaid woollen cloak around his impressive build. The trousers he wore kept the chill from his legs. Really they should be part of a legionary standard kit, he thought, taking in the naked, hairy, goosebumped legs of his soldiers.

"Talos!" he called.

"Yes, sir," replied the young slave from the region of Caecina's right elbow. It was a position he'd taken permanent residence in.

"Ah, there you are," said Caecina, still surprised by the proximity of his aide. "Trousers."

"Sir?"

"Trousers, Talos. Can we get some for the men. It is very chilly and I know they'll fight better with a nice soft wool against their skin. One feels very Germanic in trousers. Like a bear."

"I'll look into it, sir."

He wouldn't. In his short tenure working for Philo, Talos had learned from his mentor that the Roman elite possessed a tendency to demand ridiculous things. The good assistant's role was to determine how compliable this demand was, whether the demand was of value, and how long the demander would recall they'd demanded it.

Talos quickly assessed that finding 40,000 pairs of trousers at the top end of a non-trouser-wearing country in winter was unfeasible. That the lower half of the legions was unlikely to be a determining factor in any forthcoming battle. And that Caecina was likely to forget his idea within the hour.

"Excellent," smiled Caecina.

Talos felt his knees go weak from the sight of Caecina's perfectly straight teeth.

The young general sucked in the cold winter air. It cleansed him. Staring round, he saw his soldiers busily constructing the camp by heaving huge sharpened tree trunks to the perimeters. He could hear the yells of the centurions and the grunts of labour. Caecina felt at peace.

Boy, was he glad he was out of Rome. Here the air was pure, clean. Not the cloying, thick-scented air of the palace. Here the soldiers toiled happily, having shaken off their drunken ways. Things were good.

He'd known they would be, hadn't he? He'd known as soon as he got them marching they'd be fine. There'd been a bit of grumbling at first. But once Caecina had stood before them, all six feet plus of trousered self, with his cloak billowing in the wind, they'd soon been won over. It was a hard man who wasn't dazzled by Caecina's staggering good looks and oratory skills. Close persistent contact with Caecina revealed his many deficiencies of intellect. Fortunately, the nearest the average legionary got to the Adonis was several lines back while the handsome man addressed them.

Leading the men out of Rome, Caecina was reminded of their march from Germania. Those days of excitement and peril when Caecina had felt he'd truly found himself. His nostalgia took a knock when he discovered he'd somehow picked up two of Valens' legions.

An administrative error, Talos had told him with cringing apology. Caecina hadn't even had him whipped. There was no need, not when the alien legions were so well behaved. Caecina couldn't help but remember that these were the soldiers who had mutinied against his colleague. He couldn't understand it given how loyal and hardworking they'd proven to be on the road. It had to be down to Valens' deficiencies. It was the only explanation, as Caecina saw it.

Still, he'd made good with Valens, sending him a polite note in regard to this error. His colleague's reply had been less than polite. Caecina pursed his beautiful lips at the memory of that bitter diatribe. The angry accusations that Caecina had deliberately taken his troops and that he intended to use them to glorify himself at Valens' expense. Or worse, perhaps he'd turned traitor and was stealing his men to add them to *that man's* considerable forces. Caecina had been so mad at this he'd thrown Valens' letter into the fire and vowed not to communicate with him again. This vow had lasted less than a day before he was angrily dictating his reply to Talos. Damn Valens! He sucked the cooling air into his lungs.

A clatter of hooves alerted him to an arrival.

The animal came pounding out of the fog, its rider wearing the crested helmet of a tribune. He was quickly surrounded.

"I'm a Vitellian!" the tribune complained as he was forcibly ejected from his saddle.

"Unhand that man, men!" cried Caecina, striding forwards. "He's one of ours!"

The tribune shook off the hands from his cloak. Seeing Caecina he said, "I am Aelius Laminius, commander."

"Come to my tent, tribune, and tell me what news you possess."

* * *

"Verona is lost?"

"I am afraid so, general," said Laminius as Talos handed him a cup of hot, spiced wine.

"I was born in Verona. It's where I grew up," said Caecina, aghast.

"And now it's in the hands of the Vespasians. They're a filthy bunch, half mad the lot of them. And that commander of theirs, Primus," Laminius shook his head. "He personally marched me down the ranks of his men to show me their strength. That's why he let me go. So I could tell you how many of them there are."

Caecina shook himself out of his daze. "I have the German legions! They are the finest fighters in the empire."

"That's not what Primus thinks. He's told his men they've gone soft."

"Rubbish."

"There's ex-Praetorians joined his camp," said Laminius. "They've fed back stories about the state of Rome, the state of the emperor."

"Oh," said Caecina.

He understood now why Primus was so convinced of his superiority. Vitellius had picked from the German legions to stuff the ranks of the new Praetorian cohorts. This had left the forces Caecina had marched upwards much smaller than those he'd initially marched down. Plus, with several months of Roman dissipation they were nowhere near as fit as they had been back in the spring.

"Primus reckons your men will give up."

"Never!"

"He thinks they'll not fight for Vitellius when they could be fighting for the conqueror of the Jews."

Caecina scratched at a trousered leg, then tossed his gorgeous head upwards.

"My men are loyal to me. And always shall be," he declared.

Laminius took a sip of wine. "I'm glad to hear that, commander."

Caecina smiled, but it was a smile lacking its usual warmth.

Talos slipped through the tent flaps. He walked through the camp, towards the latrines and then a small outbuilding that housed the administrative staff of the army. Behind this stood a figure in a long grey cloak. On seeing Talos, she pulled her hood off her head to reveal raven locks and a face of the most exquisite beauty.

"Talos, good to see you again," she smiled, leading to another weakening of the scribe's knees. "What news have you?"

Talos bowed his head respectfully, then said, "He's beginning to waver."

Nymphidia Sabina gave another of her dazzling smiles. "Oh my dear handsome stud, we need to get you on the right side before it's too late."

FIFTY-THREE

Philo winced as he concluded the report.

"And that's what the troops have been up to," he said, rolling up the scroll.

Flavius puffed out his cheeks with a hmph. Epaphroditus looked to Caenis.

"I agree it's not ideal," she said.

"Not ideal?" said Epaphroditus lightly. "Somewhat of an understatement. They're acting like a swarm of locusts. I doubt there'll be much left of the Italian countryside with Primus' lot rampaging about the place."

"The damage appears to be more extensive than that caused by the Vitellian troops on their march down."

"Yes, Philo it does," said Epaphroditus, his eyes on Caenis.

She fiddled with her shawl and pushed her slippers further onto her feet.

"Primus is acting on his own initiative. Naturally, such incidents occur when there is no plan. Mucianus is en route to intercede and incorporate him into our own forces."

"And until that point they are free to sack all in their way?" asked Epaphroditus.

"It may work to our advantage," said Caenis. "A fearsome reputation might cause Vitellius' troops to pause."

"And the people of Rome might decide they'd much rather stick with that fat pig of an emperor, thank you very much."

"Might be a boon to our plans for young Caecina," interjected Flavius, the peacemaker. "If he sees the destruction of Primus' men, it might turn him the quicker from his course."

"It might," conceded Epaphroditus, sitting back in his chair.

"Besides which, I can assure you the city cohorts are very much on our side. Nerva has sent word. They are sworn to follow me."

"Sorry, Flavius. Of course they would. They remember what an excellent commander you were," said Epaphroditus.

"I don't like this Primus situation any more than you do," said Caenis. "It has thrown all our careful arrangements out. But he is doing what he's doing, and it is at least—oh, hello darling."

It was Domitian, with his Mina-shaped shadow stood beside him.

"I was wondering what time lunch is," he said.

"Cook said in an hour," answered Flavius. "I believe she has a very tasty ham roasting."

"Good," he murmured and departed, followed by Mina.

When he was gone, Caenis said, "As I was saying in regards to Primus."

Epaphroditus, looking at the space where Domitian had stood, interrupted her. "Are you going to involve him in any of this? He is the emperor's son."

Flavius gave another hmph. "The less he knows the better. I'm still not convinced Vitellius' better nature will last given what's coming. I don't want Domitian put in unnecessary danger."

"He's the face of Vespasian. When the troops get here, they'll be looking to him."

"Mucianus knows what has to be done," said Caenis.
Epaphroditus and Philo exchanged looks.

* * *

It was a question Epaphroditus picked up on their walk back to the palace.

"Why don't they trust him? Domitian, I mean. He's young but not that young. Attractive enough to stick in front of the troops and make an inspiring speech at any rate. Why are they keeping him out of it all?"

"I think it may partly be down to guilt at the situation they've placed him in," said Philo, as they walked through the covered colonnade beside the lake in the new palace grounds. "But I think that there may be some internal family concerns over his maturity and judgement."

"He's not much like his brother at the same age. Titus knew where to aim his charm even as a child of ten," said Epaphroditus.

"He's inexperienced and a little young for his age, from what I've seen. Times being what they are."

"Tricky?"

"Yes, sir. Tricky is the word I think. It is very tricky and delicate and I believe they fear if they involve Domitian in the plans he may—"

"Take on the mantle of Caesar and fuck things up?" suggested Epaphroditus.

Philo gave a small cough. "Something like that, sir." Philo added quietly a judgement of his own, "I think they're wrong, sir. I think he's cleverer than they give him credit for."

Epaphroditus hadn't seen enough of Domitian to tell what the young man might be capable of. But he trusted Philo's judgement.

"I think you need to start preparing him for what is coming."

Philo nodded. "He's the emperor's son. He needs to know how the palace works as a bare minimum. Otherwise, how will he cope?"

"Well, Philo, there's a good project for you. Training the emperor's son up to the standard you desire."

Philo thought for a moment and then said, "I think I'll enjoy that."

FIFTY-FOUR

"He's meant to be waiting in Aquilia for Muscianus!" cried Caenis, squishing the scroll in her grip. "What's he playing at? He's ruining everything we'd planned."

"I believe he's making a play for prominence," answered Flavius.

"He's not going to get it," Caenis said. "Does he think rampaging down Italy will commend him to Vespasian?"

"I imagine he thinks he'll take the city and my brother will be grateful for his victory."

Caenis pulled a face. "I don't want Primus anywhere near Rome, not if he's going to treat it like Verona. Ye gods!" She stared upwards at the ceiling of Flavius' study. "We had it all planned. A bloodless victory. We would cut off the grain supply whilst working on turning Caecina. There is no need for all this."

"Yet it has happened."

"You are always so calm," "smiled Caenis"—would she smile? "You are always so calm," commented Caenis.

Flavius sat forward. "Primus is a liability and I quite agree that we don't want him claiming such a bloody win. It'll taint my brother from the outset. But all is not lost if we can persuade

Vitellius to step aside before Primus and his bloody band get here. Vitellius has lost his keenest advisors. Valens, Lucius, and Triaria are all travelling towards our forces,". "From what we've heard, courtesy of Philo and Epaphroditus, I'm not sure Vitellius wants it enough to fight for it personally. Oh, he likes the trappings of being emperor, I grant you. But he's no ruler if he has no inclination to rule. We know the urban troops are on our side, and with Primus butchering his way down we have the perfect bargaining chip."

Caenis' eyes brightened. "Step aside or die." Then, "Do you think he'll go for it? Do you think he'll step aside?"

"I think it's got to be worth trying. This latest request of Primus, I'll admit, unnerves me."

Caenis was in full agreement. "I'm not sending him Domitian. I don't care if he's on our side. I don't trust him."

"Me neither," said Flavius. "So let us secure Rome before he can butcher us all."

* * *

Domitian could hear the rain pounding against the roof, sloshing out of the gutters. Into the darkness of the room, he said, "What will happen to me?"

He was not looking for an answer. It wasn't a question. More a voiced fear. One born of the dead of night when such thoughts bubble upwards. He had thought Mina asleep, but she mumbled into the pillow, "What will happen what?"

"If Vitellius' army defeats my father's," said Domitian to the ceiling. "I'll be killed, won't I?" Mina shuffled onto one elbow, tucking her loose wavy brown hair behind her ears.

"I doubt it. Otho kept Vitellius' family safe and Salvius, Otho's nephew, is still wandering about the place being alive. Besides which, I've vowed to protect you. Nothing is going to happen to you."

She rolled off her elbow onto her side. "Get some sleep, grumpy posh boy. I want to practise my archery tomorrow, and I want a mounting or two. I need you refreshed. Sleep!"

Domitian dutifully closed his eyes. Then popped them open again. "I snuck into my uncle's office. There was a letter from this Antonius Primus man. He was instructing Uncle Flavius to hand me over to him."

Mina yawned. "You're still here, so I'm assuming your uncle declined."

"What's going to happen when Primus and his men get here? What will they do to Uncle Flavius if he refuses to hand me over?"

"Urgh," said Mina, sitting up in bed. "What is it?" she demanded of him. "What is it really that's making you worry? Because you know that your uncle and stepmother would never let you be hurt. You know that Philo and Epaphroditus are working at the palace on your behalf. You know that both I and the city cohorts are sworn to protect you. So what is it?"

Domitian struggled to articulate the whirling emotions inside him. "I have this position I didn't ask for and it's put everyone in danger. And I'm not sure I'm up to it, being an emperor's son. What do I say to all those soldiers who are fighting for father? What are they going to think when they meet me? What if I mess it all up? What if something I do unravels father's entire plan?"

Mina rubbed the sleep from her eyes. "Gods, you don't half worry. I swear Otho didn't worry this much about the 70,000 men marching in his direction. Look, let's be frank."

She'd never been anything but in Domitian's company since the day he'd met her.

"There is nothing to be done about any of that right now. You may as well go to sleep."

She lay back down again and turned on her side away from him. Domitian lay on his back staring into the darkness. He was going to mess this all up, wasn't he?

He sort of wished he could talk to Nerva. Nerva, he felt sure, would have more practical advice than Mina. Nerva would know the exact things an emperor's son needed to do to be respected. Nerva knew stuff like that. He stared into the blackness. He wished Nerva was with him.

FIFTY-FIVE

"Sir, sir."

Caecina opened his eyes to see Talos' nostrils flaring above him.

"Another tribune has been released by Primus. He's in the mess hut."

"Another one? How many is that now?" asked Caecina, sitting up in bed, the blanket slipping off to reveal his naked, muscled chest.

Talos swallowed hard and concentrated on retrieving the relevant facts. It was a useful distraction from the sight of Caecina standing totally naked as his body slave rushed to bring his clothes.

"Err, I believe it's six now," said Talos.

"I wonder what he'll tell us."

As it happened, pretty much the same tale as the previous five soldiers released by Primus. The enemy legions were multiplying and they were determined.

"Primus is boasting that he's going to take Rome within the month."

Caecina felt his stomach muscles tense. "He does know that I have the mighty German legions, doesn't he?"

"He knows alright," said the soldier. "And he isn't frightened. He gave me a message to pass on to you personally."

"Oh yes?" enquired Caecina as casually as he could manage.

"He told me to tell you that Vespasian will welcome you and your legions to his campaign."

Caecina threw his head back. "He has the cheek to suggest treason to me! To suggest my legions would give up without a fight! Who does he think he is? Who does he think I am? The audacity!"

Caecina exited with a sweep of his plaid cloak.

Talos found him pacing outside his tent.

"Sir?" he enquired.

"This Primus! This Vespasian!" stormed the handsome man. "How dare they! How dare they think that I would switch sides just like that. How dare they! I am loyal to Vitellius, always. Admittedly, I may have switched allegiances once. But only once. And only because Galba had committed a heinous act by overthrowing the rightful emperor, Nero. I am no traitor. That demonstrates I'm no traitor. I turned on my own mentor for the good of Rome! The good of Rome!"

"And Vitellius is the right emperor for Rome!" said Talos, adding an apologetic "sir" to his declaration of loyalty.

"Yes, yes he is," replied Caecina. "He is the rightful emperor. The Senate have declared such. This Vespasian is a usurper. Nothing more. A traitor and a usurper who would do no good for Rome. None at all. Vitellius will lead us to—" he paused, and thought for a moment.

"He will lead us to, sir?" prompted Talos.

"Err, yes. Sorry, what was I saying?"

"Vitellius is the rightful emperor who will lead us to...?"

"Yes, who will lead us to—" Caecina paused again. Unsure in his thoughts. Or even whether he had any thoughts.

The name Vitellius conjured up a fat man lying on a couch, stuffing meat into his mouth as eunuchs whirled around him. Thoughts on eunuchs brought back memories of that eunuch that had hanged itself. Caecina had been present when they cut it down. Asiaticus cursing it as it hung against the wall. Its feet dangling, still encased in beautiful, glittering golden sandals.

Caecina had rather liked that eunuch. It could certainly dance. Yet there it hung. It was such a pity. Such an unnecessary death. Picturing Sporus dance reminded him of those other, less talented dancers who gyrated at all times through every meeting, no matter what the context. Except that there weren't that many meetings because the emperor was frequently too drunk to participate. Just as his drunk soldiers lying comatose scattered throughout the palace corridors.

Caecina was hit by an unexpected emotion. He stared wide-eyed at the ground. No longer the figure of action but one of inaction. A whirling of sensations he couldn't place and one singular image: a grotesquely fat man lying drunk on a couch, snoring.

"I'm back to bed," he told Talos.

He pushed open the flaps to his tent. Stepping inside, he saw her. Caecina froze. Partly from shock but also from her stunning beauty. She was dressed in a loose chiffon gown of the lightest of peach shades. Her dark hair falling in ringlets down the nape of her neck. Round that neck, a heart-shaped pendant dipped into the gap between the swell of her breasts.

"Salonina!" he finally managed to gasp.

She held open her arms. "My stud. My lover. My darling."

He walked into her embrace, resting his head on her shoulder as she hugged him.

"I've missed you," he said. "I've missed you so much."

Nymphidia kissed his head. Stroking his hair, she told him, "I've missed you too, my darling. But I'm back now. I'm back for always."

He raised his head up and with troubled eyes said, "I don't know what to do anymore."

She pushed his head back to her shoulder. "You need my help, my darling, and I'm here to give it."

Outside the tent, Talos gave a smile. He rushed off to write to Philo: Nymphidia was in place.

FIFTY-SIX

There was no talking until the morning. The evening was for one purpose only: lovemaking. Actively and repeatedly.

Nymphidia awoke just as a tiny slither of light penetrated the tent. She reached out a hand. It met no firm flesh, just a space.

Sitting up, she said, "Caecina?"

"Here."

Her eyes adjusted to the morning gloom. He was sitting in just his trousers by the desk, a scroll on his lap.

"The naval fleet at Ravenna have defected. They have declared themselves for Vespasian."

Nymphidia reached for her gown, and pulled it over her head. "Then there is no time, my darling. You need to act now."

Before she had left Rome, Caenis had provided her with a very pretty speech to deliver, complete with many sensible and detailed points on why Vespasian would make a better emperor than Vitellius. Nymphidia had read it through and then thrown it back at Caenis, telling her friend, "It's wonderful, dear, but there are too many words. He'll never sit still to the end of it. Let me talk to him how I see fit. I know him too well."

Nymphidia talked of the inevitability of Vespasian's triumph and the increasing number of legions backing him. Of Antonius Primus' bloody path through Italy and what might happen if he got to Rome.

"Think of your men. Will you risk their lives against Primus? They can't win those back again. Once they're dead, they're dead. Look how easily Primus is capturing men to send to you. I ask, is it worth it? Is it really worth it for a regime that will collapse the moment they get to Rome? The city troops are loyal to their previous commander, Flavius. They'll not fight for Vitellius. Rome is a done deal. Why risk all for such a hopeless cause? It's a waste of all these good men. And it's a waste of your talents."

Caecina listened to this, still naked aside from his trousers and a sheepskin he'd hung over his shoulders. His face betrayed his inner torment. Nymphidia ramped it up a little.

"On my way here, all the talk was that Primus wants to capture you and Valens to display in his triumph."

Caecina gave a gasp and looked upwards. "My gods!" he breathed.

Nymphidia reached over and clasped his large hands in hers. "My darling, you need to get on the right side of this. Think how Primus will view you if you bring over so many men to add to his forces. Think how grateful he will be. And Vespasian, when he hears. This could be the decisive, turning point of the war and the glory is all yours, my darling. All yours."

There was a moment's silence as Caecina digested this. Then he said, "You're right. You're always right."

He kissed her on the lips and they were momentarily distracted in a grapple of some passion.

"My darling, Salonina," he gushed as he nibbled at her neck.

"My handsome buck!" she sighed, one hand reaching for his most receptive of spots.

There followed a rampant fucking against the desk. Nymphidia sat on it, soft buttocks safely away from sharpened pens, legs spread wide as Caecina thrust into her.

He gave a cry of triumph as he exploded inside her, matched very much by Nymphidia's exaggerated scream.

"Oh my darling that was—"

She was cut off by Caecina. Pulling his trousers back up, he said, "I'll do it. I'll win it for Vespasian."

Nymphidia embraced him, smiling behind his head.

FIFTY-SEVEN

Valens' journey had not been a comfortable one. Though he'd affected a rapid recovery from his illness, his stomach muscles were still raw from their spasms. Every jerked movement of his horse was a painful reminder. Still, that couldn't be helped. At least he was on the move. On the move with considerably fewer men thanks to that bastard Caecina. But on the move nonetheless.

It was good to put some air back in his lungs. To be out of his bedroom where he had rolled and moaned for a month now. It was good to be soldiering again. To be poring over maps and discussing plans with his associates. It was what Valens was good at.

It was At Falerii, Valens was told of the Ravenna fleet's defection.

"Traitors!" yelled Valens, slamming a fist on to the table. The map lying on it jumped a clear inch upwards. It was hastily pinned back down with glass paperweights by a slave.

"Sir," said tribune Popius. "If we move today, we could reach Cremona and join with the legions there."

"It would force a reckoning with Primus," said another advisor. "Joined together, our forces would far outnumber his. We will crush him."

All four men present leaned over the map and began plotting their route.

"Two days marching maximum."

"If we march double time and rest the men overnight, all will be decided by the nones."

"Wait!" said Valens straightening himself. "Those legions are the ones under Caecina's control, right?"

"Yes, sir."

"We wait," said Valens. "We send word to Vitellius asking for reinforcements and we wait for them before moving."

"But sir, we already have forces in place at Cremona. If we move quickly to join them, we have an unbeatable army. The same size as the one that crushed Otho."

"No," said Valens. "We wait. Caecina cannot be trusted."

He left his advisors blustering and red-faced. He didn't care. He knew Caecina. He knew that idiot boy well. In Valens' mind, there was but one course he would take. Glory-mad, he would force an encounter early with Primus and be utterly defeated. In which case, Valens' lesser force would be in danger without those reinforcements. Better to wait and then mop up the idiot boy's actions, thought Valens.

He returned to his tent where a line of young girls and eunuchs had been lined up for his selection. Valens saw no reason why he shouldn't take the trappings of the palace on campaign with him.

* * *

It wouldn't be seemly for a woman to be present. Nymphidia waited in the tent while Caecina talked to his senior officers and centurions at the camp's headquarters. He was right, she felt, to talk to the officers before the general men. Soldiers followed their superiors. Get the superiors in line first and it should be a smooth transition.

This was an erroneous supposition. Had she consulted with her fellow agent, Lysandria, she would have discovered that the men Caecina was now leading were not quite the sheep she assumed them to be. Valens, competent general that he was, had faced an outright mutiny. The troops had barely been brought back under his command. But she did not know this.

The tent flap was pulled back. Nymphidia sat up straight.

"Oh, Talos." Failing to keep the disappointment out of her voice, she added quickly, "How good to see you. What news?"

Behind his spotty skin, Talos grinned. "He was magnificent! He talked softly but they hung on his every word. He told them about the Ravenna fleet defecting and the low supplies. About how both Gaul and Spain were sworn to Vespasian. Then, when they were truly worried, he spoke of Vespasian's great qualities and how they shone in comparison with the current emperor. He concluded by saying how disappointed he was in Vitellius. How he had been deluded into following his cause by Valens. When all Valens wanted was money and women to abuse. They all swore allegiance instantly to Vespasian."

Nymphidia gave a sigh of relief.

* * *

The first the multitude of legionaries knew about this abrupt shifting of allegiance was when they returned from their day duties. Dinner being foremost on their minds, all were unaware until legionary Rusticus appeared in a barrack hut.

"'Ere, lads. Something odd just happened."

Oddness was always appealing to those who face the monotony of the march. Rusticus had a captive audience.

"I was just in headquarters handing over the roster for tomorrow. And I happened to look over to that plinth by the desk where the bust of the emperor usually sits. But it weren't there."

A collective sigh of disappointment greeted Rusticus' revelation.

"It fell off then," said Earinus.

"No, no it didn't. It's been replaced with some other geezer. An old guy. Less fat."

The consensus was that Rusticus was confused or wrong or confusedly wrong. There was much eagerness to confirm this against Rusticus' heated protests. So off they trotted to the headquarters building.

"Wot do you lot want?" enquired the centurion on duty. "Ain't you got a supper to eat?"

All eyes fell on the plinth and the bust that stood on it.

"'Ere Rusticus was right. That's not Vitellius."

"Too right it ain't," said the centurion. "We're fighting for Vespasian now. The commander has decided."

The small party of legionaries had a collective jaw-dropping moment.

"NOW GET LOST THE LOT OF YOU!" bellowed the centurion.

Rusticus and co departed before he could get his cudgel out. They were all deeply puzzled.

"It don't make no sense. Why would the commander surrender before we've even met them other fuckers in battle? We ain't lost a thing yet. And when we get hold of them fuckers, we'll extinguish the fucking light out of them."

There were grunts of agreement.

"Unless," said Rusticus, "that's been the plan the whole time."

"Eh?"

"Think about it," implored Rusticus. "Think about how we 'accidentally' marched Valens' legions with us. That wasn't no accident. It were deliberate, planned by the commander. Don't you see he's in the pay of this Vespasian and he's marched us all this way to hand us over to the enemy."

The horror of this sunk in.

"But we're the German legions!" they protested. "The finest fighters in all the empire. And he's handing us over to Primus like slaves he's purchased."

"Dishonour!"

"Treachery!"

"Disrespect!"

FIFTY-EIGHT

Nymphidia had spent the evening reassuring Caecina that he had made the right decision. This took the form of an awful lot of sex, but also a fair amount of hair stroking and soothing. He'd perked up when she'd informed him of the exact measure of Vespasian's gratitude.

"You have done a courageous thing today, my love," she told him during another bout of hair stroking. "Men will look back and see how decisive you were. How you realised the superiority of Vespasian's claim before anyone else. They will think how clever you were."

Such had been her persuasive bolstering that Caecina swallowed this whole.

"You are right. I was right. All is right."

He stood, stretching his arms above his head. Nymphidia inwardly sighed in appreciation at the six feet of man hunk that Caecina was. He was gorgeous. Gorgeous enough to be included in Nymphidia's home harem of men. He'd look perfect stood beside her handsome Hercules. She was loath to leave her handsome young buck alone in the world of palace politics. What if some brainless missy got her fingernails into him? She could guide him entirely in the wrong direction. A thought that for unknown reasons distressed Nymphidia.

Ye gods! Did she want Caecina as a project? Like Caenis and her project, Vespasian?

"What are you smiling at?" he asked.

She answered honestly, "You, my darling."

He kissed her on the lips, then said, "I'm just going out to get a bit of fresh air. To clear my head."

A slight breeze could have cleared the contents of Caecina's head. Nymphidia nonetheless agreed that this was an excellent idea.

A slave draped his plaid cloak across his shoulders and fastened the Celtic brooch at his throat.

Stepping outside his tent he found a group of twenty or so soldiers.

"Men," he murmured.

Rather than the expected salute, he was greeted by snarling faces.

"Men?"

One stood forward. He held in his hands a chain.

"Men?" said a now nervous Caecina.

"Ahh, you've got him." Fabius Fabullus strode forward.

The men parted to let him through. All twenty saluted him. Fabius Fabullus stood in front of Caecina.

"Caecina Alienus, I am here to inform you that due to your treachery, your epic treachery," the troops sneered and made low growling sounds at this, "you have been deemed unsuitable for command of the great and loyal German legions!"

Cheers.

"The men have elected me as their commander."

More cheers.

"We shall be marching to defeat Primus. You, you treacherous slug, we shall send back to the true emperor, Vitellius, the man you have so easily abandoned. Chain him up, Discus!"

Inside the tent, Nymphidia hurriedly threw on her clothes. Minerva's virginity, they hadn't anticipated this! Soldiers deciding between themselves who they would fight for. What a fatal miscalculation! Caenis had told Nymphidia to concentrate on turning the commander with the assumption that the troops would follow. She needed to get word to Caenis to warn her there were new players in the game.

The tent flaps were pulled open and in strode a tall, dark-haired man.

"This is my tent now. I am the commander. And you are, woman?"

Nymphidia calculated quickly. Then she smiled and said, "I am whatever you want me to be, master."

Talos, stood in a corner, flared his nostrils in indignation on behalf of his boss.

FIFTY-NINE

Marius Maturus, governor of the Maritime Alps, read the dispatches with a sinking heart. It really did seem all over for the emperor he had sworn allegiance to. The provinces were turning over to Vespasian at a rapid rate. And now even Valens' forces at Ariminum had declared for the rival emperor.

"Sir?" prompted Maturus' second-in-command.

Maturus gave a sigh. One with the weariness of a governor who in the last eighteen months had faced the same dilemma four times: which side are you on?

Make the wrong decision and watch an army rampage through your town and sell your citizens into slavery. What kind of world was this when Roman attacked Roman?

But maybe this was the end of this madness.

"Sir, are we declaring for Vespasian?"

"I have decided. We are declaring for V—"

He was cut off by the entry of an announcer.

"Fabius Valens."

"What? Here?"

The question was answered by the entrance of a grey-faced man dressed in military wear.

"Maturus, I have need of your assistance on behalf of the emperor," said Valens crisply.

There seemed no other path but to offer Valens a seat. Over a meal, Maturus deduced Valens had no idea that his own legions had defected. The commander had taken only four men with him when he'd heard of Caecina's defection and that of the naval fleets.

"It's all that idiot boy's fault," he spat. "That traitor! I should never have let him march without me. I knew he was a loose nut in the wheel with no loyalty, no steadfastness. You know there was some bitch in the spring. An Othonian spy. All she had to do was open her legs and he was hers to manipulate. He's no man. No commander. What commander tells his men the eve of a battle that they are going to abandon their pledge. Their honour? For all his trousers and cloak, he doesn't understand Germans at all. I'm only surprised they didn't strike him down on the spot!" He paused to take a long mouthful of wine.

"What are your plans now?" asked Maturus.

"I intend to head for Gaul. I can't face down Primus with the pitiful reinforcements I was sent. I left them in Ariminum for my troops to toughen up. I'll send for them when I have matters arranged."

"Matters?"

Valens took another sip of wine. His young eunuch slave stepped forward and wiped his master's mouth with dabs of a napkin. He was waved away with an impatient blow to his head from his master.

"I shall invoke the Gauls and Germans to rise as one and fight! How disgusted they will be with those that have turned! Traitors! I will see them punished when I am victorious. I shall see them crucified like the slaves to bribery and money they are."

The vengeance was all too evident in the spark of the grey man's eyes.

"I will embark for my ship tomorrow. Tonight, I will stay here," said Valens rising from the table.

"You are very welcome as my guest," said Maturus.

"Thank you," said Valens. "I assume you have whores. Send five to my room. I need to relax."

He strode out, followed by the little eunuch who told Maturus in a hushed whisper, "My master prefers them young. If you could, sir."

"Anything for a guest," responded Maturus and the eunuch exited happy.

"Well," said Maturus.

"Sir, every province surrounding us has declared for Vespasian," said his second-in-command.

"Yes, I am aware of that. Valens' situation is bleak. But you can't help but admire his loyalty. Would that I had the courage to take it to the very end. To the final fight in my limbs."

"Then we are…?"

"Yes, we are declaring for Vespasian. But let us get Fabius Valens off our land before we do."

"But surely if we captured him here, that would be very favourable to the new emperor."

"It would. But he is our guest, and shall be treated as such," insisted Maturus. "He leaves tomorrow anyhow. I doubt he'll get very far with this audacious scheme of his."

* * *

The boat lurched violently from side to side, the wood creaking ominously as it did. Usually this would have set off Valens' delicate stomach. Not today though. Today the commander was far too distracted to notice the storm rocking his vessel. His mind was full of one thought: vengeance.

Vengeance on Caecina for his cowardly desertion. Vengeance on his and all those legions that had abandoned their rightful emperor for that usurper. And vengeance on the entire world for ruining Valens' plans.

He had no doubts at all that he would achieve satisfaction. He imagined himself at the front of a huge army of barbarians.

One bigger than ever seen before. Bigger even than the one Julius Caesar had faced down. Except in this case, the barbarian army would triumph over the Roman one. Valens intended to sweep across Europe conquering all until he was satisfied. Then he would return to Rome and present Vitellius with Caecina's head.

Valens' thin lips twisted upwards at the thought of his handsome colleague reduced to just his pretty head. Would he look so pretty in death? Valens imagined Caecina collapsing before him. Begging him to forgive his grave treachery. But Valens would not forgive. He never forgave and he never forgot. He would have his reckoning!

"Sir!"

It was one of his attendants, clinging to the door frame to remain upright.

"Sir, the captain says we have to make landfall. The storm is growing fiercer. He's thinks we won't make it."

Valens felt the anger course through him. Thwarted yet again.

Just then the boat heaved to one side and threw both of them off their feet.

Sitting on the floor, his hand gripping the table edge in a vain attempt to anchor himself, Valens said, "Very well. We land."

It was a difficult mooring, what with the wind howling all around them. The captain warned them to stay below deck until all was secure. This Valens and his four attendants did. The commander gazed at his small party. It struck him as pathetic that a man who but a few months ago had stood at the front of 30,000 men should be reduced to this paltry number.

It was only temporary though, he told himself. Once he was before those Gallic tribesmen, he'd be all powerful again. After his successful conquest, nobody would be able to touch him! He'd be the most powerful man in the empire. More powerful than even the emperor. For what was Vitellius but a puppet?

A drunken puppet enjoying his eunuchs whilst Valens enjoyed all the power and respect men would be forced to pay him.

Last time he was in Gallic territory, he'd picked up a most beautiful girl: his Helen. Maybe he'd find another Helen to enjoy. That definitely had him smiling as he pictured all the ways he would defile her. So caught up was he in his sexual fantasies that he failed to notice that the boat's movement had changed from a violent lurch to a more gentle rolling.

He was woken from his reverie by the door above them opening.

He rose. "Captain, we have made shore?"

The man who walked down the stairway was not the captain. He was a Roman in full military wear. His eyes took in the five bodies.

"Which of you is Fabius Valens?"

Valens stood forward. "I am. And you are?"

The Roman ignored him, calling instructions over his shoulder. Ten legionaries trotted down the steps. The chamber was now very crowded.

"What is the meaning of this?" demanded Valens. "Who are you?"

Again the official ignored him. To his men, he said simply, "Kill them all."

"What are you talking about?" protested Valens as the soldiers approached. "I am Fabius Valens, consul of Rome."

"You were consul of Rome," said the official. "Our Imperial Majesty, Vespasian, will want to appoint his own consuls."

Valens was given no more time to protest. To demand. To insist. His head was taken clean off his neck with a single sword stroke. It bounced across the wooden floor and came to rest underneath the table, grey eyes staring upwards.

SIXTY

The first glimpse of Primus and his men had been early afternoon. Just a few cavalry. Fabullus sent out a small force of auxiliaries to intercept them. Throughout the day, Nymphidia watched more and more men exit the camp to meet the advancing Flavian forces. As the skies darkened, her instinct was telling her now was the time to get out.

She threw on her shawl and packed up a few belongings. Outside she saw more soldiers marching towards the gates. Surely they couldn't be intending to keep fighting through the night? Nymphidia had assumed Fabullus and his legions would soon be back to rest. To prepare. And to kick it all off again, come first light.

Right, time to go before she was stuck here with Primus' men battering their way in. Her feet did not move. Her gaze fell upon the tent where she knew Caecina was being held. The thought came from nowhere: I can't leave him. Nymphidia laughed. Oh, Cupid's bow and arrow! She was smitten, wasn't she? How utterly ridiculous. And how deliciously unexpected.

There were two legionaries guarding Caecina's prison. No match at all for Nymphidia.

"Soldiers! Soldiers!" she screamed.

What they saw was a beautiful woman, the commander's woman no less, in a dishevelled state. Her dress was torn at the shoulder. Her normally elegant hair was matted and tangled. To her head they saw a small cut.

"Madam?"

"Flavians!" she screeched. "They've penetrated the east perimeter!"

"What?!?" The two soldiers looked at each other.

"They're rampaging!"

"Oh mighty Jupiter!" swore one soldier as they both belted off to face down the invasion.

Nymphidia watched them go, then swept into the tent. Caecina was sat at his desk. Talos stood beside him.

"Salonina?" he asked, rising. "I thought—"

Whatever thought Caecina was about to divulge was lost to history. For at that moment Nymphidia took his beautiful face in her hands and delivered a kiss with all the impact of a battering ram.

Caecina was splintered.

"I love you," she said.

"I love you too," he responded.

Talos felt almost giddy with happiness.

"Right," said Nymphidia clapping her hands together. "Boys," including Talos in the conversation, "we need to escape this heavily guarded camp. Avoid the battle that is raging on all major routes. Avoid capture by either side. And get ourselves back to Rome. What do you say, darlings?"

Pulling Nymphidia to him, holding her against his body, Caecina grinned and declared, "I say it sounds like we face a thrilling adventure!"

Talos couldn't suppress a cheer escaping from his lips.

But a few miles away a fierce battle was being fought. The winner could expect to be sole ruler of the greatest of empires. The men with swords would decide who that would be.

SIXTY-ONE

"Go away, Marcia! Get out now!" snapped Philo.
This was so uncharacteristic as to elicit a shocked intake of breath from the slave.

Philo, immediately feeling guilty, not least because of the harsh look from Teretia, was giving him, quantified this with an apology. "I'm sorry, I didn't mean to yell but, errr…"

Did he really need to spell it out for her? He was in his bedroom. On the bed. In an unclothed state beneath the blanket with his similarly unclothed wife lying underneath him. A position that he'd yet to take advantage of.

Teretia had earlier announced earlier shyly, that she rather thought she wasn't sore anymore in that part. Philo, who though not entirely unsatisfied, was none the less extremely keen to resume relations of that sort. In fact, he could think of nothing nicer.

Being a loving and kind husband, he'd endeavoured to make the experience as comfortable as possible for his beloved wife. Having spent some time building her up to a suitably lubricated point, he was poised to enter what was now an urgent erection, when in walked Marcia with her crisp, "Master!"

Hence Philo's snapped response.

"I wouldn't have interrupted, Master. Only it's from the palace. The messenger that is."

Teretia wriggled out from under him.

"That sounds important, Philo."

"Yes, yes it does," he conceded with a sigh, as he rolled on to his back beside his wife. "Marcia, can you tell him I'll be there shortly. I need to get dressed."

"Yes, master."

She slipped out the door.

"Sorry," said Teretia kissing him on the lips.

Philo gave an exasperated sigh. "Later?"

"I suppose it will have to be."

He closed his eyes to avoid further tormenting himself with the alluring sight of his naked wife. Instead, he concentrated on the most unerotic, unalluring, positively deflating thing he could think of: Straton. As usual, the picture of his now-deceased abuser had the necessary wilting effect and he was able to out of bed and get dressed.

The messenger shot to attention as Philo entered the kitchen.

"Sir!"

"Let's have the verbal summary first please," ordered Philo.

"Yes, sir. The forces of Vespasian have defeated His Imperial Majesty's forces at Bedracium."

Philo's mouth formed an O shape. Marcia ceased stirring the porridge pot. Teretia said, "Philo?"

He took hold of his wife's hand and kissed the knuckles. "This is it," he told her. "Am I the first to get this news?" he asked the messenger.

"Yes, sir."

"And the emperor?"

"Has not been informed yet, sir."

Philo ran a hand through his dark hair. "Good. I have time. I need to go to Flavius' house. We'll need to get Domitian to safety and work out what happens now. I'm sorry but I don't know when I'll be back."

"I understand," said Teretia, a little tearfully. "And I'll be waiting for you."

Philo cupped a hand round her soft cheek. Kissing her, he told her quietly in a voice only for her, "I love you. I love you so much. Please try not to worry."

She nodded, her blue eyes filling with anxious tears.

* * *

It should have been a moment of great celebration. Vespasian's forces under Antonius Primus had defeated the fearsome German legions under the command of Fabullus. This was the moment they had all been waiting for. But the mood in Flavius' house was sombre, grim even, as Caenis, Flavius, and Epaphroditus listened in silence to Philo detailing what had happened after the battle.

Cremona was a town of some 20,000 inhabitants. Citizens. There was a fair on so these numbers had been swelled by day visitors. Why they had picked on it out of all the neighbouring towns to be the subject of what Philo nearly referred to as "unsubstantiated justification" was not clear. It was true that it had been Cremona where Valens and Caecina, back in the summer, had dedicated a series of games to Vitellius. But that was a poor excuse for what was reaped upon Cremona.

Flavius, elbow balanced on the arm of his chair, openly gasped with horror as Philo read from the dispatches. Caenis was silent, her stance frozen. Epaphroditus stared at the floor, his arms and head hanging loosely down.

While Primus was allegedly at the bath house washing off the grime of battle, 40,000 of his troops had stormed through Cremona. They'd plundered as if it were an enemy city. Women of all ages, citizens the lot of them, were used by the troops to sate their desires. The most beautiful were the subject of vicious fights as to who got to rape them. Sometimes the soldiers were reasonable and decided they should share this beauty. The beauty did not survive such forceful and repeated attentions.

Age was no protection, with reports of old ladies, grandmothers, abused by the troops. Along with toddlers and even babies. And here Philo had to pause to compose himself. Neither was gender a barrier to their lusts. Freeborn men and boys were subject to the same "sport".

Any lucky enough to survive their experience had been taken into slavery.

"They're citizens," said Flavius. "They can't be sold. It's against the law."

Epaphroditus gave a snort. "What law?"

Philo cleared his throat. Epaphroditus made a hand gesture for him to continue.

"There's nothing left. Nothing bar a single temple to Mefitis. They burned down every other building. There is no town of Cremona anymore."

Flavius blew air through his teeth. "In four days. That's what they did in four days."

"It'll be interesting to see how long it takes them to do the same to Rome," said Epaphroditus.

Philo's face was one of pure panic.

"Mucianus is only a day or two behind them now," said Caenis. "He'll get them back under control."

"I admire your optimism," said Epaphroditus.

"Now, now," said Flavius. "Let's focus on what needs to be done. I still believe there's a good chance of persuading Vitellius to step down voluntarily. He's not going to want to be at the mercy of those Cremona troops. He'll want to take the easy way out."

Epaphroditus ran a hand across his jaw. "What of his troops? We know from Nymphidia they're starting to have opinions of their own."

"They will change sides once they realise there's no hope and that victory is absolute."

Epaphroditus gave a, "Hmmm."

"Sir, the emperor has yet to be told about what's happened," interrupted Philo.

Epaphroditus got to his feet. "This is our moment, Flavius. Let's see if we can get the fat pig to step down."

Flavius got to his feet. "He has an infant son. That gives us something to bargain with."

"Maybe. Maybe not."

SIXTY-TWO

Caenis broke the news as gently and as calmly as she could. Domitian's eyes opened wide and his face moulded into a singular expression: terror.

"I have to leave? Why do I have to leave?" he asked.

"Because it is common knowledge that you are being held at your uncle's house. We need to move you somewhere else."

"Why? Why do I need to be hidden? What are people wanting me for? I haven't done anything. I'm nothing to do with any of this."

Caenis placed her hands over his.

"Domitian," she said softly. "You are the emperor's son. You will be a figurehead for some. An enemy for others. But I swore to your father I would keep you safe. And I shall. Artemina?"

Mina nodded. "I'll not let anything happen to you, grumpy posh boy. That's my mission."

Domitian did not look any happier.

An apologetic cough at the door announced Philo.

"Caenis, I've had the Praetorians recalled to the palace. I told them about Cremona and how the emperor is requesting all troops to comply with new orders."

"Good."

"Flavius' city troops are outside. They're waiting to take, ermm…" He threw a look at the distraught Domitian.

"Caenis, you're coming with me, right?" asked Domitian. "I don't want to go without you."

"Darling, you're going to be fine. You have Artemina."

"Too right! Ooh, I need to get some things." She dashed out.

"And Flavius will join you once this business with Vitellius is sorted."

Domitian didn't look any calmer, so Philo said, "I could go with you. Get you settled in. If that's of any help?"

Domitian's shoulders very slightly relaxed. "Please," he said.

* * *

Outside the front door, in the street, were six city guards. A ssmall-enough number not to be alarming when moving across the city. On seeing Domitian stood in the doorway, flanked by Caenis and Philo, they stood to attention and saluted.

Their commander stepped forward. Bowing his head he addressed Domitian, "Young Caesar, we are here to accompany you to safety."

Domitian was startled slightly at the title. Caenis squeezed his shoulder.

"Off you go."

She embraced him tightly, saying, "I am so very proud of how you have handled the last few months. Your father will be proud too."

Domitian doubted that. Feeling tearful, he turned away from his stepmother and went to join the guards. Artemina ran out. She had two bags filled with arrows and clubs slung over each shoulder. In her hands she held two bows.

"Because you never know!" she said.

As she passed Caenis, the older woman whispered to her, "His life is worth more than yours. Remember that. I will hold you to it."

Mina bowed her head. "I have a mission. I shall carry it out. You can trust me."

"Young Caesar, we have a litter for you. It is the most unobtrusive way. It will be thought you are some senator with his own protection," said the commander.

Domitian and Philo got into the litter. It was hoisted upwards by four bearers. Caenis walked over.

"This will soon be over."

"And then what?" asked Domitian. "I can't go back to my old life, my old home, can I? Everything has changed."

"Madam," prompted the commander.

"Yes, yes. You go."

She raised her palm up in a farewell. Then pulled the curtains of the litter shut.

The small party, Mina walking at the rear ever alert, departed through the Esquiline streets. When she could see them no longer, Caenis went back into the house.

"Tesca!" she called.

The slave appeared almost instantly. "Mistress."

"Organise a litter for me, please."

"Where to, mistress?"

"The Caelian Hill. Julia Lysandria and Gaius Baebius' house."

SIXTY-THREE

Epaphroditus had never asked an emperor to step quietly aside before. The usual way to remove an unwanted emperor involved high-level violence or a trip to see Lysandria. This was to be a wholly novel meeting. Walking through the palace corridors, accompanied by a small number of urban troops, Flavius possessed no doubts that they would succeed.

"The last year has surely given him enough examples of the prudence of stepping aside rather than fighting for it," he said.

Epaphroditus did not share Flavius' confidence in Vitellius' capitulation. He was of the firm opinion they should get Vitellius to cease being emperor the traditional palace way. There was nothing better than a well-ordered plot. As Nymphidius Sabinus could have attested. If he hadn't gone mad the previous summer and been offed by his own men.

Strangely, Epaphroditus didn't share such concerns with Flavius. He realised that no matter how infeasible it was, he really did want the city prefect's plan to succeed. It was the only way to stop further bloodshed, the likes of which had been seen in Cremona. Surely even Vitellius wouldn't want to inflict that upon Rome?

"Here we are," said Flavius, stopping outside the great doors to the banqueting hall.

"Here we are," repeated Epaphroditus, staring at the huge double doors. "Here we are indeed."

* * *

Vitellius lay on a couch. Not reclined on one elbow. That involved too much effort. Rather, he lay propped up into position by cushions. It could be day, it could be night time. Vitellius had no idea. Similarly, he had no idea how long he'd been in this room. True, the torches on the walls were half-burned down but they could have been replaced by slaves. They might have been replaced several times. Which would mean he had been there a very long time. Perhaps he had.

What had penetrated his stupor that day, or days, was the news. There had been a lot of news. A lot of messengers darting in and pronouncing.

First, there had been news that Caecina was near to Primus' troops. Then, that Caecina and his troops had gone over to Primus' side. Then, that Caecina had been arrested by his own soldiers who had remained loyal to Vitellius.

This flurry of events had barely scratched into Vitellius' consciousness when there came a series of demands from Valens. Closely followed by accusations as to where his reinforcements were. A further flurry of messengers told him, with increasingly grave voices, the status of several legions. Those loyal were few and diminishing. Those turning themselves over to the other side were many and growing.

It was too much to take in. Vitellius struggled to comprehend the vast change in his fortunes. That was when the final messenger arrived: bearing news of both Valens' execution and the defeat at Bedriacum.

He'd ordered everyone out after that. The flapping advisors who had no advice. The jingly eunuchs. The naked girls. Even the wine boys. And there he lay. An emperor or not an emperor? He was no longer sure. He gazed about at the palace walls, sipping at his wine and wondering what would happen now.

From the corner of his eye he saw a movement. He turned his fat head slowly. It was that announcer. The blond one whose mother used to do Agrippina's hair.

The announcer cleared his throat and said in that melodically deep voice of his, "Titus Flavius Sabinus and Tiberius Claudius Epaphroditus."

The two walked in.

"Ahhh, I have guests," said Vitellius. "Sit, sit. Do sit."

They obliged, sitting upright on a couch beside Vitellius' own.

"Welcome, friends." His gaze was far from friendly, more leering. "I've been ill, did you hear? Some stomach issues. Minor but inconvenient. I took myself to the villa in the Servilian Gardens. I thought the change in scenery would aid my recovery. It did. But while I was there, lying in my garden, I heard noises. Laughing and merriment. I sent my slaves to find the source. Apparently, Julius Blaesus was entertaining when his emperor lay sick." Vitellius gave a grunt of disapproval. "I had him killed. Such a lack of respect for one's emperor is unforgivable." His eyes rested on his visitors. "I had him poisoned. I had my slave pour it in his drink right in front of his own eyes. Then I told him to drink. How could he refuse such an order? Gentlemen, truly have I feasted my eyes on the spectacle of my enemy's death."

Epaphroditus could not suppress his instinctive shudder but he kept the neutral expression on his face.

"Vitellius," said Flavius. "You will have no doubt heard the news. My brother's forces have defeated your own at Cremona."

"I heard."

"I have letters here from my brother, from Primus, and from Muscianus." Flavius looked to his slave, who handed the round scroll box over. "All are in agreement. If you step down now, there will be no harm to yourself or your family. You can live out your days in a comfortable retirement in a location of your choice."

Ignoring the scroll box, Vitellius said, "And what if I said Rome as the location of my choice?"

"That is not on the table as an offer," said Flavius. "This is a good deal. A practical deal. Read the letters. See how much we all want a blood-free solution."

"It's just one battle," said Vitellius. "Who is to say I won't win the next one."

Epaphroditus leant forward. "Imperial Majesty," he said, respectfully, born of nearly fifty years of dutiful imperial service to men he secretly did not rate. "The provinces are changing sides one by one. Spain. Gaul. Britain. Judaea. Egypt. Syria," listed Epaphroditus. "The empire is turning to Vespasian's side and there is nothing you can do to stop it. The best decision you can make is to stand down now. It will secure your safety and that of your family."

Vitellius scratched at his stomach. "Is that an order? My entertainments coordinator giving me an order? What a world this has become when the likes of you feel emboldened enough to issue orders to your betters. Though I suppose it is Saturnalia, perhaps it is fitting."

"It is a strong suggestion, Imperial Majesty, based on the facts available to me. I advise you to stand down for the good of Rome," said Epaphroditus.

Vitellius gave a barked laugh. "The good of Rome? What Rome? My Rome or your Rome? You think I don't remember you, don't you?"

Epaphroditus' jaw stiffened.

"But I do. I remember everything. Everyone. It's odd isn't it, Flavius, how we struggle up the career ladder from post to post. The endless electioneering and securing of patrons. The vast sums of money distributed. Sitting through the dullest of dinner parties with the men that matter. All to secure a position worthy of our birth. It's hard work. It really is."

"We do all of that so that Rome may be run by the best men," said Flavius.

"All those years of toil to get where we are now," continued Vitellius. "Yet all they have to do is suck the right cock at the right time." He looked directly at Epaphroditus. "And bang, they are chief secretary. I sometimes think you slaves have it easier."

Epaphroditus linked his fingers in his lap to stop them flying up to his neck. It was with exhausting self-control that he managed to say in a still-polite, respectful tone, "I urge you to consider this offer, Imperial Majesty."

"Vitellius," prompted Flavius into this poisonous atmosphere. "This offer is the best you will receive."

"Primus and his troops are en route to Rome. They will kill you, Imperial Majesty. They will kill your family."

The emperor belched loudly, a stench wafting from that red mouth. Epaphroditus flinched backwards in disgust. This made Vitellius laugh. A deep merriment that wobbled his chins.

"I should have finished you off when I had the chance," he said. "Fucking bum boy." Then to Flavius: "Noble gentleman, tell your brother and his associates I shall accept his kind offer. It's his. All of this is his." He swept a fat arm in the air. "You look shocked. Did you think me braver than this?" He grinned, his eyes flashing with amusement. "I am not. I have no desire to risk my neck, even for these facilities. It's been fun. A lot of fun." Another grin. "Shame about that eunuch. He was quite delightful. Positively the best buggering I've dished out. Better even than you." He was looking at Epaphroditus again.

"You have made the right choice," said Flavius. "My brother will be generous, you can be sure of that."

"How generous? I want a villa. A big one by the sea. And enough money that I need not grubby myself any further."

"It shall be so," said Flavius. He held out a hand. Vitellius' chubby fingers gripped it and they shook on it. "You will need to announce your abdication to your troops. That way there can be no misunderstanding that you made this decision freely."

"I did," yawned Vitellius. "Now if you would kindly get out. I want to enjoy my dancing eunuchs one last time."

That was how they left him. The emperor that no longer was. Prostrate on a couch as eunuchs danced all around him.

Outside the door Flavius gripped Epaphroditus' shoulder in support.

"Vile man," said the secretary.

"A vile man who'll live out his days on the coast because he finally did one good thing," said Flavius. To Epaphroditus' sceptical face, "Why he decided to step down doesn't matter. He did so, and he's saved many lives as a result."

Epaphroditus shook off Flavius' hand. "I don't trust him."

SIXTY-FOUR

Domitian stared out of the window, down to the Forum, then up again to the spectre of the palace's looming presence.

"Why here?" he asked. "I can see the palace from here. I can practically wave to Vitellius. It doesn't seem very safe."

"Oh, I don't know," said Mina, wandering about, sizing up the room. "From up here on the Capitoline Hill, we can see all around. No fucker can sneak up on us."

"Your uncle felt it an easier ground to defend," said Philo. Seeing Domitian's face fall, he quickly added, "If it should come to that. And, if it does come to that, the Temple of Jupiter is next door. It would be sacrilege of the worst kind to attack the god's temple. Jupiter would be sure to wreak vengeance on the perpetrators." Philo gave a shudder.

Mina's eyes brightened. "Will there be a massive battle? In Rome itself? Cool."

"Hopefully it won't come to that," said Philo. "Flavius should be able to talk Vitellius into abdicating and a peaceful solution found. The urban cohorts are positioned around the building and area for your safety."

"Thank you," said Domitian.

The young Caesar sat down on the chair beside the window. He looked troubled.

"I wonder when my father and Titus will get here. I hope they've set off already. It's a long way from Judaea." He gazed out of the window again.

"What's he like, your father?" asked Mina. "If he's going to be my master, it would be nice to know a bit more about him."

"Well, err," struggled Domitian, picturing a bald man appearing intermittently in his life, "I don't know really. He's just my father. That's all."

Mina made a pish noise.

"He's a good man," said Philo quietly from the door.

"You know him, my father?"

Philo nodded. "I travelled with the emperor, Nero that is, in Greece. Your father did also. I got to know him a little."

Mina turned to Philo. "What is he like, the new master? Tell me all." She patted the space beside her on the bed. Philo chose not to use it. "Go on. I want to hear. I know all about what happened in Greece from Sporus." She paused at the mention of the eunuch, needing a moment to compose herself. "He recounted in great glee all the shenanigans that took place. We used to sit in Alex's room, the three of us—me, Alex, and Sporus—and he would tell us tales of his wedding in Delphi or the chariot race at the Olympics." Though her eyes were moist, she smiled at the memory. "Alex and I were never sure how much of it was true."

"All of it, I should imagine," said Philo. "It was quite a trip."

"He never mentioned a Vespasian. Though actually he never mentioned you either, Philo, or anyone else much. It was all about him."

Philo gave a small smile. "That sounds like Sporus."

"Yeah, it does," said Mina with a strong hint of sadness. She shook this off with an enforced brightness. "So, grumpy posh boy's dad, what's he like? Gossip please. I need it. Please."

Giving into her pleading, Philo said, "He was nice. Polite to the staff. Kind. Caring, even."

Domitian's eyebrows rose. "Caring?"

That definitely didn't sound like his father. He was brusque, offhand, and critical of Domitian.

"He, err… Well, he was kind to me. At a difficult point. When he didn't need to be. I appreciated it. It meant a lot to me. At that time."

Mina, her forehead wrinkled, spoke for the room when she said, "Eh?"

Philo shuffled his feet. One hand on the door handle. Eyes firmly fixed on the floor. "I wasn't very happy," he explained cautiously. "Not back then. Not at all. I didn't want to come back. Not to Rome, and the palace, and things as they were. I was going to… I'd decided not to come back. Your father talked to me. He persuaded me that things weren't always going to be as they were. And he was right." Philo looked up. "I met Teretia. And we had Horace. And that would never have happened if I had—"

"Killed yourself," completed Mina.

"Yes," admitted Philo, sadly.

Mina wiped at her eyes, "Well, that didn't cheer me up in the slightest."

"Sorry," said Philo. "I think he'll make a good emperor. I wouldn't have done any of this if I didn't think that."

"That's good enough for me," said Mina. "Anything to add, grumpy young Caesar?"

"He said the same thing to me," said Domitian. "About things getting better. When my mother died and I was sad. He told me not to worry because things would be better in the future. That things always were. I thought he was callous because now he could spend more time with Caenis. But he wasn't at all."

He looked thoughtful.

"Making things better," said Mina. "That's what he's about, isn't it? He thinks things should always be better. When they're not, he steps in to make them. That's what he's been doing.

He's been watching for what happened after Nero died, to see if they were better. And when they weren't, he decided he would make them better."

"Father is a doer. Caenis is always saying so."

"That's it then. He knows how we've all been suffering. He's come to rescue us and sort it all out!" declared Mina. "He's going to be the best emperor ever! Isn't he, Philo?"

Philo thought of diligent, decent Flavius and how alike the brothers were. He thought of the dispatches he'd seen on Vespasian's military expeditions. He thought of a man who had sat with a slave in the pits of despair until he was convinced he would not kill himself. He had sat the whole night with Philo when he could have been anywhere else. He could have been with the emperor. Or the other senators. Or even Caenis. But he hadn't. He'd sat with a slave that wasn't even his, the whole night long.

Philo looked to Domitian. "Your father will be an excellent emperor."

SIXTY-FIVE

Lysandria chewed on a fingernail, watching as Caenis read the tablet. She handed it back to the messenger.

"Thank you. You are dismissed."

"Well?" demanded Lysandria.

Caenis smiled. "He's stepping down! Flavius and Epaphroditus talked him round."

Lysandria gave a squeal and embraced Caenis. "Excellent. Excellent."

"It is," beamed Caenis. "It truly is. For once, something has actually gone to plan. I don't mind admitting that I am relieved." She held a palm over her heart. "Very relieved."

"What happens now?" asked Lysandria.

"Vitellius is going to leave the palace first thing tomorrow. He will make a short address to the crowd and leave the Palatine an ordinary citizen."

"Wow," breathed Lysandria, sitting herself down on a couch. "That is really to Flavius' credit he's achieved this. It's not how we usually get rid of emperors."

The two palace old-hands shared a look born of decades of exposure to deadly imperial politics.

"The dynasty that great Augustus founded is dead. This is a new time. A new era," said Caenis. "Things will be done differently. They will be done better."

* * *

It was Epaphroditus who managed all the arrangements for the emperor's abdication. It had meant further exposure to the man shortly to be dethroned. He wasn't sure what he had expected. Some contrition? Regrets? He supposed he'd expected at least some torment of emotions given the circumstances. But Vitellius had exhibited none of this. He'd been more concerned over his choice of toga than the news of Valen's death.

Even Epaphroditus had struggled to disguise his shock at this. It was Valens who'd first pushed Vitellius as emperor. Who'd marched down tens of thousands of men from Germania. Who'd led the successful victory over Otho's forces. Without Valens, Vitellius would never have become emperor. Yet Vitellius' reaction to his death was one of nonchalance: he couldn't give a fuck.

This strengthened Epaphroditus' resolve for an orderly transition of power. This man should not be emperor. Galba, he knew from Philo, had genuinely believed only he could sort out a post-Nero Rome. Otho had become emperor accidentally but had been determined to do the right thing, to rule wisely. Vitellius had no such thoughts. Rome was his pleasure palace to enjoy. He had no thoughts further to this. He had to go.

To this end he'd kept his cool through the multitude of points to be agreed. Despite Vitellius' frequent references to his wine boy past. He stood on the steps of the palace, his breath misting out from his mouth, watching the traders set up their stalls in the Forum below. He'd arranged a small crowd to be present. A selection of carefully vetted people unlikely to set off a riot. That was one reason why the abdication was taking place so early in the day. Epaphroditus wanted no flurry of rumours and half-truths to seep into the city before Vitellius spoke. He wanted the thing done. To be seen to be done. Then Flavius could seamlessly take up the reins of power until his brother was in situ.

A noise behind him alerted him. He turned to see Lysander.

"I'm ready, sir."

"I hope your voice is good. This will be the final time you get to announce Emperor Vitellius."

Lysander was too well-practised in palace politics to offer any pleasure or displeasure at this. His face betrayed nothing. Lysandria had brought her boy up well to survive the fierce political palace factions. Lysandria had no allegiance to anyone. She took the money and she acted. Which is why, no doubt, Caenis moved to secure her services early.

"I suppose this is it," said Epaphroditus to the air. Then, to Lysander, "The emperor is ready?"

"Yes, he's waiting at the door with his family."

The addition of Galeria and Vitellius' young son had been Epaphroditus' idea. A guarantee that Vitellius would stick to the agreed script. After that he was free to leave with his family and depart for the promised seaside villa. It wouldn't be much fun in December, Epaphroditus thought, but the cash handed over would provide enough to keep Vitellius in entertainments until the summer hit.

The hand-picked crowd were ready and waiting, shuffling from foot to foot to keep warm. It was time to bring the emperor out.

The great doors of the palace were swung open followed by the blare of a trumpet.

"I said no trumpets!" Epaphroditus said to Midas.

Midas gave an apologetic shrug. "Sorry, sir. It's that Boethius, he gets carried away."

"Report it to the overseers. He can have five lashes. I distinctly said no trumpets. This needs to be low key. We don't want to attract attention."

"From one trumpet blast, sir?" queried Midas. Spotting Epaphroditus' displeasure, he said, "I'll get Boethius' whipping organised."

"Yes, you do that."

* * *

Magnus sat up with a start. "What was that?" he asked his colleagues.

"Sounded like a trumpet blast," murmured Acer, rolling over and going back to sleep.

Magnus lay back down, but found sleep eluded him. He got up and leant against a nearby wall. His head hurt. In fact, it pounded. He'd had a few drinks, hadn't he? More than a few. A many. The thought had him retching.

And he wasn't in the Praetorian camp either, was he? The Praetorian camp did not have walls so pretty. The frescoes swirled in front of Magnus' eyes into one mush of colour. Urgh.

Looking about, he determined he was in a Corridor. Surrounded by his fellow soldiers, all slumped asleep on the ground.

Ahhh, he must be at the palace. It all came back to him. The drunken gambling. The fights. The endless booze. The passing out in the corridor. A usual night.

"Never again, hey Acer?"

He gave Acer a kick with his boot.

Two slaves trotted passed Magnus.

"Epaphroditus is saying five lashes I'm afraid, Boethius."

"Five? Really? Just for a single note?"

"I have no sympathy. You were told no trumpets. So why did you trumpet?"

"It's like a habit. I can't help it. My trumpet fingers twitch and my lips purse and then parp! I've gone and done it. Anyway, it seemed fitting. It's not every day an emperor is forced to abdicate. It seemed fitting."

Magnus blinked. "What?" He called after the departing Midas and Boethius, "What was that you said? About the emperor? What did you say?"

The two slaves turned.

"What did you say?" demanded Magnus.

"He's stepping down as emperor, Vitellius is," explained Midas. "Vespasian will be emperor now."

Magnus' hungover brain struggled to process this. When it had, he said to the space where Midas and Boethius had been. "Says who? Who says Vespasian is emperor?"

He kicked a boot into Acer. "Wake up, you fuckers! Wake up now!"

SIXTY-SIX

It was, Epaphroditus conceded, quite a performance. Perhaps not wholly unexpected from a man who'd convinced five emperors he was a kindred spirit. Vitellius had walked down the palace steps dressed in black, surrounded by palace slaves who'd been instructed to weep, or face a punishment that would definitely bring tears to their eyes. Beside him had walked Galeria, pale of face. Their young son had been carried alongside in a litter, as if being taken to his own funeral.

It was a vision designed to show abject surrender. Nobody should believe that Vitellius had any hope of remaining emperor. Thus, the transfer of power to Vespasian should be smooth. Or so Epaphroditus calculated. There were two things he hadn't factored into this plan. First, just how good an actor Vitellius was. When he made his speech of abdication, even Epaphroditus began to feel sympathetic. Especially when Vitellius, with tears in his eyes, held up the tiny figure of his son and begged the crowd to be merciful and care for him.

And second, that his well-selected crowd might grow. Grow it certainly did. It started with a few soldiers who melted into the group. Somehow, word must have leaked out what was happening. The select handful of witnesses began to swell in number. Epaphroditus, stood a few feet behind the Imperial family, watched in alarm as a positive mob began to gather.

"And so, my friends, my subjects, I must step down from this position of servitude to you and to Rome," announced Vitellius. He drew from his belt a dagger, the very insignia of empire. "Behold!" he cried. "I resign my empire. I shall place it in the Temple of Concord. A fitting resting place until it may be taken up again by another."

The emperor that was no more held up the dagger and began to walk towards the temple accompanied by his household. The doors of the temple were opened by a priest, as prearranged. The priest in his white robe stood ready to receive the very empire into his hands and safe keeping.

Magnus had watched the unfolding ceremony with disbelief and then a burning anger. Why was the emperor standing down? It made no sense when he had them, the German legions, in Rome ready to protect him. It was shaming that he was being forced to resign without even a good battle. It was shaming to the German legions to let this travesty continue.

Vitellius was only a few yards from the temple doors when the shout came from the crowd.

"NO! DON'T DO IT!"

Vitellius stopped and turned to face the crowd.

"STOP! DON'T!" came another yell.

Epaphroditus, scanning the gathered citizens, quickly identified the soldiers at the back as the culprits. He was about to order the Guard to intervene when something strange happened. His witnesses picked for their very stoic nature began to yell out too. There were cries of, "Imperial Majesty!" and declarations of love for their emperor, for their empress, for the little Caesar. Vitellius' act had aroused their pity and they begged him not to go through with it.

Then a few of the soldiers present took it upon themselves to physically impede Vitellius, standing between him and the temple. They were joined by civilians, old and young, who wept and begged their emperor to be their emperor still. A few prostrated themselves at his feet.

An alarmed Epaphroditus watched as the Praetorians present involved themselves in this spectacle. His eyes fell on the emperor. The emperor looked back at him, and smiled. Vitellius opened his arms wide as if to embrace the crowd.

"My subjects!" he declared. "My beautiful, loyal subjects."

"Err, sir," said Lysander. "What happens now?"

As Vitellius was cheered and revered by all, Epaphroditus' brain was a whirl of panic. Then it hit one particular image.

"Oh Jupiter, greatest and the best! Flavius!" he cried. "I need to warn Flavius. He thinks it's all settled. He's going to walk straight into a trap!"

* * *

"Right, friends," smiled Flavius. "Let us do this!"

This was greeted by a series of determined faces. While Epaphroditus had been organising the emperor's abdication, Flavius had been here in his Esquiline home organising the smooth transition of power. Most pertinently, that of the thousands of troops still in Rome. He'd sent messages out to the tribunes informing them to keep their men in barracks. Once the allotted hour of Vitellius' abdication was reached, he would send out his urban troops with the news that Vespasian was now emperor.

They'd spent the hours carefully crafting each message to the legions. Flavius being a thorough sort had then listed all the potential issues they may face in taking over the city. Nowhere in that detailed document was it featured that Vitellius might change his mind. They therefore left the Esquiline house brimming with positivity. This was going to be a smooth transition. There was going to be no needless bloodshed.

On this point he was to be proved horribly wrong.

It was decided that they would make their way to the palace to settle matters there. Afterwards, an address would be made to the Senate. They'd just passed the Basin of Fundanus when the messenger caught up with them.

He skidded to a halt on his heels with a brisk, "Flavius, sir! A message from Epaphroditus, sir!"

"I'm just on my way to the palace. I'll speak to him personally."

"It's urgent, sir!" barked the messenger.

Flavius, seeing the messenger's red-faced agitation, took the scroll from his hand.

Having read it, Flavius looked up. "We need to get back to the house, now!"

"Flavius?" queried Atticus.

From behind a house came a yell. There appeared ten soldiers, swords raised, running straight at them. Flavius' urban cohort troops unsheathed their own swords and ran to meet them. Flavius stood in the street gutter protected by three bodyguards, a spectator to the skirmish.

A clash of swords, of grunting pushes, of force against force played out in this narrow street of Rome. Flavius' troops got the better of so few Vitellians. With three of them bloodied on the ground, they chased the remainder away. The troops came back into view, shouting their triumph.

"This is but the starter," said Flavius. "We should expect a Vitellian-sized banquet."

SIXTY-SEVEN

It had been Philo's habit since the spring to visit Domitian at the second hour. Even an emperor's abdication, novel as it was, would not keep him from making this appointment. He found the young man troubled and anxious.

"Has my uncle spoken to you? Has Vitellius stepped down?"

"He was like this all last night," said Mina. "He can't relax for even a moment. Not even during sex. It was most distracting."

Philo, ignoring Mina, said, "Epaphroditus has been talking with Vitellius all of last night. Everything is in place." Seeing Domitian's troubled eyes, he added, "I am sure it won't be long before you are able to leave here."

"And go back home?"

Philo looked confused. "To the palace," he explained. "You are the young Caesar. There will be much for you to do in your father's absence."

Domitian flopped down onto the bed, cradling his head in his hands. He looked at best despondent, at worst despairing. Philo looked to Mina for an interpretation. She gave a shrug.

"When's my father going to get here?" Domitian addressed to the floor.

"From the correspondence I've seen, he doesn't look like he's moving until the spring. Which makes sense. It's far too dangerous to sail at this time of year."

"What?" bleated Domitian, looking up. "But he's the emperor! He should be here emperoring! I don't know anything! I don't know what to do."

"You sign whatever Philo puts in front of you. You do whatever Epaphroditus tells you to. And you wave nicely to everyone at the games. Easy," said Mina, sitting beside him. She placed a hand on his thigh. "Would it help if we had sex again? It might ease the tension. Plus, I may as well enjoy you now before you're officially an emperor's son and there's a queue."

"What do you mean?"

Mina grinned. "Girlies. Lots of girlies. They'll be flinging themselves at you. Every girl wants to be an empress."

Domitian let this sink in for a moment.

"See, Philo, he's perked right up now."

* * *

Philo left Mina helping Domitian to compile a list of what he liked in women, with a promise to report back from the palace immediately.

Walking through the Forum, he mentally noted it was quieter than normal, but gave it no further thought. He had too much else to think about. Reconstructing the private secretary's office to function how it ought to. Briefing and calming the staff on the situation. Generally making sure nothing was forgotten in this new regime. It was a challenge Philo was looking forward to. Flavius had given him a mandate to organise the administrative staff how he saw fit. Philo was already building a power structure in his head, as well as wondering whether this was his moment to introduce a new filing system.

He noted a number of guards moving with haste down the corridors but thought nothing more of it. Pushing open the door of his office, he found Lysander sat at his desk.

"Hullo?"

"He didn't do it," said Lysander. "He didn't step down. Vitellius is still emperor."

"What?" Philo gasped, feeling his knees weaken.

"He's still emperor," repeated Lysander. "The crowd begged him to stay. So he did."

"But they shouldn't have done that," protested Philo. "It was all arranged. Everything was arranged. Epaphroditus said—"

"Epaphroditus has fled," interrupted Lysander.

Philo sat on a stool. Unable to express his shock and the multitude of questions running through his head he looked entreatingly at Lysander.

"What happens now?"

Lysander shrugged. "No idea. But I suggest we stay here tonight. There's soldiers searching the city. It won't be safe to leave. Best stay here. With the door closed. Staying out of everything."

Philo looked about his small office. There wasn't a lot of room to camp out.

"We should send word to Teretia and Verenia that we're safe." Then he paused as something from Lysander's words struck him. "You said the soldiers are searching. What are they searching for?"

"His son. They're searching for Vespasian's son."

* * *

"Erotica. She can be anything you want. She's super flexible too," said Mina, a note tablet on her lap. "Shall I put her on your list?"

"Is she hairy?" asked Domitian. "I don't like hairy women."

"She sometimes gets a little moustache of soft hair above her top lip." Mina placed a finger on her own lip to demonstrate. "But I can get the pluckers onto that. Hey! That could be my new job!" she declared brightly. "I could be your personal bodyguard and vet all the entertainments to ensure they match your specifications. I'd be super good at that."

Domitian, standing by the window, distractedly said, "Consider yourself employed."

Looking down at the Forum, Domitian saw a flash of colour. Then another. Then movement. A moving mass. Men. Men running across the Forum.

"Mina!"

"What is it?" she asked, as she indented Erotica's name into the wax. Giving her a full ten out of ten for shagability.

The crowd of men were heading towards the Temple of Saturn. Running with urgent speed.

"Mina!"

"What?" She got up and walked over to the window, and stood beside Domitian.

"Look!" he pointed downwards.

Mina followed his finger and saw the Forum rapidly filling up with fleeing soldiers. No, not soldiers. Not Praetorians either. But whatever they were they were headed towards the Capitoline Hill.

She flung the tablet down. Pulling her whip from her belt she commanded, "Get under the bed! Now!"

Domitian, transfixed by the spectacle of so many people heading their way, didn't answer. There was something nagging at him about their uniform.

Mina grabbed his arm. "Grumpy young Caesar! Under the bed! NOW!"

It clicked into place. Domitian turned back to Mina. "Urban cohorts! It's the urban cohorts. They're my uncle's men."

SIXTY-EIGHT

"Primus is just outside the city, barely a day's march away," Flavius told Domitian. "All we need to do is stay put until he arrives."

This was said in Flavius' usual genial tone, both calming and assured. Domitian was not fooled in the slightest.

"They're going to attack, aren't they?"

Flavius squeezed his nephew's shoulder. "That, we'll have to see. But we are well defended here, so please don't worry. Every man here is sworn to protect this hill and we shall do so."

Domitian leant heavily against Flavius. His uncle put his arm around him and kissed his curly-haired head.

"It's going to be fine. I promise."

* * *

Standing in the square outside the Temple of Jupiter, Mina watched with interest the activity occurring all around her. Flavius' troops were knocking the statues that lined the squares from their bases. They were then carried by five or six men at a time towards the opposite side of the hill. Here there was a ramp that led up from the Forum. The statues were being dumped at the top of this as a makeshift barricade.

A smaller, less substantial barricade was being constructed a few feet from the temple complex where a stone staircase was situated. There was one further route onto the hill, the notorious Gemonian Steps where the bodies of traitors were flung down. Such were the times that it was difficult to identify who was a traitor and who was loyal. It was all a matter of perception.

Mina wandered round the back of the temple, assessing the area. She wanted a possible escape route for her and Domitian, should it prove necessary. She walked with a growing satisfaction round some of the narrow alleyways, the perfect route for disappearing.

* * *

It was dusk when Epaphroditus reached the camp. Approaching the sentries, he had no idea who these soldiers were: Vitellians or Flavians. Frankly, he did not care. He'd been on a horse all day, his least favourite way of travelling. He'd have prostrated himself before the corpse of Galba for a hot scrub and a chance to relieve his aching joints.

"I'm from the palace," Epaphroditus told the sentry neutrally. "Who is your commander?"

"Antonius Primus, sir!"

Epaphroditus' shoulders relaxed as much as their painful muscles would allow. "Take me to him."

It was time to meet Beaky.

He was led into an ample tent. It took his eyes a moment to adjust to the barely lit gloom. When they did, he saw a tall man with a hooked, beak-like nose: Primus.

"Antonius Primus, I am Tiberius Claudius Epaphroditus, imperial freedman and loyal Flavian."

The tall man nodded. "You may speak," he said.

"I'm afraid I come with terrible news from Rome. Vitellius has changed his mind. He won't abdicate."

Primus' expression did not change. "He will live to regret that," he said.

SIXTY-NINE

Philo lay on the floor of his office staring upwards. He could not sleep. Unlike Lysander, who was snoring away beside him. He couldn't get Domitian's face out of his mind. He'd promised him he'd be back with news. Except here he was at the palace, and he'd done no such thing.

Lysander was adamant that he shouldn't go back to the Capitoline Hill to warn Domitian about Vitellius' non-abdication.

"Epaphroditus has legged it. They know you and he are close. What if they followed you? They don't know where his son is. Yet. You could be the one that lets it slip."

Philo recognised the truth of it. If he accidentally revealed Domitian's location to Vitellius, he'd be devastated. The young Caesar was well guarded, hidden. All he had to do was stay hidden until Vespasian's army arrived. Which should be any day now.

Yet, still he stared into the darkness, worrying.

* * *

Antonia Caenis paced the length of Lysandria's elegant dining room. Her hostess lay fast asleep on a couch, having dropped off hours ago. Her slaves had draped a blanket over her. Caenis could not relax, could not cease her movement.

Word had reached her from Epaphroditus that Primus was only a day away. They just had to hold on for one day. Just one day. That was possible, wasn't it?

* * *

On the Capitoline Hill, Domitian wept quietly into the darkness.

SEVENTY

The slave boy shook the emperor gently. He did not stir. The boy looked over to Asiaticus for assistance.

"Slap him in the face. Hard."

The panicked expression on the boy's face plainly showed his feelings on this order.

"Just do it. Or face the cross."

The boy pulled back his hand. And, SLAP, right across Vitellius' fat cheek.

The emperor stirred.

The boy ran away.

"Eh, what, what?" murmured a confused Vitellius.

"Imperial Majesty. Flavius Sabinus has been located."

"Eh? Pull me up. Pull me up."

Two guards hauled Vitellius into a less horizontal position. A goblet of wine was placed in his hand. He drank it down in one.

The emperor was now fully awake and he asked, "Is the boy with him? Vespasian's son?"

"It seems likely. Flavius and his men have taken refuge on the Capitoline Hill."

"Send the troops down there. I want them both captured! Alive. Tell the men alive. Flavius tried to force me into a humiliating exit. Let us treat him and the boy to the same experience. Let them stand in front of the mob and call an end to that man's claim to my throne!"

"Imperial Majesty, the scouts say Primus is only a day's march away."

Vitellius waited while his goblet was refilled. "All the more reason, my dear Asiaticus, to get hold of Flavius and the boy. It gives us bargaining power with Primus."

Vitellius smiled and then yelled, "Food! I need food!"

* * *

It was so early in the morning that the mist was still at knee height and the moon glowing proudly in the sky. This was not traditionally an hour when one would find Praetorians. Even the sentries on duty tended to snooze until kicked awake by a superior. But up they were, lined up in cohorts in the central space of the Praetorian barracks. Their commander stood on a platform to address them. Yelling his message in ever-increasing fiery rhetoric. Thumping his fist into the air.

The guards he addressed were as outraged as he. What had happened the previous day was a disgrace. An outrage that ought never to have occurred. The rightful emperor being held hostage and forced into that humiliating speech. Every man felt the burn of Vitellius' shame. That a small party of them had managed to rescue the emperor from his captors was small consolation.

Revenge was needed. No! It was required.

"The traitor Flavius Sabinus has been located!"

The men booed at the name.

"He and his men are on the Capitoline Hill. They think they can hold it against us!."

Jeers and catcalls rang out.

"They think they are impenetrable," the commander sneered. "But we shall show them! The mighty German legions will show them!"

The gates of the Praetorian camp were heaved open.

* * *

Teretia had barely slept, if at all. Though Philo's message had been pedestrian in the extreme, something about some very important filing he needed to finish, Teretia was not fooled. Philo had never stayed out all night before. When Lysander similarly failed to return, the panic set in and took hold in the apartment. Teretia, Marcia, and Pompeia sat in the dawning light of the kitchen eating slices of bread and butter and fretting.

"There'll be news soon I'm sure, my dear," consoled Pompeia. "Philo knows how much you worry about him. He'll get a messenger to you at first light."

"Is it first light yet?" pressed Teretia, hugging the sleeping Horace to her.

"I'll check, mistress."

Marcia unlocked the shutters and pulled them back, letting in a tiny sliver of dull winter sun.

"Just about," confirmed Marcia.

The floor began to rumble and there came the unmistakable sound of marching boots.

"Probably the early shift of Praetorians going to the palace to relieve the night shift," said Pompeia.

Marcia gazed down at the street beneath. Her eyes opened wide. "Err, mistress."

Teretia and Pompeia joined her at the window. Looking down, they saw not the expected cohort of some 500 guards. Instead, there were thousands of soldiers filling up the Viminal streets.

"They're heading towards the palace!" cried Teretia.

* * *

On the Capitoline Hill all was quiet. The city sleeping, Flavius had placed sentries on the barricade to watch for activity. You could hear them before there were visible. The stamp, stamp, stamp of boots. The sentries looked about. The Forum was deserted. The Palatine Hill silent. Stamp, stamp, stamp.

"Go wake Flavius."

* * *

Domitian was in the midst of a not terribly encouraging dream when he felt his body shake. Opening his eyes, he saw his uncle looking down at him, one hand gripped on his shoulder. Seeing Domitian awake, he removed it.

"What is it?" he asked, sitting up in bed.

His uncle's face was grave. "Get dressed. We are under attack."

Domitian dressed quickly. As he buckled up his boots, he asked, "Uncle Flavius, what can I do to help?"

"You're going to stay put in the Temple of Jupiter. The priests are expecting you. Stay there and do whatever Artemina says."

"Too right," said Mina, whip ready in hand.

"But I want to help," protested Domitian. "I want to fight the Vitellians!"

Flavius gave a sigh. "Domitian, you've never fought in a battle before."

"So this is my chance. Everyone else my age is doing their military service," he whined. "I'm old enough. You wouldn't expect Titus to hide away and take orders from a slave girl. He wouldn't listen anyway. He'd be out on the front line battling!"

Titus would. He'd always been that sort of boy. Even as a child, Flavius recalled him leaping off roofs and climbing along the most precarious of branches fearlessly. His brother was of a different mettle. No matter how much he wanted otherwise.

Flavius gave his nephew a tight smile. "The next battle is all yours, I promise."

"But—"

"They are looking expressly for you," said Flavius. "Vitellius wants you captured. I can't risk you on the front line. I'm sorry. But that is my decision."

He embraced the sulking Domitian, telling him, "I'll see you soon. I promise. But if anything should happen. If we should get separated. Send a message to Philo."

Flavius' eyes were serious. Grave. There was nothing of their usual twinkle. No amusement at all.

"Yes, uncle."

SEVENTY-ONE

They came from the western side of the Forum. A massed column of soldiers marching through the narrow gaps between buildings. The troops manning the barricade looked at each other nervously. There were thousands of them. They were greatly outnumbered.

"We'll never hold them all off!" grumbled Adriaticus.

"We've got the higher ground," said his more optimistic colleague.

"Yeah, but it's not like we're in a fort, is it? We don't have no sturdy walls to fight behind. Just this." He pushed at the statue barricade.

"It just has to hold long enough," said Flavius, walking up behind them. "Casperius," he addressed his aide. "Get some men on there." He pointed to the roof of a portico that lay a few feet beneath them. "We can pelt them with missiles as they ascend the ramp."

"Yes, sir!" barked Casperius and went to organise the men.

In the Forum beneath them, the Vitellians emerged from round the Temple of Saturn. They massed at the bottom of the ramp. There came an eerie silence as both sides eyed up each other. Then a single yelled order.

"ATTACK!!!!!!"

The Vitellians ran at speed up the ramp. Casperius' men pelted them with stones and javelins and anything they could find. The pebbles bounced off their helmets as they ran for the barricade. A few of the javelins hit their mark. The unfortunate target felled and trampled beneath the boots of his colleagues.

On the hill, Flavius stood back. Yelling at his men to collect more missiles to pass on to those scrambled on the porticos.

"More javelins! Come now men. Faster. Faster! Where are the archers? Get the archers here now!"

The bulk of the Vitellians were pushing their force against the barricade. Heaving it forward. A statue toppled from its awkward angle and landed on Adriaticus' foot. He screamed. It took three men to heave it off him. The whole edifice began to wobble. Those behind it looked at each other in panic. Which way would it fall?

The archers had climbed up on to nearby roofs. From here they rained down arrows on the besiegers. Hitting indiscriminately but not enough to lessen the numbers pushing at the barricade.

"Flavius!" cried Scaeva. "Flavius!"

The city prefect followed the direction of Scaeva's outstretched arm. It took him to the far side of the hill where the Temple of Jupiter stood above the Tarpeian Rock. Here was situated a set of 100 steps ascending upwards. On them was a mass of Vitellians powering their way up. The Flavians had thought it unlikely the attackers would try such a narrow entrance, so the barricade was not nearly sturdy enough. They were but 50 steps from it and barely a handful of soldiers defending.

"Follow me! Follow me!" yelled Flavius holding his sword aloft and running at speed towards the steps.

The troops ran beside him trying frantically to get to the barricade before the Vitellians could.

By the ramp the larger of the two defences wobbled, then crashed to the ground trapping the men beneath its weight. It now made an awkward crossing for the Vitellians to pass. They stumbled over the statues and brickwork while the archers fired at them.

By the second barricade, Flavius was ordering a desperate defence. The archers firing lit torches at speed to deter the ascent. One legionary hit in the face with an arrow screamed as his whole body was engulfed in flames. His agonised form crashed into his colleagues, setting off a chain of fire that raced down the steps.

Flavius allowed himself a relieved breath as the attackers collapsed in chaos amongst the flames. The stench of smoke was strong and his eyes began to water. Then he realised that above all the calamity there was another sound. One that wasn't a human being in pain. It was a crackling noise. Flavius turned round and to his horror saw that the Temple of Jupiter was now being licked by flames. Quickly spreading across the roof on to the other buildings. Ye gods! The whole hill could go up!

Then he remembered that was where he'd left his nephew.

"Oh gods. Domitian!"

"Flavius." A hand tugged at his sleeve. "They've broken through."

Indeed they had. The first barricade was breached fully. Vitellians poured through. Swords raised, ready to slash their way through the defenders. Beneath him, the Vitellians at the bottom of the steps were regrouping. All around, the buildings were rapidly surrendering to the fire.

Flavius wiped his brow and issued the order. "Abandon the defence! Tell everyone to get out however they can."

He looked over to the Temple of Jupiter and ran towards it. He could feel the heat of the flames the closer he got, but this was of no concern. All his thoughts were on his nephew. This was why he didn't hear the pursuing pack of soldiers behind him. Not until they felled him to the ground and all went black.

SEVENTY-TWO

Domitian kicked at a grain sack.

"This is shaming. Absolutely shaming that I'm hiding in this grain store while there's a battle going on out there!"

Mina, who had heard this complaint repeatedly, rolled her eyes but kept her ear pressed against the door.

"You can bet Uncle Flavius wouldn't insist Titus hide out this way, like a woman! This is just so typical of my family. They never let me do anything. They treat me like a child!"

Having spent an hour listening to him whine, Mina could well understand why. Her sympathies were beginning to sway towards Titus.

"Urgh!" he grunted, giving the sack another kick.

"Urgh," said Mina, removing her ear from the door. "I can't hear a thing . "

Domitian sat himself down cross-legged on a grain sack. Mina plumped herself beside him.

"Anything could be happening out there," she complained.

"Maybe we should go take a look?" suggested Domitian.

Mina laughed. "I'm not going to fall for that one! We go have a look and all of a sudden you join the battle."

"I wasn't thinking that."

"'Course you weren't," said Mina, sceptically.

"How long are we going to stay here?"

"Until it's safe to leave."

"And we will know that, how?"

Actually it was a good point. The first he'd made for an entire hour.

Mina got to her feet, taking her whip from her belt. "I'll go see. No, you stay here."

"But—"

Mina fixed him with a hard glare. "Your uncle said you had to do what I say. And I say, stay here while I go check on the situation. Here," she bent down and picked up a bow, handing it to him, "Have a practise."

"Alright," he said grudgingly.

Mina had her hand on the door when he said to her, "What do I do if you don't come back?"

"I'm coming back," she said. "I promise."

She opened the great door of the store room and slipped out. Situated as it was a level down, she had to ascend a stone staircase. Halfway up she was assailed by a cacophany of noise. The sound of men fighting against men. Of screams and yells and heaving crashes. It reminded her of the day Galba had fallen. When she'd been stuck in the Forum with a bloody massacre all around.

That was not a happy memory, and she opened the door at the top of the stairs cautiously.

As soon as she did, she was engulfed in thick black smoke. It stung her lungs and she bent over coughing. Her eyes streaming. A sudden crash. But a foot in front of her lay a wooden beam, black and mottled.

"Minerva's pointy trident!" she swore.

Mina ran back down the stairs. Pushing open the door she yelled, "Domitian! We've got to get out of here! The whole place is on fire!"

They quickly gathered up their weapons. Holding their cloaks up to their faces, they pressed cloth against their mouths to act as a mask against the smoke.

At the top of the stairs, Mina turned round and said to Domitian, "Whatever is going on out there, stick with me. Alright?"

"Alright."

Mina took hold of his hand, and pushed at the door.

Immediately everything went black. Domitian felt Mina tugging at his hand. He followed the direction, holding his breath for as long as he could to avoid sucking in the smoke.

The smoke cleared enough for Domitian to make out the great statue of Jupiter sitting upon his throne. Flames licked at the great god's ankles. Another tug from Mina pulled him away from the burning king of the gods. They ran alongside the central hallway. Mina had declared it safer. Seeing the beams crashing down in the centre of the temple, Domitian concurred with her assessment.

They made it to the great doors. Heaving their shoulders against them, they could feel the warmth on the wood from the inferno growing behind them. Domitian took one last look round and saw that Jupiter was now fully aflame. It was a terrible image: the to see the great god's face blackened behind that fire as his body was consumed.

"Domitian!"

Mina hauled him through the doors. They both collapsed on to the floor of the porch coughing. Domitian's tongue was coated with ash. He licked at his hand to clean it off. His lungs felt as if they were burning. His eyes watered down his cheeks. Beside him on her knees, Mina looked up and saw the temple square full of soldiers. Men being chased across it. Javelins thrown into their backs. As they fell with screams, they were set upon by groups of soldiers thrusting with their swords. Beyond the square, further buildings were engulfed by fflames. Masonry collapsing down on to the battling soldiers beneath.

She jumped to her feet. "Come on. Let's go!"

Domitian pushed himself upwards, wiping at his sore eyes. "Where to?" he asked. Then he too spotted the fierce fighting all around. "My uncle?" he bleated. "They've breached the barricades. Where's my uncle?"

"We can't look for him. Not now. When we're safe, we'll send word to Philo as planned. Right now, we need to get you out of here before you're recognised."

She led him down the steps and round the side of the temple into the narrow streets beyond. Domitian couldn't help but look over his shoulder behind them.

"Mina!"

She turned her head and saw as he had: a band of five soldiers pursuing them, swords drawn.

"Gods alive!" swore Mina. "We need to move faster." They both shot round a corner.

"Mina, my bow!"

"What?!?"

He ran alongside her. "My bow. I can get them."

Mina nodded her assent. "Round there," she said, pointing to the turn of the next corner.

They ran round then stopped outside a doorway. Mina put her bag down and pulled out Domitian's bow and arrows. She handed them to him. She then pulled out a bow for herself.

"You aim at their feet. Even if you miss, it'll distract them."

Mina nodded as they both loaded up their first arrow. "Alright grumpy young Caesar, let's do this."

They mouthed a count of three. Then ran back round the corner they'd just passed. In the street were the five soldiers looking about puzzled.

"Hey, boys!" yelled Mina.

All five turned, which was the signal for Mina to fire. Her first arrow hit the ground a few feet in front of the soldiers. It surprised them enough for Domitian to fire off three arrows in quick succession. One went straight through the cheek of one soldier. The second hit one square in the chest. The third penetrated an eye. There was a flurry of screams from the afflicted soldiers as they fell in agony from their wounds.

The two uninjured men, seeing their comrades so grievously hurt held up their swords above their heads. Growling a, "YARRRRRR!" they ran towards Mina and Domitian. Mina pulled out her whip. With a crack, it slapped the first soldier right across the face. Screaming, his hands flew up to his injuries. Domitian took this chance to hedgehog him with three arrows in the back.

The remaining soldier stopped and eyed up his enemies. A girl of no more than eighteen and a similarly aged boy.

"I suggest you run back the way you came," said Mina, with her hands on her hips. "Because he will kill you."

Domitian aimed his bow and fired off the remaining three arrows. They hit the soldier's chest in a neat vertical line. He collapsed on to his knees and fell face forward with a smash on to the ground.

Mina bounced on her toes. "That was awesome!" she gasped, giving Domitian a kiss on the lips. He paused for a second, wrapping his arms around her. Their eyes met.

"We should probably get out of here before more come," said Mina.

Domitian's arms released her.

A door creaked open and out stuck a bald head.

"Hello, you two alright?" he asked.

The bald man stepped out of the door revealing his white robe and a sistrum rattle held in his hand. Confirming his status as a priest of Isis.

"Priest. You're a priest!" said Mina breathlessly. "This is the emperor's son, grumpy, I mean, the young Caesar. We need a safe passage off this hill."

The priest bowed his head. "Young Caesar, you are welcome in our temple."

* * *

"This will never work," hissed Domitian to Mina.

"It will work," she insisted, holding up her sistrum up and giving it a good shake.

All around them, the priests of Isis chanted and rattled their own sistrums.

"Go on, grumpy young Caesar, give it a shake," teased Mina.

They were both dressed, as were the priests, in white linen mantles that disguised their bodies and were pulled over their heads covering their faces. The priests had elected that they walk in the centre of the throng, so as not to be noticeable.

"Not far now, young Caesar," said the priest who'd originally found them. "We are approaching the temple of Juno. There's a pathway down to the other side of the Capitoline Hill from there. The fighting is mostly on the Forum side, so we should be safe."

Passing a group of soldiers, they all bowed their heads and began to chant.

"Weirdos," said one soldier, but nonetheless let them pass.

Domitian dared to breathe. Looking up, he could see the temple ahead of them. Mina squeezed his arm affectionately. Then just in case anyone was looking, gave her sistrum an epic tingly shake.

They ascended up to the temple. At the top of the hill, Domitian cast his eyes back to the Temple of Jupiter from where they had fled. It was fully ablaze now. Consumed utterly by the flames. As were all the surrounding buildings. He couldn't see any fighting. What did that mean?

"The road down is that way," the priest told Mina.

"Thank you," she replied. "The young Caesar is very grateful. Aren't you?"

She nudged Domitian.

"Yes, very," he mumbled. Then to Mina he said, "Look." And pointed.

Mina followed his gaze to the steps at the far end of the Forum. A group of men were walking down them. Soldiers behind and in front of them. Even from that distance they could see the chains on their ankles. She knew what he was thinking, because she was thinking it too, but they couldn't stop to worry about Flavius.

She tugged at his sleeve. "We need to go."

SEVENTY-THREE

They had to wake the emperor from his late afternoon nap to break the news to him: the Capitoline Hill was taken. Vitellius rubbed his sleepy eyes. "Flavius Sabinus and the boy?"

"The guards told me they've rounded up the ringleaders, Imperial Majesty," Asiaticus told him. "They've gathered them outside the palace for your inspection."

"How very suitable," grinned Vitellius, as three small boys hauled him to his feet.

A purple cloak was placed around his shoulders. "Oh how the wheel of fortune has rotated in such a short time! Was it only yesterday that Flavius forced that humiliation upon me?"

"Yes, Imperial Majesty," said Asiaticus as the great doors of the chamber were thrown open.

"And today I have him completely under my control!" He gave a gleeful laugh. "Let Primus reject my terms now when I have Vespasian's brother and son under my control! Go gather up some of the staff. I want a good entourage to stand behind me as he grovels. The greater the numbers, the greater his humiliation!"

This was how Lysander and Philo found themselves two steps behind Vitellius on the old palace staircase. In the space at the bottom of the steps were gathered a group of men. They were chained together in a circle, held still by soldiers pointing spears a few inches away from them. Around this scene there was a growing crowd of curious bystanders.

Philo's eyes scanned over the prisoners. He saw a familiar face: Flavius. The old man stood at the front of the group. A cut on his brow dripped blood down the side of his face. His tunic was stained with dirt and gore. His legs splashed with filth. He seemed almost dazed at his surroundings, eyes unfocused.

Philo felt his chest tighten. His eyes scanned the prisoners again. The grip of anxiety eased a little when he confirmed who he couldn't see. He looked to Lysander and mouthed, "He's not there."

"Who?" mouthed Lysander back.

Vitellius stepped down to the bottom step.

The commander stood forward. "Imperial Majesty, I present the filthy traitors we rounded up."

It was said with such venom that it set off a wave of hissing from the gathering crowd. The guards poked at the prisoners with their spears, huddling them closer together.

"Bring Flavius Sabinus and that man's son before me."

Flavius was thrust forward with a push to his back. His feet shackled, he stumbled and narrowly avoided a fall.

"Ahhh, Flavius," grinned Vitellius at the battered city prefect. "And the boy. Where's the boy?"

Vitellius scanned the prisoners and saw as Philo had: a group of middle-aged senatorial men. There was no one under 30. There was no Domitian. He'd evaded capture.

"I said I wanted the boy taken too! That's what I said. I wanted Flavius and the boy Domitian," stormed Vitellius at the commander. "Those were my orders!"

"We will find the boy, Imperial Majesty. I have teams searching every street of the city. Nobody will dare hide him. He will be found. I promise you, Imperial Majesty. But we did find the arch traitor. This organiser of treason."

The commander gave Flavius a further push. This time the city prefect stumbled to the ground.

"What do you wish us to do with the arch traitor, Flavius, Imperial Majesty?"

Vitellius, his eyes on the fallen Flavius, said, "Bring him inside and get him cleaned up. We have the usurper's brother. It gives us the upper hand in negotiations. Help him up."

The commander's expression drooped. He looked at the emperor in confusion. "Clean him up? Help him up? Imperial Majesty, this is a traitor responsible for the deaths of many of my men on the Capitoline Hill this very day!"

The guards gave a murmur of agreement.

Underneath the sleeves of his tunic, Philo felt his arms goosebump. It had nothing to do with the cold. Lysander was similarly affected. He whispered to Philo, "I don't like the look of that crowd. It has more of a mob about it."

Philo was inclined to agree. Dotted heavily with the victorious soldiers, it was increasing rapidly in size and edging closer to the palace.

"Help him up," said Vitellius. "He's grovelled enough. He truly is pathetic."

Flavius looked up at the emperor from his crushed position on the ground. He levered his elbow, trying to raise himself.

"Help him up!" insisted Vitellius. "And take him into the palace. He and I have much to discuss."

The commander shook his head. "Imperial Majesty, there is a set way to deal with traitors. You set an example. You don't discuss. This isn't the time for talk. There could be hundreds of these Flavians crawling out of the ground. Amassing ready to kill more of my men. They need to be stamped on. Hard!"

There came more murmured agreement from the crowd. A shout or two. A bit of shoving.

A redness flowed upwards from Vitellius' neck to his face. "You question my orders, soldier? You question the emperor?

My orders are that Flavius Sabinus be helped up and taken into the palace. Where he will stay."

The commander raised his head and looked straight at the emperor. It was a hard look and the emperor visibly wobbled under it.

"I have lost men today because of that man," he raged, pointing at Flavius, who now knelt on the floor before the palace steps. "What am I to tell their families? That brave men of the German legions died so that you may invite their murderer into the palace as a friend?"

There was no Imperial Majesty tacked on the end. There was no respect. No honour. The crowd edged together. Philo froze as it suddenly all became clear to him. He was their figurehead. He was their front. He had been the whole time. Vitellius was nothing but a puppet for the German legions. An instrument to extract the honour and reward they felt they were due.

Valens and Caecina had tapped into that resentment as Galba and his legion gained imperial glory. They'd promised them it would all be theirs instead. They'd delivered on that promise. But Valens and Caecina were gone. All that was left was this empty shell of an emperor, who rather than raising them had insulted their honour. The legions with Caecina had turned on him the moment he'd dented that honour by changing sides. They were going to do the same to Vitellius.

"Lysander," bleated Philo.

Lysander was transfixed on the events below. The crowd were now openly chanting, "Traitor. Traitor!" in ever-more deafening yells. The emperor's eyes darted about, unsure what to do next. The commander had no such hesitation. Turning back to his men and the mob he stated, "The Rhine Legions declare the traitors shall die!"

A line of Praetorians formed at the bottom of the steps.

"Best you go inside, Imperial Majesty," said the commander. "While we deal with these traitors."

The Praetorian line took one step upwards and then another, forcing the emperor and the palace staff up the steps. This they continued to do until they were at the great palace doors.

Huddled close together, with the Praetorians pressing them backwards, they were all forced back into the palace. Philo took one last desperate look at Flavius. Saw the commander standing over him with sword raised. Then the doors were slammed shut.

Vitellius stood in the great entrance hall surrounded by his panicked and fearful staff. He seemed confused.

"They're going to kill him," said Philo to Lysander. "They're going to kill Flavius."

From outside the door came a terrific cheer and a chant of, "Death to traitors."

"I think they just did," said Lysander.

Philo gave a bleat. Lysander put his arms around him and hugged him tight.

Asiaticus touched the emperor on the arm. It seemed to snap him back to reality.

"Dear gods," he said in a hushed voice to Asiaticus. "They killed Flavius."

"They did, Imperial Majesty." Asiaticus chewed at his misshapen lower lip.

"That wasn't supposed to happen. I needed him alive. That was the plan." He rubbed a palm over his face. "Primus is not going to be pleased by this. He's going to want vengeance on Vespasian's behalf. I'm not going to get my seaside villa!"

He stamped a foot.

"Perhaps if we sent word to Primus, Imperial Majesty."

"Yes, yes. Let's do that. You! Indian boy! Stop hugging and scribe for me."

SEVENTY-FOUR

The letter Philo scribed for Vitellius made his stomach turn. It made no mention of Flavius' execution or that Domitian was missing. He similarly withheld the mutinous behaviour of the troops. Rather, he asked for a day's grace from Primus for Vitellius to arrange matters, and then the city was his. Philo couldn't deliver such a pack of lies. So he added in a note of his own. Warning Primus that the German legions were preparing to fight in the defence of the city. That Flavius Sabinus had been executed. But that the emperor's son had escaped with a protector. As the Vestal Virgins had been charged with delivering the message, Philo had every faith they wouldn't open it prior to delivery and see his treason.

He took his scroll down to the House of the Vestals and explained the mission to the chief Vestal. As a group, they should have less trouble getting through the city than anyone else. Nobody would dare touch a Vestal, surely?

Leaving the House of the Vestals, Philo could see a crowd gathered by the Gemonian Stairs that led up from the Forum to the Capitoline Hill. He knew what they would be looking at. This was the spot where they displayed the bodies of traitors. It was where the corpse of Epaphroditus' former master and arch-villain Sejanus had lain for the mob to give it a good kicking. It was where the body of Nymphidius Sabinus had lain before Honoratus had managed to gain possession of it and return it to his mother, Nymphidia. Philo knew this would be where Flavius had been left.

He'd been a kind man. A decent man. A man Philo had admired and enjoyed working with. He had no desire to see what the soldiers had done to a man he was pleased to have known. He wanted to remember the twinkly eyed, silver-haired Flavius sitting beside Caenis in the courtyard garden of his house laughing and smiling.

* * *

Domitian looked about. "Hey, I know this street. I know someone who lives here."

"Trustworthy?" asked Mina suspiciously.

"We can trust him."

Mina shrugged. It was getting dark. They needed to go somewhere. So far on their journey they'd successfully evaded the soldiers. She didn't want to push that success. Even with the blessings of the goddess Isis, courtesy of their priest friends. "Let's go," she said.

Domitian led her to a quiet side street and an unobtrusive dark-blue door. He gave it three sharp taps with his knuckles, then looked about anxiously in case the action had attracted any attention. The street was deserted. Any sensible person was inside with their slaves, armed and the door barricaded. Which probably explained why the blue door was opened so cautiously. A head stretched out.

"It's me," hissed Domitian to the slave. "We need to come in."

The door was opened fully and they were hurried inside by the slave.

"I'll take you to the master."

The slave led them through to a dining area lit with three-legged lamp stands. Mina narrowly missing setting fire to her sleeve from one. A man reclining on a couch got to his feet on seeing them. He was thin, middle–aged, in possession of a long noble nose and an unusually small mouth. His hair he wore in a rounded, fringed cut. Mina, checking out his high cheekbones, mentally cast him as reasonably handsome.

"Domitian?"

"Nerva, I didn't know where else to go.

"You did the right thing," said Nerva. "Come in. Sit. Nestor, bring wine and refreshments for our guest."

"Yes, master."

The man led Domitian to a couch. "You're pale," he commented.

"It's been quite a day," said Domitian. "My uncle. We don't know what's happened to him. Do you, Nerva?"

"I've not heard anything, I'm afraid. But I can see what I can find out." He clicked his fingers and delivered instructions to a slave.

Mina looked about the room. There were three exits. To Nerva she said, "Is there a back door to this house. A way to get out if they come for us."

Nerva looked to Domitian, who explained, "This is Mina. She's protecting me."

"I have lots of slaves, some pretty burly ones among them. You are perfectly safe here."

Mina looked sceptical.

"We won't stay long," said Domitian. "I don't want to put you in any danger."

"Nonsense," said Nerva. "You can both stay as long as is necessary. You are safe here."

"We need to get word to Philo," said Mina. "He'll sort everything out. You should get some rest, grumpy young Caesar. It's been quite a day. We both need to be sharp."

She looked to their host.

"There is a spare bedroom. You know the way," said Nerva to Domitian. Then to Mina, "If you have any messages my slaves can deliver them for you."

Mina narrowed her eyes. "Can we trust him?" she asked Domitian.

"I'm a family friend of many years' standing," said Nerva.

Mina gave a barked laugh. "As if that's any recommendation these days! I've watched types like you switch from Nero to Galba to Otho to whoever else."

Nerva's mouth pinched, pulling his jaw tight. "What choice do you have? Either you trust my slaves with your message or you deliver it yourself and trust Domitian here with me."

Mina weighed it up.

"She's ordered to stay with me always. My uncle said," piped in Domitian.

"That is true," said Mina. She looked at Domitian enquiringly.

"We can trust him," he said. "I'd trust him with my life."

* * *

Lysandria held Caenis' hands as she wept.

"Not Flavius" she cried. "This is all my fault."

"It is not," said Lysandria softly.

"It is. I should never have involved him in our plans," she said wiping a tear away. "And where's Domitian? What's happened to him? Is he an unidentified corpse on the Capitoline Hill?"

"Philo thought he and Artemina had got out. I think we should accept his judgement."

"I wish I could."

* * *

Primus received the audience from the Vestals politely. He made no reaction to the message they handed him until they had departed. Then he turned to Epaphroditus.

"We are going to have to fight the Germans street by bloody street. The bastard has killed the emperor's brother. There shall be no mercy for anyone. Not any more."

SEVENTY-FIVE

Vitellius took a sip of wine. It was like vinegar on his tongue and he swallowed it with difficulty. Before him on a low table was laid out a dish of every possible food imaginable: from cooked goose to roasted piglet, from pickled artichoke to sliced beetroot, and sweet pastries fashioned into animal shapes. Vitellius hadn't touched any of it. Instead he lay in semi-darkness sipping at his bitter brew eyeing *them* up.

Them being the guards that lined the walls of his chamber. *Them* that had made him emperor. *Them* that were holding him hostage in the palace. Because effectively he was their prisoner, wasn't he?

They'd killed Flavius expressly against his wishes. He had no doubt they would do the same to Vespasian's son when they found him, despite his orders otherwise. Which gave him what to negotiate with Primus and Muscianus? Absolutely nothing, that was what.

The two commanders would be itching to avenge the murder of the emperor's brother. They would be coming for him. And it was only *them* that stood between Vitellius and Vespasian's vengeance.

Vitellius didn't trust *them* at all. He didn't trust any of *them*. He wished he had Valens or even Caecina by his side.

They knew these men. They could command them, control them. Vitellius' words were just air.

There he lay, the emperor who didn't want to be an emperor. Surrounded by men who were determined he would not lay down his garland for any man.

* * *

Nerva gave the door three gentle taps, then said, "Domitian, it's me. Can I come in?"

The door opened and out stepped a barefoot Mina, her whip gripped in one hand.

"He's asleep," she yawned.

Nerva noted how her hair was tangled and knotted at the back. You didn't get that by just lying your head on a pillow.

"I see," he said tersely. "Nestor has returned with a message from Philo."

Mina looked back over her shoulder, then whispered to Nerva, "Is there news about his uncle?"

Nerva nodded, his lips tense.

"It's not good, is it?"

"No," said Nerva. "It's not."

It was excruciating to witness the change in Domitian's expression as Nerva relayed Philo's words: from excitement, hope, worry, concern, and then ultimately to despair.

"Uncle Flavius!" Domitian exclaimed. Burying his head in his hands he began to weep.

Mina put an arm around him, saying, "I am so sorry."

Nerva sat down on the edge of the bed. "He was a good man, Flavius. One of the best. What times are these that good, honest men are slain like cattle?"

"I hate him," said Domitian.

"Vitellius?" queried Mina, rubbing supportively at his back. "Yeah, so do I."

"No, my father. I hate my father," said Domitian, looking up at them both. "If he hadn't declared himself emperor, Uncle Flavius would still be alive. Uncle didn't approve of what father did. He just went along with it because he had no choice, like me. Now he's dead and it's all father's fault. I hate him."

There was no doubting his sincerity. It was written into the redness of his cheeks, the tenseness of his jaw line, and the heat in his eyes. Nerva looked at the floor, clearly uncomfortable.

"You know I don't like to hear you talk about your father like this."

"It's the truth. If he'd never tried to be emperor, Uncle Flavius would be here now."

"If Vitellius had never tried to be emperor, Sporus would be here right now," said Mina. "If Otho had never tried to be emperor, Straton and Daphne would be here. If Galba had never tried to be emperor, Alex would here now."

Her voice choked a little. "But this is where we are. This is how things are."

Domitian looked to Nerva.

"She's right," said the older man.

Mina got to her feet. "Excuse me. I'll just go and—I need some air."

After she had gone, Nerva said, "You forget slaves have family and friends. That they experience the same sense of loss we do." Then after a pause, he said, "You slept with her tonight. In my house. Didn't you?"

"It's not anything," mumbled Domitian.

"Like I wasn't?"

Domitian met the older man's eyes. They burned with an intensity he well remembered.

"This isn't the time. This is far from the time. You are grieving for your uncle. I will leave you be."

Nerva made to stand but Domitian put his hand on his arm.

"I'm sorry," he said. "I'm sorry for everything. For treating you the way I did. For disappearing like that."

"It would help me to know what I did wrong." His face displayed his hurt.

Domitian gave a sigh. "You did nothing wrong. Nothing at all. It was me. It was all me. I'm sorry. I am so sorry. I should have told you to your face. But I was a coward. I am a coward all over. So I didn't. I just hid. Like I'm hiding now."

Nerva's long fingers fiddled with the bed sheet. "So it is truly all over?"

"Yes. I'm sorry. I have my public career to think about and now—"

"And now you are the young Caesar." Nerva forced a smile. "I understand. I know those same pressures of office, of reputation. I would never have given in to my desires had I not loved you."

He reached up a hand and tucked one of Domitian's curls behind his ear. His lips twisted into a fond smile. "At least I had you for a time. For a time you were mine."

"I will never forget it, or you," Domitian assured him.

Nerva gave a strained smile. "Nor will I," he said. "Not ever."

The emotional intensity of this moment was broken by Mina bursting in. "There's soldiers outside. They're searching every house."

"Quick! We need to get you two hidden."

* * *

Nerva hurried them to his kitchens and to a storage room adjoining it.

"Here, there's a cupboard. If we pile up the grain sacks in front of it they'll never know it's even here."

He pulled open the cupboard door and pushed Domitian and Mina in, shutting the door on them. The space was instantly dark. So dark their eyes did not adjust and all was black around them.

"You know he could lead them straight here and say we forced him to take us in," said Mina, clutching at her whip. "We used up all the arrows getting here. I'll just have to whip the bastards. Maybe a bit of heavy clubbing. Is my bag near you? I can't see a thing. I want to get my goodies out ready."

"Nerva would never hand us over to Vitellius."

"He's a senator, isn't he," said Mina, as she fiddled about in the dark trying to locate her bag. "They switch sides quicker than a man with fleas in his mattress."

"I trust him with my life."

"I don't," said Mina bluntly. "Ah, here's my bag! And my clubs. Excellent."

Into the darkness Domitian said, "If they find us. And well … I wanted to say, thank you. For protecting me."

"Meh. Philo ordered me to," dismissed Mina. "But thank you for teaching me how to shoot arrows into poles and fruit."

"Thank you for the sex."

"No, thank you for the sex."

"And the company."

"No, just the sex, grumpy young Caesar."

They shared a laugh and in the darkness fumbled until they found each other's hands.

"I'm expecting big rewards, grumpy young Caesar, when you are installed at the palace."

"You shall have them," said Domitian. "Everyone shall: Nerva, Philo, those priests of Isis, the keeper at the Temple of Jupiter. Everyone who stood with my uncle against that beast. You shall all be rewarded for your assistance and loyalty."

"Gosh, as Philo would say, you sounded pretty near imperial then."

"I did?"

"Yeah, you did. And I've heard loads of emperors speak. I know my emperor talk."

"Thank you."

Domitian squeezed her hand and shuffled closer to her. Arms pressed together, hands gripped, they waited. Then came voices from outside.

"I don't know why you have to go disturbing my slaves' rest by fidgeting about their quarters," Nerva was saying. "They need their sleep. They have to get up early."

"It is the emperor's orders," came another, deeper voice. "Magnus! Check that big cooking pot. It's suspiciously large."

"Yes, sir!"

"Oh really, soldier. Is this necessary? Is it really?" said Nerva.

Domitian gripped Mina's hand tighter as they heard the soldiers banging and clanging about as they searched Nerva's kitchen.

"Nothing, sir."

"What's through there?"

"A food cupboard."

They could hear the approach of footsteps. Domitian held his breath as he heard Nerva say, "See, food. And grain. That's all."

"Hmmm," said the soldier. "What's behind the grain sacks?" he asked, to Domitian's horror.

"A wall," Nerva was saying. Though all Domitian could hear was the thumping of his own heart.

"You can see I am not harbouring anyone, commander. Kindly leave my home so that my staff and I can go back to bed."

There followed a pause so tense that Domitian's short life flashed before his eyes. Brief snatches of his deceased mother and sister. His little niece Julia giggling. Titus calling his archery lame. His father telling him to stop sulking for Jupiter's sake. Tidying up the study with Uncle Flavius. Caenis hugging him. Naked tussles with Nerva. Rampant rogerings with Mina. And onwards to his daring escape from the Capitoline Hill.

"My apologies, senator. Soldiers! Let's go!"

Domitian exhaled his breath.

A few moments later the cupboard was flung into light. Mina and Domitian blinked from the glare. In the door frame stood Nerva. "They've gone," he announced.

Mina bounced on her feet and embraced the very surprised Nerva, kissing him on both cheeks. "You absolutely brilliant man!" she declared, grinning.

"I told you we could trust him," said Domitian, smiling at Nerva. "He's the best. The best ever."

The senator's cheeks flushed pink with pleasure.

SEVENTY-SIX

Vitellius could not sleep no matter how much he tried. No matter how much he drank. He remained wide–eyed, casting suspicious glances at the guards in the chamber.

He'd never thought much about them before. Never really paid any attention to their perpetual presence. Now he was acutely aware of every damn one of them posted in his vicinity. A creak of leather, a shuffle of sandals had him on high alert, twisting his fat neck around.

Oh yes, there they stood. Two of them in their purple-plumed helmets and scorpion breastplates: his jailers.

"Imperial Majesty." Asiaticus bowed his head. "I regret to inform you that Vespasian's son has not been located."

"Then I am dead," responded the emperor quietly. "I have nothing of any worth to offer Primus."

"Don't lose heart, Imperial Majesty."

"How can I not? Primus is en route to kill me. And how long before the Praetorians decide they'd rather have someone else as emperor? I am caught."

Asiaticus placed a low stool in front of the emperor's couch. Leaning forward he said, "They are clearing out the palace grounds, the soldiers. They are packing up their camps to go fight Primus. When Primus gets here, to the palace, they will be too busy defending to worry about you."

Vitellius shifted on his couch. "You have a plan?"

Asiaticus nodded. "I've spent these past hours studying routes out of the palace and off the Palatine Hill."

"And you've found one?"

Asiaticus leaned forward and whispered, "One where they will never find you."

Vitellius pressed his fleshy hand on top of Asiaticus' and grinned.

* * *

Philo opened his eyes and gave a yawn, stretching out his arms.

From beside him in the bed, Teretia said, "Stay home today. It's too dangerous for you to go to the palace."

Philo was poised to mutter something noncommittal but was interrupted by a cry from beside the bed.

"I'll take him into the kitchen," said Philo, lifting Horace from his cot. "You catch up on some sleep."

"Make sure you take his blanket. I don't want him getting cold."

Philo wrapped the blanket around his son. Then instead of taking Horace to the kitchen, he gave Lysander's door a soft knock and entered.

Lysander rolled over onto his side.

"What is it?" he asked through half-closed eyes.

Philo sat down on the bed. "Teretia says I shouldn't go to work today."

Lysander pulled himself upwards. "You were actually thinking of going to the palace today?"

"Teretia says I shouldn't."

"Of course you—we—shouldn't. You told us last night that Primus is right outside the city walls. You said you expected him to attack at first light. He has masses of legions and he's headed straight for the palace. Why would you want to go to work?"

Philo held Horace up against his shoulder, rubbing at the boy's back gently. "What about the slaves? What will happen to them? There's no Felix to tell them what to do."

"They're palace, aren't they? They'll run. You and I being there isn't going to change their natural instincts."

"It feels wrong," worried Philo, "that we are all safe on the Viminal and they're facing what they are."

Lysander lay back down and rolled on to his side facing the wall. "I was at the palace the day Nero fell. I was there the day Galba fell. There's not a chance I'm going to be there the day Vitellius falls. Go back to bed."

Philo looked at little Horace snuggled against him, his eyes closing. He kissed Horace's cheek softly and said. "Daddy's staying at home with you today."

"Your Daddy is being very sensible," responded Lysander, shutting his eyes.

* * *

"Wot is it?" asked Felix.

Midas opened the lid and sniffed. "I have no idea but it smells like something a sea of nymphs would place before great Neptune along with his flagon of ambrosia."

"That'll be Vallia's fish stew. She makes it well."

Midas passed the oblong container through the bars to Felix.

"She well?" enquired Felix. "And Gany? He doing good? He ain't getting skinny or nothing?"

"They both seemed well," said Midas. "Felix, Vespasian's forces are outside the city. They're going to attack today."

Felix, halfway through a mouth of stew, made an incomprehensible but nonetheless loud noise.

"Right, Midas, lad," he said when he'd swallowed. "You tell my stock to get outta the fuckin' way. Lock yourselves away in the slave complex. You don't owe that fucker Vitellius anything. Just get the fuck away. I ain't losing a single one of my slaves to this. So you tell 'em, Midas. You fuckin' tell 'em."

* * *

Midas had never disobeyed a Felix order before, and he certainly didn't ignore this one. With the assistance of the overseers and the senior freedmen, he managed to evacuate the entire household staff back to the slave complex.

There they waited, thousands of them: secretaries and fan boys, dancers and hairdressers, polishers and flute girls. Waiting for the battle to pass and for whatever lay next for them.

* * *

"Imperial Majesty."

Vitellius looked up to see Asiaticus hovering above him.

"Now is the time to move. The Flavian forces are getting closer."

SEVENTY-SEVEN

"It's very quiet still," said Philo, peering down at the street below.

Lysander, immersed in the very important task of filing his nails, said, "Thank you for that. It's been nearly three blinks since you last updated me."

"Do you think they're still fighting? Or maybe it's all over and Vespasian is emperor."

Philo's brow furrowed with anxiety.

"Look, why don't you do some praying to Hanuman," suggested Lysander, pointing his nail file towards the household shrine where the lares mixed freely with the likes of Apollo, Minerva, Hanuman, and Kali. "It might calm your nerves."

"Hmmm, maybe."

"Right. I'm off," said Pompeia, appearing in the kitchen encased in a thick winter cloak.

"You're going out?" squeaked Philo.

"Just round the corner to my sister's. Truth be told, she's having issues with that idiot husband of hers. I won't be long."

"But there's a battle going on," protested Philo.

"Oh," said Pompeia. "Is it happening on the Viminal?"

"No," said Lysander. "It's happening at the palace most probably."

"Good job you boys stayed home then. See you later!" She gave them a cheery wave.

"She'll be fine," Lysander assured Philo. "She's going to the next street. And there's nothing kicking off anywhere near here."

Philo did not feel reassured. He checked the window again.

Unbeknown to the master of the apartment there were some further reassurances being given.

"I'm just so worried!" wailed Marcia.

Teretia rubbed at the slave's back, making soothing noises. On the floor sat Horace happily sucking on the end of one of his mother's hairbrushes.

"Magnus is out there fighting. He could be hurt! He could be dead! And I love him so much," said Marcia, sobbing into Teretia's shoulder.

"It's because you love each other so much that he's sure to let you know he's alive. You'll be the first person he comes to," said Teretia. "I know just how horrid this feels. Last year my darling Philo was arrested and I didn't know if he was alive or dead. It was horrible thinking he could be suffering and there was nothing I could do to help him."

Marcia gave a muffled sob accompanied by a nod on Teretia's shoulder.

"But you see Magnus is so much better off because he's a professional soldier. He can fight his way out of any danger. I know he can."

Marcia, extremely red of eye, said hoarsely. "He's so brave and strong."

Teretia forced a smile. "You see. He'll be fine!"

* * *

Asiaticus hadn't factored Vitellius' great weight into his escape plan. He'd assumed they'd take a litter or a sedan chair, but with the palace staff mysteriously absent, there was no one to transport the emperor. Thus, they'd walked through the endless corridors and chambers. Vitellius waddling along and frequently stopping to get his breath back.

Asiaticus' fingers twitched with impatience as Vitellius lay down on a couch.

"I can't go any further," he moaned. "My legs are too sore."

"Imperial Majesty," barked the freedman. "We have to keep moving. Otherwise, we're not going to be able to get off the Palatine Hill before the Flavians get here."

"We have plenty of time. You go see. You go see where they are while I rest here."

Asiaticus ran down the corridor, his sandals slapping on the marble until he found an exterior door. Opening it, he exited on to the hill. The noise informed him of the worst. Walking to the edge of the terrace, he stared down into the Forum and saw a mass of bodies below filling every corner of the space. Soldiers clashing sword on sword. Shields thrust against shields. Horses amid the chaos with their riders slashing downwards.

They were too late. The battle had been brought to the palace. Asiaticus looked backwards to the great palace walls. He could run, leave the emperor behind. He'd have a far greater chance of survival if he did. What did he owe the fat fucker anyway? He'd been abused by him since childhood, ripped and torn until he was just an empty shell of a man doing his bidding. He thought of the pretty eunuch and how he'd looked when they cut him down. Asiaticus' first thought had been regret at the loss of such beauty. And then a sort of envy as he realised that he, not Sporus, would be the butt of Vitellius' anger for this.

What to do?

In the end, the decision was made for him. Lost in his thoughts he hadn't seen the soldier approaching. The sword was thrust into his back and Asiaticus fell to his knees and then on to his face.

"Legionaries!" screamed the soldier. "We have the palace! It's ours."

They streamed up the ramps and pathways that led from the Forum. Up the great steps of the old palace where they faced 30 or so Vitellians attempting to defend. These were cut down easily and they stormed into the building. Here in the great hall, a cohort of Vitellians had been pushed back and a fierce fight ensued as more and more soldiers pushed through the doors. The carnage was taken further into the palace, through the corridors and chambers. No space was sacred as the Germans tried desperately to hold off the tide of Flavians. It was impossible. The odds were too great. The blond giants who'd marched and looted their way down from Germania were hacked into pieces, their limbs and extremities scattered across the marble floor.

SEVENTY-EIGHT

From Primus, Epaphroditus understood it had been a fierce battle. The Vitellians had kept the Flavian forces outside the city gates for four whole hours of intense fighting. Even when they'd broken through, the fight continued in the narrow residential streets, with residents leaning out of their windows yelling encouragements.

"We fought the bastards street by bloody street. Damn, those Germans were tenacious. They wouldn't back down over a single damn cobble. You have to admire them. Gutsy they were. Bloody gutsy. Even at the palace when they must have known all was lost."

"But they are repelled? The city is taken?" asked Epaphroditus.

"That is nearly the case. They are defeated. The survivors have been pushed back to the Praetorian barracks."

Epaphroditus' ears pricked. "The Praetorian barracks? My assistant lives on the Viminal."

"Great Jupiter, man!" swore Primus. "We've got a whole city to take. We can't worry about your damn assistant."

Epaphroditus quickly changed tack. "Philo was cared with looking after Domitian, Vespasian's son. He will know where he is. He might even be with him."

That caught Primus' attention. "I instructed Flavius to send the boy to me so he might be safe from all this. He ignored me and this is the result. The emperor's son stuck in the midst of battle."

Epaphroditus, who'd been party to these discussions, knew why Flavius had held on to Domitian. He didn't trust Primus. Neither had Epaphroditus but up against Vitellius he was now beginning to realise the foolishness of that stance. Flavius and Domitian should both have got out while they'd had the chance. They'd been stupid to think they could talk Vitellius round. Very stupid. Now Flavius, decent kind Flavius, was dead. And Domitian was stuck in the middle of a bloody battle for supremacy.

"Right, you, legionary."

"Yes, sir," said Lucullus.

"Get yourself and some men to the Viminal to this Philo's abode. Which is …?"

Primus looked to Epaphroditus. "First floor above the pan shop opposite the butchers," he supplied.

"He either has the young Caesar or he knows where he is. He needs to be moved to safety."

* * *

The first yells were heard just before dusk.

Philo shot over to the window. On the street below a group of soldiers ran, pursued by a further group of soldiers.

"What is it?" asked Teretia, joining her husband by the window.

More soldiers were now appearing, filling the main street from the side alleys. There were yells and screams as groups were caught and despatched.

Philo hastily closed the shutters.

"I think we should all sit down and, ermm, try and think about something else."

Which was easier said then done given the noise.

"Philo, I don't like this," said Teretia. "What's going to happen?"

Philo squeezed her hand tight. "They must be headed for the Praetorian camp for reinforcements. We'll be fine here if we just stay put."

"Verenia's house is near the Praetorian camp," said Lysander, a hint of worry in his voice.

"I think she might have left for Greece by now. It's meant to be any day now," said Teretia.

"What? What are you talking about?" said Lysander. He didn't give Teretia time to answer, saying, "Verenia's not leaving Rome."

"She's going to Greece with Uncle Verenius."

Lysander's eyes bulged. "Verenia can't leave Rome. What about us?"

"You split up," replied a confused Teretia.

"No we didn't. I was taking some time to think things through," he insisted.

"Oh," said Teretia, her cheeks pinkening. "I rather think Verenia thought you'd split up. That's why she decided to go to Greece with Uncle Verenius."

Lysander's face betrayed the torrent of emotions rushing through him. "No. No, we didn't." He grabbed his cloak off the peg. "I'm going to talk to her. She cannot go to Greece."

"You can't go out," said Philo. "There's soldiers everywhere!"

Lysander paused at the door. "I have to go. I can't let her leave."

He passed through the door. Philo followed him, yelling as Lysander ran down the stairs, "Stop! Come back! Please come back."

"I have to go," came a voice from the bottom of the stairs, followed by the slam of the front door.

* * *

Epaphroditus walked up the palace steps.

"There's really no sign of Vitellius?" he asked one of Primus' soldiers.

"There's no sign of anyone. Anyone alive that is."

Epaphroditus frowned at this, but the truth was revealed when he entered the grand entrance hall. The marble floor design was hidden beneath dozens of corpses scattered about. Gashes on the columns told of a fierce battle.

"So where do you think he is, Vitellius, sir?"

Epaphroditus, stepping over a body gingerly, replied, "He's here. He'll be here. You just need to know where to look."

* * *

The door to the slave complex was firmly shut. Epaphroditus gave it three firm knocks. He could hear shuffling behind it.

"It's me, Epaphroditus. It's safe to open the door."

The door slowly opened and Midas' curly-haired head appeared. "Sir? Is it really all over? We heard some awful stuff."

"It is over," smiled Epaphroditus.

Walking into the refectory, he found the staff huddled together. They looked up at him with wide, worried eyes.

"All hail, Imperator Vespasian!"

There were cheers and the worry replaced with relieved smiles. Hugs and kisses were exchanged.

Epaphroditus clapped his hands. "Right," he said rubbing his palms together. "Who wants to help me track down a certain ex-emperor?"

A sea of hands shot up in the air.

SEVENTY-NINE

Magnus knew he had to get out and get out quickly. They'd opened the gates of the Praetorian camp to the fleeing Vitellians. They'd recounted the tale of the bloody battle for Rome, alongside informing them that they were being pursued by the victorious Flavian legions. The gates to the camp were strong but not that strong. Not keeping out several legions with siege equipment strong.

Looking round at the high, thick walls topped with spikes, he saw not safety but a prison. He had to get out! His eyes strayed to the back wall, still thick, still topped with spikes but there was a wagon parked next to it. Clambering up on its cargo he might be able to pull himself up and over the other side. 'Course, he might be killed jumping off the other side, but better that than pinned down here and slaughtered by the Flavians.

* * *

Lysander was suffering a swirl of mental turmoil, so he was rather thankful for the distraction of avoiding the soldiers. He pressed his back into a shop doorway to avoid the ballista that was being rolled towards the Praetorian camp. He hoped they weren't intending to light their missiles. Otherwise, the whole of the Viminal could go up in flames like the Capitoline Hill.

* * *

It took seventeen repeated rolls of the battering ram to break open Felix's cell door. The wood splintered inwards and Felix stepped through the mess.

Seeing Epaphroditus and Midas waiting, he asked. "Right, wot now?"

"Want to help us find Vitellius?"

Felix rolled up his sleeves. Cracking his knuckles, he said. "'Course I fuckin' do! Let's go."

* * *

The battle for the Praetorian camp was perhaps the bloodiest of all the fighting of that day. Magnus had been right to flee. The Flavian siege equipment broke the gates down quickly and the Vitellians were swarmed upon by the invaders. Nobody was left standing. Some, in desperation rather than honour, chose to take their own lives, hanging themselves from the ramparts.

At the conclusion of this bloodbath, the victors gazed about at each other. Beyond the glory of victory they had only one other thought. For they were soldiers down to their nailed boots. Loot! They spilled onto the Viminal streets, keen to secure their share.

EIGHTY

Having successfully made it to Verenia's house, Lysander was relieved to see it still standing. Such had been his preoccupation during his hazardous walk that he'd failed to work out what he was going to say.

Something he rather regretted when admitted to see Verenia. He blurted out, "You can't go to Greece!"

"Why?" she enquired.

Lysander's mouth opened and closed several times under Verenia's hard stare. "Because it's not sailing season!"

Verenia turned her back on him to instruct Doris with the packing. "I am going by land. It'll take much longer, naturally. But I don't mind that. Father's gone on ahead."

"You can't go," repeated Lysander.

Verenia turned around to face him. "Why?" she asked again. "What is there for me here?"

"There's, there's," flapped Lysander. "There's everything. Everything and everyone on the Viminal."

Verenia gave a tight smile. "The girl with the broken marriage and broken engagement. I suppose I do provide them with their daily quota of gossip. And act as a useful warning to their daughters: 'Don't end up like Verenia!'"

Her eyes began to fill with tears.

"Please don't leave."

"There's nothing for me here," said Verenia, wiping at her eyes with the sleeve of her gown.

Lysander stepped forward. "There's me."

Which was the touching, tender moment that the doorkeeper burst in on. "Mistress! Mistress! The soldiers are on the streets! They've gone wild!"

Lysander blinked, then said, "We need to barricade the entrances."

* * *

A similar operation was taking place further down the Viminal Hill.

"Marcia, help me lift this table."

Philo and Marcia carried the kitchen table, wobbling, and pushed it against the front door. Teretia stood in the space where it had stood, bouncing Horace on her hip.

"My mama," she fretted.

"Marcia, let's move the chairs too and pile them on top," instructed Philo. He gave Teretia a hug. "Your mother is with her sisters. They have enough menfolk between them."

Teretia's chin wobbled but she managed a brave nod, hugging her son close to her.

Philo peered round the shutters to the street one storey below. A street that was rapidly filling with soldiers. He watched as one kicked at the entrance to Tadius' butchers, then leaned over his shoulder and yelled for help to break in.

Philo closed the shutters. "Best stay away from the windows. We don't want to attract their attention."

"I hope Lysander made it to Verenia's in time," worried Teretia.

Marcia, standing by their makeshift barricade felt a searing pain in her bosom. Was Magnus alright?

* * *

Epaphroditus peered under the couch. Empty.

"You really think that fat fucker could fit under there?" queried Felix, kicking down a screen to reveal nothing more than a chair.

"I guess not," he said. "He's in the palace. I know he is. We found Asiaticus dead outside. I think he took flight back in here."

"We'll find 'im. We got every fuckin' slave searchin'. Every soldier of Primus' searchin'. We ain't gonna miss something that size. If he's here, we'll find him."

Checking behind the door, Epaphroditus said, "He's here alright."

EIGHTY-ONE

Verenius had taken most of the household with him. Others were elsewhere making the necessary arrangements for Verenia's departure. That left just four of them: Lysander, Verenia, Doris, and the aged doorkeeper.

There was no choice but to chip in. The alarming noise from outside spurred them on as they heaved furniture, amphora, barrels, and anything else they could find against the doors. Lysander's main fear was the large wooden double doors that Verenius used to move his wagons into the courtyard. The one remaining wagon they'd pushed against those doors.

Having moved everything they could, the four of them stood in the centre of the courtyard facing the double doors. Screams from outside drifted over the walls. A cry of "No! No! Help me! Someone please!"

"It's Fidelia from next door," said Verenia.

Fidelia shouted repeatedly for help and then came a scream, long and shrill. Verenia took hold of Lysander's hand. On his other side Doris gave a stifled sob and Lysander reached over for her hand. Doris did the same for the doorkeeper and they stood in silence, the four of them hand in hand, waiting.

Verenius' house, though cramped in Lysander's palace-born eyes, was one of the larger dwellings on the street. There was little chance of soldiers set on pillaging ignoring it. They just had to hope their barricade held.

"Do you think Fidelia—"

Lysander cut Verenia's question off. "Probably best not to think about it."

Doris gave another sob. The doorkeeper began to recite prayers and promises to the gods. Verenia squeezed Lysander's hand tight.

From outside a yell of: "'Ere lads, wot about this one? The bigger the door, the bigger the booty I reckon."

Lysander held his breath as the doors rattled.

"Locked. Really must be some good stuff inside."

"Girls?"

"Bound to be. Bagsy I get the first fuck. Lads, let's break 'em down!"

There followed a series of thumps as the soldiers attempted to get through the wooden doors. Doris gasped at each bang. In Lysander's hand, Verenia's hand trembled.

The bangs increased in frequency and volume as more soldiers joined in the attempt.

BANG. BANG.

The doors rattled on their hinges and creaked. But the wagon and other items piled up against them held them firm.

"Thank you. Thank you," mouthed Lysander to the gods, even Philo's weird ones.

Much frustrated language was heard as the doors thwarted the soldiers. Eventually they heard.

"Fuck 'em! There's plenty else going free."

A muttering of agreement. A final thump. Then silence.

Lysander expelled the breath he'd been holding. Doris gave a squeal and threw her arms around the aged doorkeeper. Verenia exchanged a relieved smile with Lysander.

"They've gone."

"They have," he said, then paused as his nostrils twitched. "What's that smell?"

He turned back to the double doors. The soldiers had gone alright. But they'd left a parting gift. The announcer watched in horror as the flames spread upwards and across the wooden doors.

* * *

Magnus pressed his back against the wall and pulled his cloak over his head waiting for the soldiers to pass. It had been his plan to blend in with the Viminal Hill residents. There was no reason, dressed as he was, that anyone should realise he was a fleeing legionary. No reason at all.

His plan failed at the first lap. There were no Viminal Hill residents to blend in with. Anyone with any sense was in their home with the door barred and a club within easy reach. Which left only Vespasian's soldiers and Magnus.

Plan number two: evade them. Which was easier said than done. They were everywhere. Taking up all the opportunities the Viminal offered: goods and women. Magnus could hear their screams and the impotent yells of their male kin. He prayed to the gods that his Marcia was safe. If one of those brutes laid a finger on her…

* * *

"Could we open the shutters a little bit?" Teretia asked Philo. "Marcia and I thought we might do some knitting to occupy ourselves. The light really isn't good enough."

Philo chewed on his lower lip as he looked upon his womenfolk. Chiefly on his mind was what had happened at Cremona. How the soldiers had run amok, violating girl and boy, woman and man, young and old, with no discrimination. And now those self-same troops were in Rome.

"No," he said. "It's not safe. When they arrive, we don't want to give them any indication that anyone is at home."

There came the sound of feet pounding up the stairs. Philo froze. Maybe they won't stop here, he thought hopefully. He was instantly disproved by a banging on the door. Marcia and Teretia squealed. Philo pressed his finger against his lips, a warning for them to stay quiet.

BANG. BANG. BANG. The pounding on the door was almost in sync with the pounding of Philo's heart. BANG. BANG. Then a hissed call.

"Marcia. Marcia. It's me."

"It's Magnus," said Marcia.

"Philo, we need to move the table to let him in," said Teretia. She clasped Marcia's hands, telling her. "I told you he'd be alright."

"Who's Magnus?" asked Philo.

* * *

"So you see, they are just terrifically in love," concluded Teretia.

Philo struggled to process the information presented to him. His eyes fell on the six feet of muscle that was Magnus. Marcia stood beside him, holding his hand.

"Philo?" prompted Teretia.

Philo blinked. "You knew all this and you didn't tell me?"

"I couldn't. It was all a terrific secret."

"Why? Why was it a secret if this relationship is such a marvellous thing?"

Teretia paused and chewed at her lower lip. "You're not cross at me, are you?"

Philo thought for a moment, then said evenly. "Yes. Yes I am cross."

Teretia began to tear up. Seeing this, Philo gave her a hug and kissed the top of her head. "I'm not cross with you."

Well, maybe he was slightly peeved at her for not telling him that Marcia's relations with the soldier had gone quite so far.

But not cross. He could never be cross at Teretia. She was perfect in his eyes. Even her gross romanticism that had caused this current situation, Philo saw as being born of her loving upbringing. Philo had been raised in the palace, a quite different upbringing. His inner palace cynic rose to the surface.

"I am not cross with you," he reiterated. "I'm cross with him."

His eyes fell on Magnus. And the German was subject to, what was for Philo, a fairly withering stare.

"Sir," began the German. "If I could—"

He was cut off most uncharacteristically by Philo. "We will not talk of the great danger you as an enemy soldier have put my household in by coming here."

"We love each other!"

Philo ignored this passionate declaration from Marcia. His focus was on Magnus.

"You've got, what, twenty years left to serve in the legions? During which time you can't officially marry. During this time you could be posted anywhere in the empire. Warring Judaea maybe. Or wild Britannia. And what happens to Marcia? She can't live with you in the barracks, so does she become a camp follower living among the hawkers and the prostitutes that trail the legions? What kind of company is that for a young girl? What kind of life is that? And what if you're killed? Where does that leave her? Maybe the army might dish out some coinage. Or maybe they'll send it back to your mother instead. Leaving her stranded in a foreign land with no means to support herself."

During this speech Magnus' head had slowly lowered, the bravado seeping out of him. Philo concluded with, "Marcia is my slave. I have a duty to care for her. To ensure that she is happy, safe, and well."

Marcia looked at her German lover cringing before her slight master. Then she said, "Master, I don't want to leave Rome and live in an army camp with prostitutes. I want to stay here with the mistress and little Horace!"

"I don't want you to leave either," burst out Teretia. "I'd miss you so much!"

"I'd miss you more," wailed Marcia.

Slave and mistress embraced each other while competing in declarations of affection.

"I'll go," Magnus said to Philo.

"Yes, you will. I wish you a safe journey and may Goddess Abeona protect you."

Magnus took one final look at Marcia. Then he left.

EIGHTY-TWO

It was at the seventeenth bedroom that Epaphroditus finally snapped.

"Why in Venus' fucking cunt do they make palaces so fucking big?!"

He sank his buttocks on to the bed.

"That were an invective worthy of me," smiled Felix, sitting beside him on the bed.

His weight shifted Epaphroditus a good half-foot higher.

Felix patted his shoulder. "We will find him."

"You know, I'm not so sure now. Primus has given up. He's sent some of his men to every gate in the city to see if he's fled."

"He's gone nowhere," said Felix. "Minerva's pointy fuckin' trident, haven't we spent the last few fuckin' months getting fuckin' litters to haul him along to the next chamber? Three quarters of my fuckin' bearers have done their backs in from his fuckin' bulk. He ain't walked nowhere. 'E's 'ere alright. And we'll find him. You found Nero when he was hiding in the palace, didn't ya?"

He had. Didn't that seem like a long time ago now, years even? A time when he'd been secure in his position as the emperor's private secretary. When he'd had a wife and a family. A time that made sense. Nothing had made sense since that spring day the previous year.

"It all started that day," said Epaphroditus. "Nero. Then Galba. Otho. Vitellius. It all started that day. And all because of Nymphidius Sabinus. Who'd have thought he'd have such an impact on events?" said Epaphroditus, picturing the square-jawed son of Nymphidia who'd overthrown Nero.

"Now he were a queer fucker," said Felix. "Good prefect. I'll give him that. But odd as fuck."

"He was certainly that. I sort of miss him." He looked at Felix. "Is that odd?"

"No, that's fuckin' sensible. Sabinus would never have tolerated what the Guard have become. What this palace has become." He wrinkled his nose with distaste. "But I reckon that craggy-faced bastard Vespasian might have big-enough balls to sort it all out." Felix pushed his hands on to his thighs. "Right, we can't sit here nattering all day. We got to find this fuckin' emperor. Where did you find Nero that day?"

"With Sporus," said Epaphroditus.

"Sporus?" mused Felix. "The thing he most loved. Yeah, that makes sense. What does Vitellius adore most in the whole world?"

Felix and Epaphroditus thought for a moment then in unison went, "Ha!"

Turning to each other they said in exact synchronisation, "Food! The kitchens!"

* * *

"I just wanted Marcia to have what we have," Teretia explained as she tucked sleeping baby Horace under a blanket. "She's had such a horrible time. You know her previous master made her make his man part all hard with her hand. And he scolded her awfully!"

If the worst of Marcia's life was being yelled out and compelled to masturbate her master, Philo rather felt she'd got off lightly.

"I know," he told her. "And one day we will look into that for her. But not yet. She's not ready to be freed. I was thirty when I was freed and you know how much I struggled. She's not mature enough yet."

Also he wanted to get his money's worth out Marcia, which Philo didn't say to Teretia.

"I think you're right," said Teretia.

They walked down the corridor back to the kitchen. Marcia was stood wide-eyed. In front of her were two legionaries.

Dear gods! In all the excitement of Magnus' visit, they'd neglected to re-barricade the door. The soldiers' eyes fell on Teretia.

"Brilliant, Gleber, we get one woman each. Bagsy I get the big-titted one."

"Fuck you, Reginius, we'll draw lots for who gets a go at her first."

* * *

The smoke was getting thicker. It stung at Lysander's throat, choking his breath. The barricade of items that had saved them from the pillaging soldiers now trapped them. The flames had rapidly licked from the doors to the wagon pushed against them and then to the other items they'd piled up. All were now ablaze and the flames licking onwards to the walls of the house that backed on to the streets.

Verenia nudged Lysander. "Now what?"

He found himself under the gaze of six hopeful eyes. Now what, indeed. Lysander didn't know. All exits were ablaze. Behind them was solid wall. Either side was a rapidly spreading fire. His eyes began to sting. He told himself it was the smoke and not the feeling of utter helplessness that had encased him. Oh gods! Now what?

"Lysander!" said Verenia, coughing.

She held her shawl over her mouth to stop the smoke choking her but still it burned at her lungs, as it did for Lysander. They could feel the heat of the flames now, even in this December chill. They were licking ever closer as they destroyed Verenia's home.

"Lysander!"

He looked at the wall of flames in front of him. He felt the wall behind him. Which left? Glancing to his right he saw them. The stone stairs that led up the side of the house to the upper floor.

Up! They could go up.

"Come on," he said, taking holding of Verenia's hand and pulling her towards the stairs. "We can get to the roof from there. And maybe on to another non-burning building."

The four of them ran up the steps, choking and coughing as they did.

At the top, Lysander stood and assessed. The roof was about a foot higher than the door to the upper level.

"Furniture! Is there a chair or something we can get to that I can stand on?"

The aged slave pulled open the door and was immediately lost in a fog of thick black smoke. All of them could feel the heat. Hear the crackling from within. And then a sudden crash.

They slammed the door shut.

"Do you think that was the floor collapsing?" asked Verenia.

It was a distinct possibility, thought Lysander. Which meant they had to get off the roof as soon as they could. Before it too was eaten up by flames.

"Very well. Nothing to stand on. But maybe. That drainpipe. I can climb up that."

Lysander was not one to go to the gym much. He found the ascent harder than he'd anticipated. When he got to the top, he fell on to the roof on his back. Then jumped up as he felt the heat burn through his cloak.

Looking across, there was a perhaps two-foot gap between Verenia's house and the house next door. Jumpable. He looked down at the remaining three. Two women and an aged man. Would they even make it up the drainpipe? Could they jump across safely?

The thought penetrated his brain. He could make it. He could make it easier on his own.

He looked down at the party of three. Verenia's golden hair showing beneath her scarf. Doris' hopeful eyes. The aged doorkeeper's panicked expression. He couldn't leave her. He'd done so once before when the Guard had stormed the banqueting hall. His palace instinct had kicked in and he'd run, leaving Verenia behind. Not today though. Not now he knew what it felt like to be without her.

"Doris. You kneel down and let Verenia step on your back. I'll grab your hand from here and pull you up. Then you, Doris stand on the doorkeeper and we can all pull him up."

The lift up from Doris' back had Verenia three-quarters of the way to the top of the drainpipe.

"If you put your foot on to that bracket and push yourself up I'll be able to grab you."

Verenia did so. Lysander grabbed hold of her forearm.

"Kick upwards and use one hand to grab the side of the roof."

With one hand gripping at a tile and the other onto Lysander, the announcer just about managed to pull her up.

Doris being thinner was easier. The doorkeeper then surprised them all by nimbly ascending the drainpipe.

"Used to climb trees when I was a nipper," he told them. "You never lose the knack."

"Right. We need to jump. I'll go first so I can catch you all on the other side."

Verenia stared down at the gap. "Lysander, are you sure you can get across?"

He wasn't as confident as he had been earlier. Now he was up close. But he hid this behind a forced smile.

"'Course."

He walked upwards across the tiles, standing at the roof's peak. He began his run up before any further doubts could set in. The tiles slipped slightly beneath his feet. A gust of wind availed him as he ascended off his right foot. A brief soar. Then thump on to the other side. He shot to his feet.

"I made it!" he declared across the divide, smiling. "You next, Verenia. I'll catch you. I promise."

Verenia's eyes were fixed on the chasm of space between the buildings.

"I can't," she said. "I can't do it."

Seeing the smoke billowing behind her, Lysander pleaded, "Please darling. You have to."

Verenia shook her head, frozen to the spot.

"Mistress, let me go first," said Doris. "Then there will be two of us to catch you on the other side."

"I'm not moving from here until you are with me. I'm not leaving without you," called Lysander. "Doris."

Doris walked up to the pinnacle of the slanted roof, then ran down the tiles. She leapt across and was caught by Lysander in an embrace.

Both turned to face the other two.

"You can do it, mistress. It's really easy," encouraged Doris.

"Verenia, please. You need to jump."

Verenia turned and walked up the roof. She stood on the top for a moment. The trouble was once she started running down there was no choice. She'd have to jump. Jump or fall. She bit her lip, looked up to the grey sky and then ran.

She could feel the tiles slipping under her feet as she moved. She tried not to think about what she was about to do. At the edge of the roof she leapt. A moment of nothingness beneath her. Then, thump, into something solid. She opened her eyes to see Lysander smiling down at her. His arms holding her tight.

"You did it!" he said, kissing her.

"Portus!"

The doorkeeper was already making his ascent up the roof, ready to jump.

"Portus," called Verenia. "We can all catch you. Don't worry."

"I ain't worried, mistress," he smiled, showing off his black, gappy teeth.

He looked about to set off when there came an almighty creak.

"What's that noise?" asked Doris.

The final word was drowned out by a shuddering crash that reverberated beneath their feet.

Verenia held onto Lysander to right herself. She looked across to Portus to check he was alright when there came another thundering creak. Portus looked down at his feet. Then CRASH. He was lost in a plume of smoke.

"Portus!" yelled Doris.

"Portus!" yelled Lysander.

When the smoke cleared, there was no sign of Portus.

"Where is he?" asked Verenia.

Lysander, peering across, saw it. "The roof fell in."

A further crash sent tiles tumbling off the roof opposite them.

"Oh, Portus," wailed Doris.

EIGHTY-THREE

It had taken Vitellius a while to realise that Asiaticus wasn't coming back for him. He'd had choice thoughts about his freedman then. Namely, how he was going to hold him down and pull a sword across the unscathed side of his face.

Then he'd wandered the corridors, unsure as to what to do or where he was going. With the staff fled, there was no one to ask help from, so the emperor waddled along all on his own.

Turning a corner, he was assailed with a beauteous smell. One that set his stomach off in a rumble as loud as thunder. He'd decided to follow that delicious scent. Which was how he'd ended up in the kitchens. He soon demolished all the food within easy reach. Then he wandered about, opening cupboards to see what other delicious morsels he could find.

He'd filled up a plate of towering goodies when he heard a voice. He stepped behind a door, clutching onto his plate.

"Epaphroditus wants us to search the west wing of the palace for Vitellius," said one voice.

"I pray to Mercury that we are the ones that find him," came a second voice. "I want to stick it to that pig."

Behind the door, Vitellius swallowed a mouthful of pastry. They were searching him out. The battle must be over. He was no longer emperor. The joy at this change of status was tempered by his current predicament.

What to do?

He looked down at his plate of food. If they were searching the palace, was there any point in moving? He'd be much safer here. They wouldn't think of looking for him elsewhere than the flashy bedrooms and dining rooms.

Carrying his plate, he took a tour of the palace kitchens for the first time in his life. They were amazing. Who'd have thought they'd be so substantial? Not Vitellius, certainly. He'd neither wondered nor cared how and where his food was prepared, so long as it was placed in front of him.

There was a door set in an arched alcove that looked interesting. He opened it to reveal a pantry lined with shelves that held various condiments. Vitellius looked down at his plate heaped with food. It could do with some garum. This seemed as good a place as any to sit it out. Thus, the ex-emperor sat on the floor of the pantry pouring garum sauce over his snack. He left the door pulled almost shut, letting in just enough light to see his food.

* * *

"I want every fuckin' door opened. Every fuckin' cupboard. Every fuckin' pot lid lifted. Every fuckin' corner searched!" ordered Felix as he, Epaphroditus, and five soldiers powered their way to the kitchens.

Turning into them Felix yelled, "Get fuckin' to it!"

The soldiers began their search. Kicking over pots, ripping shelves off the walls, wrenching open doors. Epaphroditus and Felix moved into a second room. Epaphroditus, ducking onto his knees, looked underneath the work bench. Felix pulled open a pantry door.

"Well, fuckin' well. Look what I found."

Epaphroditus straightened himself and went to where Felix was standing. On the floor of the pantry sat the emperor, a chicken leg suspended midway to his mouth. He looked up at them with piteous eyes. "I'll pay you whatever. Whatever money you want to let me go."

"It wouldn't be enough," said Epaphroditus. "It would never be enough."

Felix demonstrated his brute strength by the ease with which he grabbed hold of the collar of Vitellius' tunic and hauled him to his feet. Their faces were a few inches apart. Epaphroditus braced himself for a full-on Felix rant. Except it didn't come. Instead, the overseer spoke in an almost quiet, measured tone.

"You are the most pathetic creature I have ever fucking seen. Call yourself an emperor? Hiding away here? Stuffing your mouth while there were men outside dying for you. You are contemptible. Absolutely contemptible."

He let go of Vitellius' tunic, pushing him away. Epaphroditus moved forward. He looked straight into Vitellius' face. At its gross expanse. At its greedy little eyes. He felt a rage growing in him. An anger he had never before known. He had not the words to express it. Instead he spat a mouthful of phlegm directly into Vitellius' face. It hit his nose, dripping from it in globules.

"That's for Flavius," he told Vitellius. "And for Sporus. And for every slave boy and slave girl you have ever hurt in your entire depraved life."

He looked away, disgusted, and called out, "Legionaries! We found him."

* * *

They tied his hands behind his back and led the former emperor through the palace corridors. Two soldiers in front, then Vitellius, two further soldiers, Epaphroditus and Felix. As they walked along, the slaves paused to gawp at their former master. Word quickly spread of this strange parade. Soon the corridors were lined with imperial staff in their snow-white uniforms. As Vitellius passed them, they hissed and booed and shouted out insults.

Vitellius kept his head low. He didn't look at them or acknowledge their presence.

"What about Sporus?" yelled Midas. "You bastard! What about him? You killed him. Murderer!"

"Murderer!"

"Murderer!"

"Murderer!"

It was chanted again and again as Vitellius was led to the old palace doors. As they were opened, the two soldiers behind Vitellius gave him a shove. He staggered and almost fell. There, on the palace steps, he was met by a further party of legionaries.

"We'll take him from here," said one, thrusting a sword under Vitellius' chin, forcing him to look upwards. "Hullo emperor," grinned the soldier at Vitellius' trembling features. "We got a whole city who'd like to express exactly what they think of you."

Vitellius was given another shove and he tumbled down the palace steps to much laughter. At the bottom he was hauled upright and again the sword was thrust under his chin to jeers.

At the top of the steps were gathered members of the imperial household watching the spectacle of Vitellius being dragged off to his end.

"You gonna to watch it?" Felix asked Epaphroditus. "Reckon they'll take him to the Gemonian Stairs to kill 'im. If he makes it that far."

They both looked at the gathering crowd waiting in the Forum as Vitellius was shoved and kicked down the pathway. Some of them had objects clutched in their hands ready to throw at Vitellius.

"No," said Epaphroditus. "And you?"

Felix scratched at his beard. "Got too much to do getting stuff ready for the young Caesar."

He turned round and bellowed at the slaves, "OI! YOU FUCKERS GOT WORK TO DO! GET THE FUCK TO IT!"

They jumped on cue and scuttled back into the palace.

EIGHTY-FOUR

The soldiers were busy arguing over the best method for settling who got to rape Teretia first. This gave time for myriad thoughts to race through Philo's mind. Beside him, Marcia was crying. Gods, how he wished he hadn't sent Magnus away now! Teretia's main concern was Horace.

"What if he wakes up and cries?" she whispered to Philo. "What will they do to him?"

Philo couldn't bear to think about it. He tried to block out every report he'd read on the legions' atrocities. None of that would help them now. He had to do something. But what? He couldn't fight them off his wife. They'd kill him in a heartbeat. Which was no help to Teretia, Marcia, or his son. Crying for help was pointless. They'd never be heard above the din of the Viminal Hill being thoroughly ravaged.

What could he do? What would Epaphroditus do in this situation?

"Six!" yelled the one called Reginius, holding the dice in his companion's face.

Gleber batted it away. "You lucky fucker."

"I certainly shall be," he said, licking his lips as he eyed up Teretia. "Oh, this is going to be delicious."

A hand squeezed at Teretia's left breast. She gave a whimper.

"Stop!" said Philo.

Reginius glared at him.

"Stop," repeated Philo.

He had no idea what he was about to say. The words sort of slipped from his lips without any prior examination. "Have me instead. I'm trained in the arts of that sort of thing."

He realised after he'd spoken, that rather than replicating how Epaphroditus would have handled their dire plight, he'd instead channelled what Sporus would have done. Still, there was no backing out now. The words had been spoken. He'd have to go with it.

"I was a catamite at the palace for Emperor Nero," continued Philo, amazed at what was coming out of his mouth and bemused by the very Sporus-like sassy tone he'd adopted. "I was his favourite. His very favourite." Philo found himself winking at Reginius. "He completely threw women over in the end, Nero did. He said he didn't need them. Not when he had me."

Reginius and Gleber exchanged looks. Philo certainly looked to their eyes exactly what a palace catamite should look like. He was of a slight, feminine frame with dark exotic skin. Perfect bum-boy material.

"I can't think why you'd want these mere girls when you could have me. Both of you," Philo suggested heavily.

His plan, such as he had one, was to keep both soldiers occupied. Thus giving Teretia and Marcia a chance to get Horace and get out. He was now mentally recalling all the tricks Straton had forced him to perform. He could do this. He had before. Repeatedly. Anything to save his wife and son from the horror. Anything.

Reginius and Gleber conversed. "What do you reckon?"

"I've never had a bit of palace before."

"Me neither."

"I bet he knows sophisticated stuff."

They both looked at Philo. "I bet he does."

Gleber shrugged. "Alright. You go first, then the girls."

Teretia pawed at Philo's arm.

"It's fine, it's fine," he said to her. To Marcia, he said in her native tongue, "Run! Take Horace and run. Find somewhere to hide and stay there."

To the soldiers he explained, "She doesn't speak Latin. I was just explaining that I'm first. She likes soldiers." He forced a smile on to his face.

"Alright, Indian Boy. Let's experience these palace moves of yours."

"The bedroom is that way," said Philo, mentally telling himself that two, youngish, fit legionaries were far better than Straton. "Follow me."

He was leading them to Lysander's room when there came through the door another soldier. Oh gods, thought Philo, three? Teretia screamed. Marcia began to sob.

"Hullo Gleber. Hullo Reginius. Wot you doing here? I've got a message for the geezer that lives here." His eyes fell on Philo, and he straightened his stance. "Sir, I'm Lucullus. I've come from Antonius Primus and Epaphroditus."

Philo experienced a blessed soar of relief. "Lucullus. Good to see you, soldier," he said firmly. "Now, if you could get your commanding officer to arrest these two recruits who have threatened my wife and family."

"Hey?" said Reginius and Gleber in unison.

"Oh, bloody Vesta's hymen, what in Hades' name have you two been up to?" said Lucullus. "I'm sorry, sir, but the discipline's been right shoddy since we entered the city. This is Philo," stressed the Praetorian. "He were at Plancentia with us. He were on good Emperor Otho's side. He's one of ours. The gods know what the new emperor will think about you treating his staff like this."

"I have been tasked with keeping Vespasian's son, Domitian, safe. I am prepared to forgive this transgression and not to report it to the young Caesar if you can provide safe transport to me and my family to Primus, where I will then reveal the young Caesar's location."

Philo said this with an assured authority that broached no disagreement. Reginius and Gleber affected a parade stance, albeit one with a confused glance at Philo.

"I had no idea these were the true emperor's troops," Philo said to Lucullus. "I thought them Vitellius' men so I dared not reveal my position lest I endanger the young Caesar."

"Very wise, sir. There's a right ruckus going on up the Palatine Hill with those lot. They're hanging on by their bloodied fingernails, the lot of them. Right you two, let's get an escort arranged."

As Gleber and Reginius passed by, Philo said, "You are lucky Lucullus came in when he did. That bedroom is where I keep my weaponry."

The Praetorians paled and offered up more humble apologies before departing with Lucullus.

"Horace!" cried Teretia and disappeared down the corridor.

Philo leant against the kitchen wall and exhaled, pinching the bridge of his nose between shaking hands.

"Master," said Marcia.

Philo couldn't look at her. He concentrated hard on making his reply sound as normal as possible.

"Yes, Marcia," he said with an audible tremble.

"That was the bravest thing I ever saw."

Philo looked up.

"What you did, what you were prepared to do to save the mistress and me. It was so courageous. Thank you."

Philo found himself the recipient of a surprising kiss to the cheek. Marcia gave a wobbly smile.

"I'll not forget this, master. Not ever," she said.

Philo had rather hoped she would forget. He was planning to pretend this whole ghastly year had never happened.

"He opened his eyes just as I looked over him," said Teretia, returning with a gurgling Horace.

Philo embraced his wife and son tightly. "I love you. I love you all."

"I know you do," sniffed Teretia. "We're all alright. That's the important thing. We're all alright."

"Sir!" barked Lucullus, appearing in the doorway. "I've rounded up twenty men for you."

"Thank you."

Philo looked at his wife, his son, and his slave. His family. They were all alright.

"Let's go," he said.

* * *

"Do you think he felt anything?" Verenia asked Lysander.

"I shouldn't think so. I imagine it was very sudden and absolute."

They were sitting at the far end of the roof. Deliberately, so Verenia wouldn't have to witness the total destruction of her home. Lysander had his arm around Verenia, cuddling her close to him.

It had been a cold day, and now it was dark and freezing.

"We'll climb down in an hour or two. Just in case there are any soldiers left," Lysander told the girls.

"Where will we go then?" asked Verenia with a hint of sadness in her voice. "We don't even know how my aunt and cousin have fared this day."

Now their immediate predicament was resolved, this was worrying Lysander too. From their rooftop vantage point, they could see the destruction of the Viminal. A plume of smoke in the distance suggested all was not well at the Praetorian camp. If the soldiers had tried the same trick at Pompeia's apartment, there would be no escape for the inhabitants from the fire. And that was the best-case scenario Lysander could picture. He pushed the thoughts downwards.

"I'm sure they are all safe like us," he said, using his best announcer tricks to sound convincing.

Verenia leaned into him.

"Servius Sulpicius Lysander!" came a shout from below.

Lysander's ears pricked up.

"Servius Sulpicius Lysander!"

Lysander got to his feet and walked over to the street side of the roof.

Looking down, he saw a group of tough-looking men. In amongst them, and the one doing the yelling, was his stepfather.

"Baebius!" he called down. "Up here. We're all up here!"

Baebius' eyes turned skyward and met with Lysander's silhouetted figure.

"Thank the gods!" he said. "I promised your mother I'd find you."

* * *

Lysandria had endured a terrible few hours. When her husband had brought her news of the storming of the Viminal, Lysandria's hands had gone to her heart.

"My boys!" she'd wailed. "And their girls! And baby Horace! Gaius, you have to do something!"

Gaius Baebius, successful merchant, was a man used to doing things. He was also of that wealth bracket that could afford their own army, if called to do so. He was therefore able to quickly muster a sizeable and strongly built search party.

Lysandria had fluttered about her ample mansion house waiting for news. She'd been both thankful and relieved when Teretia, Horace, and their slave had arrived at her home with a soldier escort, alive and unhurt. They'd brought news that both Philo and Domitian were safe. Caenis had exhaled a breath at this and, muttering a prayer to the gods, rushed off to compose a message to her stepson.

But for Lysandria, even the presence of the adorable Horace couldn't distract her mind away from her missing son.

If anything had happened to her boys… Well, the gods had better protect those responsible because Lysandria was coming after them. She would make revenge her mission. Gaius Baebius she would ditch one way or another to free her up for her duty to avenge. The Furies had nothing on Lysandria. Beneath an outward presence of a benign fluffy ex-hairdresser lay a heart of absolute steel. She'd been one of Agrippina's closest associates. You didn't survive that without a solid streak of ruthlessness, as all who had stood in the way of her son's route to chief announcer could attest. Or would do, had they not all died from a variety of sudden and unexpected illnesses.

The doors to the lounge were pushed open. In walked her husband.

"Gaius?" she asked, her hands at her throat. "Did you find them?"

Baebius stood to one side to reveal the party of three.

"My boy!" cried Lysandria.

"Mother!"

Mother and son embraced tightly.

"Oh Verenia!" exclaimed Teretia. "I've had the most awful time."

"Me too," said Verenia with a slightly crooked smile. She hugged her younger cousin. "But we are all here now and that's what matters."

"I've been so worried," said Lysandria, stroking her son's hair.

Lysander broke the connection. He looked over to Verenia, who came beside him and took hold of his hand.

"Mother," said Lysander. "I am marrying this woman and no one is going to stop me."

Lysandria blinked. "Well, of course you are, my darling. And why in the gods' names would I try to stop you?"

It was Lysander's turn to look confused as Verenia was given a warm embrace from his mother.

"I am so pleased," gushed Lysandria.

Baebius embraced Verenia, saying warmly, "Welcome to the family."

Verenia looked over her shoulder at Lysander and smiled.

EIGHTY-FIVE

The doors of Nerva's house were pulled open and out stepped a cautious Domitian. The soldiers in the street saluted in unison. At the front of the party, head bowed, Philo said, "Young Caesar, I am here to accompany you to the palace."

Philo stepped to one side and gestured to the imperial purple litter waiting for him.

"Nerva? Mina? You're coming too?" asked Domitian.

Nerva smiled. "If that is your command, young Caesar."

"Err, it is," stumbled Domitian.

"Excellent," grinned Mina.

* * *

Throughout the litter ride, Domitian did not dare open the curtains. Even when cheers rang out all around him, and calls of "Young Caesar!" He sat on the cushions nervously fiddling with his fingers. Mina, walking alongside the litter, the other side of the curtain, helpfully gave him a running commentary on all that was happening outside.

"There's a group of girlies on this corner," she said. "Nice dresses, quite pretty. They're throwing rose petals for the bearers to walk on. I wonder where they got them this time of year?

Oh, more girlies coming up. Super veils and very posh frocks. They seem very happy and jolly. Load of soldiers calling out your name and blessing your father as a saviour. That's nice. I can see the palace. Yep, there it is!"

The litter was lowered to the ground, the curtains pulled open.

"Young Caesar." An imperial slave dressed in white offered a hand for Domitian. He took it and pulled himself to his feet. A terrific cheer erupted. Domitian looked around. He was at the bottom of the palace steps. Nerva was beaming at him and Mina too. Even Philo sported a slight smile.

Arranged on the palace steps were the Praetorian Guard in their purple-plumed helmets. Seeing Domitian, they saluted by thumping their fists on their breastplates. Another cheer erupted. All around, behind a further line of Praetorians, were crowds of civilians shouting and cheering for him.

Standing at the top of the stairs he could see a familiar figure waiting for him: Caenis.

"Young Caesar."

Domitian twisted his neck around to see Epaphroditus. "Young Caesar, it is time to take you to your new home."

Domitian looked up at the towering edifice of the palace of the Caesars. "My home," he said.

EPILOGUE

Spring AD70

"Faustina, will you stop teasing your sisters!" admonished Epaphroditus. "Callista, take this chap will you."

Rufus was handed over to the slave as they approached the huge double-doored entrance. The two doormen either side of them were dressed in a flashy red livery with gold fringing. Between them was a small boy dressed as cupid with golden painted feathered wings. Epaphroditus smiled. Already he could tell this was going to be the most palace of weddings.

"Tiberius Claudius Epaphroditus," he said to the boy. "And family."

The boy took in the gaggle of children standing behind him. "Please follow me."

The boy led them through the atrium to the large courtyard garden at the centre of Baebius' ample home. Epaphroditus could see guests milling about, most notably Pompeia and her sisters who were ogling the impressive fountain of Neptune and the water nymphs. Seeing Epaphroditus, she gave him a friendly wave. He waved back and she yelled over.

"Bigger than your fountain, hey? Right big one it is."

"Massive," agreed Pompeia Major. "A whopper, ain't it? I wonder how much water it uses up in a day?"

The sisters conferred and then decided to set off to find the gardener to ask him.

From behind a flowering bush appeared the hostess. Lysandria was dressed in a white gown with a green shawl around her shoulders. Emerald bracelets, earrings, and a studded necklace of the gems still could not compete for attention with her hair, which today arched a good foot upwards.

"Darlings!" she gushed, embracing Epaphroditus warmly. "Go have fun," she said to the children.

"Not too much fun," warned their father, giving them what he hoped were stern, restraining looks as they ran off.

"I'm so glad you came," said Lysandria.

"Apologies we missed the ceremony. It's quite a thing to get seven children organised, even with the help of slaves. I did Julia's plait. That's why it's lopsided," he explained.

"How was Baiae?"

"Peaceful. And restful. And probably what I needed," he admitted.

Lysandria linked onto his arm and led him into the courtyard. "I am so pleased you're back."

"I wouldn't have missed it," he said, looking over to where the happy couple stood talking, Verenia leant against Lysander. "I'm very happy for you both."

Lysandria followed his gaze. "He's so much like Hypheston, don't you think?"

Epaphroditus looked at her, this friend (usually) from childhood. "I haven't heard you mention him in a long time."

Lysandria smiled, a smile tinged with sadness. "I've talked about Hypheston a lot with Gaius Baebius since Nero died. Now it's safe to talk about him. I think it's important to talk about them. It keeps them real."

Their eyes met with mutual understanding.

"I miss her," he said.

"And you always will, I'm afraid, darling," she said, squeezing his arm. She glanced across to the entrance. Her eyes opened wide. "Well look who it is!"

Epaphroditus followed Lysandria's gaze to see Nymphidia arm in arm with not only her usual man, Hercules, but on the other side, Caecina. Both were dressed in patterned celtic trousers. Though Caecina had at least matched his with a tunic. Hercules' broad, oiled chest was on display for all to see. It was certainly attracting the attention of the Pompeias who were ooh-ing in appreciation.

Nymphidia kissed both men on the cheek.

"Typical Nymphidia," smiled Epaphroditus.

"I'd better go say hello," said Lysandria.

She kissed Epaphroditus on the cheek. "Catch up with you later."

"Later," he agreed, thinking that if Baebius was happy to accept a notorious prostitute like Nymphidia into his home, perhaps Lysandria should hold on to him.

His marital musings were interrupted by a bump to his shin. Looking down, he saw a baby had crawled into him. He now had a fat little bottom parked on his foot. The child looked up at him with warm brown eyes that complemented his tanned skin and dark hair.

"Now I know who you are," he smiled, scooping up the child in his arms.

"Horace! Horace!" came a familiar voice. "Marcia, you really do need to keep a closer eye on him. He's so fast at crawling now."

Philo appeared from behind a bush. "Sir!" he gasped at the sight of Epaphroditus.

"Would you be looking for this little chap?" he asked, holding Horace upwards.

Philo took his son from Epaphroditus.

"Philo has a new job," said Teretia, proudly appearing beside her husband.

"That right?"

"Keeper of the archives," said Philo. "I think it suits me," he said quietly.

Epaphroditus, imagining Philo surrounded by books, his legendary memory and translation skills being put to the test, said, "It sounds perfect."

"No more horrible politics," said Teretia.

She rubbed at her stomach. It looked a little plumper than Epaphroditus remembered.

Seeing his glance, Teretia smiled. "In the autumn," she announced proudly.

"Horace is going to be a big brother!" burst out a grinning Marcia, taking Horace from her master.

"Congratulations to all of you," said Epaphroditus.

The two women wandered off towards the Pompeias.

"Is there any sign of the new emperor?" Epaphroditus asked Philo.

"Late autumn, we think. Just before the new baby is born probably."

Epaphroditus looked at him inquiringly. "I bet you know what I'm going to ask."

"You want to know how the young Caesar fares," Philo responded with a slight smile.

"I need your unique insight and analysis."

"There are some seats there, sir."

"Excellent!" said Epaphroditus, rubbing his palms together.

They each took a glass of wine from a passing wine boy and settled down on a bench.

"Soooo?"

Philo cleared his throat, "Well sir, it's like this—"

AUTHOR'S NOTE

The key question around Vitellius' short reign which I sought to answer was whether he was a puppet emperor. Was he pressured by his commanders, Valens and Caecina, into declaring himself? And then held hostage by the legions to remain on the throne?

I came to the conclusion it was a mixture of the two. For surely, the successful old palace hand Vitellius could not be so easily manipulated by the likes of Valens and Caecina? This was a man who had survived and prospered under the reigns of Caligula, Claudius, and Nero. It seemed to me just as likely that he took advantage of their skills and ambitions.

However, it is certainly true that it was the legions that prevented him from abdicating when he intended to, leading to the brutal and bloody battle that raged on the streets of Rome.

This was the lesson of AD69: an emperor ruled with the permission of the Senate and the army now. The latter increasingly removing those they did not approve of. This would have a catastrophic impact on the empire in centuries to come.

As with previous books, I've kept as close as possible to the recorded accounts of events. Though for the sake of coherence I've left out some of the frantic politicking and events elsewhere in the empire that Tacitus and others faithfully record.

So, yes, sadly it is true that Sporus, the beloved favourite of Nero, killed himself rather than perform for Vitellius in the arena. Similarly, Flavius Sabinus was brutally killed on the steps of the palace and his body put on public display. Shortly after the events of *Vitellius' Feast* both Vitellius' brother and infant son were executed.

However, fleeing from the battle for the Capitoline Hill, Domitian did not stay with Nerva as I have depicted but another family friend. There is absolutely nothing in the sources to suggest that Caecina and Nymphidia ever met each other; it is wholly my invention. The background of Epaphroditus is not known. He first appears in the historical record in AD65, so his connection to Antonia Caenis is again entirely my invention.

The year AD70 began with a new dynasty, the Flavians. Vespasian ruled Rome for nine years and is considered one of the best of all the emperors. He was succeeded by his elder son, Titus. In AD81 Titus died and Domitian became emperor.

Evidently his experiences in AD69 were keenly remembered by Emperor Domitian. On the site where he had hidden from Vitellius' soldiers, he dedicated a temple to Jupiter the Preserver with a marble altar that depicted his adventures. He also built a large temple to Jupiter the Guardian with an effigy of himself under the protecting arm of the god. He ruled for fifteen years.

Thank you to everyone who has read and enjoyed *The Four Emperors* series. It was sometimes despairing, often jubilant, and always enormous fun to write. What kept me going through the endless edits and rewrites was knowing that there were people out there as keen as I was to find out what happens to the likes of Philo, Epaphroditus, Mina, Sporus, and my far too long a cast list of characters. So a big thank you to everyone who berated me for killing off their favourite character or who left reviews and comments. It was appreciated.

L. J. Trafford

Milton Keynes UK
Ingram Content Group UK Ltd.
UKHW021340030924
447832UK00025B/471